New York Times and *USA Today* bestselling author Charles Grant depicts the coming Millennium in this thrilling novel of the beginning of Mankind's end.

"Grant is a spine-tingling storyteller with a riveting style."
—David Morrell

"One of a small circle of quality authors whose elite numbers include Stephen King, Peter Straub, [and] David Morrell."
—*Rocky Mountain News*

"It comes as no surprise that the leading exponent of subtle dark fantasy would have the apocalypse begin not with worldwide war, pestilence, and famine, but with the eerie tolling of a church bell on a quiet summer night in rural New Jersey."
—*Publishers Weekly*

"[The ending] whets the appetite. Grant has a gift for suspense. It is hoped that the rest of the series will be published soon so readers won't have to wait too long for the answers."
—Associated Press

CHARLES GRANT

SYMPHONY

TOR®

A TOM DOHERTY ASSOCIATES BOOK
NEW YORK

This is a work of fiction. All the characters and events portrayed in this book are either products of the author's imagination or are used fictitiously.

SYMPHONY

Copyright © 1997 by Charles Grant

A Tor Book
Published by Tom Doherty Associates, Inc.
175 Fifth Avenue
New York, NY 10010

Tor Books on the World Wide Web:
http://www.tor.com

Tor® is a registered trademark of Tom Doherty Associates, Inc.

ISBN: 0-812-56283-6
Library of Congress Card Catalog Number: 96-42992

First edition: February 1997
First mass market edition: January 1998

Printed in the United States of America

0 9 8 7 6 5 4 3 2 1

Part 1

BRASS
AND VIOLINS

1

1

The night was made for werewolves.

A newly full moon washing color from the ground and stars from the sky, not bright enough to read by, but bright enough for shadows to spread and grow an edge.

A steady silent wind riding down the slopes, skating across the high desert, not sand but dust and dirt, low brush, barren arroyos, a stubborn twisted tree whose roots had found water and refused to let it go. A coyote trotting across a two-lane road, tail dragging, eyes dull. The shed skin of a rattler, dead white in the moonlight, fluttering on a flat rock. White bones, tiny bones, trembling in a ditch.

The temperature cold enough for March.

Dark between the mountains.

No lights at all.

2

Sunday, just shy of midnight.

A woman sat on a lawn chair, the chair on a square of

cracked concrete outside the dented door of a trailer resting on cinder blocks and wood, fifty yards from a narrow paved road hardly anyone ever used. She wore scored boots and worn jeans, flannel shirt, and an open denim jacket lined with fleece. Long black hair pulled severely to the back, covering her ears, carelessly bound with a rawhide strip. A lean face with angles where once there had been curves.

In her right hand, a cigarette; in her left, a .45, Army issue and loaded.

She had been waiting every night for nearly a month, sitting, smoking, sometimes drinking coffee, sometimes drinking beer. Watching the road that shot down from the north, passed her by, heading straight for Albuquerque, who-gave-a-shit-how-many miles away.

If she was lucky, she'd never see it again.

If she was really lucky, the Anglo who had brought her out here with flowers and candy and words just as sweet, with hands that knew her before they even touched her, would come back with his little boy expression: forgive me, Lupé, I've been a total jerk.

When he did, she would kiss him, maybe even let him touch her, then put a bullet between his eyes.

She wasn't often a fool, but this man had done it to her. Gold, he had said, and maybe a little silver, some pure-strain turquoise. He had the maps to prove it, and signed papers from assayers and a professor at the university and a surveyor who swore that any claim would be theirs, the government couldn't touch them.

A long shot, the man had told her, being honest, kissing her throat; but what else, he wanted to know, did they have going for them these days? His low-level job at Sandia was precarious at best, and she had just been laid off.

Pool the money, get the trailer, hit the road, dig the mine, and even in horse races long shots sometimes won.

He didn't hit her the first night, or even that first week.

But when the snows came, and the gold didn't, the isolation broken only by a small TV and a crackling radio, he drank a bottle of discount bourbon and nearly broke her jaw crying out at his rotten luck. She didn't forgive him, but she knew how drunken men behaved when their women tried to fix them and the world didn't care, didn't do what they dreamed.

She knew it was the way her mother had died.

But his hands were too good, and his lies were too good, and she had dug through the rock and watched the snow and waited for spring, and when he came out of the shaft four weeks ago and threw the pick and shovel as far away as he could, she knew they were beaten.

Only in movies did two amateurs strike it rich.

He was sober that night.

He hit her that night.

When she woke up, he was gone, with the money and the car and the TV and the cheap stereo and half the food and all the liquor.

When she healed, when she could walk again without sobbing, she considered standing down there by the road, to hitch a ride to anywhere but here. With nothing left, she had nothing to lose, and she could probably pick up something in the city; the pay wasn't important, just as long as it fed her until she found another way.

That was the last time she had cried, shaking her head at the boulders, at the scrub brush, at the birds that wheeled too high overhead. When the tears stopped, when God didn't speak to her or send her a sign, she plopped the lawn chair onto the concrete square and spent the first afternoon cleaning the gun, the second afternoon practicing her aim, and every afternoon and evening after that, waiting.

She was patient. Very patient. Sooner or later he would grow curious. Sooner or later, he would wonder about her, wonder if he could get anything for the trailer, for what was left inside, and he would come back.

He would die.

She shivered a little and drew her chin toward her chest, lay the gun in her lap and smoothed her hair back over her ears. She wasn't afraid of him, or of pulling the trigger; she wasn't even all that angry anymore.

The waiting, and the killing, had become something she had to do.

She stared at the gun, and felt nothing; she looked up at the moon, and a coyote bark-howled somewhere in the distant dark.

A corner of her mouth pulled back in a crooked smile.

You and me, *amigo*, she thought; you and me until it's over.

The first thing she would do after getting out of this place would be to find a judge to change her name; and if she couldn't find a judge, she'd damn well do it anyway.

Lupé, for Christ's sake.

At school they called her "Loopy."

But Lupé Valez had been a movie star long before Lupé Viejo was born, and her mother had insisted the name would bring her good fortune.

It brought her "Loopy" and a battered face and a battered soul and a .45 in her lap, that's what the hell it had brought her.

It had brought her mother a broken neck, and her father life without parole in the state prison, up near Santa Fe.

She flicked the cigarette away, watched the flailing sparks, and lifted her face to the slow coasting wind. Smelling spring. Smelling green. Smelling twenty-six years slide away into the dark.

She smiled and closed her eyes.

Aw, poor *niña*, she whispered without making a sound; poor little thing, feeling sorry for yourself? He hit you and you stayed, he hit you again and you stayed, he hit you and said things and hit you again and you stayed, and for this you want someone to feel sorry for you?

Stupid bitch.

Grow up.

Get a life.

The coyote called again, farther away.

She lit another cigarette, yawned, coughed, and saw the headlights.

They came out of the mountains, stabbing the sky, raking the brush-and-rock hillsides where no one lived but her.

She listened for the engine, but couldn't hear it for the wind.

When she stood, she cursed. Her knees were weak and stiff, her stomach jumping, and a shudder stiffened her spine, as if an ice cube had touched her neck.

She crushed the cigarette out beneath her boot, grinding it, kicking it away, and set the gun against her leg as she walked down to the road, watching the lights steady, hearing the engine at last, eyes widening when she realized how fast the car moved, stopping and ready to turn when it stopped, too, without pulling out of its lane.

It was long, it had to be old, they sure didn't make them like that anymore, but she couldn't tell the color because the moon took it all away.

The passenger door opened.

A woman's voice said, "Lupé, you'll catch your death out there. Come in and sit a while."

The soft sound of a hand patting the seat.

There was no reason in the world why she should, but it was a relief to hear someone's voice besides her own. She got in, but caution kept the door open, one foot on the ground, catching her breath at the soft leather, staring at the driver, who didn't look at her. All she could tell was that the woman had short hair, not very dark; the shadows and dim dashboard light played games with the rest.

"You want a ride?"

Lupé didn't, she had things to do, but to be polite, she said, "Where?"

The woman laughed softly, quickly, her hands sweeping around the beveled steering wheel. "Lots of places."

"I don't think so, thanks."

"It'll be better than sitting out here, talking to the coyotes and bugs."

Lupé glanced into the backseat, saw nothing at all but the red glow of the taillights. Kind of like fire; kind of like blood. "Do I get paid?"

"In a way."

Lupé rolled her eyes. "Meaning?"

The woman pointed at the gun. "Well, you might get to use that once in a while."

Lupé almost laughed. She'd been too long in this place, too long without seeing anyone but the man she wanted to kill, too long without listening to a single note of music except the songs she tried to sing in a voice that sounded on a good day as if she had a vicious sore throat.

Stir crazy, that's what she was. Maybe just plain crazy.

Coyotes and moonlight will do that to a woman.

The driver turned her head.

Dashboard glow, shadows shifting, and Lupé felt a sharp hitch in her lungs, a whisper of ice. She braced herself to run, stomach jumping again, her mouth open, her fingers tightening around the gun.

"Jesus," was all she could say.

The woman leaned away, just a little, and Lupé rubbed a hand quickly over her face.

Stir crazy, nothing; Jesus, I'm worse off than I thought.

"What did you see?" the woman asked, amused but not unkindly. "A ghost?"

Lupé grinned, feeling stupid. She didn't mind answering: "No, no ghost." She patted the flat of her chest to calm herself.

"What, then?"

"It's dumb."

The woman waited, the question clear and unasked.

"Okay." Lupé shrugged; what the hell, you're crazy, right?

"One of them things, you know? Like in the movies. Wolf. Werewolf. You know what I mean?"

"Sure." The driver faced front and gripped the wheel, fingers flexing slowly. "Close the door, Lupé. Please? It's too chilly out there."

That's not what she meant, and Lupé stared at the trailer, dull even in starlight, and saw the lawn chair, and the concrete square, and the nights waited and waiting.

He's not coming, you know. You can stay here until you fry, but he got what he wanted, and he's not coming back.

Still, there was a long hesitation before she pulled in her

leg and closed the door, and the car moved away so smoothly she was hardly aware that she was gone.

"This is nuts," she muttered, suddenly conscious of the gun and not knowing what to do with it and so tucked it beneath her right leg.

A crooked mile passed, warmth and silence.

"Where are we going?"

The woman shifted. "East."

Lupé stared out the windshield. "East? But—"

"Anytime you want to leave, just say the word, and I'll stop." A low chuckle. "Not in the middle of the desert, either, by the way. Or the mountains, for that matter. You won't be abandoned, just let off."

For no reason in the world, Lupé believed her.

Another mile or two, taking roads she hadn't known were there.

"So why east?" she asked, stifling a yawn. "Why not west? California."

"There's someone we have to see."

"He know we're coming?"

She sensed a smile when the woman answered, "I don't think so, no."

She leaned back then, her eyes half closed, her left hand slowly unbuttoning her jacket. The tension that cloaked her began to shred; the questions she had didn't seem too important anymore. It was crazy, but what the hell, it was, like the woman said, better than talking to the coyotes and bugs. And it wasn't as if she couldn't take care of herself. The lady tried anything, she always had the gun, and the knife in her boot, and her fists.

Digging had made her strong; hating had made her stronger.

The moon coasted, and the automobile raced.

Suddenly the woman said, "Werewolf," and exploded into laughter, head back, rocking side to side.

Lupé watched the road leap at her from the dark, the mountains blacker than she had ever seen them.

The laughter faded.

The laughter died.

"Okay, I'm sorry, okay?" Lupé snapped, anger deepening her voice.

"Oh, don't be sorry, please." A hand touched her leg, tapped it once, an apology. "It's my fault. I shouldn't have laughed."

Lupé said nothing.

"The thing is, hon, by the time this is over, you'll probably wish I was."

3

Violins nudged her close to awakening, the menace of deep horns lurking behind. She opened her right eye, but not very much, she wanted to keep sleeping as long as she could, and through the tinted window saw the flat of the desert, and a mesa midway to the horizon, bleeding in first light.

The music played on.

She wasn't sure what it was; it sounded familiar, maybe something one of her grade school teachers used to play, to wean them away from bubblegum rock.

The eye closed.

"Hey," she said, her throat a little dry.

"We'll be stopping for breakfast soon. Sleep. You deserve it."

"No problem. But . . . you have a name?"

Tires hummed; violins and cellos.

"Susan."

The left eye opened, half expecting to see a kid, or a crone in pearls and furs.

What it saw was a woman with light brown hair short and smooth and straight to her shoulders, large eyes, small mouth; a plaid shirt, and sleeves rolled halfway to the elbows, jeans, tennis shoes. No jewelry and no furs and no watch.

"No werewolf," Susan said with a lopsided grin.

Lupé grinned back and closed the eye, drifting and sinking, listening to the violins.

4

"After we eat, then what?"

"East, remember?"

"Last I heard, there was a heat wave going on. Couldn't we go someplace cool?"

"Like Alaska?"

"Yeah. That sounds okay to me."

"Sorry. We're going east."

"Straight through, huh?"

"Oh, no, there're a few stops along the way."

"More people?"

"That's right."

"We gonna party?"

"Not quite, dear, not quite."

2

1

The heat slipped in with June barely started, tolerable at first, nothing special, it was summer, until it began to climb.

A degree a day.

Taking its time.

By the end of the first week, night and day were little different. Moon and sun were white, all color gone.

By the end of the tenth day, nobody cared that records had been broken, that water was scarce, that brownouts swept the state, the whole Northeast, like lightning-set brushfires, that earthquakes and floods tore at other parts of the world.

Nobody cared.

There was only the heat.

It turned streets to treadmills and steps to endless mountains; muscles drained and lungs strained and infrequent patches of unmoving shade became places to stand in and stare blindly and gasp.

The hills and mountains were no better—the ground was warm, lakes and ponds still and tepid, and the air smelled less like grass and flower than copper and sweat and things left to die; the beaches were almost worse, sand too hot to step on to get to the water still too cold to stay in for very long.

Vacations took families from one furnace to another.

By the eleventh day there were no games, in corner lots or parks.

By the twelfth, there was only sound—sharp music turned dull; dull voices turning sharp.

A drop of rain; that's all they wanted.

A single cloud.

2

The sun never set, not even at midnight; the heat only shifted from white to dark. Like the shift of a slow saxophone from low note to lower, the effect was the same—the heat never let go, it only eased back and waited, taking its time, knowing the score.

Casey reached over to the end table and switched the radio off. The music died, didn't linger, and the silence left behind was a tangible weight.

He picked up a book lying on the mattress, flipped it open, read a word, and dropped it on the floor.

His eyes, deep-set and dark, closed for a moment as he sighed, as much for the sound as for the note of self-pity. But he figured he was entitled; being stoic was no fun when there was no one around to watch it.

He shifted, and sighed again.

He had been in bed, or on the living-room couch, for six miserable days, and he was almighty tired of reading, of soap operas and game shows, magazines and the local, mostly-ads newspaper; not to mention the ceiling plaster above his bed. He had memorized every crack, noted every loose flake, had blurred it all into patterns only a fevered man could see; but when he began to see faces that looked back at him and winked, he decided he had had enough.

He sat up slowly and gathered the sheet across his lap, rubbed his eyes with the rough heels of his hands, and waited to see if the familiar dizziness would take him back to his pillow. The bare floor was cool and clammy under his feet. A harsh cough made him grimace, but it was brief, more a bark, and no bubbling in his chest. That was a good sign. At least it didn't sound as if he were driving his lungs into his hands, and there was no longer a tight pain around his ribs or a burning band around his head. He coughed again, another bark, and still the dizziness stayed away.

He had been feeling awful since the beginning of the month, shortly after the heat wave had begun, hacking more than coughing, losing strength and weight, but when the fever dreams began, he had swallowed his pride and visited Doc Farber, who told him what he had was a classic case of walking pneumonia.

He grunted, shaking his head, pushing his hands back through his hair.

Walking pneumonia. How the hell can you get walking pneumonia in the middle of a drought? In the middle of a goddamn heat wave?

The doc said it was easy—too much hard work, he was run down, he smoked too damn much, he caught a cold ducking in and out of air-conditioned buildings, and he wouldn't stop to rest. The prescription was easy—antibiotics, stay off your feet, eat right, plenty of liquids, and for God's sake don't answer the phone.

Friends and neighbors came by for the first two days, bringing chicken soup and casseroles, reminding him that the isolation of the house didn't mean he was alone.

They didn't return because he cranked at them, asserting his independence while flat and groaning on his broad, stupid back.

They understood; they stayed away.

Six days; Sunday now, and he was ready to shoot someone, just for something different.

It didn't make any difference how late it was, he had to get up. He had to *do* something. Besides, he realized as he glanced around the bedroom, he actually did feel better. So much so that he only now understood how truly awful he had felt before.

Still moving slowly, not yet ready to take on the world, he pulled on black jeans and stumbled into the bathroom to splash cool water on his face, changed his mind and took a cool shower instead. Brushed his hair. Wondered if he could get away with getting a crewcut in the morning. He doubted it. There had been too much of it, dark and thick and thickly curled to his shoulders, for far too long; he would just have to wait for it to fall out.

Still feeling slightly weak, he walked into the front room and used the wall switch to turn on the lamps.

It wasn't a fancy place, but it was comfortable—thirty-five feet long, half that wide, with a slightly vaulted, raw-beam ceiling. A large brick fireplace in the back wall, with the television and stereo in its mouth. The door to its left was the only bedroom, a doorless entrance to the kitchen on the right. Bookshelves on all the walls. Two short couches at right angles to the hearth, with a coffee table between them. A round, white pine dining table and ill-matching chairs set off to one side, his desk as well as the place where he ate. The house had been a summer bungalow like most of the other original buildings in town, and like them had long since been converted to year-round living.

Yet despite the fact that all the windows were open, it was still warm, still muggy. He walked past them all, straining for a breeze, shaking his head at the moths clinging hard to the screens. Dopes, he thought, flicking his finger at one.

It fluttered, but didn't leave.

"Dope," he said aloud, and went to the kitchen, stood at the squat refrigerator and stared. His stomach told him to forget it, don't push your luck, so he grabbed a cigarette from the pack on the table instead and, after switching the lights off again, stepped out onto the front porch, pushing the slightly warped screen door shut behind him.

"Jesus," he gasped.

It was like stepping into a room lined with damp cotton, and it dismayed him to think that this was only June.

July or August would probably put him in his grave.

He lit the cigarette and sat on the railing, ankles hooked around the spindles below.

The yard was wide, not very deep, with a flat-stone walk, a quartet of old giant oaks that did their best to give him shade, and a low and weathered picket fence that swung around the house to the corners of the much larger backyard. A one-car garage to the left at the end of a short dirt-and-weed driveway. Nothing but woods across the road beyond the fence; the nearest neighbor a hundred yards to the left, nothing but trees and shrubs between.

One hundred yards to the right, the road curved sharply and dipped down to the Delaware River.

He drew circles in the air with the cigarette's tip.

He watched a spark linger, winking out without falling.

He looked up at the stars.

He closed his eyes and listened to the night, but the leaves didn't move, and Star Creek had almost dried up, and even the crickets had given their songs a rest. Nothing hunted. Nothing stirred.

He was convinced, at that moment, he was the only living thing on the planet.

"Oh boy," he whispered, and smiled when a shooting star flared over the woods. He made a quick wish for a break in the weather, finished the cigarette and caught himself with a laugh when he nearly crushed it with his bare heel. He ground it out on the railing instead, and stuffed the filter in his hip pocket.

He was ready to return inside, when he saw a light across the road, bobbing between the trees, sweeping upward, aiming down. Two of them, then three, heading his way.

He frowned and moved to the steps, clammy wood reminding him again he wore nothing on his feet.

Faint voices, one of them laughing until another hushed it.

He backed up until he reached the door, opened it just enough to slip inside and grab a pair of boots from beside one of the couches. He pulled the boots on, head tilted and listening, watching the beams dart across the windows on either side of the door, and slipped out again, moving to the far corner so he could duck between the porch swing and the wall.

They came out of the woods.

White lights, pointing at the ground now, almost-shadows behind them.

"Shit, ouch," one of them muttered.

"Will you shut the hell up?"

"Turned my ankle, stupid."

"Just shut up, okay? He's sick, he ain't dead."

Casey almost laughed aloud, it was so easy.

Reed Turner, Nate Dane, and the other one, the silent one, must be—

"Not through the gate, you jerks. It's rusty."

He smiled. Cora Bowes.

Still complaining, they climbed over the fence and made their way toward the porch across the grass. One light swept across the front, paused at the door, and slid away over the floor and three steps.

"How the hell are we going to do this?" Nate asked, his voice too high for a boy his age.

"Jesus," Cora said, "we only went over it a million times."

"But suppose he catches us?" Reed demanded, keeping his voice down.

"You don't think you can outrun him?" Cora was scornful. Casey knew that tone; it was her weapon of choice.

They stopped at the steps, flashlights off, only a faint glow of starlight giving them form.

He tried to figure out what they were up to, unable to make out what they carried in their free hands. Spray paint wasn't their style. Most likely it would be manure or something in paper bags, even though he couldn't smell it.

They moved up the steps, testing them for sound.

Hissing, pointing, while Casey waited until the moment he was sure they would turn the flashlights back on.

Then he rose from behind the swing.

" " "Vengeance," " " " he boomed, " " " "is *Mine*," sayeth the Lord!' "

3

He didn't know who screamed first, but it was enough to send them all flying. They might have escaped had Reed not tripped as he grabbed the porch post to launch him down the steps. He landed flat on his chest, and Casey was over him before he could recover. He grabbed the boy's shirt and hauled him effortlessly to his feet, snapped the hand from shirt to nape, and squeezed.

"Stop!" he yelled, ignoring Reed's squirming.

Nate did, halfway over the fence.

Cora, light and fleet, was already on her way back up to town, no intention of stopping.

"Cora!" His voice, rough and deep.

She ran on a half dozen steps before she threw up her hands and slowed, and turned around.

"With me, boy," he said to Reed, and pulled him back to the porch, where he turned on the single bulb over the door.

The moths stirred.

He let Reed go, aiming him gently but firmly toward the swing. The boy didn't argue; he sat, glowering at Nate, who dropped sheepishly beside him.

"Pussy," Reed said.

Nate glared. "Who ran first?"

"Oh, shut up," Cora told them, stomping angrily up the stairs. She didn't look at Casey until she'd hip-shoved a space between her friends, and even then she made it clear she wasn't about to talk.

Casey stepped to the porch post, slipped one hand into a pocket, and looked pointedly at the brown bags left scattered in their flight. The aroma was strong; he had been right—horse shit.

"Look—" Cora began.

"Hush," Casey told her.

He straightened, deliberately slowly, and swallowed a grin when the two boys tried to push their way through the swing's laddered back. He was used to the reaction, and though it had caused him much trouble most of his life, he had also been able to turn it in his favor.

He was a tall man, five inches over six feet, and broad from shoulders to thighs. He wasn't as solid as he'd once been, things softened and he was growing a paunch, but no one in Maple Landing ever doubted his strength. Yet it was his face that usually cowed them—the heavy brows, the once sharp nose, the high cheeks and dimpled chin that never hid the bad times he had suffered, never softened the blows they had taken. And the lines age had laid there only made him seem more fearsome when he kept himself from smiling.

These kids were in their late teens, but now they looked like children when he stood before them. Hands on hips, looking down. Meeting their gazes, making their gazes drift away.

"Seems to me," he said at last, "you're trying to take advantage of a sick man."

Reed looked up, wide-eyed in disbelief. "But you *were* sick."

"That's right."

"So what was it?" Cora sneered. "A miracle or something?"

"Antibiotics," he answered blandly.

Nate's hands danced nervously in his lap, long fingers drumming, then twisting around each other, then drumming again until Casey covered them with his own hand and pressed them hard until they stopped.

"We didn't break any laws, you know," Cora said defiantly, arms folded under her breasts.

"That's true."

"You can't keep us here."

"That's not true."

Reed and Nate exchanged nervous glances behind Cora's head. But for the difference in their heights—Reed was taller and dark-haired, Nate slightly thinner and fair—they could have been brothers. Neither looked at the girl.

Casey gestured at the bags. "Was I supposed to stomp on

them when you lit them? Or were you going to smear the house with all that shit?''

Nate gulped.

Reed bowed his head, shook it once. ''Stomp on them,'' he admitted quietly.

''Oh . . . Jesus,'' Cora said.

''Jesus,'' said Casey mildly, ''had nothing to say about this.''

Nate's lips almost grinned; Reed's did, but it didn't hold.

Casey stepped back. The boys visibly relaxed; Cora was harder, but he could see her shoulders slump. Just a little. Just enough.

A moth flew at his face; he swatted it, and Nate jumped.

''Oh, for God's sake,'' Cora snapped. ''He's not going to beat you up.'' She looked at Casey again, defiance returned, a pretty girl turned ugly. ''I'm going to tell my father, you know. You're keeping us against our will.''

Again he almost smiled. ''Cora,'' he said, ''shut the hell up.''

Her face reddened.

Reed looked steadily at the house wall, a muscle jumping in his cheek.

''So tell me, Nate,'' Casey said, ''what did I do to deserve this particular honor?'' He looked at the roof in mock concentration. ''It's not Halloween, not my birthday, it's not your birthday yet, and . . .'' He looked back at him. ''Don't tell me—you've started a club, and this is the initiation?''

Nate shook his head, misery working his hands again.

Reed, on the other hand, was angry, but not at him. ''Look, it wasn't our idea, okay?''

''Oh, I know that,'' Casey answered mildly. ''But you were stupid enough to do it anyway, weren't you.'' He took a long stride toward them, heel loud on the flooring. Nate had sense enough to cringe; Cora only glared. ''It's *my* fault there's no camp, *my* fault there's no trip to the Poconos, *my* fault there's nothing for you poor kids to do around here but watch TV and swim and hunt and boat and . . .'' He drew himself up, full height, eyebrows down. "Screw around when you think nobody's looking."

Nate choked when he tried not to laugh.

"*And,*" Casey continued, a little louder, "it's probably also *my* damn fault that it's *so* damn hot your own damn *brains* have probably *fried.*"

The boys' heads were down, but they were finally grinning without caring about the girl.

He made sure they heard his exasperated sigh, made sure they saw him glance heavenward in search of divine patience, before he pointed again. "Take those . . . *things* off my porch. I don't care what you do with them, just get them out of here. And go home, okay?" he added as the boys jumped to their feet, Cora moving deliberately slower. "I'm an old man, a sick old man, and I need my beauty sleep."

They hustled, giggling, until the bags were fetched, then hurried down the steps.

"And use the goddamn gate this time!" he yelled after them. "It's not that rusty!"

Reed exploded, laughing so hard he could barely work the latch, and after the others were through and on their way, he raced back to the porch. "I'm glad you're feeling better, Reverend Chisholm, really," he said breathlessly, and raced away again.

Oh, I'll bet, Casey thought as he watched them merge with the dark; I'll just bet you do.

But he smiled.

He couldn't help it.

4

Midnight was long gone when Casey opened one eye, listening to the dark.

Dreaming, he figured; the church bell hadn't rung, a single peal that seemed heavier than the humid air.

The eye closed.

Not dreaming, he decided miserably.

He groaned and sat up, grabbed his jeans and boots and a shirt from the closet, stumbled into the front room and dressed. Taking his time. There was no real hurry; whoever it was would be gone when he got there, but he wouldn't be able to sleep unless he checked. Those kids were going to be the death of him; the shit trick didn't work, so now they weren't going to let him get a decent night's sleep.

He lit a cigarette, grabbed his keys, and walked out to the road, walking down the center of the blacktop in a half-formed dare for someone to try to run him down. It made him smile. A dare was a kid's thing, but this place had done that to him. He wasn't sure why, and he wasn't complaining. He was lucky to be here at all.

He was lucky to be alive.

That had nothing to do with good health or the Lord; it had everything to do with the man who had held the gun to his head so long ago it seemed now to be a fragment of a nightmare, nothing substantial, nothing real, nothing to do with the late winter night he had walked into the food mart in South Carolina and raised a blue-cold fist to the poor child behind the counter. It might as well have been a gun the way she cringed and wept as she fumbled to open the cash register, the way she trembled and leaned heavily against the counter when he asked her politely to hurry, the way she screamed when the door crashed open and the cop crashed in and the gun jammed against his temple and drove him to his knees before he had a chance to turn around and tell the man he was sorry, he didn't mean it, he was just so goddamn hungry.

So goddamn cold.

Boots on the blacktop still soft from the day's heat.

The last of the cigarette dying in orange sparks beneath his heel.

The night had weight, but he refused to bend.

The night watched him, he felt it, but he looked directly ahead, seeing the houses appear and fade, drifting past him.

Knowing every one, inside and out.

5

Maple Landing had begun as a settlement tucked into the edge of state forestland, mostly hunters and fishermen who never stayed the year round. When they did stay, finally, they renovated, but only enough to suffer the seasons hot to cold.

The original section was little more than a straight downhill road with six straight streets branching off it, none the same length, none completely developed, all ending in the grip of the forest. The road leveled to a broad step where a handful of businesses found a hold and held on. A second, shorter slope leveled just long enough below Casey's house to accommodate a wide meadow on the north side, a place for deer and buzzards and wandering black bear; a place for watching the stars without trees to block them; a place that had no name.

When the road, Black Oak, dove a third time, below the meadow, it didn't stop until it reached the Delaware, and the maple-choked landing that had given the hamlet its name.

Before the slope began, up over the crest, newer houses had been built, development-style and a handful of prefab log cabins, and a small grade school, a coin laundry, a video store, deli, the volunteer firehouse with its single creaking engine.

Unequal sizes; but equal reasons for living in a place that had been ordered by the state not to grow anymore.

A hideout, Casey believed; in here, buried in the forest, visited only by tourists looking for a ride on the river, some fishermen and nature lovers, the world didn't much matter.

It was out there when you needed it; that's all the Landers needed to know.

6

He walked on, through the intersection with Hickory Street, glancing at the darkened Moonglow on the corner to his right,

Vinia Leary's pharmacy on his left; checking Mackey's Bar on the corner across Hickory, attached to Tully's hardware store and gun-and-tackle shop, Mabel Jonsen's grocery on the right. A wooded lot past Mabel's place, then Mel Farber's clinic and an empty shop whose window was blinded with sun-faded posters of fishing contests and rock concerts. Past the empty shop and a second empty lot to Ozzie Gorn's gas station, where a black shepherd once spent the nights guarding until Ozzie got tired of climbing out of bed to calm the animal down—it barked at every kid, every critter, every twist of the breeze. Casey couldn't remember its name; he could only re-member its eyes as it barked, wide and frightened. Tail wag-ging and fangs bared.

He might have taken it for himself had not Ozzie been quicker, with a bottle and a gun.

Houses again, set back from the road, and on the left, in the center of a well-kept lawn bounded by a low, gateless picket fence, Trinity Church, a small white building with a steeple and belfry, behind it an ancient graveyard surrounded by a low stone wall. The building had been a meeting house in the original community; someone bought it, sold it, and now, with the steeple and the bells, it was a place to talk to God; for some, another hideout.

He stopped and looked at it, shaking his head as if weary of scolding a mischievous child. Cora? he wondered with hands on his hips. He checked the belfry as best he could from below, half expecting to see one of the boys dangling help-lessly from the slate roof, a little disappointed when he didn't.

The death of him.

Absolutely.

He crossed to the flagstone walk, took the three steps to the broad stoop, unlocked the right-hand door, and stepped into the vestibule, a fair-sized room with a long pew bench against the front wall, a table near the entrance to the sanctuary for handouts and such. On the left, a narrow door that opened onto a winding staircase to the choir loft and belfry, another that opened on the sexton's closet, used to house what was needed to keep the place clean; on the far right a door that led to the changing room and behind it, the office he seldom used.

He switched on the overhead light and checked the nave first, walking slowly down the wine-carpeted center aisle, glancing into the pews, turning to look up at the loft, turning again when he reached the altar rail. Polished wood and polished brass, catching the light and holding it like trapped brass stars.

He scratched his head, glanced at the cross on the simple altar draped in white cloth, and shrugged.

Empty.

And not quite empty.

He wasn't sure if an animal had gotten in—it wouldn't be the first time, raccoons and skunks were maddeningly canny— or if someone was hiding somewhere in the building, but he couldn't shake the feeling he wasn't alone.

The half dozen stained-glass windows along each wall were closed; the rose window above the loft was undamaged. With a brief frown, he lifted the center rail and passed in front of the altar to the right; the door in the back wall was locked. He opened it, and stepped into his office, standing in the dark, listening.

No one here.

Back in the church he almost smiled as he checked the hollow beneath the tall, ornate pulpit, a gift from the estate of a woman he had never known. It more rightly belonged in a cathedral, but he liked its solid feel when he leaned on it to preach, liked the bas-relief carvings of saints and symbols that shone even when the wood hadn't been touched by polish.

No one there.

He returned to the vestibule and switched off the inner lights, leaving nothing behind but the faint glow of the cross.

The choir's changing room was empty, and no one cowering in the wardrobe.

Empty.

Not quite.

He opened the staircase door, and flicked the wall switch. Nothing happened.

"Great," he muttered. He hadn't thought to bring a flashlight.

The vestibule's light took him up the four steps to the landing, but it didn't reach around the corner. He peered into the darkness above, shook his head at the waste of time, and began to climb, the cracked plaster walls nearly touching his shoulders, the single railing sliding damply beneath his palm. Halfway up he lit a match, and climbed again, scowling as the flame danced near to extinction, filling the walls with the hulk of his shadow. Just before his fingertips burned, he snapped the match out and lit another, which took him to the top and the low door on the right.

He tested it; it was unlocked, as it should be.

He pushed it open, climbed two more steps, and stood in the belfry.

Nothing moved.

The match went out.

There was enough glow from stars and streetlamps to let him see the three heavy bells several feet above his head, bolted to a single thick pipe at the end of which was a large wheel. A rope from the wheel dropped through a small hole in the floor, all the way down to the cleaning closet. When the rope was pulled, the segmented pipe turned over, each segment in turn. The bells rang, one at a time. Not a carillon, but music nonetheless when the church needed a voice.

It was impossible for only one bell to ring.

He grunted.

He stepped gingerly around the tiny space, only eight feet on a side, taking care not to look through the pointed openings in each wall, each wide enough and tall enough for a man to walk through, and fall through if he had a mind to. It was a beautiful view, he'd been told; you could see over the trees straight down to the river. He took their word for it; heights were not prime on the list of his phobias to conquer.

Eventually he reached the rope, touched it, brushed it, pulled it slightly and felt the mechanism that turned the pipe prepare to follow through. The three bells shifted. He released the rope and wiped his face with a forearm.

What the hell was going on around here?

He supposed somebody could have used something, a stick or a bat, to give the largest bell a whack, but that wouldn't have sounded right. It was also possible a stick or broom had been used to give the clapper a hard enough swing to make it strike, but whoever it was would have had to be quick and strong enough to stop it from striking twice, even three times.

It was possible, though, he thought, lighting a third match and peering into the bells' mouths. They were only a foot or so above the reach of his hand. It was possible. It was also an awful lot of work just to ring a stupid bell. Cora couldn't have done it, Nate hadn't the strength, and he didn't think either of them could get Reed in here on a bet.

So who the hell was it?

He descended quickly, and checked the closet door—it was locked, and except for the sexton, he had the only key. He looked in anyway, just in case, and found only the rope dangling to its coil on the floor, a pail and mop, a pair of brooms, and a shelf of neatly arranged cleaners and polish, a stack of clean rags, a box of short candles.

"Well, hell," he said as he relocked the door.

He turned off the lights, stood in the dark, puzzled because he had been so sure he wasn't alone in here.

Unless, he thought as he went outside, he was just plain tired. Still a little fuzzy in the head. That would do it. He had definitely heard the bell, but the rest was all fancy. He yawned, locked up, and headed back down the street, the keys bouncing thoughtfully in his right hand.

Another fancy: he wore a gunbelt, spurs, and a pulled-low hat with a sloping brim, walking through his town, making sure the bad guys knew he was there, and knew he'd be trouble if it was trouble they were after. A tall man in black. With flowing black hair.

Less a fancy than a vanity, and one difficult to control. This wasn't his town, but it felt like it; the people didn't depend on him for protection, but it felt like it; there was every chance he wouldn't be here until retirement, but it felt like it. And he wanted it.

A place to call home.

A place to hide from the demons.

He looked down at his feet, and noticed the way his arms hung, away from his sides, fingers curled, wrists slightly inward, everything ready to draw when they came.

He laughed, his head back, face to the stars.

Black Casey Chisholm, wanted in fifty states, dead or alive. Your reward in the next world; there's not enough money in this one.

The laugh was easy, slipping to a grumbling as he stuck his hands in his pockets. Coughed once and cleared his throat. Whistled a single note, high and sweet. Kicked at a pebble, and chased it, kicked again, trotting now and not minding the sweat that broke across his face. Black Casey Chisholm, heading straight for the goal, feet deft, herding the pebble without missing a beat until he reached his gate.

He kicked hard.

He scored.

He held his hands high and laughed again at the stars.

And when the bell tolled, just once, he told it to go to hell.

7

The dream hadn't come in almost five years.

Ponytail girl, all angles and bones, red-checked shirt and fake satin slacks, scrabbling at the cash register drawer, tears dripping from her chin to the floor, lower lip trembling as she whispers, *please don't hurt me, please don't kill me, please don't, please don't,* until he wants to scream.

A dollar bill flutters to the counter, slips to the floor.

Panicked, she looks at him helplessly, can't see him for the tears, streaks of mascara like claw marks on her cheeks.

Please don't, please don't, Jesus save me, please don't.

He hears what sounds like a hundred mirrors breaking, and lowers his fist as he half turns toward the door.

When she screams, he can see her teeth and her tongue.

When the gun mouth clamps itself to his head, he falls to

his knees without having to be told, chin clipping the counter's edge on the way down, blood from his lip, light shimmering before his eyes.

Goddamn bastard, the cop yells; *goddamn bastard, lie down, hands behind your back.*

He's too dizzy, his mouth hurts, the girl is still screaming, and the gun presses hard, forcing his head to one side, a cramp teasing the side of his neck.

Goddamn bastard, lie down!

He lies down awkwardly, swallows blood, feels a sharp knee in the small of his back, feels rough hands and handcuffs, a kick to his ribs, his left shin, the girl screaming softly.

Keening.

The gun to the back of his head.

Goddamn bastard.

His head begins to vibrate with anticipating tension as he waits for the bullet, listening to the girl sobbing now, saying, *please don't, please don't hurt him.*

The cop doesn't care.

The last thing he hears is the explosion in his brain.

8

Casey sat up, sweat on his chest and back, tears on his cheeks. He wiped a hand across his mouth, across his eyes, and fumbled his way into the living room, into the kitchen where he stood in front of the open refrigerator, letting the cold wash him, not minding the shivers as he grabbed a pitcher of water, and grabbed the empty glass beside it.

He poured and drank.

The cold hurt; it gave him a headache.

He drank another glass, found his cigarettes, and stood on the porch, testing the morning that looked too much like night.

Five minutes gone before he lit the match.

Then he said, "Dear Jesus," and dropped limply onto the swing.

A couple of hours to dawn, he figured, which wasn't soon enough.

The last time he had had the dream was the year the Delaware had backed up because winter's ice hadn't melted, great blocks of it stacking atop each other, flooding the lowlands all the way down to Philadelphia; the year Todd Odam at the diner had been clubbed with a loaf of stale bread by Mabel Jonsen for laughing at her UFOs; the year the bishop down in Newark had agreed that Casey could stay on in Maple Landing for however long he wanted.

He smiled then at the last memory. The liberals in the Church had been relieved and hadn't hidden it; the conservatives had been dismayed because Casey, they claimed, was a mortal danger to his parishioners' souls and shouldn't be anywhere near an altar at all.

A felon.

A near-murderer.

A man of the cloth who hardly ever wore the cloth, spoke to God as if He were one of his neighbors, and . . .

The smile broadened, and he blew a smoke ring at the night.

He supposed he shouldn't have done it, that night outside the cathedral, but no one else had moved.

There had been a meeting, budgets and new members and how to fight the TV evangelicals who were promising more than a mere Episcopalian could offer, a mere Methodist, a mere Presbyterian. Promising heaven for a check instead of a prayer. A summer night muggy and threatening thunder in the middle of Newark. A gang of a half dozen swept down upon the clerics standing outside the small cathedral's doors, laughing, asking for money, jostling and shoving, until Casey finally lost his temper.

He grabbed the nearest one, the largest one, with a roar that froze half the city, picked the kid up by his leather lapels and carried him easily to the corner.

And held him there, two feet off the ground, until a cruiser came by and took the kid away.

They told him later he hadn't said a word.

The cops told him later the kid had begged them to lock him up, to save him from the giant.

There is great violence within you, the bishop had said, speaking to him in his office once the incident was over and the meeting had broken for the night.

Casey had apologized; the bishop knew the whole story.

Funny, the old man had said, beringed fingers tented beneath his chin, *sometimes I think you're closer to Him than most of those prigs out there. But there's great violence in there, son. It's a frightening thing.*

Casey agreed, and wondered what Episcopalians did with their bad seeds—excommunicated them, banished them, scourged them in print and drove them back to civilian life, Bible tucked between their tails?

So, Case, how would you like to live in the woods for a while?

Casey had accepted readily, gratefully, to escape the dreams and the politics and the perfect-haired ladies and unctuous dark-suited men who traded in preachers the way they traded in old cars, to get back to the kind of place where he had spent most of his life.

Until tonight, so far so good.

Good grief, don't worry about it, he told himself as he crushed the cigarette out on the seat beside him; it's the damn heat, boy. It would drive a saint crazy.

A bird sang briefly, in a tree he couldn't see in the yard.

Sleep, he decided, or you'll be a zombie all week.

He laughed, shook his head, and thought of the kids, his kids, and that made him laugh again, all the way to his bed.

3

1

There was a routine, and it seldom varied:

Casey unlocked the church's front doors, switched on the air-conditioning, set it to low, then propped open the doors to the sanctuary and said, "Good morning, Lord."

Sunlight on the pews and altar, on the brass cross, tinted light from the stained glass reminding him, for no particular reason, of a calliope's music, and every so often a wasp or bee bumping angrily against the ceiling or one of the panes.

Every day of the week.

"A lousy day," he said amiably, moving down the center aisle, hands in his pockets. He wore black—jeans and a loose, long-sleeved shirt with the cuffs rolled up twice—because it was expected of him; he also wore it because it was easy. A blind man could dress this way and not worry about anything not matching. But he only wore the collar on Sundays and whenever he took Communion to the hospital and the shut-ins. He hated that thing. It was like a starched noose. On the other hand, he could be a Presbyterian and have to wear a stupid tie.

"Too hot again; are You maybe thinking about sending some rain soon? The creek's near dry, and Your little guys in the woods sure could use some water. A long drink about now would spare them a lot of misery." He sniffed, and rubbed his chin, coughed into his fist. "A lot of dying out there, Lord. And the birds aren't the only ones going crazy from the heat."

An automatic check of the pews, the hymnals in their slots, noting worn spots on the aisle carpet, a few places where plaster had to be replaced on the walls.

"Speaking of crazy, do You have any ideas for me? Like who was fooling around in here last night?"

A palm brushed across the altar rail as he made his way toward his office.

It was a small room, just large enough for a wardrobe, desk, two easy chairs, a filing cabinet, and a wall-long bookcase. A single window overlooked the yard in back and, beyond it, the graveyard, with headstones that, on occasion, were dated before the middle of the last century. A door to the outside seldom used. When he was sure nothing had been disturbed, he sat at the desk, opened the center drawer on the left, and pulled out a Bible.

The cover was pebbled black leather, the pages onionskin, and he opened it carefully. It was his first Bible, the one his mother had given him, the one that had taken its time showing him what he was supposed to do with his life, his size, that voice of his. It was the one used for his ordination, and when he had buried his mother on an autumn hillside in Tennessee five years ago. King James. He didn't care about the scholars or the accuracy or the bringing of his church into whatever century they claimed it was these days; he cared about the poetry, and about the comfort it brought to those who needed to hear it.

He read for half an hour, no specific verse, no particular chapter.

When he finished, he returned to the nave, knelt in the aisle and prayed for the day's ration of strength.

Ten minutes later, he rose, dusted his knees, and looked around one more time.

Maybe he'd go up to the Crest, and on over to the end of Sycamore Road, where Ed and Sissy Palmer had a small stable. Go riding for a while. Let the horse do the work while he thought a little. Take one of the trails down to the river and shoot the breeze with Micah.

He coughed hard, and shook his head.

Maybe not.

His shoulders rolled then, dispelling a faint shiver.

It was an odd thing, and he wondered why he hadn't noticed it before, but there was a chill in here, one that had nothing to do with the central air.

It was vaguely damp, vaguely disturbing, so vague in all respects that he scolded himself for not getting enough sleep the night before.

But when he stepped outside, the relief wasn't vague at all, and he couldn't help but feel ashamed.

2

The Moonglow, by design, was not a breakfast diner. The people who lived up on the Crest generally left for their commutes too early, and those who stayed behind ate at home. All of which was fine with Todd Odam, who never could see the benefit of starting his day in a strange place, with strange food, with strangers trying to engage him in idiot conversation about the weather or the Yankees.

For him, however, the Moonglow was home, at least as far as the kitchen was concerned. When he bought the diner fifteen years ago—a thirtieth birthday and ex-wife go to Hell present—it hadn't been much more than a worn-out shack with a balky refrigerator, stove, and a couple of rickety tables. He gutted it, expanded it, faced it with dark brick, ditched the tables in the junk yard, and made sure he never had to walk more than six steps in any direction to get what he wanted while he did the cooking.

The dining area was as simple: six dark-brown booths along the single front window, three more along the Hunter Street side, and a twelve-stool counter with the register on the end. The windows were tinted to keep out the glare, and the shelf in the wall gap between his domain and the customers' was wide enough for him to rest his arms on so he could gossip and watch people eating, and high enough so he wouldn't crack his head.

During the day, he took orders himself; Helen Gable came in at four. When it was real busy, little Rina Doyle lent a hand. Most of the time, it wasn't.

Right now, the booths were empty, and probably would be until the first batch of tourists came back from riding the river. He didn't expect any others today. Despite optimism on the radio, the heat wave hadn't broken. Ten o'clock in the damn morning, and it was already in the low eighties, Black Oak was deserted, and not even the squirrels he fed in his backyard had bothered to come around for nearly four days.

The yuppies on the Crest claimed it was global warming, and Mabel Jonsen countered with UFOs.

Todd didn't give a shit; he just wanted to get cool.

Arlo Mackey, slightly paunchy and tie-dyed from loose shirt to baggy jeans, sat at the counter's far end, nursing a cup of coffee, humming to himself. His long, gray-shot red hair was pulled back in a shaggy ponytail that reached the middle of his spine, his granny glasses forever slipping to the end of his sunburnt pug nose. Todd waited for the day they'd drop into his cup; he didn't think the man would notice.

The reverend was the only other customer. He was on what had become by default and use his personal seat—the last one by the register—polishing off the last of four eggs over medium, four pieces of toast, six slices of bacon, hash browns, and, for God's sake, a tall glass of milk.

No wonder the man was so goddamn big.

"You keep a noisy church there, Case," he said mildly, arms folded on the shelf, looking around as if there were a dozen people to keep track of.

Chisholm looked up from his plate without raising his head. "It keeps the pagans at bay, Todd. They sneak up on you at night sometimes."

"Keeps me from my beauty rest is what it does." He scratched through his thinning hair, far too short to be fashionable. "A man in my food service position has appearances, you know."

The reverend grinned, but said nothing.

Todd grinned back. He knew he wasn't a good-looking man. He was too thin, with too many planes in his face and angles in his limbs, his eyes too dark and too deep in his head, and his voice sounded edged with pieces of sharp tin. Still, there were some from the opposite, God love 'em, sex who were attracted to that not-quite-desiccated look, and he wasn't, at his age, fool enough not to take advantage.

Last night, however, he had been alone when the bell had tolled, and it had scared him half to death.

He didn't know why.

He suspected Reed Turner and his friends, out of school and bored, but it hadn't stopped him from sitting up half the night, waiting for something dark to ride on horseback down the road.

"You figure it was the kids?"

Chisholm shook his head. "Doubt it. I checked. No one was there."

"No offense, Padre," Mackey said, voice nasal and high, "but they'd be like there and gone before you even got out of bed. You being sick, I mean. You're still moving kind of slow."

The reverend shrugged.

"Not that I mind the voice of the Lord and all, you know, but it was kind of late."

"They're kids," Chisholm said calmly, staring at the coffee urn, sipping his milk. "If this is the worst they can do, you should be grateful."

"Little ones need love, man, a little respect, you know what I mean?" Mackey said, fat smile all white teeth and chubby cheeks as he pushed his glasses back up his nose, touched the corners of his mouth with a napkin. "In my day, they protested righteous. Today, all they do is whine and use spray paint.'' He made a deep-throated noise of disgust. ''Hard to take sometimes, Padre, you have to admit.''

Chisholm held up the peace sign.

Mackey nodded solemnly and returned the favor.

Todd, wishing the hell the sixties would just die and be done with it, retreated into the kitchen, running his fingers over the polished stainless steel, touching the instruments of his creations, unnecessarily checking the larder in the pantry and walk-in refrigerator.

He was nervous, hand like a cat's tail, twitching, never stopping. He knew it was the Landing. For months now, some weird shit had been going on, and he had an idea, not much more than a little instinct.

Nearly ten years ago, the Army Corps of Engineers and the state had had this plan—dam the upper Delaware, flood the nearby lowland into a lake, bring on the tourists, make a ton of money. Land was bought, people were moved whether they wanted to go or not, the plan died. One of the areas most vocal in its opposition had been Maple Landing, Casey leading the charge. The state hadn't liked it then, and he didn't think they liked it now.

Instinct, suspicion, nothing more.

Water contaminated last fall, a house or two burning despite all the precautions, a few folks on the Crest and a few down here suddenly jobbed by the state's income tax bureau. Roads not plowed after the worst winter in memory. Forestry Service honchos coming around in spring, checking things out, wondering out loud what this would be like if it were wilderness again.

It wasn't the heat; maybe it wasn't anything at all.

Nevertheless, he didn't like it.

Finally, his wandering done, he stood at the screen door in back, staring across the top of the eight-foot hedge separating the diner's short service driveway from the house beyond. All he could see was a dormer window on the second floor, curtains fluttering in the lifeless breeze.

Are you there? he asked silently; come on, babe, are you there?

3

Arlo Mackey slapped a two-dollar bill on the counter and
walked out, peace sign to the preacher, sandals slapping the
checkered linoleum floor.

Humming. Always humming his own private tune.

He closed his eyes against the heat, welcoming it, absorbing
it, then ambled diagonally across the street without bothering
to look.

Nothing to see anyway.

He had come here about the same time Odam had, thinking
the trees and the flowers, the simple life, the river, would take
care of him until he died. Don't bother me, I won't bother
you—that was the way of it, that was his rule.

It had pretty much worked out that way, too, except for
once in a while one of the traveling young would call him
"quaint" and want to take his picture. Not that he really
minded. If that was where their heads were at, as long as they
didn't ask him if he had been at Woodstock, what did he care?

Life was like that.

Peace, with a few bumps along the way.

What he hadn't figured on was winning the bar in a poker
game and having to actually work to make a living. Not that
he worked very hard at it. Bobby the Beautiful Barmaid Karnagan did most of the hard stuff anyway. And in a tucked-
away place like this, crowds were something he only saw on
TV.

He unlocked the stained oak door and stepped inside, closed
his eyes, and felt the cool, the dark, absorbed it and welcomed
it before heading over to the pay phone by the restroom al-
cove.

He slipped in a quarter and dialed.

He said, "Peace, love, all that good shit. I'm getting too
old for this crap, man." He looked blindly around the room,
dust motes hanging, the smell of beer and polish. "Sure, sure,
you got karma, I got karma, all God's chillun got karma, big

deal. Swear to God, I must've been a mass murderer in my former, you know what I mean? What goes around, though, I suppose. So get to the point, man. Just tell me when, I don't want to be here when it comes down.'' He pulled a cigarette from his breast pocket, a wood match from his jeans, and frowned at them both. "Nobody gets too hurt, dig?" He lit the match on the wall, lit the cigarette, inhaled, and coughed. "What?" He coughed again, into the receiver, and grinned. "So get another ear, you got two, right? Lord, sometimes I wish I wasn't so damn smart. Just do it, man, okay?—you got your money. Next time you see me, I'm in Arizona. Harmonic convergence gonna expand my mind, make me One with the Universe and the president of the local bank.'' He laughed. "Believe what you want, man. Millennium's coming and I ain't gonna be here when it happens. Do what you're told.'' He stared at the door. "Just do what you're told.''

He hung up and wandered over to the bar, took the first stool and stared at the smoke curling from the cigarette.

It was a shame, when he thought about it, which was as seldom as possible; a real shame.

But survival was something you either rode easy or got killed by. Sometimes a Child had to become a Man for a while, and do what had to be done.

You didn't reach Nirvana by sitting on your ass.

4

At the foot of Black Oak Road, the blacktop widened into a parking-lot apron at the riverbank, large enough to hold a half dozen vehicles. On the south end was a long shed that served as a boathouse, and beyond it a small log cabin high enough above the water to escape the occasional spring flood. A weathered dock thirty feet long, with twelve indentations, each deep enough to hold one canoe, merged with the blacktop under a stout rope fence.

An overturned nail keg against the shed's north side was Micah Lambert's throne, where he watched the river's level, the woods climbing the hillsides on both banks, and the fools who thought they knew how to handle a canoe. He wasn't a guide, and he wasn't an historian. He took the money, made sure the canoes were equipped with paddles and life jackets, made sure the waivers were signed, and did little else.

Right now, Reed and Nate were out with a small party from New York, sweeping down toward Stroudsburg with a swimming stop along the way; they wouldn't be back until near dinner. Five boats were left. If he was lucky, they'd be gone by noon. *If* he was lucky. But lately that luck had turned bad, real bad, real fast. Despite the lure of the water and the coolness it promised, few wanted to take the time to seek his place out, travel through the heat and over the hills to a backwater like this, just to ride in a canoe. It was, after all, the Delaware, not the Mississippi.

"Too old for this shit," he muttered as he lit a cigarette. "I gotta retire."

Trouble was, he could barely feed himself now; retirement meant starvation.

He rubbed a hand over his short, coarse white beard, then back under his captain's cap through his hair, thick as it was when he was thirty, forty-four years ago.

He stood, one hand massaging the small of his back, and wandered onto the dock, checking the river's level, shaking his head, thinking folks would be able to walk across to Pennsylvania if this kept up. Fish were dying. Every day for the past week he had found dead birds floating on the current. Twice he had seen black bears rumbling along the opposite bank, looking for water, for food. Normally harmless, he figured it wouldn't be long before they turned mean.

At the dock's end he wheeled and walked back, feeling the heat on his head and back, feeling the age in his limbs, feeling the chill when he heard a faint buzzing sound.

He stopped, and looked to his left.

The immediate hillside was steep, heavily wooded with little underbrush, and he could see all the way up to the meadow. At the edge of the woods, not far from where dock and parking lot gave way to the riverbank, what remained of a large oak creaked out over the water. He'd been checking it for days, but only from a distance. A large colony of bees lived in its hollow grey-bark trunk, providing him with enough honey to last most of the winter, while he bottled the rest and sold it through Mabel Jonsen. Lately, though, they barely stirred, even when he threw rocks.

The buzzing faded, and he sighed.

Another sign his life was slow-sliding into Hell.

Movement lifted his gaze above the treetops, and in the hazy sky he spotted a flock of crows circling without calling. They were in no hurry; it almost looked as if they were dozing.

Something dead up in the meadow, he reckoned; rabbit, maybe a raccoon. Those that hadn't left the area already were either too old, too stupid, or too sick to move.

The crows took their time, wheeling at different levels.

And as he watched, one hand shading his eyes, one of the birds fell, wings fluttering helplessly, as if it had been shot. He waited for the retort, the echo, but heard nothing.

He grunted.

A second bird dropped.

A third.

The rest sped away, calling as they aimed for the protection of the forest.

"Be damned," he muttered.

5

The grocery wasn't large, mainly carrying the staples Mabel's customers needed so they didn't have to drive fifteen winding miles to the nearest Acme or A&P. On the left wall a rack of magazines, comics, newspapers, and cards; on the right wall a long, multi-glass-door refrigerator with milk, soda, ice cream, and beer. Once she had completed the inventory, she moved behind the counter in back, leaning forward on her elbows.

Moss Tully stood at the door, one hand in his hip pocket.

"So?" she said.

He squinted at the thermometer she had fixed to the outside window frame. "Eighty-five, gonna hit a hundred, no question about it." A smooth voice, mostly monotone. "You walk out there today, you're gonna fry like an egg." He shook his head, bald from chemotherapy almost a decade ago and never recovered. It was his badge. He bent his knees so he could peer up at the church steeple. "Bet you five hundred it was that damn Turner kid and his gang last night. They got no respect for religion anymore."

"Doesn't make any difference, it's the UFOs anyway," she told him, her voice like dark honey. She wore a patched cardigan caped over her shoulders against the fierce wind of the air-conditioning, a shapeless print dress, her mostly brown hair pulled back in a bun and corralled with a hair net. Reading glasses perched on her nose. A face round and flushed, with small emerald eyes that seldom stopped moving, checking, even when the store was empty.

Moss glanced over his shoulder. "UFOs?"

"Of course." She picked up a copy of *Weekly World News*. "They're coming, can't you read?"

She ignored his scoffing snort. Moss, like most of the other simpletons around here, never paid any attention to anything but making enough money to last through the winter. She, on the other hand, when she wasn't at the tables in Atlantic City, read constantly, rapaciously, forgetting nothing, sifting everything. The UFOs were a fact, even the Air Force said so, and what with dead birds and critters all over the place, the church bell ringing all hours of the night, it was obvious something was going on here, and just as obvious the UFOs were involved. All she had to do was figure out how. And where. Once she did that, those casino bus trips would be history. She'd have enough money from selling her story to head for Arizona, Alaska, any damn place she pleased. Fifty-one years old, it was time to start thinking about packing it in, unloading this store and getting herself a life.

She flipped the tabloid's page and shook her head. 'Course, this crap about kids eating their mother alive on Mother's Day, that was made up. She knew that, she wasn't stupid. She

couldn't figure out how a newspaper like this could print gar-
bage like that. If it wasn't for the UFOs, she wouldn't even
stock it.

"There goes old Arlo," Moss said. "He looks stoned, per
usual." He chuckled. "Guess that bell scared the hell out of
his customers last night." He laughed. "Get it?"

She could barely see him against the sun's glare, his outline
making him even skinnier than he was, older than he was,
which was only a couple years younger than her. Hiking boots,
low-slung jeans, a plaid shirt worn from too much washing.
Taut, that's what he was.

When he turned around, it seemed like the clothes vanished,
and her breath shortened as she blinked against the illusion.

"Something wrong?"

"Nope."

He smiled, face falling into sun wrinkles that gave his face
the look of fine leather. "Bet I know what you're thinking."

"I'm thinking," she said sharply, "you should get your
skinny butt out there and see what's going on."

He sauntered down the center aisle, thumb hooked in his
belt. "I don't think so."

She straightened, a hand fussing unnecessarily at her hair.
"For God's sake, Moss, there's people out there."

He didn't stop. "So?"

Out of the glare, clothes back, sly smile, left eye as always
partially closed. "So?" he repeated.

"Damnit, I want to know about the UFOs."

"Jesus, Mabe."

She pointed a slender finger at the door. "You want something? You gotta get me something."

He stopped, corner of his mouth twitching. He inhaled,
ready to say something, then shrugged elaborately, winked,
and turned around.

Mabel almost told him to stop, she was ready anytime he
was, but the UFOs were important. She could always get laid
later, after he had found out what, or who, had rung that stupid
bell.

He said nothing as he left, and in that glare he was almost

transparent. Enough so that she caught her breath, pressed a hand to her chest.

Good God, maybe he was one of them.

Maybe he wasn't really Moss Tully at all. And that stupid beagle of his wasn't really a dog. Christ, all it did was sit on the bench outside the hardware store, watching the people, watching the birds. Damn thing didn't even have a name. Maybe because they didn't give their pets names.

Son of a bitch, she thought; son of a bitch.

6

They stood far enough back from the bedroom window so Todd couldn't see them through the screen and blowing curtains.

"They all think we're queer, you know." Bobby raised herself onto her toes so she could see better. "Even him, sometimes."

Tessa shoved the shorter woman off balance. "They do not." She waggled her thick eyebrows. "Just weird, that's all."

"I am not weird. I am independent."

"In this place, that's weird."

They giggled like schoolgirls, and Helen, standing just behind them, wanted to smack them across the head a few times. The trouble was, they were probably right. Three women in one rented house barely large enough for two had been, she knew, the topic of nightly conversations at Mackey's and the Moonglow since she had returned to the Landing last fall.

Not that she cared anymore. She had been born and raised here, had left to go to college, and hadn't even considered coming back until her husband of nine years had decided he had had enough of her, of his stultifying Tucson job, and life. In that order. Luckily she hadn't found his body, hadn't seen what the shotgun had done to his head; unluckily the only message he had left was the phone number of his mistress, and two words: *the end.*

The money and house had been taken when his clumsy embezzlement had been discovered; her impatience with Arizona ran out the first time she tried to get a decent job and the personnel director called her "honey" five times in two sentences, and "little lady" three times.

There had been only one place left to go, unless she wanted to stand beneath a streetlamp and hustle passing cars.

"He's going away," Bobby said, disappointed. "Shoot, and I was going to strip for him, too."

Tessa punched her arm, and they mock-wrestled each other onto the single bed.

Helen watched, sighed, and left, not understanding how they could both be going with the same man at the same time and not tear each other's throat out, even though the man was Todd Odam. He was a nice guy, a decent boss, but he spooked her, moving too quickly and quietly for her peace of mind.

But then, lots of things spooked her these days.

Even her own shadow.

In the small, mostly green kitchen she made a peanut butter sandwich and stood at the back door, watching the lawn die. She rubbed her neck absently, glad she'd gotten the haircut, even though Tessa had wept for what she had called the desecration of her womanhood. So it was short, almost masculine, so what? It was cool, it brushed into place with only a couple of strokes, and it fit her long face, accentuating rather than emphasizing.

Her arm folded across her stomach.

Besides, Casey seemed to like it.

Tessa came up behind her. "If you went to church once in a while, maybe he'd notice you more."

Helen closed her eyes, seeking the strength not to strangle the woman. "Just drop it, Markowski, okay? You guys have been on me for weeks, and it's getting a little tired."

"Hey, okay by me. But the house committee wants you to know we're getting a little tired of you moping around. Either get a second job, or get laid, one or the other."

Helen turned in deliberate slow stages, but Tessa had already retreated to the doorway, round face flushed trying not to laugh, one hand up as a false gesture of peace.

"You die," Helen told her, lowering her already deep voice.

Tessa cupped a palm around her ear. "What? Can't hear you, lady. The air-conditioning's too loud."

"It's broken, jerk."

"Right. And you were supposed to fix it today, remember?"

Helen did, just then. It was part of the threesome's rental agreement—she would pay a smaller share than the others so long as she kept the place from falling down and the appliances from running amok. There were times, though, like now, when she hated the skills her daddy had taught her. If she had only had a brother—

"Oh, don't give me that look," Tessa said in mock disgust. "It ain't gonna work. Just do it, huh? Before we all melt?"

Helen finished the sandwich and wiped her hands on her jeans. "You know," she said, kneeling at the cabinet under the sink, "if you watched me once in a while, you could learn cool shit, too."

Tessa rolled her eyes. "I am on vacation. The only cool shit I want is beer on ice."

"And a man!" Bobby yelled from the staircase.

Tessa ignored her and leaned against the door frame. "Why do you put up with us?"

Helen pulled out her father's old toolbox. "Because we grew up together."

And more; they were more sisters than if they had the same mother. Tessa knew that; Bobby probably did too, but wouldn't admit it.

"Yeah, but . . ."

Something in the tone made her look up.

"She wants to marry him, Hel." Tessa's eyes shone, her lower lip stiffened so it wouldn't quiver. "She'll move out."

"Okay. Assuming Todd's crazy enough . . . so what?"

"So you won't stay here forever either, right?"

She didn't answer right away. She hefted the toolbox onto the kitchen table and flipped back the lid. The smell of oil, grease, sawdust, her father. Nothing of her mother at all, except every time she looked in a mirror.

"Hel?"

"Christ!" Bobby yelled.

Tessa looked over her shoulder. "What now?"

Bobby pointed indignantly at the front door. "There's a zillion dead moths all over the porch." She made a face. "God."

"So you know where the broom is, dope. Put on some shoes and broom." She looked back at Helen. "There's something wrong here, you know."

Helen grinned. "Right." She picked up a screwdriver. "You want to help?"

Tessa didn't smile. "I'm not kidding." A nervous hand tangled itself in her blonde curls. "I don't mean the fires, the water, that stuff. I don't mean that. It's something . . ." A wan smile and a shrug. ". . . I don't know—else."

"It's not that hard." She tucked the box under her arm and headed for the living room, pausing to put a hand on Tessa's shoulder. "What's wrong here is three grown women living in a shoebox during a wicked heat wave, getting on each other's nerves. What's wrong here is two of those grown women messing around with the same guy. And," she added softly as Tessa opened her mouth, "what's wrong here is that instead of going on your Canadian trip, you stayed here to look after poor little Helen, who got dumped by a cheating husband and was made a widow, all in less than a couple of weeks." She kissed the woman's cheek. "I've been here for nine months, honey. If I was going to crack, it would have been long before this."

Her friend's expression was a protest, but Helen didn't allow her to voice it. She rattled the tools, yelled at Bobby to stop whining and get the broom, and marched into the living room where the air conditioner dared her to do something about it.

A challenge, she told herself; think of it as a challenge. If you blow it, you can always leave.

"Aw . . . gross!" Bobby cried from the porch.

Tessa slammed impatiently through the screen door and groaned, ''You were supposed to put on shoes, you jerk.''

''I forgot!''

On the other hand, Helen thought, who'd take care of the kids?

7

Star Creek meandered through the woods, across the meadow, and down to the river. When it had more than a trickle of water. Now, what moisture it held barely moved, and the raccoon on the bank only stared at the weeds growing in the shallow bed. It sat for nearly an hour, just staring, half its tail gone, its right front paw lifted stiffly off the ground. It didn't move when a crow landed not five feet away; its fur barely rippled when a warm breeze coasted across its back; its eyes didn't blink when a mostly brown leaf bumped against its nose. When it toppled, there was hardly a sound. Had there been water in the creek, it would have drowned. As it was, it just died, and the crow flew away.

Part 2

PERCUSSION AND REEDS

1

The night was made for vampires.

A full moon washing color from the ground and stars from the sky, not quite bright enough to read by, but bright enough for shadows to spread and grow an edge.

A slow constant wind slipping through the trees of the Blue Ridge Mountains, skating across the grass, scurrying grit from the shoulders of the interstate onto the tarmac. Dust devils short-lived, dancing in the black. Dead leaves slapping across windshields and clinging to blades, fluttering, scraping, slipping away in shreds. A paper cup rolling into a ditch. Pebbles stirring.

The temperature cool without being cold.

Dark between the exits.

No lights but a pair of headlamps.

No lights at all.

2

Stan Hogan knew things.

He knew how to slip through a town North or South without getting arrested; he knew how to check neighborhoods and malls for work without someone calling the cops and calling him a prowler; he knew how to make canned food last twice, three times longer that it was supposed to.

He knew how not to die.

He also knew, as he trudged along the interstate, Roanoke on his right and behind, swimming fast toward midnight, that if he didn't catch a ride soon, he was going to have to spend another damn night in this damn place, and that would probably make·him mad.

He hated it when he got mad.

He did stupid things.

It wasn't as if he didn't know what he was doing; it was simply that as he was doing them, he knew they were dumb.

Sometimes he stole, sometimes he hit people, sometimes he took the little money he carried and went into a bar and drank that money into a ball-peen hangover that more often than not landed him in a cell, some guy calling him a vagrant, maybe some other guy, seeing he didn't do drugs and wasn't as old as he looked, calling around town trying to find him work so he wouldn't be a vagrant anymore.

It didn't happen often.

Three, maybe four times a year.

Three, maybe four times more than he wanted.

Like the traveling, it was something he did.

Not that he minded the traveling part. Hell's bells on a reindeer, hadn't he been doing it since God knew when? Hadn't he seen damn near every state in the Union over the past ten years? And damn near every jail?

Nah, he didn't mind it much at all, usually. Come down to it, he'd rather be doing this than sitting in an office, wearing a goddamn noose, suit, polished shoes, matching socks. Come down to it, he'd just about rather be doing anything else at all than that.

Except doing it like this, in the middle of the week, slumping along the interstate, hardly anyone on the road, empty stomach, tired feet, the backpack adjusted but his back killing him anyway.

A nice night, at least, the moon, the stars; at least it wasn't like walking down a dead tunnel like it was sometimes when the clouds crept in and took the light from him because he hadn't been paying attention. Air just right, just cool enough to hold back the sweat, just warm enough to hold back the sweat, just warm enough to ward off the shivers.

Slumping along.

Singing a song.

He laughed aloud, and loudly.

Guy he had met, not long after he'd hit the road, he had called Stan a natural. Not very tall, a little on the round side, but a face that would charm, the guy said, the mother side of every woman in the country. Although, Stan had to admit, not the eyes. They were bigger than a man's ought to be, and when he widened them, he looked less like the good old deer caught in the headlights than he did someone who had just had a stiletto slipped into his back.

It took him years to get those eyes to stay partially closed without him thinking about it.

They opened all the way only when he got mad.

Three, maybe four times a year.

With a quick look back, he stepped into the near lane to get around a drainage ditch, moved quickly back to the shoulder and moved on. All without half thinking about it.

A natural.

Five days out of high school, telling his old man he was gonna see the country before he headed for college. The old man wished him well. Stan hugged him, kissed him on the cheek, never saw him again. Never saw college, either, for that matter.

He liked the road too much.

Natural.

Singing a song.

Side by side with the night and the moon and the stars and the wind.

So when he saw the lights slipping down the hill toward him, he flipped a coin he didn't have and prayed it wasn't a state trooper. They were nice down here most of the time, but they had a job, and part of that job was making sure little round guys with big eyes didn't hitch on the federally funded highway.

The way the lights grew, he knew there wasn't much time.

After settling his backpack, he swept a quick practiced hand over his trench coat, dusting as best as he could before pushing the hand back through the thatch of pale blond on his head. Touched his beard, trimmed once a week. Smoothed his mustache, trimmed once a week. Blinked several times before he found the right expression, the one that said, I'm okay, I ain't gonna knife you, all I want is a seat before my legs fall off.

Hard to do in the dark.

Stan was good at it.

A natural.

But no thumb. Never a thumb on a road like this.

It was a technical point; he could argue he was just walking, officer, easier here than on the side roads, those things got him lost most of the time. Some cops grinned and let him go; others glared and let him go; a handful now and then, especially in winter when they didn't want to stop and let in the cold, yanked him in faster than a trout on a thin line.

A look over his shoulder.

The look.

Hoping the driver would glance his way as he passed, sixty, seventy miles an hour in the middle of the night in the middle of the invisible gut of the Shenandoah Valley.

He heard the car, saw the dark ahead begin to fade in the approaching glow.

He made sure there was plenty of room between himself and the right-hand lane, just in case it was a drunk, or a kid, or an idiot who wanted to play matador, see how close he could come without taking off Stan's hip.

He also made sure there was a stretch ahead wide enough for the driver to pull over if he was of a mind. No sense trying to hitch on a bridge, or along a ditch, or on a short curve. Not good in broad daylight; suicide at night.

Then, as the glow brightened and he grew a shadow, he looked.

The car pulled over smoothly and stopped.

Behind him.

Wheels crunching on the gravelly dirt, lights too white, making him squint, shading his eyes with one hand, half turned, slightly hunched, legs trembling for the action call.

Stan Hogan knew things.

And he knew this wasn't right.

Nobody stopped before they got a good look at him, checking him out on the way by.

Pinned to the night, now, like a moth on black velvet.

Still, the constant wind was getting ready to give him a headache, and his stomach had already growled a half dozen times in the past ten minutes. And it sure wasn't as if he couldn't take care of himself; Jesus, he'd had enough practice. And it wasn't as if whoever was behind the wheel, just sitting there, waiting on him to move, couldn't see that he wasn't starving, that he wasn't a shrimp.

What the hell, he decided when neither he nor the car moved after a full minute; beggars and hobos can't be choosers.

He smiled just enough, and trudged back, keeping to the shoulder, lowering his hand to prove he wasn't really afraid. Moving. Just moving. Coming up and around and finally away from the glare and stopping before he got to the door.

Oh, my God, he thought; my God, would you look at that, for God's sake, Daddy, would you take a look at that.

Shadow behind the windshield leaned over, and the door opened without a sound, not a creak, not a groan.

Stan nodded, just once, and moved up, hand braced on the top and leaned over. Not in. Never in. No threats here, just a guy.

"How far are you going?" the driver asked. Quietly.

"Do you know," he said, breaking all the rules, "this is the biggest goddamn car I've ever seen in my life?"

The laughter was quick and light, the same as a thank-you, and he could see her now, the dashboard just bright enough, and not bright enough to show him her eyes. But he knew there was no fear in that car, that cavern on wheels, that magnificent Continental gunboat nearly as white and silent as the moon, silver horse in full gallop fixed on the hood. So he grinned, and eased his backpack from his shoulders, slid in, set the pack on his lap, closed the door as gently as he could, and shook his head slowly. Keeping his hands carefully folded in his lap, feet flat on the rubber mat.

Looking straight ahead; it wasn't right to stare.

When the car moved, he barely felt it.

Not a sound.

Not a goddamn sound.

3

"So," she said, reaching over to switch on the radio. "How far are you going?"

"Wherever," he answered, as honest as he could.

Some kind of symphony almost too soft to hear; but he could hear the clarinets, bassoons, and something else behind them. Timpani, stately and steady.

She nodded, hands at ten and two. "I'm leaving Virginia."

"Okay by me."

He looked then, and saw a young woman's profile, sensed more than saw short dark hair, jeans, and a light jacket not denim.

She glanced over and smiled mischievously. "Every male's fantasy, right?"

He didn't answer.

"I mean, getting picked up by a woman."

He didn't answer.

"She gets tired, maybe suggests a stop for the night. And why bother with two rooms since he obviously can't afford it, and she doesn't want him sleeping in the car or someplace outside. It wouldn't be fair. Coffee maybe, if the restaurant's open.''

He couldn't answer.

"They talk a little, nothing deep, right? Then they go to her room, she suggests maybe he'd like a real shower for a change.''

A soft voice, a soft accent; South, maybe, but he couldn't tell exactly where.

Saxophones, and bells.

"After fussing around a little while, a little embarrassed, for crying out loud, he gets in, and nearly faints from all that hot water and perfumed soap, and he's thinking that if he's really died and gone to heaven, she'll suddenly yank back the shower curtain and join him.''

He knew things.

"Maybe," she said, looking over, ignoring the road, "she'll offer to soap him up if he'll soap her. I mean, she's been driving all day and most of the night, and she's stiff. It's the least he can do for the ride and the room. And all that water, Stan, pounding on his head, maybe it's making him a little dizzy." She laughed almost soundlessly. "It's sure as hell making him horny, wouldn't you say?''

He knew she was driving too damn fast; there was no way he could jump out without killing himself.

He knew that she was just talking, there was no fantasy here.

He knew that she shouldn't have known his name.

She turned her smile toward him, and it must have been the dashboard's dim light, the shadows, the weariness, the growling in his stomach, the long hours on the road.

It must have been.

Because her teeth were too sharp.

"Stan," she said, parting her lips just a little, "tell me what you're thinking.''

"Vampire," he blurted, and felt like an instant fool. A kid, instead of an old man not quite thirty. "For a minute there I thought you was a vampire.'' He chuckled and ducked his head. ''Or a werewolf, something like that.''

She didn't laugh, but she looked back to the road.

''I'm sorry,'' he said. ''I guess I'm . . . I'm sorry.''

''A vampire?''

He nodded.

''Stan,'' she said, ''even if that were true, it would be the least of your problems.''

4

He knew he wasn't alone.

With a smile so false he was positive it was insulting, he checked slowly over his shoulder. It was too dark back there in that mansion-sized rear seat, but not so dark that he couldn't make out someone tucked comfortably into the far corner, and someone else curled up right behind him.

Oh God, I'm gonna die.

The driver *tsk*ed as she glanced at the rearview mirror. ''You're scaring the man. Introduce yourselves before he climbs through the roof.''

He heard quiet laughter, and some giggling.

''Not fair,'' the driver said, scolding with a smile. ''Stan's not stupid, you know. And you're not invisible.''

A second after the giggling finally stopped, he heard a woman call herself Lupé, and saw the hand reach out of the dark. A nice hand. A little tough when he twisted around to grip it, lots of hard work there in those fingers, nearly as strong as he was, nearly as large.

Another hand reached out, much younger, softer, but he couldn't tell if it belonged to a boy or a girl, and the owner only giggled, didn't give him a name, didn't come into the dim light.

He nodded. ''Stan Hogan.''

''Nice to meet you, Stan,'' Lupé said.

Giggling again, and a whispered, ''Likewise.''

A moment and a smile more for courtesy, and he faced front

again, gripping the pack hard, crushing it to his stomach.

I'm gonna die.

The driver reached out and patted his leg. "You've been on the road a long time, haven't you? It must be hard to be around people."

He shook his head. "Nope. No. I'm—"

"Don't be. I'll make you the same offer I made the others— if you want to leave, just say the word and I'll drop you off." He sensed the kindness, the genuine offer. "At an exit where you can get something to eat, maybe some sleep, by the way." She laughed. "I sure won't drop you off with nothing but farms around for miles."

He thought, what the hell, and nodded. "Okay."

Another mile driving too damn fast.

Horns, and violins.

"How old are you, Stan? Twenty-seven, twenty-eight?"

His eyes widened before he could stop them. "God, you're good!" Realized immediately how loud he sounded, how softly she spoke.

She shrugged. "Practice, that's all. Lots of practice. I mean, you've probably been more places than ninety percent of the people in this country, and I'll bet you can tell at a glance what most of those people are like."

He shrugged one shoulder. "Well . . . kinda."

"You pretty much know who'll give you food, or some work, things like that, right?"

Another shrug. "Well . . . I guess."

"So . . . what do you think?"

He didn't know; he didn't say.

"Have you been on the road long?" Lupé asked, staying back in the dark.

"Yes."

The driver turned toward him, half her face gone, half touched by the dashboard glow. "What can you tell me about me, Stan?"

"Well, you sure ain't a vampire."

Three laughs, and a giggling.

Reeds, and soft percussion.

"Get some rest, Stan. We've a long way to go."

5

"You know, Sue—"

"Susan."

"Yeah. Sorry. But no offense, I really could use something to eat."

"We'll stop as soon as we get into Maryland or Pennsylvania, okay?"

"Sure, no problem."

"Then we can all get cleaned up, refreshed, be ready to go."

"You know, you still haven't told me where we're going."

"Have you ever killed a man, Stan?"

"Nope. Well . . . I guess maybe. I'm not really sure."

"Well, that's where we're going."

2

Babysitting wasn't exactly the way Cora had hoped to spend the summer, but with the guys working the river, and Rina working at the diner most of the time, it was at least a way to earn a few bucks, and stay away from her father.

Besides, it was kind of fun. The Balanovs had a large pool behind their mock Tudor, they let her have the run of the house, and the kids weren't much of a hassle at all. Sonya spent most of her time in the huge sandbox, building elaborate castles for her dolls, while Dimitri, when he wasn't trying to talk to the birds, played ball in the little schoolyard across the street.

Every so often, though, she felt a bit lonely, but it seldom lasted. Sonya would decide it was time to play in the water, or Dimitri would shriek into the one-acre yard and try to tackle her out of her chair, and before she knew it, the Balanovs would be on the redwood deck, watching with some amusement, and bewilderment, as the seventeen-year-old girl gangwrestled with their children.

Today had been better than most.

The heat wave had bent, the temperature dropping out of the high nineties for the first time in two weeks. The radio still talked about weather-blamed riots in Boston and New York the night before, about the explosion of drive-by shootings in suburban New Jersey and Philadelphia, but it was all too far away.

Everything was too far away.

"Oh, Christ," she muttered, and sat up.

"Bad word," Sonya scolded, scowling as she tried to fix a tiny flag to a not quite perfect tower. Skinny like her brother, and like her brother, topped with curly black hair that made her large black eyes seem enormous. "I'm telling Momma."

Cora rolled up to her knees. "Oh no," she begged in a high-pitched voice. "Please don't tell, Sonya. I'll do anything." She started crawling toward the sandbox. "Anything."

Sonya ignored her.

"Pleasepleaseplease?"

She heard a giggle.

"I'll never say a bad word again as long as I live, okay?"

The girl's hand shook as she tried to reset the flag.

"I swear."

Cora's palm came down on a sharp pebble. "Damn!"

Sonya shrieked a laugh, rocked back on her heels and shrieked again when she lost her balance and toppled off the sandbox ledge onto the grass.

Cora pounced. "Now," she said, face close to Sonya's, "I will be forced to torture you, girl." She lifted one eyebrow. "You know of the infamous Bowes Water Torture?"

Sonya tried to wriggle free, but she couldn't free her arms, couldn't stop laughing.

"Ah, I see that you do." She stood, lifting the nine-year-old with her. "Too bad." She turned toward the pool. "Because *I have not yet fed the sharks!*"

As Sonya cried to her dolls for help, Cora leapt into the water. Cannonball. Releasing the girl when her feet touched bottom, pushing her up, following her to the surface and staying right behind while she dog-paddled to the edge.

Laughing; still laughing.

Cora deepened her voice and hummed the theme from *Jaws*.

Sonya shrieked again and tried to haul herself up to the rose-tile lip. Cora pawed at her waist, causing Sonya to slip back, whirl, and catch her on the jaw with a tiny fist. A punch, not a slap, and much harder than it should have been.

Laughing; still laughing.

Surprise dropped Cora under for a moment. Her temper flared, and before she realized it, she had reached out again, this time to drag the child under with her, teach her a damn lesson. But as soon as her fingers closed around an ankle, she released it and floated up.

Sonya scrambled out and sat with her legs dangling. "Stupid shark," she said.

Cora spat, treading water, rubbing and poking at her jaw gingerly to be sure she had all her teeth. Exaggerating, but not by much. Man, that kid was strong. She tasted blood and watched droplets fade in the water. The little creep had cut the inside of her lip.

Sonya's eyes widened. "Did you get hurt?"

"I'll live." Tasting blood.

A lower lip curled under and trembled. "I'm sorry."

"It's all right," Cora said flatly. "It was a mistake."

Sonya lifted her chin. "You can hit me if you want to."

Cora tightened her jaw to keep from smiling. "It's tempting, you little twerp. Never tempt the shark."

Sonya kicked one leg halfheartedly, the splash not going very far. "I'm sorry."

A lazy breaststroke took her to the girl's side, a kick and pull brought her out of the pool. They watched a breeze cast a ripple across the surface. She spat on the grass, not stopping until the blood did, the sun warm and cool on her shoulders. At the back of the yard a stand of trees mostly birch and oak hissed at them for a moment, dancing shadows on the grass.

Then Sonya said wistfully, "I wish you were my sister."

"Me too," she answered without thinking, giving Sonya a hug.

" 'Me too' what?" a voice asked.

Dimitri crossed the lawn. T-shirt and shorts, and a baseball cap turned backward. He was a year older than his sister and two inches taller, but with those eyes and that hair he was too pretty to be a boy. It had gotten him in trouble, and she hoped he'd bulk up before he reached high school, or they'd eat him alive.

"Cora's gonna be my sister," Sonya said.

"Oh, yuck."

He walked past them, and Cora sighed when he didn't try to knock down the sand castle or push her in the water. Something had happened. It wasn't his expression, but the only time he went near the trees on his own was to talk to the birds; he only talked to the birds when something had upset him. She hustled Sonya to the sandbox, and followed, not pretending to do anything else.

There were sparrows up there, no more than a handful, and he cocked his head as if they were talking just to him.

"So?" she said quietly.

He shrugged. "Nothing."

She rapped his skull with a knuckle. "Talk."

One shoulder lifted this time; she rapped him again, a little harder, and knelt beside him, keeping her face turned to the birds, glancing over and startled to see tears in his eyes.

She touched his back lightly. "What do they say?"

Dimitri sniffed, and wiped an arm across his nose and mouth.

"Are they telling you when it's going to rain? I hope so. We could sure use it."

A tear slipped, but she didn't stop it.

"That bad, huh?"

"Die."

She wasn't sure she heard him. "What?"

"We're all gonna die."

Oh man, this was the part she really hated. This was when the kid needed his mother, not her. This kind of stuff she didn't know anything about.

"Oh." She stood, putting an arm around his shoulders and forcing him to turn with her. "I suppose we are, in a way. In a couple hundred years." She nudged him toward the house. "Of course, I don't know about Batman. I mean, he seems pretty good to hang on for, I don't know, a couple of weeks."

He didn't smile.

He twisted away and ran, climbing the deck steps two at a time, yanking open the kitchen door and vanishing inside.

The only thing she could think of was that someone had said something to him, either in the schoolyard or on the street. It made her mad. Kids don't need to think of things like that. God, it was bad enough as it was just trying to grow up in a noplace town like this. She shoved her feet into her flip-flops, ordered Sonya to stay where she was, and marched around the house to the front. Across the road to her left, the single-story square brick school was silent. No one in any yard she could see. So where had he gotten such a crazy idea?

A car drove by, heading west, and a hand reached over the roof to give her a wave.

Her arm was up before she realized who it was, and she froze.

Son of a bitch. Reverend Chisholm. That son of a bitch hick bastard. Looking at her like that, making her feel strange.

Making her feel.

He waved again, and her hand closed into a fist, and when he checked the rearview mirror she had already turned her back, making him wonder if it wasn't time for them to have a little talk. But not so little, he knew; not so little at all.

He remembered Sunday night, her attitude, her face. He had known her too long to believe she had grown into that; she had been forced there, and he had a sickening idea who had done it.

His breathing grew shallow as his anger surged, and it took several whacks of his fist against the seat beside him before he beat the anger back, ashamed for not feeling compassion first.

Two blocks later, he parked in front of a brick ranch house nearly buried by flanking pines. Across Black Oak was a deli, the Video Pavilion, and a coin laundry, all housed in a flat-roofed, hideous yellow clapboard building that wanted repainting. He trotted over into the video store and headed for the counter on the right. No one was there, and he rapped the bell beside the register, shave-and-a-haircut.

A glance at the window blocked with movie posters, half expecting to see Cora stomping by. Half hoping, even though now wasn't the time. On days like this, weariness had never refused a ride home.

He shook his head and unbuttoned his suit jacket. He had been at the hospital, and he was, as always, equally depressed and elated. Elated because Georgia Williams had survived her third back operation in eighteen months, no mean feat for a woman in her eighties; depressed because he could do nothing about the others. Weak and wizened, staring blindly at a wall-mounted television, or simply staring at the ceiling, mumbling to themselves.

Waiting.

Just waiting.

When they looked at him, recognized him, saw the plain gold cross on the plain gold chain hanging against his chest, they always had the same question even though they didn't always ask it: *what did God say, Reverend? Am I going to go home?*

He had dozens of answers stock and glib, and had used them all at one time or another. None of them, however, was *it's His will, whatever happens*. He didn't believe that one for a minute.

Sometimes he wished he did; it would make his job so much more simple.

"Why," a woman's voice asked crossly, "do you always come in here when you've hit the hospital and shut-in trail? Is it my karma or something?"

"I need a good laugh, Kay," he answered honestly, leaning a heavy hip against the counter.

"Yeah, maybe, but you always make the rest of us so damn depressed." Kay Pollard wandered out of the back room and over to the comedy section on the back wall. "Besides, you've already seen most of these." A glance over her shoulder. "Twice."

He didn't move. He would rather watch her move, and grinned when she read the faint smile on his face.

"You're a preacher," she scolded, coming toward him. A

head shorter, too much weight without being fat, baggy slacks and blouse hiding her true figure. Deep brown hair and feathery bangs, a pleasantly round face he suspected would never get old. "You're not supposed to be thinking stuff like that."

"Like what?" he asked innocently.

She passed him, thumped his stomach with a loose fist, and pointed toward the new releases on the opposite wall. "It's Wednesday. Two-for-one. Go find something there before you make me want to cut my throat."

"I didn't say anything," he protested, and obeyed anyway.

She sidestepped behind the counter. "You don't have to. The collar is still on, the jacket is still on, that ugly face is still on. You could wear a sign, but it would be redundant."

He turned his back to her and scanned the titles.

"How are you feeling?"

He waggled his right hand. "So-so. I'll live."

"You should rest, eat."

"I'll eat in a few minutes, rest later."

She mumbled something he didn't catch, then said, "So, you hear about that stuff down in Arkansas? That town?"

He nodded; it had been all over the hospital. A tiny roadside community leveled by fire and gunfire. Its own people killing each other, burning each other out, the survivors claiming they were cleansing the spot for the Lord, for the end of the world.

It wasn't alone; there had been others.

"So what do you think?"

He coughed, not badly. "I think I'm a little tired of reading about things like that, I guess." A shrug. "I'm not surprised, if that's what you're asking."

"You're not?" Her voice said she was.

A glance over his shoulder. "Not really. Too many people, too much pressure, too much heat, too much of just about everything. Something's bound to give."

"Yeah, well, how about saying it's just the end of the world?"

"Okay. It's the end of the world."

He braced himself for something—a thrown box, pencil, pen, wadded-up paper.

It was paper.

He grinned, and leaned over to read the titles near the bottom, thinking only midgets would ever know what was down here.

"So how is Georgia?"

"Fine." He kept reading. "She ought to be home sometime after the Fourth." Nothing there, and he straightened, lightly rubbing his chest. "What do you suggest?"

"Violence."

That made him look. "What?"

She smiled sweetly, sinking dimples into her cheeks. "Nothing you take ever makes you laugh anyway, right? So get some old-fashioned, extreme, gratuitous violence. Something where people are blowing other people away. Buildings blowing up." She spread her arms. "Entire cities leveled. Countries destroyed." A tap to her temple. "Trust me, it works. Vicarious death and destruction, guaranteed to make you feel a whole lot better."

"About what?"

"About not being a stunt man."

He laughed silently, slipped his hands into his pockets and wandered around the store, reading posters and boxes, checking the rack of candy and microwave popcorn, and finally staring pointedly at the unmarked red notebook she kept beside the register.

"No," she said hastily, snatching it away to tuck under the counter. "No way."

"Why not?" All wide-eyed and hurt.

"I don't rent porn to preachers. It's a rule. And it's probably a law."

"Maybe," he said quietly, "you shouldn't be renting it at all."

"Oh no." She shook a finger at his chest. "Don't start with me, Casey Chisholm. It's bad enough Enid comes in two, three times a week, preaching about ruining the lives of our children, destroying their precious morals. I don't need you, too."

He nodded knowingly. "Ah. Came in before she left for work today, did she?"

Kay sneered. "I swear, one of these days I'm gonna deck her, the pious bitch." She didn't apologize for the language.

He understood. Enid Balanov was a member of his church, and a preeminent member of the Ladies' Guild. They furnished flowers for the altar, polished the silver, decorated for the holidays, planned picnics and suppers, ran rummage sales, and tried, in the bargain, to run the church as well. She and her friends knew everything about everybody, and they made sure he knew it too.

Even Job, he suspected, would have cracked under the pressure.

"I'll have a talk with her," he promised, knowing it wouldn't do a damn bit of good.

Kay knew it too by the skeptical, and grateful, look she gave him. She winked as she reached under the counter. "Here."

Puzzlement sketched a frown as she tore off the plastic shrink-wrap, trying and failing to read the title upside down. "What is it?"

"Chinese movie. You'll love it. Ghosts, demons, chop-socky in slow motion, stupid subtitles," she lowered her voice, "a little sex," and handed the box over, "and something called a hopping vampire."

He stared at the cover, a woman in flowing white, floating above the ground in a skeletal forest. "A what?"

"You heard me."

"That's what I'm afraid of." He reached for his wallet, but she stayed him with a touch to his arm. The finger lingered, stroking the black cloth to his wrist before sliding away. He smiled and tried to think of something to say. It was easy to be quick with a bunch of kids, or the guys at the Moonglow; it was something else to find wit or substance in a woman's presence. For all his size, they made him feel like a teenager still trying to figure out what hormones meant, and what he was supposed to do with them once he found out.

Kay wouldn't help him. She watched his discomfort until she couldn't stand it anymore, then propped herself on her elbows and fed him the latest hot gossip—that Mabel and

Moss were going to be married in two weeks. She giggled at his expression, and told him Mabel had come in only an hour ago with the news; she was also hunting for Casey.

"Me?" His hand went to his chest. "Dear Lord, surely she doesn't want me to . . . not . . ."

She nodded. "Absolutely. Cheaper than a judge is what she told me."

"Wonderful. What a recommendation."

"You'll love it, and you know it," she told him as he nearly ran for the exit. "She figures the UFO guys will be at the reception."

He opened the door and paused.

She waited, but he said nothing, just shook his head and left.

She watched him drive away, and cursed herself for not asking him to dinner. It had been her day's plan, ever since Doc Farber had told her Casey was on his rounds. Experience had taught her he'd be back just before five, that he'd be sad, feeling helpless, and starving because he would have forgotten to eat anything since breakfast. But just like all the other times, she had lost her nerve the moment she saw him—not just the size of him, but the sheer *him* of him. He overwhelmed her just by standing there, making her wish she had Cora Bowes's figure or Helen Gable's quick sharp tongue; then she'd at least be able to make a dent in him, one way or the other.

As it was, he was gone, and now she'd have to contrive to see him at the diner, or in Mackey's, or . . .

"Shit," she said, angrily tossing the shrink-wrap into the wastebasket. "Shit. Shit!"

She stormed around the small shop, straightening the empty video boxes, swearing fiercely at customers who didn't put them back in the proper place, damning UPS for not delivering the new titles on time, cursing distributors who never sent her the right numbers of the top films that kept her business going, marching into the back room where all the cassettes were kept in coded black cases and nearly screaming when she saw that Nate had mixed up an entire month's worth of returns, which meant he'd probably screwed it up in the computer, too.

She stormed to the back of the long narrow room, to the black metal desk where she kept her ledgers, the computer, and what seemed like four hundred empty boxes of tissue paper. Next to it was a door that led to a bathroom barely large enough for its sink and toilet. That was probably filthy too. Which was what she got for hiring a kid instead of someone like Tessa or Bobby.

The problem was, Bobby didn't know from movies, and Nate had apparently seen every one ever made. The perfect recommender. People trusted his judgment, just as she trusted him not to rip her off.

Before she reached either place, however, she stopped, panting, sweat on her brow, sweat running between her breasts, and realized she was wrong.

Nothing was out of place.

Nate had even dusted.

She felt the tears then, frustration bitter.

"Okay, be cool," she whispered. "Be cool. It's not the end of the world."

A calming breath, and a vow to apologize to Nate as soon as she saw him. He wouldn't get it, but it would make her feel better. Which would be something of a rarity these days. Being unable to rent her two cabins had put a hell of a crimp in her budget, increasing the pressure she had put on herself to succeed. Nate, the poor darling, was often the brunt of her short-lived tempests. God, if he were only ten years older. Hell, five.

She giggled.

"Nice talk," she told the tapes. "Cradle robber." She giggled again. "Horny bitch."

She was about to head for the bathroom to splash some water on her face, when she heard the door's bell warn her of a customer. "Damn," she whispered, and with one hand brushing uselessly at her bangs, she returned to the front.

"Hey," she said.

Dimitri stood by the counter. "My mom said to bring these back." He nodded to a pair of black cassette cases he had placed by the register.

She took a step toward him, and stopped.

In his other hand he carried a gun.

Her eyes widened. "Dimitri?"

"Gonna die," the boy said, no expression at all.

She wanted to smile, to show him she got the joke but didn't think it very funny. But she screamed instead when, holding the gun in both hands, those beautiful big eyes wide and unblinking, he fired, taking a gouge from the jamb by her shoulder.

She screamed again when he fired again, putting a three-inch furrow in the floor, not far from her right foot.

She threw herself into the back room when he fired a third time, knocking over a half dozen cases, cassettes skittering across the floor when the cases snapped open. She fell on her hip, seeing too many colors and too much light, wondering why the hell nobody else was here; Jesus Christ, couldn't they hear?

She pushed herself backward on her rump as he stepped over the threshold.

"Miss Pollard, you okay?"

No gun.

"Dimitri, I think . . ."

No cases on the floor, no furrow.

Oh my God, she thought, shuddering violently; oh, God.

"Miss Pollard, I . . . I have to go now."

No gun; just the boy.

She reached out, hoping he would help her to her feet, but he only backed away uncertainly, then bolted for the exit. He didn't know what was wrong with her, why she had started yelling and running and jumping like that, but he sure didn't want to be here anymore. And once outside he also decided he didn't want to go home right away. His parents were home now, but it didn't look like supper would be coming real soon.

He headed west instead, balancing on the uneven curb, thinking maybe he could talk with Arlo. He liked Arlo. Sonya thought he looked stupid with those beads and headbands and his hair longer than their mother's. But Arlo was silly, and he could do magic. Maybe he could tell him why Miss Pollard had gone all weird. He giggled. She sure did look funny, scooting away on her rear end like that. Maybe she was on drugs or something. Arlo would know. He knew just about everything. Except maybe why the birds talked. Well, not really talked. But when they sang, he could tell what they were singing. So maybe Arlo could tell him why the birds were singing they were all gonna die.

Maybe he couldn't.

Ahead, Black Oak began its first step toward the river. He could see people walking, going in and out of the Moonglow and weird Mabel's store, an old lady coming out of the sick place with a white hat on with a white veil, a white purse in her white-gloved hands. He knew who she was but he couldn't remember her name. She called him ''child'' all the time, and he didn't think she could see very well.

A blue jay glided swiftly across the street, scolding, vanishing into the trees beside the church.

Moss Tully's no-name beagle sat on the bench in front of the hardware store, wire tail wagging a zillion times a minute.

He heard hoofbeats behind him.

Now that was weird. Mr. Palmer never let his horses ride anyplace but on the trails. Maybe it was—

He looked over his shoulder and nearly stumbled off the curb.

The horse walked slowly down the center of the street. He didn't know what the right names were; this one was dark brown, its mane and tail long, its head high and bobbing with each step.

Hooves loud on the blacktop.

No one rode it.

No one walked beside it.

''Wow,'' he whispered, looked for someone to help him, then decided he would have to catch the horse himself. But it was so big. Bigger than any horse he had ever seen in his life. His hands fluttered as he tried to decide how to stop it. Maybe jump in front of it and wave his arms, yell at it, tell it to go home; maybe grab its mane and swing onto its back and ride it home.

He took a deep breath and stepped into the street. "Hey," he said, remembering to keep his voice friendly and not make any sudden moves. "Hey, boy, you lost or something?"

The horse stopped, and looked at him.

He smiled broadly and held his hands away from his sides. "See? I'm okay. You don't—"

It tossed its head, mane slapping its neck.

The smile faltered, and he swallowed nervously. Maybe this wasn't such a great idea. Maybe he should just run down to the Moonglow and get one of the men to do this.

He took a step back, and the horse instantly lunged into a charging gallop, huge teeth bared, ears flat back.

Dimitri froze for a full second before he bolted.

He didn't think to head for the nearest house or tree; he ran as fast as he could down the slope, screaming, waving his arms, not looking back because he could hear the horse right behind him, snorting, hooves pounding, so big and so fast that he knew he would be trampled, knew he was gonna die, which made him scream louder, vision blurred now with tears, chest burning, legs not moving nearly fast enough, screaming until an arm grabbed his waist and swung him off his feet.

He shrieked, beating the air with his heels, hearing the horse bearing down, hearing the breathing, hearing the hooves, seeing an unfocused face nose-to-nose with him, hearing a voice tell him to calm down, it's okay, what's the prob, man?

His legs went limp, with exhaustion, not relief.

"Hey, buddy, what's going on?"

"There!" he yelled, pointing up the hill.

Reed Turner followed the finger. "Mrs. Racine?"

Dimitri gaped.

The horse was gone.

The only thing he could see was the old lady all in white, crossing the street with tiny, careful steps.

"But . . ." He wriggled impatiently until Reed set him back on the ground. "But I saw . . ."

"It's the heat, Dimmy," Reed said, squeezing his shoulder quickly. "You run full-out like that, you know you're going to get nailed by the heat."

He blinked several times, looked up at his friend and was suddenly swamped with a dismay that sent him racing back toward home. He cried out once.

"What?" Reed called after him.

The boy didn't answer, so intent on his flight that he nearly collided with Mrs. Racine, who didn't even notice him.

"Dimmy!" Reed called again, worried now that something was wrong, that maybe the other little kids had been after him, and all he had wanted was a little protection.

"It's all right."

Reed looked at the Moonglow entrance. "What do you mean? He was scared to death."

"Has a right to be," Odam said, chewing on a toothpick. "Scary shit going on around here lately, boy, or hadn't you noticed?"

Reed hadn't, but he didn't feel like asking questions. He could see the man was in another one of his pissy moods. It was better just to mumble, give him a vague wave, and head for home. Besides, he was tired. His arms ached, his legs as they carried him past the diner down Hickory Street were wobbly, and his face felt as if it had been baked in an oven; his own fault. The temperature drop, the cool breeze, had tricked him into thinking he didn't need much protection on the river today. Wrong. Real wrong. Nate had teased him all the way back, until Reed's scowl had sent him on his way, muttering, then laughing loudly.

Jerk, he thought, maybe at Nate, maybe at himself, and lifted a disgusted hand when a large moth dove out of the shade at his face. He swatted it away, feather touch against his knuckles, and swore when it came at him again a few seconds later. He hit it, saw it fall, and crushed it beneath his sole.

It didn't make a sound.

Whole world's going nuts, he decided, wiping the back of his neck, drying his hand on his shirt. Yesterday, some dumb-ass Philly tourist tried to drown his wife just because she wouldn't sit in the back of the canoe. It took him, Nate, and Micah to pull the man off and calm him down.

Two weeks ago, a fight in Mackey's Bar had sent three men and a woman to the hospital, and closed the place down for a day so Arlo could patch up the walls and scrub up the blood; and Cora had snuck into the church Sunday night and rung the· damn bell.

Maybe not scary shit, but it was definitely weird shit.

Halfway home, he turned and walked backward, thinking the world's most beautiful woman might be back there, following him to see where he lived. Naked. Real naked.

"Yeah," he said, grinning. "Tell me another."

He faced front and walked on, keeping to the middle of the blacktop. No chance of anything coming. Except maybe a woodchuck searching for water.

He whistled a single note soft and low, glanced behind him, saw the tree shade moving, looked away and whistled again.

Nothing naked back there.

He giggled, and slapped his hands against his legs.

In the middle of the block he passed a streetlamp, and slowed. Even though it was still a while before sunset, it was on and the bulb under its metal hood was nearly dark with moths of all sizes swarming frantically over the surface, dozens more fluttering wildly around it, swinging away and swinging back while the dead spiraled to the ground, some of them still, others flopping over the grass on curling burned wings.

He was tempted to check it out, but the distant sound of a screen door slamming moved him on, angling to the left until he reached the man-high stump of a tree split and hollowed by lightning not long after he'd been born. A slope of grass served as a curb. Beyond was a two-story house with a pair of dormers on the roof. A brick walk to the porch.

He looked at his watch and sat, his back against the dead tree. He hadn't been there a minute before the front door opened, and a man came toward him.

Reed looked up. "Hi."

"Hi," his father said. "You're home."

"Right on time."

"Any trouble?"

He shook his head. "The water's so low, I could've walked the whole way."

Harve Turner scratched his chest under his shirt, and belched. "I'll tell your mother you're here."

"Okay."

"You coming in?"

Reed shook his head. "Not for a while, if that's okay. It's too hot in there."

Turner grunted, scratched again. "I'll be fixing the air conditioner tomorrow. Damn thing's working too hard, all this heat, you know what I mean?"

"Yeah. I know."

Turner walked back to the house. "Not too late, all right? Your mother wants her supper soon."

"Sure."

The door opened, closed quietly, but not before he heard his mother ask a question.

He reached between his legs and grabbed a handful of grass, crushing it and throwing it at the space where his father had stood. Then he closed his eyes and rested his head against the stump. Maybe he'd get lucky and fall asleep; maybe he'd get lucky, and his father would fall asleep; maybe the ground would open and swallow the whole town.

The son of a bitch was already drunk again.

And someone was watching him.

He felt it, like a feather barely touching the back of his neck.

He snapped his eyes open and looked around quickly, feeling like a jerk when he saw nothing but trees and empty lawns and, up the street, the moths still killing themselves, still falling.

Dimitri, he decided. Whatever had spooked him must have rubbed off.

Shit, he thought, and pushed himself to his feet. A glance at the house, and he decided to bum a meal off Nate and his mother. And while he was there, the world's most beautiful woman would walk in the door, take his hand, drag him upstairs, and—

He laughed. "Yeah. Right."

3

Dusk to full dark. Pale streetlamps, one to a block, washed pallid grey through the black. On Birch Street, on the Crest, a loose shutter on an empty house creaked and sighed with the slow evening breeze. In the stables at the end of Sycamore Road, a roan gelding pawed monotonously at the floor, a faint fleck of foam bubbling at the corner of its mouth. On Hickory Street, Harve Turner stood at the screen door, scratching his belly, wondering where the hell his snotnose kid had gone. In the woods at the north end of Hunter Lane, a black bear and her undersized cub tore at the carcass of a yearling buck, lapping its blood. The river whispered through tall reeds that hadn't been there two weeks ago.

There were no crickets.

There were no tree frogs.

8:45 P.M.

Casey wondered if, in canon law, there was a loophole which would, when activated, permit him to strangle a bride-to-be.

It was wishful, no doubt sinful, thinking, but he couldn't help it.

From the moment Mabel had walked into his office, it was clear this wasn't going to go as well as it should have. Moss was no help, either. All he did was sit there and grin, nod, and grin again.

They sat in the easy chairs, Mabel with her hands prim in her lap, Moss suited, slouched, and comfortable, his bald head gleaming as if he'd just shaved it. Which, Casey figured, he probably had.

On the desk was a typewritten schedule of the way Mabel wanted the service to go. When he glanced at it a third time, just to be sure it said what he feared it did, she smiled warmly.

"You like it?"

He leaned back, the gold cross sliding across his chest. Since returning from what Kay had called his "rounds," he hadn't had a chance to change. He should have. He should have changed into a Corvette and sped the hell out of here.

"Well?"

"Mabe," he said, careful with his tone, "while this is certainly an . . . original concept—"

"They told me, you know." She looked to Moss, who nodded solemn agreement. "Told me how it was to be. To make it right."

"Yes. Well, be that as it may, I'm afraid . . ." He made sure his expression and slight shake of his head implied strong regret as well as sympathy. "Let's put it simply, okay? No sense beating around the bush. There are specific liturgical reasons why, for example, I can't wear . . ." Beneath the level of the desk, his right hand dug into his thigh, to keep the laughter stillborn. "Silver."

Mabel's hands fussed in her lap. "But they *said*, Reverend."

"I'm sure they did, Mabe. But you have to understand that, while I'm allowed a lot of flexibility here, there are some things I'm forced to stick with. My robes are one of them."

Disappointment pushed her back into the chair, and she stared at the ceiling while working her lower lip between her

teeth. Moss nodded, and Casey took a second to glare a scolding at him for going along with this nonsense. The man only
winked, with the eye away from his intended.

Okay; he was on his own, no help from the groom. He
cleared his throat and sat up.

"Look, Mabe, consider it like this: your friends want more
than anything to understand us, am I right?"

"Of course, Reverend. It's not like they want to zap us or
anything." Her lips twisted in disgust. "That's only in those
stupid movies you see on TV."

"Of course. So what better way to know how we think,
how we feel, than to witness one of the Lord's most solemn
ceremonies?" He spread his hands to encompass both the
schedule and his Bible. "Marriage is a sacrament. And since
it's the first time for both of you, my own feeling, without
meaning any offense, is to do it up brown, as my momma
used to say. Full-blast organ, my fanciest vestments, fresh
flowers all over the place, bridesmaids and red carpet . . . and
when it's done, we'll ring those bells right out of the belfry.
Mabe, I guarantee you there won't be a town up and down
the river that won't know what's going on and won't be cel-
ebrating right along with you." He looked squarely at Moss.
"And you, you lucky dog, you're going to be absolutely
amazing in your morning coat."

"My what?"

"Tuxedo, silly," Mabe told him, close enough to giggling
to make Casey wince. "It's a kind of tuxedo you wear in the
daytime, ain't that right, Reverend?"

He nodded.

Mabel shifted to the edge of the cushion. "What about the
music?"

"Your choice, darlin'," he said. "Fancy classical, tradi-
tional, contemporary, a combination . . . just let Helen know
so she can start practicing."

There was a moment, then, when he thought he had put his
big foot square in his equally big mouth. The two women
weren't exactly the best of friends, although he didn't know
why, and he hoped mention of Helen didn't ruin the spell.

Mabel smiled sweetly. "Of course. I'll head on over as soon as I get changed." She stood, gripping her small purse in both hands. "Reverend, I can't thank you enough."

He rose, waited for Moss to get glumly to his feet, and guided them into the church rather than the short hall that led to the vestibule. He wanted her to see it as it would be—the carpet, the flowers, the afternoon sunlight through the stained glass, and to hear the music soaring to the rafters. He could tell by her eyes she was doing just that. He said nothing. He followed them up the aisle, bade them good-bye at the inner door, and watched as they left.

Then he faced the altar. "Lord, forgive me, I am shameless, and I know it. But if You'll forgive me again, no way am I going to wear a silver spaceman jumpsuit."

9:15 P.M.

Arlo sat at a corner table, watching Bobby the Beautiful Barmaid wipe down the bar as she chatted with two couples who had thought they could cross the river here, and had decided to stop for a drink before finding their way back to civilization. Polo shirts. Bermuda shorts. Colors he thought had died with his flashbacks. Matching tennis shoes, for crying out loud. They flashed the green, though, so as long as they didn't start singing, he supposed he could stand them a while longer. Besides, the men had their eyes practically glued to Bobby's chest and the buttons that barely held her white shirt together, which was why he had hired her in the first place, not being exactly young anymore but not being a total idiot either. The fact that she could run the business better than him was, he figured, a miraculous bonus.

His left hand ran a quarter deftly over his knuckles, around his fingers. It happened automatically; he was barely aware he was doing it. Parlor tricks he could do in his sleep if he had to.

A glance around, and he sighed contentedly.

The other tables were taken, two dozen or more locals stop-

ping by after strolling in the unaccustomed cool or finishing
a late meal and sick of reruns on the tube. The Weavers on
the jukebox, crossing the River Jordan. Concert posters on the
wall, Jimi Hendrix and Janis. Joan Baez and scruffy Bob, harmonica forever caught in his mouth. Look up and there's a
faded white peace sign painted across the whole ceiling.

It promised to be a quiet night.

Until a man came in, open-neck shirt, slacks, polished ox-
fords. He found Arlo right away and walked over, sat without
speaking, and stared.

"Peace," Arlo said calmly.

"Up yours, too, Mackey." A man of clear Hispanic descent,
with a sharp widow's peak, and a long face pocked with the
scars of a hard adolescence. Long fingers that slipped around
Arlo's beer bottle and brought it to him. Arlo did nothing but
signal to Bobby to bring him another pair.

"Christ," the man said. "It's dark in here."

"The better to see you with, my dear."

The man grimaced and drank, and said nothing more until
Bobby had brought the order and left. Then he emptied his
bottle, picked up another and used it to point.

"Now you listen to me, you old fart." Voice low, smooth,
a crocodile's smile. "My office got a call this afternoon from
that doctor—what's his name, Farber?—wanting to know how
come he's getting money and there's nobody in his house."

"A natural question for a man who rents property."

"He wanted to know what was going on."

"A natural question."

The bottle pointed again, beer slopping from the mouth. "A
natural question, you shithead, investigators will be asking
when this is over. You were supposed to be writing letters,
remember? You were supposed to be covering."

Arlo's expression didn't change. "You drove all this way,
man, just to tell me that?"

The man sneered as he fingered the top button of his shirt.
"Look, you screw this up, hero, you aren't going to converge
with Arizona *or* Mars, you understand? That's what I came to
this dump to tell you. In fucking person."

Arlo shook his head sadly. "Bad vibes, man, bad vibes." He gestured toward the Make Love Not War posters on the walls, the lava lamp on the table between them. "A place of peace, that's what this is. I don't like anybody disturbing my place of peace."

The man laughed without mirth. "Shit, where you're going, you old fart, if you screw me over, you'll get all the frigging peace you want, *comprende*?" He drank, wiped his mouth with the back of his hand. "So what're you going to do about it, huh? How you going to fix this?"

The move was smooth and unhurried.

Arlo snatched the bottle from the man's hand and brought it down alongside his skull. Unlike the movies, the bottle didn't break; unlike the movies, there was blood on the table as the man slipped to the floor.

"Bobby," he called in the midst of the resulting confusion, "get hold of Doc Farber, okay?" He looked at the floor. "Seems this dude has had himself an accident."

9:35 P.M.

They sat on the bench under the fringed awning at Tully's, Reed on the end, Nate beside him, Cora and Rina on the other end. Watching the street wind down. Watching the heads in the Moonglow. Micah Lambert drove up in his pickup, parked in front of Mackey's and waved to them as he walked in.

"I. Am. So. Bored!" Cora announced. "Why didn't we go to the movies?"

Nate stretched out his legs. "Because we went last weekend, and there isn't anything new playing."

"You're so lame, Dane." She plucked at her T-shirt. Despite the night, the heat had crept back, and with it the humidity that encased the streetlamps in faint fog. "That's not the point."

Nate shifted, but Reed nudged him, don't bother, she's still pissed we got caught. He sat forward, clasping his hands, resting his arms on his thighs. He couldn't get Dimitri out of his mind, the kid's fright and his flight. That wasn't like him. Maybe he was too pretty to be a boy, but Reed and Nate had spent a long time teaching him to defend himself. Which, as they'd seen in the grade school yard, he could do pretty well for a shrimp his size.

So what had frightened him so much?

"So the least you nerds could do is buy us something to eat."

"Not hungry," Nate said, and glowered when Reed nudged him again. "What?"

Reed puffed his cheeks in exasperation. Nate was his best friend, and could, like the Reverend says, shoot the eye out of a gnat flying south on an eagle, but sometimes he was so dense, Reed wanted to scream. Didn't he see the way Rina looked at him? Christ, did she have to strip in the middle of the street to get his attention? It wasn't like he already had a girlfriend, for God's sake, was it?

He blinked.

Did he?

Nate said, "You know, I've seen *The Thing*, the Carpenter one, nine times?" He snapped his fingers. "And I've seen the giant-carrot one almost twenty."

"Life," Reed muttered.

"What?"

"I said, 'Life.' "

"What about it?"

Reed looked at him. "Get one, for God's sake."

Cora stood and stretched, making sure they saw how much flesh she could expose between the cut-off T-shirt and her shorts without exposing too much. Then she moved to the curb and wrapped an arm around a lamppost. "I think we ought to try again."

Reed's head snapped up. "Oh, no. No way."

"Well, we know he's not home now, right? He's sitting right over there with Gorn and the slut."

"Her name is Tessa," Nate said stiffly. "She isn't a slut."

"Oh, right." Cora swung around the post. "She walks

around in halter-tops all day, her boobs practically right out there, and I've seen her practically throw herself into Odam's lap a zillion times.'' She spat dryly. ''You guys are so dense, you know?''

''I think . . .'' Rina said quietly. ''I think Nate's right.''

''Oh, Jesus, you too?'' She spun around twice and flopped to the curb, elbows on her knees, hands on her cheeks.

''Thanks,'' Nate said.

Reed wanted to strangle him. Thanks? That's it? He turned slightly and tried to catch his friend's eye. What was wrong with him? But Nate refused to look; instead, he hooked his left foot onto his leg and started to pick at the sole of his deck shoe. Reed saw Rina shift. Tall, too skinny for his taste, with long brown hair parted in the middle and hanging straight down to the middle of her spine. As long as he had known her, she had never worn anything as tight as Cora did, or as revealing. Everything hung on her loose and easy.

Nate found his shoe too fascinating for words.

''So, Rina,'' Reed said loudly, ''did Nate tell you how he single-handedly saved that lady the other day? The one the guy nearly drowned?''

Rina looked at him shyly, hair falling over her eye. ''No.''

''Who cares?'' Cora said. She nodded toward the clinic across the street, a small stucco building, three windows and all of them lighted. ''I want to know who smashed that guy.''

''So go ask,'' he said.

''Maybe I will.''

He made a face—*big deal*—and tried to get Nate to tell the story. He had heard it a million times already, but he figured that even if Rina had heard it too, she would want to hear it from Nate anyway. The way it was going, though, neither one of them was going to say anything. Unless the jerk started on movies again.

Cora rose, dusting her rump slowly. ''I'm going over.''

''Okay.'' He grinned when she looked. ''I'll watch for the cops.''

She stuck out her tongue, said, ''You coming?'' to Rina, and started across the street.

Rina didn't move.

Reed scratched through his hair, wondering what Cora was trying to prove. At least she had dropped the idea of trying to get back at Reverend Chisholm. What she hadn't been able to see was that their colossal failure had been funny. Sneaking through the woods, sneaking up to the porch, and getting the crap scared out of them when Reverend Chisholm jumped up like that. He wouldn't admit it, but he had almost pissed his pants. That voice booming out of the dark, just like on Sundays. No microphones for him; he could probably be heard all the way to Philadelphia.

What he didn't get was this thing she had against the minister. It was getting a little intense; it made him uneasy. The main reason he had gone along the other night was to keep her out of trouble—Cora Bowes, walking in the woods alone, would have probably ended up in the river. For a kid who had lived here most of her life, she had absolutely no sense, or sense of direction.

"What happened, Nate?" Rina asked, sliding over an inch.

Reed stood, ignoring Nate's panicked expression. "Don't leave anything out, okay? I'm gonna see Cora doesn't get into trouble."

He trotted across the street, watching as Cora hopped over the curb and stood indecisively for a moment before ducking into the trees in the wooded lot beside it. He rolled his eyes and followed, knowing she had heard when she jerked a look back. She didn't stop. She eased closer to the drive that separated the lot from the clinic, aiming for a lighted window at the rear corner.

That's all the light there was.

Nothing else but trees and shadow.

He stood behind her, relieved and disappointed that the blinds were closed; they couldn't see a thing.

She leaned into him, taking his right hand, pulling it to her stomach. Raised it a little. She wasn't wearing a bra.

He held his breath.

She twisted her head around; he could almost see her face.

"We could do it right here, and nobody would notice."

A little higher.

"Cora . . ."

She pressed her buttocks into his groin.

His hand drifted farther across her stomach, and there was faint buzzing in his ears. He pressed, she sighed, and suddenly winced and broke away.

"What?" he said. Head down, she headed for the street, but he caught her arm. "What?"

When she looked up, he couldn't see her eyes, but he could see the tears.

"He hit you again, didn't he."

She didn't answer.

Never where anyone could see it, she had told him once, swearing him to secrecy; never where anyone could see and make a fuss. Which was why she was with Rina tonight—she'd be spending the night there.

He took her hand and squeezed it, let her lead him out of the trees and up the street, away from Nate and Rina, Nate's hands gesturing while Rina's floated around her hair and lap.

"I'll walk you," he said, feeling helpless, feeling rage.

Cora nodded.

"You want to come on the river tomorrow?"

She looked away, and finally, "Sure, why not?"

Into the dark between the streetlamps.

"Reed, would you have . . . you know, back there?"

"Are you kidding? With you? Gimme a break."

"Fuck you, Turner."

He grinned. "You wish."

He couldn't hear the whispered answer.

9:50 P.M.

Enid Balanov sat in the center of the three-cushion couch and watched her husband watching a baseball game from his leather club chair. He was quite tall, and quite thin, and, she believed, quite the savior. In the middle of the recession, Petyr had saved their computer business by diversifying into prognostication and business scenario–building, making them more successful than ever; he had saved himself by fleeing the Soviet Union before the roof fell in; and he had saved her from a life of taking care of her ailing parents. In return, she had given him herself, and Dimitri and Sonya. A harsh-looking man who was extraordinarily gentle.

She waited until the inning was over.

"Darling?"

He stirred as if waking, and smiled at her.

"Something's the matter with Dimitri."

He waited patiently.

"He . . ." She wasn't sure how to put it. She didn't want him to think their only son was unstable. "I don't know where he gets it, certainly not from us, but he has a notion that we're all going to die. Soon, I think. I'm . . . concerned."

He covered his mouth with one hand thoughtfully, parted the long fingers. "He is learning mortality?"

"No. This is . . . oh, dear." She faltered.

"The birds?"

Her mouth opened. "How did you know?"

"I hear him in the yard sometimes." He left his chair to sit beside her. "Sonya has her castles, Dimitri has his birds." He rubbed her back in slow small circles. "Maybe he has read about Dr. Dolittle." He laughed as he always did, not making a sound.

She nearly wept with relief and leaned back into his hand. Petyr knew; Petyr would save her son.

Just like always.

"That woman still rents pornography," she whispered, her eyes half closed. "The Lord knows I try, but she only laughs at me."

The hand moved to her shoulder, massaging.

"She distresses you?"

"I do my best." She could barely speak. The crack of a bat on the television, the roar of the crowd, the touch of his hand as it snaked down to her breast. "Father Chisholm appreciates me. He says so often. But that woman . . . one of these days, she's going to make a mistake, and someone's poor child will see that filth. Our children, Petyr. Maybe they'll see."

"It is a hot summer," he said, close to her ear, breath warm, hand moving, constantly moving. "You see on the news the strange things people do in hot weather." Constantly moving. "Sometimes to themselves."

A pleasant chill closed her eyes, made her sigh.

Petyr would save the children.

Just like he had saved her.

10:05 P.M.

The excitement was long over, jukebox blaring, Arlo back in his chair, Bobby fussing around the others as if the problem had been all her fault. Kay watched her move smoothly from table to table, and took another pull at her beer. On her right, Tessa stared glumly at her glass; across from her, the Palmers described in excruciating detail the birth of a foal at their stable last week. They were thin, leather, and plain, and it was all she could do not to reach out and pinch their cheeks to see if they were actually human. A smile as she ducked her head— maybe this was something she could tell Mabel. Aliens renting horses right here in town. But she hadn't told anyone about Dimitri and the gun. Or, more accurately, her hallucination about Dimitri and the gun.

Bobby brought another round.

When she danced away with a wave, Tessa looked up and muttered, "Bitch."

The Palmers ignored her.

Kay felt like slapping the woman a good one. She couldn't figure out why Todd Odam, of all the men in this town, had two of the most eligible, prettiest women pining like they were part of some stupid country song.

The door opened and a man walked in, heading for the bar.

She was halfway out of her chair before she realized it wasn't Nate.

Tessa stared at her oddly. "You okay?"

She nodded weakly and sank back.

"So tell me something," Tessa said, nodding toward her housemate. "What's she got that I haven't?"

Ed Palmer said, "Nice legs."

Sissy Palmer said, "Solid flanks."

They looked at each other and laughed hysterically.

"You know," Tessa said solemnly, "maybe you guys ought to get out more."

Kay laughed with the others, but she couldn't stop thinking about how she'd been mistaken. First Dimitri and the phantom gun, now the stranger who wasn't Nate.

It scared her, and made her ashamed.

Mostly, however, it scared her.

10:15 P.M.

Casey sat on his stool and glared at his cup of cold coffee. He had ordered it shortly before all hell had broken loose in Mackey's. He had helped carry the stranger to the clinic, and when Farber shooed them all out except Tessa, his part-time nurse, he had returned to find the coffee still there, Helen in conversation with two couples in the far booth, Todd practicing his guitar in the kitchen, and Ozzie Gorn sound asleep in the booth by the door. No one asked about the accident. No one asked what he had thought when he had seen the man lying on the floor, and Arlo sitting in his chair, humming to himself.

You're being unreasonable, you know.

But he knew a bar fight when he saw one, and he knew Arlo Mackey wasn't nearly the flower-child idiot some thought he was.

"The Millennium," Todd said from the serving gap.

Casey held up his cup, tapped it with a finger. "Can I get another? This is cold."

"Nobody, but nobody insults my coffee," Helen declared, swinging sharply around the counter. She snatched it from his hand. "You better pray you're right."

He watched her sip, grinned when she grimaced, and winked at Todd when she swished away, slapping a towel against her leg.

"Millennium," Todd repeated.

Ozzie snored, snorted, snored, and groaned.

"Jesus, Hel," Todd complained, "will you move that jackass outta here?"

"Move him yourself," she said from the coffee urn. "I've got my reputation here to think about."

Todd made himself comfortable, and Casey thought, why not? So far today he had had sick people, dying people, a recovering old lady who played poker with the interns, spacemen slated to join him at a wedding, and Ozzie Gorn smelling like gasoline and snoring in public. So why not the Millennium, too? It almost made perfect sense.

He adjusted his *I'm listening* expression and waited.

"Basically," Todd said, loud enough for everyone to hear, "every time one comes around, people start acting weird."

Casey couldn't argue; he waited.

Helen slipped a fresh cup in front of him, dared him to complain again, and returned to the far booth.

When Ozzie sputter-snored, Casey swiveled around, stepped to the booth, and leaned as close to the man's face as he dared. "Ozzie, customer!" he bellowed, and stepped nimbly aside when Gorn threw himself out of the booth and the diner without saying a word.

Then he returned to his stool, picked up his cup, looked innocently at Todd and said, "That's it? People act weird?" He was aware that Helen's friends were staring at him. Helen stared as well, but not in astonishment. She, he knew, would be thinking of a good way to explain him. "Every thousand years people act weird?"

Odam nodded.

"It took you all day to figure that out?" He sipped his coffee, added a spoonful of sugar, and sipped again. "Todd, the Lord surely knew what He was doing when He sent me to you.'' He smiled broadly as Helen failed to stifle a laugh, and Todd blustered as he stomped back to his guitar.

When the couples left, he was alone, listening to Todd's awful playing, and to Helen's footsteps as she swept through the booths, gathering dishes and cups, glasses and glass ashtrays.

''So who rang the bell Sunday night?'' she asked, taking a damp cloth to the tables.

''I don't know.''

''I wouldn't put it past Cora or Nate.''

He shrugged. ''Like I said.''

She dropped onto the stool beside him, and kissed his cheek. ''How you feeling?''

''Wrung out.''

She nudged him. ''You want a date?''

His head swung slowly toward her, and he blinked when he realized their noses were nearly touching. ''Why is it that you're the only one around here who doesn't treat me like I was different?''

She didn't smile; she didn't turn away. ''You're a preacher, you're not God,'' she answered simply. ''So what about that damn bell? It woke half the town. Do you have any idea how much a woman my age needs her beauty rest?''

He hated it when she did that—answered a question with something he felt he ought to address, then changed the subject to something he could answer without having to give a sermon. By the time he sorted everything out, she was, like now, on her way to somewhere else. In this case it was the kitchen, hips deliberately, mockingly, twitching, and he heard her tell Todd to lay off the cranky cook bit because the place was empty.

She was as bad in her way as Kay was.

''Well, thanks for nothing!'' Casey called.

She poked her head through the gap and frowned as she looked around. ''The only people ever in here are the ones who like my coffee.''

''My Lord, don't you ever forget anything?''

When she smiled, he nearly blushed.

When she laughed at his discomfort, he threw his hands up in mock surrender, dropped a bill by the register and bid them both good-night. Once on the street, he stretched and started for home, deliberately not looking at Nate and Rina sitting on the hardware bench, forcing himself not to go over to the bar and demand that Arlo tell him what had really happened.

Spacemen, UFOs, bar fights, and women, he thought, slipping his hands into his pockets; I am truly blessed.

He kicked at a pebble, and missed.

Oh, and don't forget the hopping vampires.

He considered heading on down to the river, let its whispers and rushes work its magic on his nerves, but the thought of climbing up the hill again changed his mind. He would go home, watch the movie, get some sleep. He had a checkup with Farber in the morning, and he didn't want to give the doc any excuses for still not feeling well.

The gate squealed.

He hummed tunelessly as he unlocked the front door.

He frowned when he heard something on the road, thinking with an impatient silent sigh that Cora had rounded up her gang again. Bracing the screen door open with his foot, he turned to make sure before he yelled.

Moonlight; nothing more.

Still, he heard something, and several seconds passed before he realized it was hoofbeats.

Unhurried; unshod.

A careful step to the railing, squinting into the dark, searching the moonlit road.

Nothing there.

By the sound, the animal was close, but he was puzzled when he couldn't spot it.

You're hearing things.

Unhurried; unshod.

There's nothing out there.

Near the gate, but the road was empty.

The warm night took a chill.

He stepped back from the railing, left hand slapping his leg slowly, lightly. He should have been annoyed, perhaps even angry, but all he could feel was a winter touch on his arms, on his nape.

It stopped.

It was out there.

He couldn't see it, but it was out there.

And just as suddenly, it was gone.

10:50 P.M.

William Bowes sat on the front steps of his single-story ranch house. Even in the yellow light from the bulb above the door, he was huge. Fashioned from slabs of flagstone from his face to his hands. Marine-cut brown hair. Fatigue pants and black T-shirt. Bare feet.

A tarnished wedding band on his right hand.

Tears on his cheeks.

Come home, Cora honey, he pleaded to the dark; please, darling, come home, I'm so sorry, I'm sick, I need help, come home, I need you, don't leave me alone, not again, I'm sorry.

He sobbed aloud.

Please. Please.

A dog barked.

William snarled.

11:45 P.M.

Micah drove slowly back to the landing, parked beside the boathouse, and made sure the place was padlocked.

He was halfway to his cabin when he heard the buzzing.

Couldn't be, he thought, walked on, and stopped.

Too many beers in too short a time. That was always his problem. He never had learned the knack of nursing.

He checked over his shoulder.

A shifting, fragmented black cloud hung above the river.

No; but he ran anyway, despite the fact that bees don't fly at night.

12:01 A.M.

The church bell rang.

Part 3

CONDUCTOR

]

1

The night was made for ghosts.

Mist coiled and curled over the interstate lanes, hung in the trees, sparkled in the headlamps. In some places it seemed to have a pulse and glow of its own; in others it took on the color of night.

Nothing moved but the moon, hazed and fading.

Leaves sagged for want of a breeze; debris on the shoulders hardly stirred when trucks passed, barely once an hour; a long stretch of construction narrowed two lanes to one, reflecting signs and red-flagged poles and striped barrels and a dump truck squatting behind a sawhorse fence; a deserted car, a scrap of limp cloth hanging from the driver's window.

Nothing moved but the moon.

Not a sound.

2

The Continental swept across the flatland out of West Virginia, and Stan checked to the right, to the glow of tall lights beyond the exit and the trees. He had been here before, maybe three years ago. Hagerstown. A quick ten-minute drive between West Virginia and Pennsylvania. Motels, restaurant, gas stations, fast food. He didn't know what else was here. He had only seen it at night.

His pack was on the floor between his feet, although he didn't remember how it got there. He had slept, though; he was sure of that. Got in the car, said a few words, drifted off to the music that still played on the radio.

When the car drifted to the right, aiming for the exit, he was surprised. He was glad. He hadn't eaten since probably forever, and maybe Susan would finally give him the meal she had promised.

Mist swept over the windshield.

The car slowed.

"We gonna eat?" he asked hopefully.

"In time," she answered.

He shook his head wearily. "Man, I'm starving. I don't mean offense, but you said."

"I know."

Stirring in the backseat.

He still hadn't seen who was there with Lupé, and he still wasn't sure he wanted to know.

"I second the starving," Lupé said, close to his ear, making him jump. She had folded her arms on the back of the seat, rested her chin, and when he looked, his eyes nearly crossed. She grinned. "Steak, home fries, beer."

His tongue touched his lips. Soup and scraps, that's what he was used to. "Yeah."

They swayed into the long arc of the exit ramp, slowing, but not by much. No one followed them; there was no one ahead.

"You married, Stan?"

"Nope. You?"

"No way, *amigo*. I am a free woman."

He watched the road brighten as the tall lights came nearer, not wanting to watch her. She made him nervous. But he could smell her, a mix of some kind of flower and some kind of soap. It was faint, but it was there. She also smelled warm.

She tilted her head to bump his shoulder. "You always wear that coat?"

He shrugged. "Don't have anything else." His left hand glided down his chest. "It does all right, though. I don't look so much like a bum, you know? I keep it clean. People don't talk to you if you look like you just climbed out of the sewer."

She nodded, rocking her chin on her arm.

The car stopped.

They were near a crossroads, stop signs and another highway. A blind spot for the tall lights. They were stopped in the dark.

Stan waited for Susan to say something. He hoped she would say it was time to raid the kitchen. Or maybe, almost but not quite better, time to sleep in a real bed in a real room. He yawned without warning, too late to cover his mouth, coughed to try to cover it, and choked a bit instead.

"You okay?" Lupé asked.

"Yeah." He choked again. "Yeah."

Semis cranked and backfired down the highway, heading for the interstate entrance. A handful of cars crawling back and forth. The mist hanging from the lights, from the telephone poles, from the wires.

His eyelids sagged, and he shook himself to keep awake.

"Stan."

It was Susan.

A nervous glance to Lupé before he looked over, wishing he could see her more clearly, thinking maybe this was the time to change his mind. Nobody had told him anything about anything, but he wasn't fool enough to believe that what was coming was anything good. Still, he had been asleep and no one had killed him, robbed him, anything like that. So maybe he would just—

"Stan."

He cleared his throat to prove he was listening.

She stared out the windshield, hands on the steering wheel, ten and two, engine humming.

"I'm going to drive into that gas station past the corner

over there." She paused; he didn't speak. "When we get there, Lupé is going over to the Burger King." Another pause; he didn't speak. "This is where you make your choice."

He tried to look like he understood what she meant, but there was no clue in her voice and no clue from Lupé, who only nodded and slipped away, back into the dark.

"I'm sorry," he said, feeling himself grow tense as if in fear of a whipping. "I don't get it."

He didn't see it, but he felt the smile.

"As I told you before, if you don't want to stay, you can leave. Here. There are plenty of places to eat, places to sleep. You could hitch another ride, although I don't know how long it will take this late at night." Her hands shifted. "This early in the morning, I guess I should say."

His feet tightened around the pack.

A hand touched his leg, patted it once.

"So if you want to go, that's fine. No hard feelings. That much I promised."

He didn't know what to say. Instinct usually took over about now, guys or women giving him rides, sending signals or not, hard times and good times teaching him all the way. But now, with this woman, in this palace of a car, he was lost.

For the first time since the first time, he was utterly lost.

"What . . ." He rubbed his cheek, shifted his rump. "I mean, what happens if I stick around?"

Funny thing. He was lost but he wasn't scared. Not like he was before, not knowing who was in the back, not knowing what this lady was up to, not knowing where he was going. Curious was what he was, and he was pleased to know it. Curious was okay. He learned things then, poking around, reading stuff, seeing stuff. Sometimes it got him trouble, him and his mad, but most of the time it got him somewhere he hadn't ever been before.

"I mean, you're a nice lady and all, okay? But no offense, I hardly never got something for nothing, you know what I mean?"

She nodded, nothing more.

She wasn't going to tell him.

And she wasn't going to wait until dawn for him to make up his stupid mind.

If only he knew who was in the backseat with Lupé.

Susan's hands stopped caressing the wheel. "Stan, I have to go. And you have to decide."

No threats; a simple choice.

He felt dumb then, really dumb. Too many parts of him pulling too many different ways. He was no good at this, never was, never would be. All he wanted was the road, singing a song, meeting the people, seeing the sights. He was no damn good at this, and it made him feel dumb.

It made him angry.

It made him take a deep breath and stare at her, hard, not caring about the heat he felt inside his head.

She waited.

The heat grew, blurring his vision, turning it colors, making him wonder where the hell this bitch got off, teasing him this way, forcing him into a corner, who the hell did she think she was, some kind of goddamn queen or something?

"Stan," she said mildly.

Who the goddamn hell did she think she was?

Then she looked at him, through the mad, through the heat; she looked at him, and he knew.

3

Lupé stood just inside the Burger King entrance, thinking this was a real strange place to stop. Hardly anyone here, it being long past midnight. Two guys behind the counter, another in the kitchen that she could see. White tourist family at a fake-wood table over by the window, two adults, two bored and exhausted teens picking at their food. Two black women arguing at another, hissing at each other, not wanting to yell; tight jeans and tight T-shirts, too tight for their sizes, one with dreadlocks, the other damn near bald.

She smiled to herself and strolled back to the restroom, ignoring the glare of the oldest counterman. She went inside, nose wrinkling at the disinfectant, and stood by the single sink, staring in the mirror, taking her time, thinking she wasn't looking half bad, even after all this time on the road. Not half bad at all.

She didn't concern herself with the time; she knew what would happen.

It did.

Not two minutes later, one of the arguing women came in, stomping, huffing, cursing to herself, slapping a hand at her dreadlocks, beads clacking at the ends.

The second one followed.

"Larone, you dumb bitch, what the hell you doing?" she snapped.

Lupé turned around just as Larone ducked into the stall and pointedly locked the door.

The second one pounded on the frail wood. "Bitch! Get the fuck out here!"

Lupé moved up behind her.

The woman snarled, "What the hell you want?" over her shoulder.

Lupé smiled, and showed her the knife.

"Fuck off, Bee," Larone said from the stall. "I got nothing to say to you."

Bee stared at the knife, at Lupé's sweet smile.

"Bee?"

"I ain't got no money," Bee said in a hoarse whisper, eyes wide, no place to go as the knife drifted slowly in front of her chin.

"Bee, damnit, who you talking to?"

"Just me," Lupé called softly.

The knife moved, smooth and quiet.

Bee sagged to her knees, one hand at her throat, the other covering her eyes.

"Who the fuck are you?"

"End of the world, honey, end of the world."

The stall door slammed open; Larone had a knife too.

"What the fuck you—" She saw her friend topple forward,

forehead smacking on the floor, saw the blood, one hand drumming the floor without a sound.

Larone screamed, but no one heard it.

The explosion buried it in shattered glass and roaring gas and the screams outside from the white tourist family blown out of their seats, piece by piece.

Lupé opened the restroom door and walked out, heading for the front entrance, batting an irritated hand against the smoke hot as steam that billowed through the room. The night had turned to fire, and one of the countermen grabbed her arm, face dripping blood.

"What the hell happened? Jesus, what the hell happened?"

She pushed the hand away and walked on, just as Larone screamed out of the ladies' room, T-shirt soaked and dark.

The counterman had a gun.

Larone only had the knife.

Lupé heard the shot as she stepped through the glassless door; she didn't pause, didn't look back.

She walked down to the highway, wincing at the heat nearly burning her back from the fires that stretched from the gas station to the moon. By the time she reached the car, two top-floor windows of the Days Inn blew out, followed by instant smoke and flame; by the time she slid into the backseat, a second gas station blew up, and a man with a rifle stood near the entrance, shooting without aiming at anything that moved.

She sat behind Susan and closed her eyes, leaned back, listened as Stan fell into the front, gasping, laughing a little, singing a song she didn't know.

The passenger door opened, a shadow slipped in, and the car pulled away from the shoulder, shuddering at an explosion, trembling when a piece of flaming metal bounced off the hood, another off the roof.

She opened one eye and saw Stan in the firelight, hugging himself; she knew how he felt.

In Arkansas she had thought she was going to die, simple as that. But all that had happened was that she had burned her arm a little when a kid all afire fell against her before she could dodge him.

She had thought she was going to die, but all she had done was laugh.

"Wow," Stan said, shaking his head, shaking like a leaf in a high wind. "Wow."

They glided onto the interstate, into the mist not quite a fog.

Behind them the sky exploded.

4

What we're going to do is, Susan told them, eyes straight ahead, voice spider silk and calm, we're going on to Carlisle. There are some nice motels there, so we'll get a couple of rooms. You're tired of riding, I'm sure. So am I. You need your rest. So do I. You need something decent to eat. It'll be just about dawn when we get there, and you'll probably want to sleep all day. That's okay. I'll take care of it, don't worry about money or being disturbed. If you've been hurt, we'll get you fixed up, but it looks like you're all right. So sleep, and when you wake up, get yourselves cleaned up. When you're ready, come to my room. I'll take you to supper. I'm not sure we'll be moving on right away. I have to think about it. I'll let you know. Whatever we do, I'll have to get you all some new clothes. It'll be hot where we're going. Hot and dry. Stan, you'll have to pack up that coat. Lupé, you'll need something besides that flannel shirt or you'll drop a dozen sizes before you take two steps. Little one, don't worry, you're just fine the way you are.

I'm going to turn on the radio.

Listen to the music.

Close your eyes.

We're almost there.

2

1

Casey moved through the woods, following Star Creek's deathbed toward the river below.

He was not in a good mood.

The bell's tolling nearly had him out the door at a run until common sense restrained him. They would be gone, whoever it had been, and he would only make himself look like a damn fool, charging up the hill for the second time this week. It was what they wanted, and he wasn't about to give them the satisfaction, or himself a relapse. But he hadn't forgotten, especially after spending half the morning crawling around the belfry, looking for some kind of clue until a splinter had rammed into the heel of his left hand; it had taken all his strength not to let loose right there in the church.

By the time he returned home, the temperature was back in the nineties, the humidity smothering, and a cold shower hadn't done the least bit of good. Neither for his comfort nor his temper.

He decided he needed the woods, no people and no problems, and with a baseball cap crammed on his head, he went out to check the creek.

It was worse than he had thought.

Only tiny pools a few inches across were left here and there, mostly there, connected to each other by threads of weak brackish water clotted with dead leaves and weeds. The rest was baked and cracked, puffing to dust when he touched it with a toe or a heel.

The partially eaten body of a raccoon, the remains of a snake, several baby birds covered with ants.

At the meadow, he stood in the doubtful shade of a canted pine and followed the creek's meander until it was swallowed by brown grass that looked like brown nails. One hundred yards ahead the forest began again, and it didn't look any cooler there than it was standing here.

Still, he figured that to be in New York now, or any Eastern city, would be even worse. The networks and local news, even CNN, spoke of murder and suicide rates soaring to new records from Portland down to Washington, riots that broke out over a hat or a soda or a token being snatched, and brownouts that had turned buildings old and new into ovens. Leaders spoke of keeping the peace, urging patience and restraint until the weather broke. Casey had finally turned it off; he couldn't stand the desperation in their eyes.

To his left he could see the road, and wondered if he had the energy to walk up to Ed's, take a horse, let him and the beast wander for the rest of the day.

A drop of sweat slithered into his eyes, stinging as he rubbed at it.

Nope, not today.

So he figured now was as good a time as any to pay a visit to Micah. If nothing else, the old man would have a goodly stock of cold beer.

He moved along the treeline toward the road, wincing as the grass snapped beneath his boots. He wore a thin pale shirt, sleeves rolled to the elbows, and was tempted to take it off. But that way lay quick sunburn, an annual bit of torture he definitely didn't need now.

Besides, he was probably sweating out the last of his walking stupid pneumonia. In which case he ought to be Superman by dinner.

At the road he paused, looking down a five-foot embankment that seemed like fifty. Jump or slide, nobody's looking.

He grinned—*don't be an idiot*.

A breeze kicked dust across the blacktop and ice across the back of his neck.

He turned his head slowly.

At the north end of the meadow a young buck stood just inside the trees. Shadows behind it suggested a family, doe and fawns. He watched it test the air, lower its head and turn its antlers.

The breeze kicked again.

Ice again.

The buck was gone.

He waited a few minutes before slipping down the embankment, arms out for balance, running a couple of steps along the blacktop before he corralled his momentum. In a way, he was pleased to see the deer. It meant something was still alive back there, although he didn't want to think for how long.

When he came around the bend, Micah was on his nail keg, a cigarette in one hand, beer can in the other. Casey, forced into another run by the steep slope, panted by the time he reached the graveled parking area. He climbed over the thick rope and dropped onto one of the pilings poking chair-high from the dock.

Micah reached into a cooler beside him and tossed him a can. He opened it, held it to his brow, and sighed before he drank. A sip at a time. Then he nodded toward the empty slips.

"Full house today?"

Micah spat into the river. "Do I look rich? They're still in the boathouse, except for two. Damn fools wanted to go up to Port Jervis."

Casey looked to his right, the Delaware sweeping around a far bend. "Against the current?"

"Told you they were damn fools. Had about a dozen cam-

eras, said they were looking for wildlife.'' He snorted, drank.
''If they stick to the shallows, they might see a minnow.''

''Who took them?''

''Reed, who else?'' The old man drank, crushed the can,
opened another, drank again. ''And that girl.''

''Rina? I thought she—''

''No. The other one. The redhead.''

Casey couldn't believe it. Cora? Working the river? Cora
Bowes? It had to be the heat; there was no other explanation.
He tugged on the bill of his cap to block the glare off the slow
water. Less than a hundred yards to Pennsylvania, but he had
once been in the river on a dare and had felt the current lurking
beneath the surface. Strong as he was, he had barely made it
back to shore.

Micah drank, face flushed and creased, eyes narrow under
the captain's cap, cigarette burning forgotten in his other hand.

Casey watched him. ''What's the matter?''

''Hot.''

''Then don't drink so much. Or, you could get out of the
sun. That kind of makes sense, too.''

Micah's smile was brief, sarcastic. He flicked the cigarette
into the water and pointed with his chin at the blasted oak.
''Those bees.''

''No honey, huh?''

''No. They come at me last night.''

''They did what?'' He looked behind him, and saw nothing
around or on the tree. Usually there was at least a handful of
bees hovering over the hive. Still, even bees had to rest sometime, he supposed. ''What do you mean?''

''I mean, Case, I got home from Mackey's last night, and
they were swarming over the river. Chased me to the house
and hung around for nearly an hour before they left.''

Casey stared pointedly at the can in the old man's hand.

Micah shook his head. ''Nope. I had some maybe, but not
that many. Last time you saw me shitfaced was when? Five,
six years ago? Some birthday thing, right? Kay's Doc's?'' He
shook his head again. ''Don't matter. I wasn't last night.''

Casey didn't know what to say, and so he said, ''So maybe

it was the weather. Back in Tennessee when I was a kid, we had a string of heat like this one August, and this big old bear, he must've been a hundred, he came into the middle of town, sat himself down in the middle of the street and wouldn't move until somebody finally figured it out and brought him a pail of water." He sipped, quickly now because the beer was already getting warm. "Damn thing emptied that pail twice. Then he stands up, crushes it with one paw, and heads back on home." He laughed softly. "Half the town saw it and didn't believe it, the other half didn't see it and believed every word."

Micah didn't smile. "Didn't chase nobody though, did it."

"Come on, Mike, it's not like they haven't gone after you before, stealing their honey like you do."

"I harvest it," the old man insisted.

"Whatever. You take it, they don't like it. Maybe—"

A backfire turned their attention to the road.

A car more rust than wheels chugged down the slope and backfired itself onto the parking apron. It almost didn't make it, coming to a stop only when its front bumper nudged the rope. Todd climbed awkwardly out of the passenger side, wiping his face with a sleeve, sneering at the sky. A shorter man solidly round struggled out from behind the steering wheel, his gleaming midnight hair plastered straight back from his forehead, curled up at the collar in back. White shirt open at the throat, white trousers, white shoes.

"You want to play tennis, Doc," Micah said sourly, "you come to the wrong place."

"Casey," said Mel Farber, "we've been looking all over for you. Where the hell have you been? We had an appointment this morning, in case you forgot."

Casey lifted his beer in a *nice to see you too* toast.

"Rev," Todd said, "I think we got some trouble."

2

They adjourned to the cabin porch where the shade brought them the fantasy of relief. Once settled—Lambert on the steps, the others on wood chairs that creaked at each shift—Casey gazed out across the river from his perch on the railing, watching shade and shadow darken the forest on the opposite bank. A breeze drifted over the water's surface, rippling it, husking through the leaves, not cooling anything, but at least it moved.

There was no mayor, no town council for Maple Landing. No rules were written or written down; what laws there were belonged to the state and county. There were no police; once or twice a day on a good day, a state trooper drove through, or someone from the county sheriff dropped by to show the flag. When trouble arose, the longevity factor took over— those who had been around the longest and weren't feuding with half the town were consulted, arbitrated disputes, decided whether or not a higher authority needed to be informed or brought in.

As the community's only cleric, Casey had automatically been placed in that position, and after all this time, he still wasn't sure he appreciated the honor. There were, despite the small resident number, too many egos and too many muddied points of view. He felt uncomfortable passing judgment; he'd much rather sit someone down on the riverbank or in his office, on the bench outside Tully's store or in the Moonglow, and talk it out. Talk it to death, if he had to. Most times it worked, and seldom did anyone go away feeling slighted.

From the expressions on their faces, however, he knew this wasn't going to be one of those comparatively easy times.

He lit a cigarette, grinned at the doctor's disapproval, and suggested they get on with it before he fell asleep.

"It's Arlo," Todd said, stretching out his legs, folding his hands across his belly.

"What about him?"

Todd looked to Mel, who pulled at his chin, his nose, massaged the side of his neck before saying, "That man last night, the one Arlo clobbered?" He stared at the floor. "I finally took him over to the hospital for X rays, just in case he'd been handed a concussion. He didn't, as it turned out, just the laceration and a hell of a bump. But I found out a couple of things."

Micah passed out the beers. "Like what?"

"Like, his name is Cardiño Escobar."

Casey shrugged; it meant nothing to him. Nor, from his expression, to Micah either, who said, "What is he, some kind of Mafia?" No question the idea didn't bother him a bit.

"Close," Mel said. "I recognized the name, and this morning I called a friend down in Trenton. It turns out Mr. Escobar is one of those gentlemen who are generally acknowledged to be crooks of medium water, nothing like the Mob, but it seems they have ambitions of more than the modest sort. Mr. Escobar has thus far been able to evade jail time. He works for a small group of other gentlemen, mostly from South America, who apparently have established quite a reputation here and in Pennsylvania for gambling operations, most likely murder, probably real-estate scams."

Micah drank. "So?"

Todd sighed over his beer. "Jeez, Mike, use your head. What the hell does Arlo Mackey have to do with someone like that? Promoting oldies concerts?"

Lambert shrugged. "How should I know?"

"It's like this," Mel said earnestly, speaking directly to Casey. "Half this town owns most the other half, right? And we rent houses and cabins and shacks out whenever we can. Hunters, fishermen, families, the whole weekend and weekly rainbow. Lot of people's extra, sometimes necessary income comes from that. Right? Right. So, you've walked around. Have you seen many *For Rent* signs out this season?"

Casey didn't have time to speak.

"No," the doctor answered for him. "Maybe nine or ten, tops. Why? Because last autumn, Arlo went around to the homeowners and offered to act as their agent, promising higher fees and bigger cuts than they'd been getting from their ads or wherever they'd been doing business before. And almost everyone who agreed to deal with him had their properties contracted for by the first of the year."

"So what if he makes a few bucks?" Micah asked impatiently. "So what?" He chuckled. "You afraid the Landing's gonna be one of them Mafia meeting joints? Like they used to have in upstate New York?''

"So one of the people who didn't sign, you jackass, was Jack Manger.''

Micah grunted.

Casey remembered it was after Christmas, right after the first of over a dozen weekly snowstorms had hit the area. The Landing had been cut off for two days. Manger, who lived on the Crest, had been walking home from the bar on the second day. A car without headlights came out of a side street, cut him down, and sped out of town. The man's neck had been snapped on impact; Farber guessed he was dead before he hit the ground.

Neither the state police nor the sheriff's office had been able to find a thing.

"Steve Wishum used his old agency. His place was gutted on New Year's.''

"Moved to Florida right after," Todd reminded them.

Mel looked at Casey again. "Georgia Williams fell down her cellar stairs and broke her hip.''

"You saying Arlo did this?" Micah demanded incredulously. "Damn, you're nuttier'n he is.''

"I'm saying," Mel told him with exaggerated patience, "that it's awfully funny our hippie buddy Arlo should suddenly up and turn into a guitar-playing real-estate man, and the people who didn't deal with him got themselves hurt. I'm saying," he added, raising his voice to keep Lambert silent, "it's awfully peculiar Arlo all of a sudden knows a man who specializes in this stuff.'' He leaned back. "I'm saying there's something going on, and I don't think it's over.''

Casey listened to Micah argue coincidence and molehills, and as far as he could tell, the boatman was right. Not everyone who hadn't worked with Arlo ended up like Manger, Wishum, or Georgia—who had never claimed she had been pushed or tripped anyway. A dizzy spell had done it, nothing more sinister than that.

When the three finally hushed just shy of standing up and

shouting, Todd looked at Casey straight-faced and said, "So what does God think of all this, Rev?"

Casey closed his eyes, put a forefinger to each temple, and hummed a single note for several seconds before saying, "No answer. I think we've bored Him to sleep."

Micah snorted a laugh and rummaged in the cooler for another beer; Todd rolled his eyes; and Mel did his best to look stern, except that he ended up looking to Casey like a snarling puppy, which, he supposed, was the danger of such a young man falling into a role belonging to a man much older.

"The thing is," Casey told them once they had settled down, "unless we get an investigator in here to dig around, I don't see any laws broken. Arlo brokered the rent, and you got your money. Unless you think it's illegal to take it from someone like Escobar, I don't get it."

"Nobody's showed up in the rental places, Case."

"Like I said, you got your money."

"But why?" Mel passed a hand over his brow, pursed his lips and whistled once, a low note. "Case, the Landing is empty. It's empty because of the weather, sure, but also because of Arlo, and maybe also Escobar. The summer money we depend on from the stores and stuff isn't here this year, and people like Kay and Mabel, Howard up at the deli, they're not doing so well. Pretty awful, in fact."

"Okay, but don't you—"

"Now Ozzie, he's doing all right because we all need gas and oil, and Vinia, her drug store isn't hurting either, for obvious reasons."

"Yes, but—"

"It's possible that Escobar had Jack killed and Steve burned out, and God help us, did something to Georgia. And I know, I know, I can't prove it. Any of it."

"So what does Arlo say?"

He stopped himself before he said more. He already knew the answer—he saw it in Todd's sudden interest in the river, and in Mel's having the grace to look more than a little uncomfortable. He asked why with a weary gesture.

"Because you'll scare the shit out of him," Todd answered

bluntly. "If he pulls that 'flower power' crap, all you have to do is make that face and he'll have to change his drawers."

Casey was startled. "What face?"

"The one you always make just before you blow your stack."

He frowned in confusion. "I do?"

"Hey, it's not an ugly face," Mel assured him hastily. "It's kind of a . . . I don't know, like you've turned to stone or something." He nodded. "Scary as hell, believe me."

Casey had a feeling he ought to be insulted. Nevertheless, he thought it was stupid idea, and he told them so, and told them again when Micah, perversely, agreed with the idea. It was stupid because Arlo had done nothing wrong that they knew of; stupid because if Arlo denied it, there was nothing they could do about it; and doubly stupid because if they were in fact right—which he honestly doubted—they were risking a lot of trouble with a man named Escobar, who traveled in circles considerably more dangerous than the kind they could find in Maple Landing. Or anywhere near it.

Arlo was a friend to them all to one degree or another. They were taking a big chance confronting him with such accusations.

"We're dying, Case," Mel said simply, hands spread.

"Nobody cares about a two-bit place like this," Todd added. "Small people like us, we don't amount to much in their view." He gestured to the hill beside him, meaning the outside world. "Hell, it's hard enough getting people coming here as it is. We get some kind of scam, plot, whatever the hell it is, what chance do we have? And who would give a damn?"

Casey slipped off the railing and stepped away from the cabin. He refused to look at them, although he could feel their expectation. It wasn't right. He couldn't do it. Arlo was a throwback, calculated or not, and he still couldn't see any crime here at all. He took off his cap, wiped his forehead, and kicked softly at the ground.

Shook his head slowly, and licked his lips.

Nope; he couldn't do it.

Before he could tell them, however, the sound of a van broke the silence.

He could see it through the trees, and knew it was going too fast. The driver must have realized it too, because there was a sudden harsh cry of brakes, and as Micah said, "Son of a bitch," the van skidded down the slope, slewing sideways, straightening, missing a tree by the breadth of a scream, and slammed to a halt with the dock rope drawn taut around its blunted nose.

"My God," Mel said breathlessly.

"Customers, Mike," was all Todd said.

Micah pushed off the steps, and was abreast of Casey when he stopped. "Oh . . . shit."

Casey didn't see it until Micah nudged him sharply and pointed.

The bees.

A spinning cloud too thick to see through, rising like a thunderhead from behind the van.

Todd eased to his side, Mel right behind him. "Look at them," he said at last. "They've goddamn swarmed." He leaned forward, squinting. "What in the hell made them do that?"

Casey's throat seized as they moved toward the apron.

The bees settled over the van, covering it by stages, hundreds of them crawling, dozens more circling, dropping, circling again.

They didn't make a sound.

"The noise," Casey offered quietly. When Todd frowned, he pointed at the skid marks on the blacktop. "The brakes were damn loud. Maybe that was enough to set them off."

They looked to Micah, who only shrugged his ignorance and stopped, tipping his cap back on his head. "This is far as I go, guys, I can tell you."

"Well, we can't just leave them," the doctor argued, his voice high, nearly squeaking.

"You want to go over there, shoo them away?" Micah asked. "Be my guest."

"But we can't leave them," Farber repeated.

Todd grabbed Micah's arm. "You got kerosene some-place?"

Casey shook his head at the idea. "There's too many. We need smoke or something." He shook his head again. "Not enough. We'd need to burn the damn forest down."

The bees didn't seem to care. They crawled, hovered, crawled again.

Without a sound.

And now the men could hear the muffled screaming inside.

Todd flapped one hand helplessly. "Aw, man . . . Casey, now what?"

He took an involuntary step forward. Good question, he thought, feeling a rush of cold pass through his stomach.

"Damn," Mel whispered, and walked purposefully toward the dock. Todd stretched out his arm, but Farber swerved around it.

"Doc, damnit!"

"I'll think of something."

Casey followed without thinking, not daring to yell at Mel to get his ass back here. Todd joined him, jaw working nervously, fingers of his left hand patting his leg. Micah swore, and veered toward the boathouse, gesturing that the others should stay the hell where they were.

Todd glanced at Casey, gave him a sickly grin. "I kind of like the odds. A couple thousand to one, what the hell."

The three men slowed as they broke into the open.

They were close enough now that Casey could see the individuals that made up the swarm, glistening as if it had been just washed with a shower; but it was too thick to see the van, the windows, the people inside.

If only they would make a noise, any kind of noise.

This was damn spooky.

Todd leaned toward him. "They're not moving very fast."

"Starving," Farber guessed. "No flowers, nothing, they haven't eaten properly in God knows how long."

"Is that right?" Casey asked hopefully.

Mel only shrugged, he was only guessing.

"So . . . now what?" Todd said.

Which was when Micah returned with two large jerry cans of kerosene and set them down on the edge of the apron. He muttered and stepped back, unlit cigarette bouncing between his lips. Casey saw the fear, saw him measuring the distance between the van and the cabin. There was no sense using the boathouse if they had to run; it had no wall on the river side.

"Got an idea," Todd said, kneeling to uncap the cans.

Casey grunted a *get on with it,* and grimaced as the stench of kerosene rose into the heat. He felt the cold again.

"What we'll do," Todd explained, standing again, handing one can to Farber, "is we'll work around to the left. Doc, toss yours on that side, I'll take this one. Casey, you do the matches."

"Then what?" Micah asked from behind him.

"We run like hell to the cabin."

"What about the people inside?"

"They stay in there, they'll die. Once the fire starts, they'll have a chance. They got the river and the cabin, their choice."

"Maybe the Rev can preach at them or something," Micah whispered. "Bore them to death."

Casey gave him a look, received an apologetic smile and shrug, and looked back at the van.

The cold deepened, and spread.

Something; surely he ought to be able to do something.

Odam and Farber sidled toward their positions, the kerosene sloshing, as Casey braced himself and moved forward, fumbling in his jeans for a book of matches.

The bees crawled, weaving, gleaming, once in a while letting a color show through.

Casey's lips moved in unconscious prayer, felt Todd looking at him, but he didn't stop.

Todd nodded. "It sure as hell can't hurt."

The cold made Casey's teeth want to chatter; it stiffened his spine, and for a moment he thought he was going to faint, or die.

"Ready?" Todd whispered to Farber, who nodded shakily. "Okay. On three."

Farber hefted the can, one hand braced on the bottom. A few drops splattered to the blacktop.

"One."

Casey took out his matches, tore one from the packet; his fingers shook.

"Two."

Micah backed away in a hurry.

Suddenly Casey couldn't stand the cold, the silence, any longer; he inhaled deeply and stepped up to the van, heels crunching softly on the gravel. The cold burned. He was angry. Angry enough to be tempted to reach out and grab those damn bees in his fists, tear them away, tear off the doors and tear the people out.

No one moved.

Todd hissed at him to get the hell away, goddamnit, he was screwing it all up.

Casey's lungs filled, emptied, the cold warming suddenly, fire in its place, and a hazelike fog that blurred the swarm to black; floating.

"Leave," he ordered, his voice deep, singing, carrying over the river even though he wasn't shouting. "You have no place here. Leave."

Farber looked at him desperately.

"Leave!" Casey commanded, raised a hand and pointed.

The bees crawled.

A woman begged for help, muffled and weak.

Casey lit a match, held it cupped in a palm, and without warning tossed it into the swarm.

"Leave," he whispered. "Leave now."

There was no flare, no explosion, no burst of heavenly flame.

The match landed.

Farber gasped, dropped his can, and backpedaled so fast he nearly stumbled.

"Leave." Casey nodded. "Now."

Immediately, the bees rose, in pairs, in dozens, then by scores and hundreds; they swarmed overhead, and took the black cloud back to the tree.

There was no angry buzzing, no sign of attack.
Nothing at all but the ragged sound of their wings.
Nothing at all but the heat as Casey felt his knees buckle.

3

There were voices, distant and muted.

There was movement, clumsy and slow.

There was bile in his throat, but he couldn't spit it out, and a cold that settled in every bone and every muscle. A cold that burned, like fire without a flame.

He felt so damn heavy, like the worst days of his pneumonia when he wanted to leave his bed and couldn't and so had to vomit into a large bowl someone had set beside the bed. Nothing he tried then or now worked—not his arms, not his legs, and he couldn't open his eyes.

He wasn't sure he wanted to.

Lord, what happened?

No one answered.

4

Helen stood over the grill and shook her head at the mess she had made of a couple of simple, lousy cheeseburgers. They should have been patties, browned, round, sizzling at the edges. She couldn't help thinking of mud pies stepped on by a wandering elephant. The spatula didn't help; it only made the things look more obscene. Her only hope was dressing up the plate and using the fixings to hide what couldn't possibly be something meant for human consumption.

"Ready?" Rina asked from the serving gap.

Helen looked at her sourly. "What do you think?" She pointed.

Rina saw, and grinned.

Helen scowled. "Couple of minutes."

"Sure." Rina giggled. "Whatever you say."

There were six people at the counter, six more in the booths, and Helen hadn't stopped working since Todd had left, promising to be back within the hour. Two hours ago. Which, she supposed as she set up the plates, shouldn't have been a surprise. Although he hadn't said anything, she suspected some kind of meeting, and bet her miserable tips there'd be more beer than talk.

This, she thought, is a hell of a way to run a town.

But it usually worked, she admitted grudgingly, and had worked ever since she had been a little girl, watching her father traipse down to the dock with five or six others, depending on who was in town and who wasn't in trouble. No one ever talked about what had gone on, but sometimes the police came, sometimes someone left and didn't return, and once in a while a state or forestry official showed up and streets that needed paving were paved, pipes were replaced, or campers were removed from hidden glens in the woods.

She had thought then, and she thought now, that the Landing was more like a club than a town.

Her hands moved swiftly, surely, assembling sandwiches and the burgers, salads, slices of pickle, scoops of cole slaw. Turn to the deep fryer, lift the basket, shake out the fries. Turn, pour, grab the plates and slap them on the shelf.

"Rina."

The meals were gone before she had a chance to blink.

That girl is definitely not human, she decided. All arms and legs and hair, she ought to be more awkward, tripping over herself, breaking dishes, whacking her shins. Instead, she moved as though she were dancing, gliding without a single wasted movement.

It made her feel like a lump.

In fact, as she watched Rina refill coffee and take swipes at spills, she figured the only time that kid acted like a kid was when Nate Dane was around. Which at least proved she was human. Maybe.

She smiled, flicked a wave at Mrs. Racine, sitting at a booth with Mabel and Moss, and turned back to clean the grill.

Now there was a challenge—practicing the music Mabe

wanted for the wedding. Although she had been able to talk the woman out of Jefferson Airplane, Mozart and the Beatles wouldn't be moved. Even if she hadn't been Trinity's only organist, she wouldn't miss this event for the world.

"Hey, Helen!"

She looked up as she scraped the grease into the gutter at the front of the grill. "Now what?"

Rina jerked a thumb toward the street. "I just saw Dr. Farber's car stop at the clinic."

"So?"

"So they just carried Reverend Chisholm inside."

That's when she realized the diner had gone silent, and those at the counter had swiveled around to peer through the side window.

Helen didn't move. "Carried?"

"Well . . ." Rina twisted a towel around her hands. "He was walking, sort of. Mr. Odam and Mr. Lambert were kind of holding him up."

Oh, Jesus, she thought.

Figures passed behind the girl as a handful of customers left, gone before Helen could think to ask one of them to bring back some news.

"You want me to go see?"

"I . . ."

"No sweat," the girl said. "Mrs. Racine wants some pie, Miss Jonsen needs more coffee, and," she whispered, "Mr. Tully won't keep his hands off her." She snickered, dropped the towel, and took off, telling the remaining diners that Helen would take care of them, she'd be back in a second.

Helen couldn't move.

The grill sizzled.

Someone called her.

She couldn't move, didn't dare, because as soon she did, she would start to imagine all the things that could have happened. Her left hand fluttered around her hair, her right remembered it was supposed to be cleaning. Automatic. Scrape and dump. Not feeling the heat. Starting when Moss pushed open the swinging door and asked her if he could fetch the coffee himself.

"Sure," she said distractedly. "Yes. Whatever."

A wave to dismiss him.

A deep breath to calm herself, and an order to stop behaving as if she were Rina catching sight of Nate. There was no reason for it. On either side. He was a friend, nothing more, and if she started thinking the way Tessa thought she felt, she'd only land herself in one hell of a lot of trouble.

Still, she yelped when a hand touched her shoulder.

"Gawd, Hel," Todd said, taking the spatula from her hand. "You okay?"

"Yes. Sure. How's—"

He shooed her from the kitchen. "Too much beer, too much heat, the jerk almost passed out, that's all."

Standing in the doorway, heat on one side from the kitchen and cool on the other from the air-conditioning, she felt a little faint herself. She also knew he was lying, and would have confronted him had not a customer demanded service. Without thinking, she picked up Rina's towel and walked down to the end booth, glancing up when a van sped by, heading east, doing fifty at least and not slowing down.

"Idiot," Moss said, stretching his neck to follow the vehicle up the slope. "Think a bear was after him." He curled his lip. "Stupid tourists."

The quartet in the booth bridled until Helen told them not to worry, he was getting married in two weeks, didn't know up from down. They relaxed, she took their dessert orders, and numbed herself by cutting pie, leaning into the ice cream vat, serving, moving down the counter to see that everyone there was satisfied.

When Rina returned, Helen's legs nearly cramped as she forced them not to run. Instead, she leaned back against the shelf, folding her arms, feeling the warmth of the coffee urn radiate to her spine.

"So?"

Heads cocked, turned, no one stared directly.

Rina fussed with her ponytail, not concerned at all. "A

touch of heat stroke.'' Automatically she reached for a customer's empty cup. ''No big deal. He has to rest for a little
while, then Doc's sending him home.''

''Big men like that shouldn't move around so fast on a day
like this,'' Moss said.

Mabel slapped his arm lightly. ''He's not fat.''

''Didn't mean that.''

Another slap that turned into a caress, and a suggestion they
leave, there were things to be done, plans to be made for a
week come Sunday.

Rina turned her back, making a face. ''Gross.''

Helen, however, had seen Todd's reaction to the news. A
slight sagging, clear relief.

''Hey, can I pay my bill here?''

Plastic smile as she tended the register; plastic farewell; staring unseeing at the street until she slammed the drawer closed
and marched into the kitchen. Todd looked up from the
butcher's block, scowling, then backing away when she
rounded it and forced him without touching him to the back
door, to the stoop outside.

''Helen, what the hell?''

''Tell me,'' she said, keeping her voice low. ''Tell me, or
I'll smash that damn guitar over your damn head.''

5

''How long do I have to stay here?''

''Until you stop looking like uncooked dough. And until
people stop sneaking around out there, trying to figure out
what happened.''

''Doc, I'd rather go, if you don't mind.''

''I do mind, Casey. If you collapse on the street, it's my
ass. Not to mention my malpractice insurance.''

''It's not your insurance I'm concerned about.''

''I know, Case, I know.''

''Man, I feel awful.''

''You should. You haven't been out of bed a week, you're

clumping all over the place, drinking, smoking—''

"Chewing, cursing, I know, I know."

"Case, it isn't funny. People have died from less. Drink."

"I have any more water, I'm gonna float."

"Just drink it. And stop worrying about it."

"Just like that?"

"Case, it was a fluke. They were ready to leave, and you happened along at the right time. Or the wrong time. You start thinking it was anything else, you're going to drive yourself, and the rest of us, nuts. Now, if you were one of those TV preachers, or a born-again, I would worry. But you're not. Sometimes you talk like them, but you're a whole different breed."

"That doesn't mean I don't believe."

"No, but it means you know the difference between a fluke, a coincidence, and a miracle."

"Yeah, well—"

"Besides, what would you call it? The driving out of the bees? No offense, Rev, but it doesn't quite have that ring."

"Doc, I have to—"

"What you have to do is rest a little. What I have to do is chase Mabel away from the front door. I'll tell her it was UFOs, getting ready for the wedding."

"Thanks."

"Don't mention it."

6

He closed his eyes, waiting for the cold, the burning cold, to return; he reached for the sensation of floating, drifting, as if treading easily through water; he waited for a sign.

Nothing happened.

He waited anyway.

That was the easy part, the waiting. When he had to, he could be as patient as a rock. This time he had to be. This time it was more important than Doc could possibly know.

please don't please don't hurt me please don't

on the floor you goddamn bastard on the floor
please don't
on the floor
please
His eyes opened when the cold returned.
But it wasn't the same.
This cold was something else.
This cold was fear.

7

Kay took her time getting back to the Pavilion. The Moonglow
had been jammed, practically everybody talking about what
had happened to Casey. She had been lucky to find a counter
stool, luckier still to catch Rina at a mercifully slow moment.
The speculation had run to everything from parting the Delaware to falling off the dock in a drunken stupor. Heat stroke,
however, was something she could deal with.

She could certainly empathize. Even now, going on seven,
simply walking up the street made her feel lethargic. By the
time she reached the shop, she was gasping, sweating, and
made a face at Nate, who looked up from the counter and said,
"Ugh."

She slumped toward the back. "You're fired, little boy."

He laughed. "You fire me all the time."

She slapped the air with one weary hand while she held her
hair away from her neck with the other. She wondered if
skinny women like Helen or Tessa ever sweated like an elephant, or how chubbos like Farber managed to live through
the day without their hearts exploding.

The air-conditioning raised gooseflesh on her arms, but she
was still too hot. The back room was cool—it had to be, because of the tapes—but the tiny bathroom was a sauna because
she insisted the door be kept closed.

Her reflection told her Nate was right. Ugh. No question
about it. All that hair gone to string and frizz, flushed cheeks
making her look like a chipmunk. No wonder Casey didn't do

anything but talk. A woman like that didn't deserve anything more.

Oh, Christ, let's not start, okay? the reflection scolded; it's too damn hot.

She unbuttoned her short-sleeve blouse, grabbed a wash-cloth, and soaked it under the cold-water tap.

Hot. That's what she was, all right, and not only because of the weather.

She wrung the cloth out and passed it over her forehead, her cheeks, her neck. Slowly, to the flat of her chest. Shuddering at the coolness, feeling the heat. Soaking it again and wringing it out and daubing at her breasts, shivering and smiling at a trickle of cold that slipped into her bra.

If you had a slave, she thought.

Her left hand gripped the sink's rim.

"Hey, Kay?"

How young would he be?

"Kay?"

Big mistake, letting him call you by your first name. Not good business. If he gets too familiar, how are you going to let him go? If you let him go.

Slowly, over her chest, across her stomach.

The cool was lukewarm.

She didn't care.

She might well have to let him go. Without that extra rental money, this place barely allowed her to eat, much less turn a decent profit. Thank God for the savings account; some judicious withdrawals were the only things that had kept her going this season. And the fact that Nate, when he worked here, worked for free rentals.

Soak the cloth, wring it out, start again at the top.

Slowly. Very slowly.

How young?

"Kay? Look, I—Oh."

She didn't jump, didn't turn. She looked square in the mirror and saw him in the doorway, doing his damnedest not to look, and failing so miserably it was almost comical.

"What?" she said gently.

Washcloth still moving; slowly, very slowly.

"Um . . ." He glanced away. "Mr. Balanov's coming."

"Okay."

The washcloth moved, pushing across the tops of her breasts; slowly, very slowly.

What can he really see? she wondered; what does he want to see?

"Nate," she said evenly, maybe a scolding, shifting her gaze to her chest, then back to his eyes.

He got the message. A hasty nod and he was gone, and she watched the beads of water shimmering on her neck, on the push and rise of her breasts, on the back of her hand.

You've been watching too many of those movies, she thought; young studs, older women, who the hell died and made you sexy?

A smile for the mirror.

A deep breath, and she wondered.

When the bell rang, she folded the cloth and draped it over the sink, fussed with her buttons but didn't tuck the blouse in, and fluffed her hair, grimacing when it didn't do anything but hang there. A step back revealed water spots on the blouse, darkly translucent. She didn't care, and even if she did, there was nothing she could do about it now anyway.

She reached the front the moment Petyr Balanov walked in, and she bristled automatically. Enid may be a royal pain in the ass with all her moralizing and preaching, but he was far worse. He never preached, never lectured, but his disapproval was abundantly clear. His manner didn't help either—tall, always impeccably dressed whether in a suit or, as now, in casual and expensive clothes, and always with a deliberate air of condescension.

He was lord of the manor; she was little more than a peasant and he never let her forget it.

"Hi, Mr. Balanov," Nate greeted from the register. "How's Dimmy and Sonya?"

The man ignored him. He stood just inside the threshold and waited, hands at his sides, head slightly back, eyes reminding her of a hawk who had spotted its prey and was taking its time.

"Can I help you, Pete?" she said, knowing he hated that.

He said nothing. His gaze glanced off Nate.

Games I have no time for, she thought, and used a jerk of her head to send Nate into the back, making sure her expression let him know she didn't want to. When he was gone, she leaned against the counter, arms folded carefully under her breasts.

He still didn't move, the outside glare darkening his face, making him seem taller, fleshed out with shadow. "I am asking you, Miss Pollard, to remove those films from your store."

She didn't need to ask. "Sorry."

"I do not think it an unreasonable request."

She shifted slightly, not having to look to realize she hadn't buttoned the blouse all the way up. His eyes didn't move, but she knew that he saw. "Are you a spokesman, Pete? I mean, for a group or something?"

He shook his head.

"Then I can't help you."

"Can't?"

"Look," she told him, "if I do what you ask—"

"Demand, Miss Pollard. Demand."

"—then I'll have to do the same for everyone else who has a gripe against one kind of movie or another. And that would leave me with nothing but Disney in here." She smiled sweetly. "I wouldn't be in business very long, now would I."

"I do not care. You have disturbed my wife, and I cannot allow it."

"Too bad."

He smiled, a toothsome, wicked smile that lasted only a second, just long enough for him to take three long steps toward her, long enough for her to see the nothing in his eyes.

A glance toward the tape room before he said, "I am giving you fair warning. If you do not remove that filth, you will regret it most sincerely."

His breath smelled of mint.

He was too close, but she had a feeling that if she pushed

him away, he would break her arm, or worse, without exerting himself at all.

"Is that a threat?"

"Oh, absolutely, Miss Pollard. Absolutely."

The smile again before he turned away and walked to the door, opened it, and looked back.

"The worst kind of threat, Miss Pollard. The worst kind you can think of. Ask Mr. Wishum. If you can find him."

She would have yelled, but he was already gone, one hand in his pocket, the other waving politely to someone she couldn't see. So calm, so ordinary. The urge to scream was replaced by a spasm that rocked her against the counter. She gripped the edge until it passed, then made her way shakily to the back. A sour taste filled her throat as she pushed by Nate and flung open the bathroom door, lurched in and sagged against the sink, willing herself not to throw up.

It was possible she had overreacted. Surely he couldn't have actually meant . . .

"Are you gonna call the cops?"

Startled, she looked into the mirror.

Nate was furious. "He threatened to hurt you. Do you want me to call the cops? I could be a witness or something."

Her eyes closed, and her knees gave way. A small involuntary cry as she scrambled to grab the basin, but his arm took her waist and she leaned gratefully against him as he brought her out to the chair. As soon as she was seated, he reached for the telephone.

She grabbed his wrist. "Not yet," she said.

He didn't say a word.

Oh Lord, Kay, what are you doing?

"Not yet."

8

Dimitri sat on the edge of the pool, feet dangling in the water, Sonya beside him, silently mimicking every move he made. Supper was over, his mother on the lounge on the other side, and his father gone. Dimitri didn't know where, and didn't ask. That was a house rule—you never asked where Papa went. Sometimes, when he came back, he brought candy or ice cream; sometimes, when he came back, he played with them in the water; sometimes, when he came back, he stood on the deck and said nothing, hands clasped behind his back, watching his family until Momma realized he was there. Then she would grab her towel and say, be good, children, and go inside.

Sometimes he heard noises after that.

Sometimes he heard nothing.

"Dimmy?" Sonya had tired of the game and kicked at her own, slow, speed.

He grunted.

"Do the birds really talk to you?"

He kept his voice low. "Sometimes."

"That's neat."

No, it's not, he thought; no, it's really scary.

She looked at him sideways. "You know what I'd say if they talked to me?"

"What?"

"I'd say, stop scaring my brother, it isn't nice. I'd say, I'll let you play in my castle if you stop it. People shouldn't do things like that, so you can play in my castle if you don't do it anymore." She nodded sharply. "That's what I'd say."

He rocked against her.

She rocked back.

He said, "Father Chisholm knows it too."

She frowned. "Knows what?"

"That we're all gonna die."

3

A voice in the dark:
  Wake up, children, wake up, it's time to go.

A sleepy mumbled question while stumbling in the dark:
  Oh, he'll know, Stan, he'll know. But by then, it won't matter.
  And quiet laughter.

A groan and protest against the shadow in the dark:
  Don't be silly, time to go. And Lupé, dear . . . don't leave the gun.
  And quiet laughter.

A whimpering, and a giggling at the smile in the dark:
  Wake up, darling, time to go. You'll like it there, I promise.

And quiet laughter.

4

1

Sunset, no clouds, the stars and moon arrogantly cold.

A car, squat and ordinary, parked on the shoulder, on the far side of the bend just before Maple Landing began. Diño Escobar wiped his face hard with his left hand, his right gripping the steering wheel so tightly it trembled. Beside him, a tree stump of a man sat placidly, gaze taking in the woodland that surrounded them.

Escobar didn't like the dark outside the car, but he didn't like more the lump of gauze and surgical tape on the side of his head. As soon as he could walk without feeling nauseated, he had checked himself out of the hospital. No one had protested, especially when Miguel Astante arrived to pick him up. They took a room in a motel by a nearby lake, and he had slept through the afternoon, Miguel waking him in time for a late supper he could barely eat. Not because he sometimes saw double, but because of his anger. He had let an old man, a smelly old man, best him. He didn't care what his employers thought; this had become a matter of honor. Young men wouldn't obey him if old men laughed and beat him.

By the time he got back into the car, his anger had flared to rage.

"Just there," he said, nodding toward the bend.

A glow beyond, outlining the trees, but even with the windows down, they couldn't hear a thing save the rumble of the engine. Not even a cricket.

"You sure?"

"It's done anyway, most of it. They won't need him. We just finish a little early, that's all. A lesson."

Miguel shrugged. "If you say so."

The voice suggested doubt, and a warning. If Escobar was wrong, they'd both better head for the nearest border.

Escobar touched the bandage, winced, hissed.

"I say so."

2

He lay prostrate before the altar.

Black cassock, bare feet, arms outstretched to either side, forehead on the carpet.

The sun was down at last, two candles on brass burning on either side of the cross. No other light, no other sound but the sound of his breathing.

He had no idea if this would do any good, but he could think of nothing else to do. Once sure he wouldn't be waylaid by well-wishers and the curious, he had left Farber's clinic and walked home, shivering, hugging himself, finally unable to stand the walls and the fireplace and the furniture anymore. For a while he had thought to visit the meadow, then changed his mind and returned to the church. He had met no one on the way. And once in his office, he had taken out his Bible and started to read. The words were there, but the comfort wasn't. The next thing he knew, he had stripped off his boots and socks, put on the floor-length black cassock, and knelt before the altar.

A minute later he was prostrate.

It seemed the natural thing to do.

What he wanted was an explanation. Everyone else had one; the only one who didn't was him.

He was, at the same time, disgusted and afraid.

Disgusted, because he had actually dared, for one horrifying second, to believe that he had somehow performed, not a miracle, but an exercise in the kind of power he had always believed a true holy man could wield. Without an ounce of humility, he knew he was not holy. He was, as Helen had said, a man, not a god. He had vices, he had sins, he had, Lord help him, pride. And that pride was what had nearly collapsed him after the swarm had left the van, because that was the second when he had thought, *I did it.*

Not afterward, when Farber blamed the heat and Micah the van and Odam the fact that the bees had already begun to lift.

Not then, when he knew that one of them, or all of them, were right.

Not afterward, when common sense and his own sense of the natural had regained control.

It was the moment, it was his voice, it was the deadening of the air and the heat and the floating.

I did it.

He had believed it.

He was afraid because he hadn't been able to stop himself— *I did it*—or stop himself from wondering if maybe his friends were wrong.

I did it.

So he prayed while the light died, not expecting a heavenly voice to chastise him for his vanity or absolve him for his pride or strike him down for his hubris; what he expected, what he prayed for, was the return of the peace that had taken him so long to nurture.

please don't

please don't hurt me

He wouldn't have.

That's what neither the police nor the judge would believe in the nightmare-frantic days following his arrest. He couldn't have hurt that terrified child any more than he could have hurt a helpless animal.

He was a coward.

He used his size and his appearance, but he seldom used his fists. And then, only when he had been attacked first.

He was a coward.

The girl had known it. She had visited him in prison, just that one time, and when he couldn't find anything to say other than to stutter an apology for making her cry, her expression told him all he needed to know.

Disgust; disgust and pity.

Even now, after all these years, he didn't know her name.

But she had known, and if there hadn't been forgiveness, at least there had been understanding.

He felt the roughness under his brow, at his knees, at his stomach; he felt the pulling at his shoulders, at his waist, at his back.

Slowly he drew his arms in, and pulled his legs up until he knelt, hands flat and loose on his thighs as he settled back on his heels. He looked up at the brass cross on its brass stand on the white altar, knowing that formal prayer wasn't needed, wasn't right. The Lord knew his thoughts, and there would be a response. Not a burning bush, or a tornado of fire, or a great sweeping wind. It would be in an inescapable sureness, and if it didn't come now, it would come some other time.

It didn't come now.

He smiled a little, cocked an eyebrow, and realized that he wasn't alone in the church.

A careful turn until he was seated, knees drawn up, hands wrapped around them.

Helen sat in the first pew, on the aisle.

"You know," she said, her voice trembling a little as if she wasn't sure she should speak, "I don't think of Episcopalians behaving like this." A vague gesture at him, and at the altar.

He shrugged, just a little. She was clearly uncomfortable, but he wasn't sure why.

"Are you all right?"

He nodded. "Yeah. It kind of threw me a bit."

"It would have scared the sh—heck out of me."

Their voices were soft, not quite whispering.

"It did, believe me."

She nodded toward the cross. "So what did you find out?"

A quick scratch through his hair as he shifted to sit Indian-style. "I found out that it's easier for a camel to pass through the eye of a needle, than for a fella like me to scare off a few thousand hungry bees."

When she smiled, he smiled back. "Aren't you supposed to be working?"

"Rina's covering." She looked away. "Todd said I'd better find you before I burned the diner down." And added quickly, "Lots of people are looking for you, you know. Reed and Cora want to tell you something, but you weren't at the house. I guess they tried here, but the doors were locked."

"Oh? So how did you get in?"

"Old locks, Casey." She looked back, shy but pleased. "I have a way with them."

He laughed and shook his head, then swung himself to his feet, slightly taken aback when she leaned away from him at the move and recovered badly by trying to get too quickly to her feet. She sat with a thud, tried again, but by that time he was beside her, holding out his hand.

When she took it, he pulled gently.

"You Southern boys know all the moves, don't you?" She glanced down at his feet. " 'Course, you wear a dress and forget your shoes, it kind of lacks something, you know?"

He pulled her into the aisle and guided her toward the office. "Stick around while I change. I could use the company."

Five minutes later, candles extinguished and cassock in the wardrobe, they left through the side door. The night was muggy, the air had weight, and he couldn't help a check of the belfry as they walked toward Black Oak Road.

A bat darted over the roof.

Down the street, music from the bar sounded dull and unhappy.

The streetlamp on the corner sputtered, and shadows became black lightning.

He stopped before they reached the fall of the light, and slid his hands into his pockets. His head lifted slightly, and he sniffed, smelling honeysuckle and dead grass, blacktop, and something else. His nostrils wrinkled. He couldn't tell what it was, but it wasn't very pleasant.

Helen remained beside him. "Kind of like an oil fire."

His surprise was a quick low whistle.

"I've been smelling it all afternoon. I thought it was something in the kitchen."

"Anybody complain?"

"Not that I heard."

She moved to stand in front of him, smooth and unhurried, as if they'd been dancing. They weren't exactly in the dark, but he couldn't see her face, not until she looked up at him and he saw the tears in her eyes.

"What?" he whispered.

She shook her head violently, and just as violently fell against him, gripping him tightly around the waist, cheek against his chest, tears against his shirt. His hands touched her waist, slid up to her shoulders, slid across and held her close. He could smell the warmth of her hair, the warmth of her neck where her collar pulled away. His eyes closed. His embrace tightened briefly before the hands slipped slowly back to her waist.

"Don't ever do that again," she said, still holding him, still crying.

"Which?" he asked lightly. "The bee thing or the church thing?"

"The going-away thing." She shifted to her other cheek. "They . . . they think maybe you've gone."

"They?" It came out before he could stop it, and when she didn't answer, he said, "I guess I'd better show my face, then."

With her arms still around him, she leaned back. "Aren't you mad at them? Todd, whoever?"

"Why?"

"For thinking you'd leave for something stupid like that?"

"I don't think they'd think I left for good, do you?"

Tears on her cheeks, none left in her eyes. "That's not the point. Mel thinks you scared yourself."

His chest and stomach jumped in silent laughter. "I did. Believe me, I did."

She sniffed, and as she released him to wipe her nose, he sidestepped and kept one arm around her waist, walking her back up the street, through the gate and across the grass behind the church. He sensed her question, and only signaled with his arm, heading for the graveyard's low stone wall. Once there, he lifted her to the top, and settled himself easily beside her, the graves at their back.

Clasped his hands in his lap and spoke to the ground.

My daddy worked for the railroad. Signalman in a tower. Not very exciting, but it was fun to say he worked with trains. We got free rides, Momma and me. We had to. He made no real money, and Momma had to take in washing now and then just to be sure we got fed. He died when I was fifteen. I hated him, you know. We went to one of those tinny-organ, no-fans churches in east Tennessee. Lots of hollering and damning of souls and no fun at all. I went to the funeral, and that's the last time I went to church.

Classic case of blaming God, I know that now. I hate to say it, but sometimes I still do. When I miss him. Which is just about every day I breathe.

Momma couldn't do anything for me, or with me. I walked out of school that October—he died in July—and never went back there, either. I fixed cars and swept floors, even thought about joining the Army, just to get the hell away. Naturally, I suppose, I got to drinking, and smoking a little dope, some minor breaking-and-entering, a whole lot of fights.

But I had this dream, you see—my idols were Waylon and Merle and Willie, the whole outlaw gang. I was going to write me a few songs, get me some money, and build my Momma a big mansion on the banks of the Tennessee.

What an idiot.

By the time I was twenty, I'd been in and out of jail so many times, I could have walked through the routine blindfolded. Couldn't play the guitar worth a lick, either. My songs were all jumbled, most of them so filled with self-pity, I'm surprised I wasn't lynched. In and out of Nashville, Memphis, cursing the fools who couldn't see my God-given natural talent.

That winter I went home for the first time in three years.

Momma wasn't there.

Neighbors told me she'd been taken sick and was in the hospital. They wouldn't let me in there, either. They wouldn't believe who I was.

Damn cold, too, that winter. I hitched and walked in any direction I could find a road. I hadn't eaten for three, four days except for a squirrel and a rabbit I caught with my bare hands. So cold and bone weary, I tried to rob a food mart with my bare hands too. You know that part. Three years in prison. I was supposed to serve ten on account of my record.

But this man, the chaplain, I don't know what he saw, but he saw something, and I kind of liked him, so we'd talk pretty much three, four times a week. He was the one who told me, as a singer I was worse than the Johnstown Flood. I believed him because he was right. And when he managed my release, good behavior and his promise, I lived with him and his wife for a year, came downstairs one morning and said I wanted to be a preacher.

I think I near killed him, but that night I heard him crying.

He and his friends got me through what I needed to get into seminary, paid my way there, made sure I knew exactly what I was getting into. A pretty late start, I guess, but amazing, you know? Dirt poor and bad-tempered, foul-mouthed and randy, I got through and was ordained.

The year after that, I buried Momma, and I buried him and his wife, murdered in their beds while I was at the beach.

North was about the only place I could think of to go, the bishop agreed, and here I am.

Sitting on a graveyard wall, wondering.

Just . . . wondering.

*   *   *

"Wondering what?"

He slid off the wall and stood in front of her; they were almost eye-to-eye.

His mouth tucked up at one corner. "Wondering what a lady like you would do if I ripped off all her clothes, right here, and made love to her on someone's grave, in there."

She glared. "For starters, she'd slap your face clear around to the other side of your head."

When he stepped back, she grabbed his wrist. "Then, when she got your attention, she'd probably let you," and she kissed him.

Salt, and heat, her fingers tangled in his hair, legs wrapped around his waist as he took her off the wall and tried not to crush her when he folded her close.

The kiss broke, and she leaned back, her expression as dazed as he imagined his was.

"Lord," she said. Then she put her fingers on his lips, and in a whisper, "No cracks. Not a word."

She kissed him again.

3

Mabel shook her head in disgust. "It's them terrorists from the Middle East, that's what it is." She stabbed a finger at the newspaper spread on the counter. "I mean, what else could it be? Motels blowing up, gas stations." She shook her head in disgust. "Hundred-twenty people dead. Jesus, a damn war zone."

Todd, from his position in the serving gap, glanced at the booth just behind her, where the Palmers sat with Moss and Enid. "Maybe it's the UFOs, Mabe." His face gave away nothing.

"Never." She didn't look up, reading the columns between a series of five photographs.

"Why?" Rina asked. She had a Boston cream pie in front of her, slicing it for Mrs. Racine's late night snack.

"Too obvious." Mabel sounded distracted, scowling at the

pictures, running a finger down the print. "You don't go hunting by blowing up the damn woods."

Todd raised his eyebrows. "Hunting?" Another exchange with the booth, especially with Moss, who at least had the sense to look embarrassed. "I thought you said they were just studying us. You know"—and he started to sing—"*getting to know us, getting to know all about us.*"

She didn't answer.

Just as well, he decided; whatever had happened in Maryland was horrible enough without him making fun. But she was such an easy target, and his self-control was so lousy. Although he supposed taking potshots was a lot better than listening to them talking about the reverend all the time. A short-lived phenomenon, it turned out to be. A mild dose of heat stroke was the perfect answer to a lot of puzzling questions, and it seemed most folks accepted it.

The trouble was, he had been there, and he still wasn't sure.

And he wished to hell he knew where Casey was.

"Can't make an omelet without breaking a few eggs," she said at last, still trying to match the reports with the photos.

Moss held up his coffee cup to Rina. "Maybe they just wanted to test their subsonic death-ray."

Todd covered his mouth with one hand.

Mabel turned slowly. "Don't make fun."

He lifted a hand. "Not making fun, Mabe honey, honest. Just making a suggestion."

Todd couldn't see her face, but he could see Moss look away, abruptly intent on watching Rina pour him a fresh cup. He had no idea what that man saw in Mabel Jonsen, but whatever she had, it was certainly powerful. Maybe just as powerful as the grip Bobby had laid on him, subtle as a spider's web and just as strong. You don't even know it's there until it's too late.

Tessa, in shorts and halter-top, walked in just as Enid said, "Have any of you ever considered the fact that this might be God's hand?"

"Terrorists," Mabel insisted, swiveling back to her paper. "Must be some kind of secret government installation out there. The CIA's always screwing around with things.''

Tessa slid onto a stool well away from Mabel, and asked for a tuna sandwich. Todd noticed she didn't look at him, didn't lean over the way she used to, making sure he could tell that her top wasn't padded with anything that hadn't grown there on its own. In fact, she looked as if she hadn't been sleeping very well—her young face looked a decade older, her neck betrayed tension.

Shit. Bobby must have said something. Shit.

"God," Enid persisted, ignoring Mabel, concentrating on the Palmers.

Sissy smiled politely. "I'm not going to argue with you, Enid. It could be."

Moss shifted into the corner, leaning against the window sill. "Enid, no offense, but sometimes you sound like one of those born-again types, you know? Holy rolling and all that stuff.''

Oh, damn, Todd thought; don't get her started.

"I mean, I didn't think Episcopalians were like that, you know? Case sure isn't.''

"Reverend Chisholm," she answered stiffly, "is a God-fearing man who has his own way. It does not mean he does not see the Hand of the Lord in terrible retribution. When he returns from his pilgrimage, he will be the first to tell you that.''

Moss gaped at her.

Todd wandered away, absently took down his guitar, perched on a stool he kept near the door, and quietly strummed a few chords. He was pretty mediocre, bordering on the awful, and knew it, yet seldom failed to soothe himself while he played. His mind roamed as his fingers did; it was almost like dreaming.

"Seems to me," he heard Moss say dryly, "if God was gonna do something like that, it'd be a big place. New York. L.A. Make a better impression, if you know what I mean. Like Sodom and that other place, see? Stuff like that there down in Maryland, it ain't gonna be on the news but a couple of days, then it's gone, something else in its place.''

He couldn't hear Enid's response over Rina's rattling cups and saucers, or the noise Reed made when he came in with Nate and Cora, laughing, hooting, giving Rina a hard time the way friends do. He glanced at the wall clock by the walk-in freezer and groaned. One hour to official closing. Why did everyone always pick one hour to official closing before deciding they wanted something at the Moonglow they could just as easily get at home?

And as long as he was griping, what was he going to do about Tessa? He hadn't thought their sack time had been anything more than an occasional bout of healthy lust. Seems he was wrong. Seems the girl had developed a bad case of he's mine, leave him alone.

He groaned again when Rina smacked the order bell. Every dime toward the retirement fund, he reminded himself as he hung up the guitar; every dime toward settling down on the porch and letting someone else do all the work for a change. Be nice; it would really be nice.

He grabbed the order from its spike just as Moss told Enid she was, no offense, out of her mind. When she replied coldly that at least she had a mind to be out of, Mabel looked up from her newspaper and said, "Todd, as long as you're making those kids some burgers, you think you can whip up one of those minute-steak-and-potato things you do?"

He wanted to tell her to forget it, that burgers and nothing else were his speed this time of night, but Tessa decided she wanted one too, forget the tuna sandwich.

Every dime for the fund.

Several more people wandered in, grinning and laughing at something that had happened in the Yankee game just finished.

The noise level rose.

Ozzie, awake for a change, turned on his stool and suggested to Vinia Leary that she'd better reopen the pharmacy, lots of people going to need some Alka-Seltzer or something, what with all this grease going down. Vinia, mock-primly patting her beehive blonde hair, suggested he buy soap instead, industrial strength, and the booths filled with good-natured laughter.

Todd slipped into cooking mode, hands moving, eyes watching, half an ear on the conversation outside.

Grease spattered on his wrist.

He swore and wiped it off, just as another shower aimed at his face. He danced aside on one foot, swearing loudly, scowling when Rina glanced inquiringly through the gap.

Shit, if he kept this up, he'd be dead before dessert.

Then he heard Reed say, "Has anyone seen Reverend Chisholm?"

As if a spell had been cast, the Moonglow fell silent, not a sound except for the meat cooking on the grill.

Hissing, like a snake.

Then Tessa, her voice slow and too steady, said, "The last time I saw him, he was on his way home from the clinic." She stared at Todd, but he knew she didn't see him. "He didn't look so hot."

"Mr. Odam?" Rina waved at him. "Mr. Odam, the meat's burning, I think."

He shook his head, once and quickly, and went to work with the spatula, filling the plates, slamming drawers, until he heard Enid say something about a miracle.

"Son of a *bitch*!"

He stomped through the swinging door so fast, it slammed back against the wall.

They stared, all of them, at the spatula raised shoulder-high, and the look on his face.

"There was no miracle," he said to Enid carefully, feeling his cheeks burning, his eyes abruptly dry. "There was no fucking miracle."

She paled, spread fingers covering her mouth.

He glared at all the others. "You hear me? There was no miracle. I was there. I saw it. Jesus Christ!" He marched back into the kitchen, grabbed the plates and slapped them onto the gap counter, snarling until Rina picked them up and hustled away.

There wasn't, he thought as he returned to the grill.

There wasn't, he insisted as he began to scrape it clean.

Then he howled when the handle snapped in two, and his

knuckles skidded across the grease. Whirling, eyes wide with rage, when Tessa slapped the door open and hurried in, grabbed his wrist and tugged him to the sink.

"Hey!"

"Cold water," she ordered flatly, turning the handle, forcing his hand under the flow.

"Jesus," he whispered, lips pulled away from his teeth. "Jesus damn!"

He tried to pull free, but she held him firmly, clucking at the furious red that spread across his knuckles.

"Damn." He tried again to get free, and again he failed.

"Will you hold still? God, you act like you lost your fingers, for God's sake."

He glowered at the top of her head. "It hurts."

"Well, yeah, it hurts, you dope." She grinned up at him. "Is this what you guy-types mean when you offer a knuckle sandwich?"

Rina giggled.

Todd glared her away, and tried to force the tension from his arms and neck.

The burning subsided.

Finally Tessa released him with a poke that told him to keep his hand where it was. "Rina, I think the kitchen's closed for the night."

"What about my steak?" Mabel complained.

"The cook is out of service."

"Hell, I can do it myself, no big deal."

Before Todd could answer, Tessa leaned through the gap. "I don't think that's a good idea, Miss Jonsen." She jerked a thumb over her shoulder. "You know how he is about people touching his stuff."

He couldn't hear the response; he had sagged against the sink, eyes half closed, feeling his hand growing blessedly numb. A deep inhalation when he heard her return.

"Listen, Tessa," he said, "I—"

"Shut up," she told him. "Just shut up, okay?"

He turned to apologize for whatever it was that had gotten her temper up, and froze when he saw the cleaver in her hand.

4

The car drifted around the bend.

Out of the woods, purring.

Escobar took his time, not wanting to hurry, wanting to be sure there were as few people around as possible. Wanting to be sure he would enjoy what was coming.

Lights in the houses, no one in the street. A few heads in the laundry, a night-light soft over the counter in the video store, the deli closed and dark.

"This is a foolish thing, Diño," Miguel said, and said no more.

The car stopped at the top of the slope, headlights reaching out above the street, and drowning in the dark.

Maybe, Escobar thought, Miguel's right; maybe I shouldn't let that stupid old man get to me like this. In a week, maybe two, it would be all over, and surely, after all this time, he had the patience not to take his reward early.

He turned to Miguel, to tell him he had changed his mind; the movement was a mistake. Fire began to burn under the bandage when skin and hair pulled across the gash the bottle had put there.

The pain nearly blinded him.

When Miguel looked back at him, Escobar's lips pulled away from his teeth. "You ready?"

After a moment, Miguel nodded.

5

"No. Casey, please . . ."

Helen pushed him away easily and slid off the wall. She looked at the church, the graves, and shook her head helplessly.

"No. I'm sorry, Case, but . . ."

He didn't speak, and didn't try to stop her when she hurried across the grass to the street, brushing at her clothes, fussing with her hair. As it was, he was having a difficult time breathing, and he had a feeling that anything he said now would be absolutely the wrong thing.

When she was gone, he slumped against the wall and slipped his hands into his pockets, waiting for his heart to stop racing.

Waiting, with a small smile, for the lightning to strike.

Your timing sucks, Case, he told himself, allowed himself a chuckle softer than a whisper, and pushed away with his rump. He might as well go over to the Moonglow, get something to eat, and kill a few rumors.

Helen was nowhere in sight when he reached the street.

We'll pretend it didn't happen, he thought as he walked toward Black Oak; we'll pretend that nothing happened, just a kiss between two people too afraid to do more.

He checked the sky for stars and moon, sighing long and loud in case anyone was listening. As a lover, he was something less than a stud, and he supposed his ego ought to be smarting about now. On the other hand, there was no question she was right. Between a church and a graveyard was hardly the right place for either lust or love.

It courted the lightning.

He looked up again, and shrugged with his eyebrows.

At the corner he stopped, suddenly apprehensive. Maybe he shouldn't go after all. If Helen was there, it might make things uncomfortable, and he doubted anyone took the rumor of his leaving very seriously, if at all. She was probably exaggerating.

Still, the diner's glow spread comfortably over the street, a neon and fluorescent welcome he sure could use about now. Take some ribbing. Take a few jibes. Make them laugh. The wise thing to do: Make yourself the fool and help them forget.

He reached into his breast pocket for a cigarette and made a face. He'd left them in his office. He started back toward the side door, and paused when he saw a car parked just this side of Mackey's. A tilt of his head. Nobody drove to the bar around here, especially this late. Then the brake lights flared and died.

He watched.

No one climbed out.

The lights flared and died again.

The streetlamps were too dim, he couldn't see inside, but he started walking anyway; the cigarettes could wait.

"It's dirty," Tessa said, dropping the cleaver onto the counter beside the sink. "Jesus, Todd, what's the matter with you now? You look like death warmed over."

Arlo stood by the bar's narrow front window, peering through the neon haze at the car sitting at the curb just up the street. He couldn't see the driver, but there were two in the front seat, and he didn't need a stargazer to tell him who it was.

Should've killed him when I had the chance, he thought ruefully; the boy's just gotta have his revenge now, can't wait his turn.

Like he ever really thought they would let him actually get away to Arizona clean and happy. But he didn't figure they would come at him so soon, the season barely begun, the money barely warm in the bank.

He rested his shoulder against the wall and checked the room. Bobby was behind the bar, washing glasses; Kay Pollard was at a corner table, empty shot-glasses ranged like votive candles in front of her; the Palmers were finishing up, Sissy already on her feet, Ed meticulously counting out the exact change to lay on the table, plus an exact fifteen percent.

Everyone else had left.

He checked the car; it hadn't moved.

Man, he thought, I don't need this shit.

He pushed away from the wall with a silent sigh and bade the Palmers a good-night as they left, stopped in front of Kay and waited until she looked up.

"Looks like early closing tonight, movie lady," he said, smiling his smile.

She didn't react; she only stared.

He gestured at the empty room. "Gonna hit the sack, if that's okay with you."

She stared, a single tear caught on the ridge of her cheek.

His shoulders sagged, and he dropped into the chair opposite her. "You got a problem, movie lady," he said gently, "maybe you ought to see the preacher man, huh?"

She fumbled in her jeans pocket for a tissue, blew her nose, tossed the tissue on the table. "I don't think so, Arlo."

"Then maybe you ought to sleep it off, it'll be better in the morning."

"Won't . . . won't make any difference."

He scraped the chair back, making it squeal across the floor. When she winced, he held out a hand. "Come on, Kay, time to go." He winked. "Bobby wants to get a man tonight."

Kay stood, and swayed a little, but she didn't smile. "Then tell her to fuck a baby. That's what I just did."

Reed looked out the diner window, only half listening to Cora complain about all the stupid rules Rina had at her house. He had seen the strange car pull up a while ago, and when no one had gotten out, he couldn't help thinking there was something not right. It just sat there in the dark.

"Cora, shut up," Nate said wearily.

That was another thing—Nate hadn't said more than two words at a time the whole night, most of them "shut up." Reed knew it wasn't anything at home. Of all of them, Nate had the most normal family, even if his father did spend most of his time traveling. Asking, however, had only gotten his head bitten off.

Shortly after he saw the Palmers head up the street, he straightened then, and smiled. "Hey."

"Dane, bite me," Cora said.

Nate only shook his head in disgust.

"Hey, you guys, look."

Cora rolled her eyes. "What?"

"It's Reverend Chisholm." He pointed at the figure slipping out of the dark. "There he is. See?"

"Well, big whoop." Cora picked up her soda glass and glared at the contents. "Did you really think he'd run away? Because of a couple of stupid bees?"

Reed ignored her. "Rina," he called; she was behind the counter. "Tell Mr. Odam he's back. Reverend Chisholm, I mean."

He looked out again, wondering if he should go out there, and this time his eyes widened. "Hey."

Cora slid out of the booth and headed for the ladies' room.

"Hey!"

A few heads turned.

Reed pointed. "That guy." He kept pointing as he shoved Nate out of the booth. "That guy. Over there by the car."

Moss looked. "Jesus damn, he's got a goddamn gun!"

Nobody moved, nobody spoke.

Todd, his right hand wrapped in a towel, pushed out of the kitchen and leaned over Reed's table.

"My God," he said.

"Company," Escobar said calmly.

Miguel looked over the car roof and saw the wide-eyed faces in the diner. He smiled a terrible smile and aimed his revolver at the first woman he saw.

Enid Balanov screamed.

Todd yelled, "Drop! Everybody drop!" just as someone turned off the lights.

Enid screamed again.

This time she wasn't alone.

Casey hesitated when he saw the short stocky man point at the diner, and stopped when he realized the man wasn't pointing, he was aiming.

When the taller one strode almost casually to the bar entrance and stepped in, he still didn't move.

When the man with the gun turned and followed his partner inside, Casey still didn't move.

He couldn't.

please

He had no weapon but his hands, had no one to back him, had nothing he could use that would stop a bullet if a bullet came his way.

please don't

He took a helpless step forward, right hand in a tentative fist at his side, then another step toward the curb, thinking to head for the diner and its telephone.

Until the Moonglow's lights went out.

Alone on the sidewalk, being watched, not moving.

I don't have a gun, he thought; it's okay, I don't have a gun.

He didn't move again until the shooting began.

It didn't last long.

It was over by the time he reached the bar at a full run, and with a glance over to the darkened diner, he shouldered open the door.

Immediately, he was slammed aside when someone barreled into him, cursed, and swung something that caught him square in his stomach. Unprepared for the blow, he gasped and doubled over, and was punched just behind his ear, toppling him to the pavement on his side, gulping for air, twisting his head around to see two men fling themselves into the car.

He tried and failed to get to his hands and knees, grunted, tried again and made it as the engine caught and the headlamps glared on, catching Reed squarely as he sprinted across the street.

No, Casey thought.

Reed froze.

The rear tires spun smoke and a squealing.

No.

The car surged forward as Reed leapt for the curb, barely missing him as it U-turned in the intersection and raced up toward the Crest.

Casey braced a hand against the wall and hauled himself to his feet. Reed called his name and ran over, yelling startled surprise when his feet skidded out from under him. Casey tried to catch him, but he could barely move, and the boy landed on the base of his spine.

"Jesus!"

Reed groaned and slowly curled his knees toward his chest, looking up, angry, then looking at the sidewalk and groaning. He scrambled away as fast as he could.

Casey frowned until he saw the blood.

"You okay?" he asked, and didn't wait for an answer. As the Moonglow's neon flickered on again, he clamped a hand across his aching stomach and pushed inside Mackey's.

"Arlo!"

He thought the room was empty.

Voices outside, calling, demanding.

"Arlo?"

Bobby Karnagan rose from behind the bar, a hand trembling at her throat. "Reverend Chisholm?"

"It's okay, Bobby, I'm here. Where's—"

Mackey moved out of the far corner, a shotgun in one hand, his other arm around Kay's waist. "We're okay, preacher man," he said, his voice shaking. Suddenly he sat hard in the nearest chair, bringing Kay slumped onto his lap. "Hell of a mess, man. Hell of a mess."

Casey grabbed for the back of a chair. "Are you all right?"

The smell of gunpowder.

Arlo nodded weakly, and placed the shotgun on the table. "They came in, man, like they wanted to rob me, you know? They—"

"Save it," he snapped.

The smell of blood he spotted in trails along the floor.

Kay Pollard threw up on Arlo's shirt.

"She's drunk and scared," Arlo said to Casey's startled look. He didn't move; he just shifted her head to his shoulder. "Bobby, honey, you want to bring me a wet cloth here?"

Tessa and Mel rushed in, Todd right behind them. Casey warned them about the blood, warned them to step easy. Then his own stomach lurched and he made his way outside, to the frightened voices that skidded to frightened whispers when they saw him.

"Nobody's hurt," was all he would say.

"I called them!" Cora yelled from the diner entrance. "The cops! They're on their way!"

He heard the distant scream of brakes.

"You didn't do anything." Petyr Balanov stepped out of the crowd. His hand didn't move, but he pointed just the same. "You just stood there, Reverend. You didn't do a thing."

Casey had no chance to answer.

They all turned at the sound of the crash, at the same time sharp and muffled. He took a step toward the Crest, another when the night began to glow.

Reed said, "The curve," just as Casey began to run. He yelled at the boy to get Todd and the others to the fire station, yelled at Moss to fetch the ambulance.

Only a few people followed.

Until the fireball spread from a webbing of black smoke.

Spread, and rose, and died.

Casey broke into a sprint interrupted when Micah's pickup pulled alongside, pacing him. He scrambled into the passenger seat, and others piled into the bed, shouting orders, thumping the roof, yelling when the truck took the slope at speed.

Lord, Casey thought, hand on the door handle; please, Lord.

The accident was easy to find.

Tiny spits of fire burned on the blacktop where gasoline had been sprayed; a pile of leaves on the shoulder burned acrid and white; the car itself was side-on to a tree, flames hissing inside, and through the shattered windows.

A man lay on the ground, face up, arms rigid at his sides.

Reed and the others grabbed fire extinguishers from the pickup, and from the old square fire truck that rolled up just as Micah braked.

Casey recoiled from the heat of the burning car, from the stench of charred flesh.

Bracing himself, breathing shallow, he knelt beside the fallen man and recognized him—the stocky one with the gun, skin black and flaking, clothes fluttering to ashes when a breeze coasted by.

The spray of fire-retardant, the hiss of water.

One eye opened.

Casey swallowed and leaned down.

"Father?"

"I'm here," he said, hoarse and nearly choking. "An ambulance is coming. You'll be—"

"He's gone," Astante whispered. "Be careful, man, he's gone."

And moaned so loudly Casey automatically placed a light, comforting hand on his chest. "Hush. Hush."

The eye closed.

"Miracle there ain't no real fire," he heard Micah say. "Why ain't these trees burning?"

"Nobody in the car," someone yelled. He thought it was Doc Farber. "Spread out, find him. He's gotta be hurt."

"Mel!" he called. "Mel, I need help here!"

Farber was beside him instantly, black bag in one hand. He winced at the sight, but that didn't stop him.

"Lord," Casey said. "Please, Lord."

Farber sagged back onto his heels. "Too late, Case. Damn. Too late."

Casey whispered a prayer and touched the dead man's cheek. No matter who he was, he didn't have to die like this; no matter what he had done, he didn't need this.

Voices around him faded as the fire was extinguished; sounds faded as onlookers decided whether to stick around for the cops, or go home; a handful of men, William Bowes their leader, loudly trying to organize a search party, the cops would be too late, anybody got a gun, just in case? Anybody but the doc know some first aid? Just in case?

Still Casey prayed, touching the cheek, the forehead, ignoring the bits of slick flesh that stuck to his fingers until the fingers moved, and the char flaked away.

He looked up then, and saw them watching, expectant.

He didn't understand.

Within the circle of her husband's arm, Enid said quietly, urgently, "Bring him back, Father. You can do it. Bring him back."

The dead man sighed, and opened his eyes.

5

1

Cardiño Escobar saw the demon, and it was made of fire.

He lay on the roadside, his face half buried in a small pile of brittle leaves that smelled of gasoline and heat. All he could hear was the liquid sound of his breathing, and a distant crackling, a muted grumbling. As he pushed swaying to his hands and knees, dazed and feeling nothing, the demon stepped out of the burning car, arms at its sides, a black figure caged in shimmering gold, with flickering pools of flame at its feet.

It was beautiful.

Everything was beautiful. So painfully beautiful that tears filled his eyes and he could barely see until the tears dried. He inhaled sharply. Something wondrous had happened to his vision. Everything had a stunning clarity to it, a vividness, that reminded him of stained glass and razors.

Then the demon turned its head toward him and opened its mouth, its head quivering violently, its hands raised to grab at the fire.

He saw the flames flow inward between those thick black-

and-gold lips, saw the eyes widen, saw the demon shudder and turn and fall onto its back.

He wanted to scream.

Instead, he staggered to his feet, and fled into the woods. The fire died quickly, cutting off most of his light, the moon only giving him dark and pale shadows. Still, he was able to move swiftly, pausing only long enough to make sure he wasn't dripping blood onto the ground. There was something not quite right with his left arm, and his right leg moved awkwardly at the hip. There was pain somewhere, he sensed it, but at the moment he could feel little more than a dull stabbing. The need to get away, however, was too strong, too urgent, for him to take stock. He had to find a place, a den, where he could rest, hide, find out what was really wrong with him before he was caught.

He was mildly surprised he was still alive.

They had charged into what he had first thought was an empty bar. Then Arlo had slid out of the shadows, shotgun in hand, and there was fire and noise and someone screaming.

A giant.

The next thing he remembered he was behind the wheel, Miguel slumped and groaning in the passenger seat, a hand clamped over his side, unable to stanch the bleeding through his shredded shirt and jacket, ignoring the bleeding from the tiny holes in his cheeks. His own hands had been slick on the wheel, and when the curve leapt into the headlights, his fingers slid instead of gripping; before he could react, there was fire and noise.

And someone screaming.

The demon.

He saw the demon.

He heard shouts and a racing engine, looked over his shoulder and saw nothing.

With luck they would think he had gone on down the hillside, as far away from this damned place as he could get. He headed west instead, slowing a little, shifting northward to avoid the houses on the first street, keeping to the trees, wondering if he would last. He fell twice and waited for the cry that discovered him; he clamped his teeth onto his lower lip when the pain began to worm out of the shock.

A second street, too many lights, and a third and fourth that looked as if every man and woman in town were standing in their yards. Some had guns; almost all had flashlights. None thought to look at street's end, in the woodland.

Dizziness finally forced him to lean heavily against a trunk, and although he couldn't see it very well, he could smell the blood on his clothes, could feel it begin to squeeze through the fingers that gripped his forearm. He held his breath and stripped off his jacket, wrapping it snugly around his arm. It wasn't perfect, but it would do, for now.

A great shout startled him, what seemed like a hundred voices raised as one, and more engines.

He didn't have to be there—they had found Miguel, and now they knew he was gone.

He took a step away from the tree, shivering uncontrollably, and the earth dropped abruptly away beneath his feet. He tumbled down a steep slope, and rolled, and didn't stop until he flailed into a large bush that scratched at his eyes and cheeks. When he moaned at the fire that wanted to consume him as it had consumed the demon, his eyes closed tightly; when he suddenly rolled onto his chest and vomited, his skin felt as if it had begun to split along invisible seams; when he rolled onto his back and stared at the night and no one found him, he allowed himself a tentative smile.

Not yet, old man, he thought, using the branches to brace him to his feet; not yet, you old fart.

He embraced another tree with his left arm and blinked fiercely against the sudden urge to sleep. Right here. Right now.

The den; he needed that den.

Through the trees, through the dark at the end of the block, he saw a car race past the intersection, heading toward the river. They must have called the cops by now, and search parties were probably already being formed. They had to be. He swallowed hard. These people were hunters; they knew how to use guns, and they knew these woods.

He had to—

He leaned his head against the tree, and he grunted.

He had been staring at the street without realizing how many of the small houses and cabins were dark. Permanently dark.

Breathing was difficult, and everything was too sharp now, sight and sound, scent and sense; simply looking around made his head ache. Nevertheless, a humorless grin came and went as he pushed away from the tree's support, keeping his wrapped arm pressed tightly to his waist.

On the right side of the block were three such buildings.

Ten minutes later, he was in the first one, crawling on hands and knees across the kitchen floor, not to avoid being seen, but because his legs wouldn't hold him anymore. There was no second floor, but there was a long couch in the front room, the drapes over the large front window already tightly drawn.

The smell of dust and absence.

Dry heat.

He crawled onto the cushions, groaning as he settled, and appreciated the irony that, of all people, he had the old fart to thank for this. Maybe later, when he had a chance to see how badly he was hurt, he would return to the bar and thank him properly.

Right now, all he could do was pray that when he woke up, he wouldn't be dead or captured.

2

The stench: burning gasoline, burning rubber.

The cry of fear.

"No," Casey whispered.

In the forest, the cry of something too long without food, too long without water.

The stench: charred metal, charred flesh.

"Please, Lord . . . please, no."

3

Something changed.

Lupé frowned, unsure what was happening, not at all sure she was fully awake. Not at all sure, in fact, she had really been awake, or anything like it, since the night she had left the trailer and the mountains. It wasn't hard to feel that way— Time and the world didn't exist inside this car. Soft music, the occasional murmur of someone half dozing, and a deep and quiet, sort of electric feeling that once in a while raised gooseflesh on her arms.

She watched the countryside slide by, she watched clouds form and disperse, she watched moonrise and sunset, and she might as well have been watching a television screen.

If it hadn't been for the bodies, she could well believe she was still inside that damn trailer, waiting for the man she still wanted to kill.

She had started out of a doze when she heard Susan grunt as if in surprise and felt the car slow down abruptly. As she rubbed her eyes, it drifted sharply toward the shoulder, leaving the Pennsylvania interstate at a T-intersection with a narrow, two-lane road. She frowned again. This was a departure, and it didn't feel right. She saw Stan turn his head in question, then glance into the back; he was afraid.

The car braked on a black gravel shoulder, nose pointing south. The headlights flared past a gas station on the right, boarded up and sagging, its pumps gone, nothing left but stains on the cracked concrete island.

Stan said, "Susan?" and all Susan did was look at him, and he cringed.

Lupé stiffened.

Beside her, in the far corner, a stirring but nothing more.

Susan shoved her door open and got out without saying a word. She ignored the handful of trucks and cars sweeping eastward not fifty feet away, kicking up dust and grit; she hesitated when she reached the hood, then crossed the road into the dark.

"What?" Stan asked, sounding close to panic.

They had never stopped before, not like this.

Lupé poked him between the shoulders, got out herself, and waited for him near the rear fender.

A hazy moon and dull stars, but there was enough light to see the high dead-grass hills that rose above the interstate on its north side. Between them, a broad river ran north to south, deep in its own wooded valley, its water dark, nothing moving on the surface. Not far from where they stood, the river passed under a high bridge and took a sharp bend to the east, sparks of moonlight marking its surface. At the nearest bend she could see what looked like factories or warehouses on the banks illuminated by sickly orange light. Maybe some houses, too; she couldn't really tell.

The far shoulder was broad and pocked with tufts of weeds. As far as she could see, the drop to the river was steep, and Susan stood at the edge, unmoving.

Stan walked a few paces north and squinted at the intersection signs. "Harrisburg?" he said when he came back.

She didn't know. She didn't care. She had never been to the East, hadn't ever wanted to, and Harrisburg or not, she had a strong feeling Susan hadn't planned to stop here.

Except for the deserted gas station, there was nothing to burn.

There was no one to kill.

I don't like this, she thought; man, I don't like this.

A chilly breeze rose out of the valley. She rubbed her arms briskly, and smiled when Stan offered to fetch her his coat. She hadn't really checked him out before. Until now he was just another one of the guys along for the ride. But even after being rousted the way they had been, he didn't look half bad. Not as round as she had first thought, his sandy hair a little on the wild side, a little shorter than she. It was the eyes that got her. Even as he squinted into the dark, trying to figure out what Susan was doing, she couldn't help thinking they were too large for his face.

"You think something's wrong?" He hunched his shoulders a little, looking at her sideways. Then he grinned, and she knew why. *Everything* had been wrong with this whole business right from the start. But Susan had made it all seem natural. Exactly the way things ought to be. No need, no desire, for any explanations. "Maybe we should talk to her."

"I don't think so." She looked around again, at the hills, the river. "You ever been here?"

"Nope. Lots of places. Not here." He hummed softly to himself. "Nope, not here."

Susan hadn't moved. She stared at the horizon.

The breeze wasn't chilly anymore, and it carried enough dust to make Lupé sneeze.

"Cars."

She didn't get it.

Stan pointed south past the gas station, the hills far beyond barely visible, black against black. "You got roads, right? I been on roads. Lots of roads. All over lots of roads. Roads have cars." He pointed at the intersection. "Cars come from down there to up here." He shrugged. "How come there aren't any cars?"

"It's got to be after midnight, *amigo*. Where would they go this late?"

"I been up late, I been up early." He hummed a little. "Always cars sometime, you know? Always cars sometime." He lifted a hand, let it fall. "You called me that *amigo* thing again. You Mexican or something?"

"Spanish," she said flatly. They do that all the time. You come from New Mexico, they think you're a Mex. Pain in the ass, but from Stan she didn't mind. "A little Indian, too, you know?"

"Wow. No kidding?"

She smiled. "No kidding."

He rocked side to side, hands in his pockets, waiting, gravel crunching beneath his feet.

A truck growled westward. Its headlights were dim; they didn't touch Lupé at all.

"What's she doing?" He rocked again, nervous.

"I don't know."

"I'm getting cold."

"So go inside."

"I can't."

She knew what he meant; they had to wait.

It wouldn't take long.

They felt rather than saw her move, gliding toward them out of the dark, the glow of the headlamps catching a smile Lupé wished she hadn't seen. She nodded to them, nodded at the car, and they hurried inside. Shivering. Waiting until she slid in behind the wheel before Lupé said, "What's wrong?"

"The guy," Stan said suddenly. He looked into the back. "The guy, right?"

"What guy?"

"It's all right," Susan said calmly, quietly. "It's all right, nothing's wrong." She inhaled slowly. "We'll go a little slower now, but nothing's changed. Don't worry. Nothing's changed."

Oh, yes, it has, Lupé thought, pulling her legs up, huddling in the corner; oh, yes, it has.

While Susan laughed softly.

And for a moment, just a moment, the headlights burned dark red.

Part 4

OVERTURE

1

1

Dawn wasn't much more than an hour gone, and the sky was already pale, the sun already white.

Casey sat on his front porch in a simple wood chair, bare soles braced against the railing, hands flat on his thighs, every so often a finger tapping the black denim. His shirt was open halfway down his chest, as if he had begun to undress and had given up the effort.

No breeze, no sound in the forest, no sound from the river. No voices.

For a while there, for hours, there had been nothing but voices.

County sheriff and state police sweeping in, asking questions; Doc hastily explaining what Casey already knew, about air left in lungs and postmortem muscle contractions; Enid screaming, half in terror, half in joy; the sheriff leading Bowes and the others into the woods; sirens; the sudden slap of helicopter blades, up there in the dark, while the night was slashed with searchlight beams; Enid, weeping, falling on her knees with at least five others, praying loudly, heedless of those who either backed away or gawked; a single gunshot, deep in the woods; ambulance carrying the charred body away; voices in his ear, requesting, demanding, begging, cajoling.

i did it

Reed Turner finally taking his arm, Nate Dane on the other side, bringing him to Micah's pickup for the short, eternally long, trip home.

On the porch: "Are you going to be all right, Reverend Chisholm?"

In the kitchen: "Here, take some water."

In the bedroom: "You okay? You want me to turn on the fan?"

And Cora, hovering in the background, saying nothing.

i did it

The moment they had left and he closed his eyes, he had seen the fire, the eyes, and he got up, went to the porch, sat, and stared.

Mel was right, of course. Enid could scream miracle all she wanted, but Mel Farber was right.

The man was dead.

And Casey had seen the life in those eyes.

He sat without moving.

He had watched flashing lights blur down toward the river, listened to the helicopter drone overhead, listened to distant voices make their way through the trees, listened to the thud and march of his heartbeat and his blood.

Finally there had been silence and nothing lit the night except the cigarette in his hand. He didn't smoke it. He had only wanted the tiny light, and the smell of burning tobacco to mask the smell of burning flesh.

The sun sucked the night into shadows, and he had prayed, "Thank You."

He shifted a little and yawned, so loud and so hard he felt his jaw pop.

A crow settled on the lawn, the first life he had seen since the rising of the sun. It preened itself, strutted, fluttered to the gate and spread its tail feathers, spread its wings. Stretching. Looking around for breakfast.

"Slim pickin's," Casey said, his voice hoarse.

The bird started, but didn't leave.

Slowly Casey placed his feet on the floor, grabbed the railing with both hands and hauled himself up, groaning aloud. The crow did leave then, a brittle fluttering of its wings, and he gave it a mocking salute, wished it well, and swayed a little. He wanted to sleep, and was frightened of it. Terrified of it. Yet he had to sleep. He could feel the sickness still lurking in his system, could feel the solid weight of exhaustion on his shoulders and across his back.

If he didn't sleep, he would collapse.

If he collapsed, they would find him, and there would be voices again.

Never-ending voices.

"Lord," he whispered as he made his way to the door, "I sure could use a big old break about now. I damn sure could use some rest."

Once inside, he also prayed for the miracle of air-conditioning, something he had never bothered with simply because it had never been this almighty, damnable hot. A pair of fans suited him when he was home during the day, and at night there had always been the woodland breeze.

Despite the humidity outside, the cabin was oven dry. Sapping him. Making him sluggish.

He wasn't really hungry, but he made himself a light breakfast—cereal and milk and two pieces of toast—scolding himself all the while because he knew he was stalling.

He was afraid.

This time of the dark that waited behind closed eyes.

All these years, and he was still a coward.

He ate, and tasted nothing, returned to the living room and dropped onto the couch and used the remote control to switch on the television sitting in the fireplace. He searched for news of last night's gunfire and accident, but even with all that, the Landing was evidently too small for caring. He waited for the weather, raising a cynical eyebrow when a cartoonlike map purported clouds on the way.

They had been saying that for a week, and people still died and thirsted and lost control and died.

Sick of it, sick of the promises, he shut the TV off and glanced over at the telephone, wondering if he dared call Helen, or Mel, to see what had happened after he had left.

Probably nothing.

Had they found the second man, someone would have come running.

He yawned, stretched his legs, wiggled his toes.

The remote slipped from his hand and bounced off the cushion to the floor. He stared at it dumbly, blinking slowly, willing himself to reach down there, that's all he had to do, reach down there and pick it up before someone stepped on it.

He stared until it blurred.

He couldn't move.

i did it

He began to weep. Softly, no sobbing. Just the tears on his cheeks, dripping one by one onto his chest, and onto the cross around his neck.

Standing in the meadow, his Bible in one hand, parchment pages flipping over by the hand of a breeze that tickled hair across his face and teased his lips with moisture;

Standing in the meadow, birds overhead, flocks of them and all kinds of them, dipping low, veering away, while deer and bear and raccoons and skunks and a bobcat and a copperhead and a lop-eared dog eyed him from the tall brittle grass;

Standing in the meadow, his voice the thunder that matched the clouds that killed the sun;

Standing in the meadow with his Bible in one hand, the other pointing at the people who stood in the road and screamed.

Standing in the meadow.

Preaching sermons to the dead.

*   *   *

Opening his eyes, stiffness in his back and the back of his
neck, his lips open, a touch of spittle at the corner of his
mouth. His head was propped against the couch's right armrest, his feet hanging over the left.

A shadow hovered in the doorway.

"Padre? You awake?"

Casey used hands and elbows to push himself up, waving
as he did an invitation for Arlo to come on in.

"Man, it's an oven in here. You trying to lose weight? You
trying to sweat out the sick stuff? You going to sleep all day?
Half the afternoon's gone already."

Realization that he was drenched made Casey grimace,
wrinkle his nose at the stench that clung to his arms and torso.
"I need a shower," he said, trying to scrub the sleep from his
face. "Why don't you wait on the porch? I'll be with you in
a minute."

"Your call, Padre."

Casey grunted, didn't bother with the hot water, letting the
cold shock life back into his muscles, and thought back into
his brain. After dressing, still without boots, he joined Mackey,
who had taken the swing; he took the chair again, turning it
to face him.

Arlo gave him the peace sign. "No offense, Preacher, but
you look like hell."

Casey almost smiled. Arlo wasn't much of a vision himself.
His jeans were too large and streaked with dark stains; his
Hawaiian shirt wrinkled as if he'd slept in it and didn't quite
hide the bulge of his paunch; his eyes were red-rimmed and
smudged with shadow, and his hair was only barely captured
in that ragged ponytail.

He leaned forward, hands clasped between his knees.

Casey waited a moment, then said, "Tell me, Arlo."

The law had taken over the diner as temporary headquarters,
and Mackey had been the last to make his statement, telling
the sheriff about two men who had barged in, guns waving
and blazing, Arlo himself grabbing his perfectly legal shotgun

and protecting himself, his bar, and his customers the only way he knew how. He didn't know the men, had never seen them before, and was grateful Casey had arrived when he had, no telling what would have happened, who would have died.

"That's what I told them." A shrug. "You think I'm, like, going to hell for lying?"

"Which one of them was Escobar?" was all Casey said, taking no satisfaction in the way Arlo sat up, startled and afraid.

"You knew?"

"Guessed some. Figured some. Doc had the clues. Is it true, Arlo? These were the men who did all the renting?"

True enough, and more. Escobar's people were indeed planning to take the Landing over. In their own sweet time. It wouldn't take much. Without funds to last the winter, he said, folks would eventually start selling and Escobar would start buying. All legal, signed and sealed. Two years, tops.

"And if you didn't sell?"

Arlo aged a decade as his hand passed wearily over his face. "I don't know. Nothing, probably. You know. The way Diño put it, who would care, a bunch of spics in the woods." His lips curved into a brief, unreadable smile. "Ordinary folks just like you, Padre. They just happen to have relatives, you know what I mean?"

"A man died last night, Arlo."

Mackey took a bandanna from his hip pocket and mopped his face, nodding.

"They nearly ran Reed down."

Mackey nodded again; the bandanna kept moving.

Casey looked out at the road, afraid of the anger that constricted his lungs. He looked away. There was no color or comfort out there, only the heat.

"Why," he said, "didn't you tell that to the police?"

"You been there, man," Mackey said without looking up. "You know what it's like. I'm too told for that shit. I just want to go to Arizona, put up my feet, watch the sun set over the mountains." He pushed his glasses up with one finger. "The cops, they don't have respect for a man's dream, you

know?'' Suddenly he raised his head. ''You're not going to
tell them, Padre, are you? Jeez, you're not going to tell them?''

''Why shouldn't I?''

Panicked, Mackey sat up, one foot tapping the floor. ''But
this is, like, confession, right? You can't tell.''

Casey shook his head. ''No, Arlo, this isn't, like, confession.'' He stood slowly, watching the older man shrink back
into his seat. ''A man died, Arlo.''

''A crash! For God's sake, it was a crash!''

please don't please don't hurt me

''You shot him.''

''Self-defense!''

The heat; he felt the heat.

''Was it, Arlo?''

Mackey scrambled to his feet, head shaking, hands out, the
bandanna waving like a red flag of truce. ''You don't get it,
man,'' he said. ''You don't get it.''

Casey didn't move to stop him when he stumbled down the
steps, said nothing to calm the terror in the man's face, in the
way his arms flapped, the way his head jerked side-to-side like
an aged bird searching for the hunter. Instead, he leaned
against the post until Mackey fumbled with the gate latch,
whimpering when it wouldn't open right away.

But as soon as he was on the road, Casey said, ''Arlo.''

Mackey turned, eyes too wide.

''Think about it,'' he said, far more gently than he felt.
''One of us has to say something. You know that.''

''They'll kill me!'' Arlo insisted loudly. ''They'll . . .
they'll . . .'' He took off his glasses, wiped his face, squinted
at the half-lenses as if they had the answer. Then he put the
bandanna back in his pocket, the glasses back on his nose, and
took a step toward town. One step before he turned. ''Jesus,
Padre,'' he said, ''just who the hell do you think you are?''

2

The next one was Mel Farber, white shirt stained under the
arms and across the belly.

"How you doing, Case?"

"I just talked to Arlo."

"I saw him on the road. Fool was practically running. He was talking to himself. What did you say to him?"

"A few words of wisdom, Mel. You were right. About Escobar."

"Why am I not surprised? And don't argue, I just remembered, but I had a talk with a friend the other day.. Come Monday, there'll be an air conditioner here for you."

"Doc—"

"Don't argue, Case, it's already done. What did Arlo say? He going to the police?"

"I gave him a choice."

"You used the look, right?"

Casey stared, and laughed, admitting the truth and embarrassed as well.

Mel was on the top step, black hair glistening with sweat, leaning his back against the post. His white tennis shoes were grey with road dust, the crease of his white trousers not quite straight. "A hell of a night, Case."

"Anyone else hurt?"

"No. Well, probably Escobar, but they can't find him. Todd talked to the sheriff about an hour ago. They think he made it as far down as the highway, probably forced himself a ride." He scratched the back of his neck, stared at his knees.

"You don't think so?"

"No. A crash like that . . . no. Not," he added reluctantly, "unless he was extremely lucky."

Casey leaned forward. "You don't think he's still in town?"

"They did a quick house-to-house, checked the dock . . . nothing. The empty ones were locked solid. I don't know where he is." A pudgy hand waved toward the woods across the road. "But he's out there somewhere. If he's alive, he's bleeding to death."

"They still looking?"

Mel's face showed nothing when he said, "Bowes, a couple

of others. A deputy's with them." The expression changed. "You okay?"

"You already asked me that."

"So?"

"He was dead, Mel."

"Yes. He was."

"He stayed dead."

Farber nodded, no room for doubt, no crack wide enough for a miracle to slip through.

The crow returned to the gatepost, feathers slightly ruffled. Casey smiled at it, wondering what the poor thing had run up against, why it wasn't with the rest of the flock.

"Mel, why are you here?"

"You're my patient, right? If I don't take care of you, you'll sue me and I'll end up like Arlo, tending bar someplace, or collecting empties for chump change."

Casey looked at him without turning his head.

Mel wiped a bead of sweat from his cheek. "Strange question, Case."

"Strange days, Mel."

The crow turned around to face them.

"Do you have to know?"

Casey shook his head.

"I didn't kill anyone, there was no malpractice, nothing quite so dramatic as anything like that."

The crow hopped to the grass, stabbed at it, stabbed again, and took off, vanishing into sunlight before it reached the tops of the trees.

"Big city hospitals, big city patients, then small town patients, small town clinic. Then, here to the Landing." He touched his breast pocket, fingered the pen poking out of the pocket. "I'm not even forty, Case, and I'm already tired. Can you believe it? Trust me, healing ain't what it's cracked up to be."

After a long minute Casey said, "It can be, you know. One patient at a time."

"They need you, Case," Mel said in response. A gesture up the road. "The church was locked this morning."

"I'm tired, Mel. Almighty tired."

"So am I." He was irritable. "But guess what? Harve Turner cut his leg open trying to jump a deadfall this morning, playing posse, and I had to stitch him up. Amazing. He was sober. And Mrs. Racine has palpitations from all the excitement, so I calmed her down, reminded her to take her nitro pills, sent her home after she cried because she couldn't give me any tomatoes from her garden. Cora banged up her arm, running around last night, I had to gauze it." He stood, hands on his hips, cheeks flushed, chin jutting a dare. "Any minute now, I expect some idiot to come in with a damn gunshot wound, my car's barely running, and you want to talk to me about being almighty goddamn tired?"

Startled, Casey lifted a quick hand in apology and retreat, but it was too late. Farber was already on his way to the car, and he didn't look back, didn't wave as he drove away.

"Oh, nice, Case," he said to the backs of his hands. "Well done. Real nice."

But Mel hadn't seen the life in the dead man's eyes.

3

He had just enough time to go inside and pour himself a glass of refrigerator cold water before he had another visitor. As he stood on the porch, sipping and sighing, he wondered what Mel was so hot about. He didn't have to go up the road; everyone was coming down here for a change.

Reed opened the gate and nudged Cora through.

They were dressed in shorts and T-shirts, sneakers and no socks. Cora had a gauze pad on her left arm, just above the elbow, wrapped around with surgical tape.

The ice water turned sour.

Casey perched on the railing. "Morning."

"Afternoon," Reed reminded him with a grin.

Cora said nothing, only stared sullenly at the ground.

Casey wiped his mouth with the back of a hand, squinted

at the sky. "Seems you were bored the other night. Can't be very bored now."

Reed toed the flagstone. "It . . ." He shrugged with one shoulder. "It was . . ."

"Not like on TV," Casey offered.

The boy nodded.

"It's what happens when things get real, son. Kind of hits you like a brick, right between the eyes."

"You can say that again."

"Don't intend to. It was ugly enough the first time."

Reed smiled again, but he kept glancing at Cora, opening his mouth, changing his mind, until finally Casey slipped down to the top step. "Reed, you know that oil can I have in the garage? Why don't you do this sick old reverend a favor, work on the gate hinges for me. That way your next surprise will be a surprise."

Reed hesitated, looked at Cora one more time, and trotted away.

Cora jammed her hands in her hip pockets. Her hair was too short for a ponytail; she used one hand, then the other, to push it back over her ears.

"Gave your arm a good one," he said, nodding at the bandage.

"Yeah. Tree."

"Should be more careful. Dark means you can't see so well, you tend to bump into things. Like trees."

"Yeah."

He emptied his glass, held it out. "You want some ice water? Plenty in the fridge."

She wavered, checked over her shoulder at Reed studiously working on the gate, then nodded, grabbing the glass as she ran past.

Reed looked up.

Casey used a hand to tell him to keep at it.

Waiting for the crow.

The screen door slammed, and he felt a wedge of cold pressed on his shoulder—a full glass for him. He thanked her and, as she started down the steps, said, "Sit, Cora."

She did, right beside him, her head just reaching the level of his shoulder.

They watched Reed for a few seconds, shimmering heat behind him, smearing the trees.

Casey sipped, smacked his lips loudly, ran the glass across his forehead, sighing at the relief, however temporary. "You want to tell me?" Tennessee soft in his voice, his expression. "Do I have to guess?"

Nothing in her voice: "What do you care?"

He shifted, putting his spine against the post, drawing up a leg, free hand on his knee. "After all this time, Cora, you have to ask a stupid question like that?"

"Yeah, right." She held her glass so tightly, he was afraid it would shatter. "It's your job, right? I mean, it's not like it means anything."

"What I do," he said, fingering the gold-chain cross that hung beneath his shirt, "what I *try* to do is make sure people don't get eaten by the wolves." He watched the sun set sparks in her hair, the anger jump a muscle under her jaw. "My job isn't something that I do. I do it, fight the wolves, because I want to. Maybe because I have to. You look at it that way, I really don't have a job at all. Not like Todd Odam, for example. Or Doc Farber. I do what I do, Cora. I do what I do."

Reed tested the gate; it squealed, and he sighed, loud enough for them to hear, and to let them know he was still working.

"What happened?" she said, working hard at a sneer. "You find Jesus in jail?"

"Nope, not that easy. In a man." He remembered a Tennessee hillside, the wind that blew that chilly, foggy morning. "And a woman."

She set her glass down on the step beside her, clasped her shins, leaned forward until her chin was on her knee. She tried twice to say something before she said, "You know what he did?"

Casey put his own glass down.

"He came back from playing hero, hunting that scum that shot up Arlo's place. He came back, he grabbed me." She moved her bandaged arm, edges of a bruise slipping away from the tape. "He grabbed me and said . . ." She swallowed hard, and choked. "He said . . ."

She closed her eyes, but not before he saw the first tear clinging to a lash.

"I tried to kill him once, you know." The tears didn't stop, and she didn't try to stop them. "Drunk on his ass in the living room. I picked up the poker and wanted so bad to hit him. Open his head, let his brains out all over the floor. I wanted to. God, I really wanted to."

Casey didn't move.

He felt the heat again.

Inside.

"You know why I didn't?"

He shook his head.

She turned her head so her cheek was on her knee, her single laugh bitter enough to curl her lips.

"I thought, Reverend Chisholm would hate me." The first sob. "I didn't want you to hate me."

And you hate me for that, he thought as she pressed her forehead to her knees and let the sobs twist her shoulders, thump her heels, until he took a handkerchief from his pocket, sat beside her again, and put an arm around her back. Immediately, she was against his chest, holding the handkerchief to her nose, to her eyes, crying and apologizing and crying and cursing.

While he rocked her.

While he watched Reed look away, a swift hand across his eyes.

While he rocked her.

And the heat expanded.

He didn't ask her how long, or how often, or how hard. He knew. He had known. And he hadn't had the blessed courage of his convictions to step in and find out, because he was afraid he might be wrong.

Sorry bastard, he thought, then thought, *sorry bastard* at himself.

He waited until she could hear him, then asked if she

thought the Doyles would take her in for a couple of days. It took a while before she finally nodded; it took longer to sit up, blow her nose, and ask about her father.

What he wanted to say was, *he may have had a part in your birth, child, but he isn't your father.*

What he said was, "I'll take care of it. I just wish you'd come to me sooner."

Not only a sorry bastard, but a liar too.

"That's what I told her," Reed said angrily, waving the oil can around. "I kept telling her and telling her, but she—"

"Hush," Casey told him gently.

He hushed.

Cora stood, a little wobbly, and walked away, suddenly smaller and much too young.

He waited until she was out of earshot, then crooked a finger at Reed. When he was close enough, Reed spoke before he could: "You going to beat him up, Reverend? Kick the excuse me shit out of him?"

Casey glared, and his voice deepened to a rumble. "You listen to me, boy, and listen to me good—you touch her, you even think about touching her the way she is now, you have no idea how angry that will make me. No idea at all."

"Reverend Chisholm!" Reed's eyes widened and blinked in shock, and not a little fear as he took a step back. "I . . . how could you say . . . ."

Casey smiled grimly.

Waited.

"Oh," the boy finally said. Realization: "Oh!"

"That," Casey told him, "is sometimes called the fear of God."

Reed grinned uncertainly, sputtered a thanks, and ran off to catch up with Cora, just through the gate. She asked him something, he shook his head and put an arm around her waist, looked at Casey, and suddenly the arm was at his side. She put a hand against his chest—*wait a second*—and trotted back to the porch.

Her face was hard, green eyes turned to stone. "Hurt him,

Reverend Chisholm,'' she begged. ''Use your powers and *hurt him.*''

4

Knowing the Doyles were no friends of William Bowes made it easier to ask Noreen for an extra bed for Cora. By the tone of the woman's voice, he didn't have to explain much beyond mentioning the father's name; when he suggested she talk it over first with her husband because there would surely be trouble down the road, she told him not to worry, they both knew how to handle bullies. Even ones with lawyers.

Next he called Mel, spent five minutes apologizing for the slight and the self-pity, and asked him to contact some colleagues to arrange counseling for Cora and her father. Preferably not together; at least not for a while.

''You're sticking your head in a beehive, Case.''

''Seems to me I've done that before, sort of.''

Farber laughed.

Casey hung up. Standing in his living room. Left hand in a fist, shaking as if he had palsy.

He stood there, barely breathing, until he felt a breath of cold slither across his back.

Lord, he thought, and hurried to the door.

At the west end of the yard he spotted the buck he had seen the other day, back in the trees. Watching the house.

The cold deepened, he heard a sound, and looked just in time to see the ragged crow hit the flagstone.

When he looked again, the deer was gone.

5

It took him five minutes to dress and make himself presentable.

It took him ten minutes standing at the door before he could bring himself to go out.

He walked up Black Oak Road, seeing nothing but the steeple, hearing nothing but his footsteps, feeling nothing but the heat.

He unlocked the church door, turned on the air-conditioning, stepped into the sanctuary, and stopped halfway to the altar.

"All right, Lord," he said. "If You don't mind, You mind telling me what's going on?"

Stained-glass light, and the whisper of soft wings.

He waited for countless seconds before squeezing between the pews to the left wall.

There, below the windows, the carpet was covered with dying moths.

The whisper of their wings.

A glance at the cross as he made his way to the other side.

Scores of them.

Hundreds of them.

The whisper of their desperate wings.

2

1

The fire demon wasn't dead.

It gnawed on Escobar's arm most of the night, making him groan in his sleep while sleep drifted into fever.

In the fever he saw Independence Square the way it was when tourists came into the city—full of cars and color, leaves and grass, the statue of Washington on his horse, the hucksters, the cameras. He had taken the train from Miami, on impulse decided not to go all the way to New York. A cabbie took him here, and he had stood for hours, blinking away the tears, the biggest damn grin in the world on his face.

He had a feeling this place was going to make him rich.

It almost had.

Until the demon came and took him away with claws made of fire, and gnawed on his arm.

He groaned again, this time loud enough to wake himself up.

He lay on his back, staring at the ceiling, his injured arm jammed between his side and the back of the couch. Carefully, hissing inward, he moved it until it was propped across his stomach. Blinked away the sweat. Licked his cracking dry lips. Smelled the stench of fear and running, and listened for sounds that shouldn't have been.

Nothing.

Nothing but his breathing.

Cursing, he sat up stiffly, favoring the arm, hissing again when a trace of surprisingly weak fire lanced up and through his shoulder and lodged in his temples. His suit jacket was in the floor, both shoes and one sock off, shirt unbuttoned down to his belt; he wondered how he did all that without waking up.

He also wondered how long he could stay here much longer without drying up like a dead leaf.

It was a small room, bedroom through one door, kitchen through another. The couch, two armchairs, a coffee table, not much more. A summer place where people didn't spend much time. He took a breath, wiped his face with his good arm, and went to the front window. The drapes were heavy, crawling with vines and flowers. He used one finger to part them in the middle, and his vision had adjusted to daylight's glare; he didn't know whether to laugh or scream.

Across the street, on the corner, was Mackey's bar.

He shook his head and stepped back. Tried to moisten his lips and realized he needed water, right now.

Still moving backward, as though someone might crash through the front door if he turned around, he went into the kitchen. A radio on the counter beside the refrigerator. A dusty glass in the sink. The light here was a little brighter, the curtains on the window and back door not as heavy as the drapes. Still, he felt too open, spotted a door to his left and opened it: the bathroom.

Nothing much, barely wide enough to walk through. A shower stall with pebbled translucent door, sink and mirror, and a toilet across from the sink. A second door led into the bedroom.

There were no glasses; he didn't care. He ran the water slowly, cupping his palms to use as a saucer, then to douse his face and hair. His reflection made him wince, bruises and scratches transforming him into a creature from the movies. His arm throbbed, his ribs and his right hip.

Okay, he thought; gotta check, gotta know.

He took off his shirt and shook it out, sneering disgust at the flurry of dirt and grass and leaves that snapped to the tile floor. Pants the same.

Then he looked in the mirror again, grabbed the sink and rising on his toes to get a longer view.

It took him a few seconds to take it all in.

And again he didn't know whether to laugh or scream.

2

From the serving gap Todd watched Casey march up the street. His first impulse was to go after him, find out how he was. His second, once he had seen the reverend's face, was think that God or somebody was in a hell of a lot of trouble, and this was undoubtedly none of his business. He backed away and returned to the grill, flipping burgers and wishing Helen would come in early for a change. Bowes and his friends were out there, bragging about their tracking skills, and bitching that Todd didn't serve beer. Mackey's was closed. How the hell were they supposed to help the cops when quenching their thirst meant drinking goddamn water?

The police had, for the most part, left town. A state cruiser had stopped by twice, but only long enough for the trooper to let him know that nothing had been found, Escobar was still on the loose, remind people to keep their doors locked.

Todd didn't think they would catch him. Roadblocks on the state and county roads had turned up nothing. The man was gone. They'd do better checking his Philadelphia places, or wherever the hell scum like that went to ground.

The screen door opened, and Helen walked in, reaching for her apron hung on a wall peg.

"You seen Case?" he asked as casually as he could, slapping burgers on plates.

Helen made a face at the noise out front. "No."

"You heard?"

She nodded, made no comment.

He wiped his hands on his apron. "At least Enid hasn't come in. I heard she went to every house on the Crest this morning." He laughed shortly. "Preaching, I heard. Telling everybody about the new Lazarus."

Helen picked up the plates without a word and took them to the front.

Oh boy, he thought; we're in a mood today.

The screen door opened again. This time it was Bobby, T-shirt and shorts, hair looking as if she'd brushed it with an eggbeater. "I'm going to the mall," she announced, keeping the door open with her hip. "You want me to look for something?"

"Nope." He smiled. "What about Arlo?"

She shuddered. "He can clean the place himself. I'm not going in there again, not until he does. Maybe not until he gives me a fat raise."

He agreed, started over to give her a kiss, and frowned when she sidestepped onto the stoop, waved, and left.

A puzzled stare at the house beyond the hedge—*damn, you ladies have a knockdown or what?*—before he closed the door and started cleaning the grill.

"Is it true?"

He saw Helen over his shoulder, leaning against the butcher block counter in the middle of the room. "What's true?"

"About . . . about Casey."

"Jeez, Helen, you know better than that."

He realized then the diner was silent. Bowes and the others had left. Grease popped and sizzled.

"Do I?" she said, biting on her lower lip.

She looked frazzled and hot. He set the metal spatula on its hook on the grill's front and stepped over to the counter. "Helen . . ." He shook his head. "It was a freak thing, okay? I was there, and it was a freak thing. Mel already told him what really happened. Something about muscles and stuff. A freak thing."

"Like the bees?"

He swallowed. "Yeah. Like the bees." Then he reached over and stopped her hands from fussing with the apron.

She gave him an embarrassed laugh, fussed with her hair, and laughed again. "I'm still not used to this," she said, meaning the haircut.

He didn't know what to say.

She headed for the swinging door. "Got to clean up. Bowes and those animals . . . slobs, they're all slobs."

He cleaned up, went to the gap, and watched her damp-dust the booths, the counter, check the coffee urn, count the money in the register, grab a broom and sweep the clean floor twice. There was no one on the street. No cars passed in either direction. The police stayed away.

"You know," he said when she started her fourth pass on the counter, "you wear that stuff through, I'm taking it out of your tips."

Instead of dutifully laughing at something he said at least twice a week, she dropped onto a stool and cupped the rag between her hands. "You remember the other night, you and Casey were talking about the Millennium?"

He didn't, not right away. When it finally came to him, he nodded cautiously. He didn't like her voice—toneless and flirting with hysteria; he didn't like the way she wouldn't look him in the eye.

"Look, Hel, we were only—"

Her look silenced him.

"Think about it," she said, squeezing the rag in one hand. "You think about the bees and that dead man, and you tell me what it means. You tell me all it means is that people act weird."

Not a request; a demand.

"Helen—"

"Then you tell me why I heard a horse on my street last night, and when I looked, the street was empty."

He forced himself to laugh and returned to his grill.

He picked up the spatula and attacked the grease again.

He remembered the night the church bell tolled, and the

unshakable, uneasy feeling that a horse was riding down the road.

He remembered the bees.

3

Casey wielded a broom from the janitor's closet.

He had already swept the dead moths from the left side of the church into the vestibule; now he worked on the right side.

Shivering.

Terrified he might find one of them alive.

4

Nate checked the inventory for the fiftieth time that afternoon, scribbling a note to Kay that Howard from the deli still hadn't returned the four red-cased videos he'd rented three days ago. When he was finished, he stood behind the counter and checked the change, the bills, rereading the receipt from the UPS man, closing the drawer, and beating out a drum solo on the counter.

Waiting.

Wondering if Kay would ever come in today.

He hoped so, because he was nervous being in here without her telling him what to do.

He hoped not, because he wouldn't know what to say.

Especially after the dream he'd had about her last night.

"Aw, man," he said, and drummed louder.

He wanted desperately to tell someone. After all, now he could brag with the rest of the guys at school, only he wouldn't be lying through his teeth, not like most of the others. He could honestly brag. But he wouldn't. Just like he wouldn't tell Reed, because Reed either wouldn't believe him, or he'd blow his stack, his cool, and everything else.

He certainly couldn't tell Reverend Chisholm. The man

would pick him up with one hand and throw him halfway to Texas.

"Aw . . . man."

Drummed louder.

Rina; what was he going to do about Rina? Seeing a woman in *Playboy* or something was one thing; seeing a woman right there in front of him, under him, on top of him, all over him was something else again. How could he ever look at Rina again . . . without wondering.

Drummed louder.

Blinked and looked at his hands.

He wasn't drumming anymore.

The sound he had made was the sound of hoofbeats.

He snatched his hands away and wiped them on his jeans, wiped them across his mouth, and decided to take inventory again. Then he would call Kay's house and find out if she was all right. Then he would . . . then he would . . .

The bell over the door rang, and Dimitri walked in.

"Hey, Dimmy, what's happening?"

Dimitri wandered around the store, touching boxes, humming to himself.

"Dimmy? What's up?"

Dimitri stopped in front of the new releases and turned around. His eyes were red, his cheeks pink.

Nate hurried around the counter and knelt in front of him. "Hey, bud, what happened? Those sh—jerks try to get you again?"

The little boy shook his head.

Nate tried a smile. "Then what? Oh, I get it. Sonya beat you up, right?" He poked the boy's stomach playfully, but there was no response. "Okay, I give up. You going to tell me?"

"The birds," Dimitri said, his voice soft and high.

Nate automatically glanced at the window. "What about them?"

"They're gone."

5

Against the wall behind the counter at the grocery was a low table Mabel Jonsen used for a desk. She never took her work home; she figured once she'd turned out the lights and climbed the stairs, she didn't want anything to do with how many cans of pea soup she had left, or day-old bread, or bags of kitty litter. She didn't want to know about electric bills or delivery bills or the credit card bills that never seemed to get low enough for her to pay off in a single check.

When she sat at the desk, only customers were allowed to interrupt her concentration.

"Man," Moss said from the front of the store, "only a couple of minutes to five, and it's still at the one-hundred, red-mercury, sweltering level."

She hunched over a sheet of paper, working on a list she'd been developing since she'd opened.

"You see Reverend Chisholm before, Mabe?"

Wedding guests. Who would be the same guests for the party she wanted to throw Sunday afternoon after church. Sort of a preview of the nuptials picnic, even if the weather didn't break. She chuckled. If it rained—*please, God*—she would hold the umbrellas herself.

"Man looked like he was ready to strangle someone."

She was pretty sure she had everyone, but there could be no mistakes. Leave one person out, and she wouldn't hear the end of it. Ever.

Mrs. Racine thumped a carton of milk on the counter, along with a dozen cans of cat food. Mabel grunted as she stood, nodded to the old woman, and rang the items up.

"How are you feeling, Tiffany?" she managed to ask with a straight face. It was one thing for a high school kid to have a fancy, silly name like that, but a woman who was surely pushing seventy if she was a day? She ought to be called Agatha, or Thelma. "Managing the heat okay?"

Mrs. Racine allowed as how she'd feel a whole lot better

once winter arrived. As it was, she and her children were doing the best they could under the trying circumstances.

"Fine," Mabel said. She bagged the milk and cat food in brown paper, hefted it, and said, "Moss, you want to help Mrs. Racine with this? It's kind of heavy."

"Kind of hot, too," he answered good-naturedly. "Sure, hon, no problem."

Mrs. Racine demurred, but only out of politeness, clasping her white-gloved hands over a matching purse at her waist while Moss grabbed the sack under one arm and offered her the other.

"Flirt," the old woman said, lips tight in disapproval, eyes smiling.

"My charm, Mrs. Racine, my charm."

He winked lewdly over her head at Mabel, who scooted around the counter and made impatient shooing motions with both hands until they were gone. At the door she watched him pretend to stop traffic as he and the old woman faded into the glare, like ghosts. He was a nice man, she thought with approval; he seemed to have assimilated very well.

When they were gone, she returned to the desk, unable to hold back the giggles any longer.

Tiffany?

She laughed aloud, picked up her pen, and gnawed thoughtfully on the inside of one cheek as she went over the list once more. And suddenly threw the pen down so hard it bounced off the table to the floor.

"Damn him!" she yelled.

She loved Moss, God knew she did, but he kept sneaking in, putting names on without consulting her. Yesterday it was that awful Bowes bastard, and this morning, after breakfast, he had slipped in Michael Rennie as a joke. She hadn't laughed.

"Mabe," he had said, aggrieved, "this heat wave has stolen your sense of humor, you know that?"

"Mr. Rennie," she'd answered stiffly, "is a respected movie actor."

"Mr. Rennie," he said, mocking her tone, "was an alien

in a science-fiction movie about flying saucers, that's the only reason you like him." On the way out he'd added, "Besides, hon, he's dead."

Mabel couldn't retort because he had closed the door too quickly, then popped it open again and grinned. "Maybe you could send Casey to fetch him." He laughed, ducked the thrown box of cookies, and left again.

Not funny, Mabel thought, glaring at the list.

And neither is this.

As soon as Moss came back, he would damn well explain to her who this Susan person was.

6

Casey slumped against the wall, puffing, glints of sweat at his hairline. The moths were at the door. All he had to do was sweep them out. A couple of times he had been tempted to pick one of the more unusual ones up, but he was afraid the wings would move.

He blew out a weary breath and returned to the sanctuary, to check to be sure he had gotten them all.

He was, but not until after he had looked under every pew back to front, under the pulpit, behind the altar, under and behind everything in his office.

It was then that it first occurred to him to wonder how they had gotten in. With all the windows and doors closed, it would have to have been—

"Magic," he muttered, and froze for a second, half expecting a bolt of lightning to strike him where he stood. His stomach grumbled instead, reminding him of meals long overdue, making him laugh silently, sending him to the front to finish the job and be done with it.

But once he saw them again, tumbled in the pile, broken, near to dust, he realized he would have to wade through them to open the doors.

He couldn't move.

7

"Today is Friday," Sonya said, not quite a question.

Cora nodded. "Yep."

They sat at the shallow end of the pool, arms around each other's waist, feet dangling in the water. A beach umbrella was jammed into the ground behind them, providing shade but scant relief.

"So . . . so why is Momma singing?"

Cora didn't know. She had been late. Rina had helped her grab her things from the house, once they were sure her father was off playing cowboy in the woods. When she got here, Dimitri was gone, and she could hear Mrs. Balanov's voice, even through the closed windows. Hymns. Nothing but hymns.

"Maybe," she said, "your momma's happy."

Sonya considered it. "Are you?"

She didn't know that, either.

"Dimitri isn't."

"Oh? How come?"

"The birds."

Oh, God, she thought, not again.

"They're all gone."

Cora started to make a joke, changed her mind, and looked around. Except for the muffled singing, the yard was silent. No breeze to move the water, no hum from the pool's filtration system, no cars on Black Oak, no noise of kids playing in the schoolyard.

She hugged Sonya closer, and for no reason she could think of, she didn't want to make a sound.

8

Arlo sat in the darkened bar, slowly spinning round and round on a stool. The cleaning was done, the air stank of disinfectant, and all he had to do was throw a switch, light the lights, and the Landing would know he was back in business.

Round and round.

All morning since the last cop boy had dropped by, he had been trying to understand why he hadn't confessed to them but he had to Casey Chisholm. He tried to understand why he had confessed at all. Big trouble coming down the road, sure as he sat here, but he would be long gone when it arrived. They would have found it out later; why did he say something now? It sure didn't make him feel any better, no closer to Arizona, no closer to Nirvana.

All it had done was piss the Padre off.

Round and round.

And the Padre had pissed him off, too. Sitting there, a giant in black, judging him, and, if the truth be known, scaring the living daylights out of him. Nothing specific, but something had changed, and the Padre wasn't just a big goofy preacher anymore, wasn't a drinking buddy, wasn't a wink-and-nod, mind-your-manners-son friend anymore.

One more night, he swore; one more night, and I'm out of here.

Round and round.

Like the moth bouncing around the peace sign painted on the ceiling.

9

time to go, children
i've changed my mind
it's time to go

10

Casey couldn't do it.

Ashamed . . . worse, humiliated, he went the other way—through his office and out the side door. Dragging the broom behind him until he reached the front step. Standing before the doors, feeling the heat of the sun on his back, the heat of the stoop through his soles.

Stupid; this was stupid.

They were only moths, they were dead, they weren't going to rise up and smother him, they were moths, and they were dead.

Hundreds of them.

Waiting for him to open the doors.

11

Diño did his best to see as much as he could of his back, but the light was dim, the shadows shifting. He fetched a footstool from the kitchen, stood on it, and checked again.

Nothing.

Madre, there was nothing.

A few bruises, a few scabs.

No burns.

He had been thrown from a burning car, clothes afire, fire demon coming, and despite the residual ache in his arm, there were no burns.

"*Madre,*" he whispered.

His toes curled on the humid-damp tiles when he stepped down; his hair dripped sweat down the length of his back as he picked up his shirt, his trousers, and searched them for scorches.

Nothing.

Nothing there.

Ignoring his nudity, he hurried to the front room and snatched his jacket off the floor. The gun rolled free, rattling dully across the hardwood. He examined the sleeves, the collar, the lapels, the inside and outside pockets.

Nothing.

Nothing there.

Madre Dios, he thought; what is it with this town?

He didn't know, he didn't care, he wanted to get out. He was not a superstitious man, didn't wear a cross around his neck or carry a talisman in his pocket. But this was beyond anything he could understand, and he didn't like it. Not at all.

The hell with the old fart, he decided, bracing himself against a chill that make his legs and arm quiver uncontrollably; the hell with them all. He wanted out. And since he didn't seem to be injured—not anymore—as soon as it was dark, he was getting out. A shower first, dress, and out.

It wasn't until he stepped into the stall and realized there was no soap that he also realized that the fire hadn't touched him.

And if the fire couldn't kill him . . .

He stood there a long time before he closed the door and turned on the water.

He stood there a long time before he began to smile.

12

time to go

13

It was mindless work, straightening the empty tape boxes so the customers would read them, but it was the only thing Nate could think of for Dimmy to do. He wished Reed were here. Reed knew how to talk to the kid better than he did. Reed and Dimmy had a connection somehow. He sighed, and tried to call Kay again, but she still didn't answer.

"Done, Nate," the boy said, presenting himself at the counter.

"Good. Great job. You want to work here instead of me?"

Dimitri shook his head solemnly. "I can't. Poppa says this is a bad place."

Your poppa is a nut, Nate thought, instantly felt guilty, and decided to make what Kay called an executive decision. All the tapes due back today were in, no one had come in for nearly an hour, and he was starving. He didn't think she would

mind him closing up for half an hour so he could grab a sandwich at the Moonglow.

"Okay," he said, locking the register. "Tell you what. It's
going on six. How about you and me, we go get something
to eat, okay? My treat."

Dimitri nodded.

"Your mother won't mind?"

Dimitri shook his head. "She's singing."

"Oh." He turned the door sign around to *Closed, Be Back
Soon*, and locked it behind them. The heat sapped him instantly, and as they trudged down the slope, he couldn't help
feeling not even an hour-long cold shower would make him
cool again. He also couldn't help but wonder when Dimitri
slipped a hand into his.

"You okay, bud?"

Dimitri didn't answer.

"Well, look," he said, pointing. "There's Reed. Maybe
he's had an adventure on the river, huh?"

Reed approached the diner from the opposite direction,
walking as if he were slogging through mud. They waved to
each other just as Nate spotted Reverend Chisholm standing
with a broom at the church's front doors. He frowned, was
about to call out, but Reed called Dimmy instead, and the boy
broke from Nate's grip and ran down to meet him.

"Hey, guys," Reed said when Nate caught up. He jerked a
thumb toward the church. "What's Reverend Chisholm up
to?"

Nate shrugged. "I don't know. Cleaning, I guess."

"In this heat?"

He shrugged again. "How should I know? Why don't you
ask him?" He would have said more, but Helen Gable came
out of the diner just then, wiping her hands on her apron. He
said, "Hi," but she didn't notice, only stared at the reverend.

"Reed?" Dimitri said.

"That's me, pal, what's up?"

Dimitri pointed skyward.

Nate looked. "Whoa. Hey."

Miss Gable looked as well. "I'll be damned," she said,

rapped on the diner window and waved at someone inside, telling them to come out, you have to see this.

"This is silly," Nate said, rubbing a crick from his neck. "I mean, this is silly."

"Yeah," Reed agreed. "But when was the last time you saw a real cloud around here?"

Arlo threw the switch.

The lights flickered on, but not before he saw a group of people standing on the sidewalk in front of the Moonglow, looking up.

Man, he thought, they looking at angels or what?

He stepped outside, waved to them, and saw the cloud.

Well, he thought, it's about goddamn time.

"Mabe?" Moss said, throwing open the grocery door.

"Just the man I'm looking for," she snapped.

"Come out here, hon, you gotta see this."

"Get in here, Moss Tully, I've got some questions for you!"

"Mabe, just look. I think we might have some rain tonight."

At first Helen thought it was only a thickening of the haze that had robbed the sky of its blue. When she looked again, however, she knew it was a cloud. A genuine cloud. Softly fluffed at the edges, darker on the west side and pale streaks across its belly. Moving slowly eastward.

When Nate said, "Silly," again, she had to agree. Here they were, grown-ups and children, standing in the street like natives watching their first eclipse of the sun. A magical thing. A godlike thing. Something that was more than simply a cloud.

"Be damned," Todd said.

She checked the horizon all around, didn't see any others.

Not that it mattered. One cloud had to mean there were others somewhere. One cloud had to mean the heat wave was close to breaking.

She looked at Casey, nudged Todd, and said, "I don't think he knows."

Reed heard her and called to the minister, got no reaction, and suggested a race with Dimitri to see who could reach him first.

Dimitri shook his head, said only, "The birds are all gone."

Helen smiled at the boy, wanting to tousle his hair, maybe cuddle him a little, until she realized he was right.

There were no birds.

There was no sound.

None at all but their suddenly hushed voices.

Dimitri edged closer to Reed, who put an arm around his shoulders.

Helen passed a finger across the back of her neck, saw Vinia Leary leave the pharmacy and walk up toward Arlo, who stood on the corner, and stepped off the curb herself, cutting across the road toward Casey.

She felt but didn't hear the others begin to follow.

She felt but didn't hear a soft *hush* in the air.

She saw Moss and Mabel up the street, in front of Mabel's store. Mabel had his arm, tugging angrily, while Moss scowled and pointed skyward.

She saw Cora and Sonya at the top of the Crest, shirts over their bathing suits, waving to Dimitri.

Her step quickened.

Without any reason apprehension began a crawl across her shoulders, in her stomach; without any reason she felt like screaming Casey's name.

She didn't know why he stood there so still, as if he had forgotten how to open a door.

Nor did she know why, when she reached the foot of the church's flagstone walk, she stopped.

Finally, "Casey?"

*   *   *

He turned around and saw them, saw them all, saw the cloud, and turned his back.

They didn't know, he thought, taking a breath, taking another; they didn't know the cloud hadn't cast a single shadow.

He tossed the broom aside.

"Reverend Chisholm? Hey, Reverend Chisholm." It was Moss, sounding as if he were about to break a laugh.

He felt the air move.

"Case." It was Todd. "Case, you okay?"

Leaves husked and scraped like the palms of old men rubbing together.

"Hey," a startled voice said. It was Arlo. "Man, it's like maybe rain, what do you think?"

Someone answered; he didn't know who.

He grabbed the doorknobs, swallowed, and thought:

This is my church.

This is God's church.

You will not keep me out.

Abruptly the breeze screamed into a high wind that filled the air with gritty dust and shriveled grass and shattered leaves and broken twigs, slamming into his side, nearly pushing him off his feet.

He planted his feet, and glared, and yanked the doors open.

The wind rushed inside.

Moths—scores of them, hundreds of them—were plucked from the floor and gathered and blown outside, forcing him to turn his head and hunch his shoulders as they swirled around him, catching in his hair, slapping softly across his neck, across his face, across his eyes.

On his lips.

Someone cursed, and someone yelled.

Grey smears of moth wings appeared on his chest and face; black smears of crushed moths appeared on the church walls; sunlight turned the dead moths dark as they spun and tumbled across the yard and through the air and down the hill toward the dying river.

When they were gone, the wind calmed.

When Casey stood and faced the others, the breeze settled

and it was cool.   After a stuttered step Helen ran up to him, although she stayed on the walk. "My God, Casey, what was that?"

And the church bell rang.

Cora and Sonya stopped midway down the slope when the wind came up and the church doors opened. All Cora saw was a dark cloud that briefly enveloped the minister.

Sonya whimpered.

"It's okay, kid," she said, putting a hand on the girl's shoulder. "Don't worry, it's okay."

"Dimmy was right," Sonya said.

And the church bell rang.

Mel heard the commotion from his reception room and yanked the door open, scowling. The heat made his cheeks feel as if they had abruptly turned to leather, and he squinted through the glare toward the crowd at the church.

He saw the moths, saw Casey beat at them with his hands, and he couldn't help it—he thought about the bees.

While the church bell rang.

Ozzie Gorn stood in the grease pit under Sissy Palmer's battered army Jeep, swearing at the things he knew he couldn't fix. A thick drop of oil landed on his forehead. He should have left this place a hundred years ago. He should have gone to his sister's, down in South Carolina. Christ, it couldn't be any hotter down there than it was up here.

Another drop of oil.

The hydraulic lift creaked, and the Jeep trembled slightly.

Right, he thought angrily; give out and smash me, you son of a bitch.

It creaked again.

The church bell rang.

*   *   *

Micah sat on his piling throne and watched the cloud ease overhead toward New York, his lips working in a silent prayer that this was a sign the drought and heat were about to end.

The beer can just reached his lips when he heard the buzzing and saw the swarm lift from the oak. Slowly. Too slowly.

Just as the church bell rang.

A red-tail hawk stumbled in the sky.

As the church bell rang.

3

1

Lupé sat patiently on the hillside, legs drawn up, hands lightly grasping her shins. Below, she watched a horse-drawn carriage move along a narrow road, a triangular red reflector out of place on its back. She couldn't see the driver, but she could see a little girl in a black dress and white cap, bobbing her head as though she were singing a song.

Lucky you, kid, she thought; I got a feeling you aren't going to die today.

A swarm of gnats rose from a thicket not far to her right, speckling the air.

A footstep crackling in the dry grass warned her that Stan had finally left the car. She didn't turn. She watched the carriage. Cows in a pasture. A pair of horses standing beneath a drooping, browning tree. Despite the drought, there was more green in this valley than she had ever seen in her life, and it amazed her. Took her breath when she tried to imagine it without all the brown.

Nothing but green, as far as she could see.

Stan crouched beside her, plucking at the stiff blades, saying nothing, humming to himself.

There was a slight breeze, but it didn't do either of them any good.

"Something's up," he finally said.

She nodded.

Although they hadn't been told where they were going, what they were going to do once they had left the interstate and headed north, Susan abruptly pulled off the highway shortly after mid-afternoon. Without a word she got out and fairly marched up the slope of a treeless hill. Lupé had followed soon after. Susan was gone. Lupé waited.

"Feel's not good."

She agreed.

At first she had thought it would be like Arkansas, like Maryland, and her hands had twitched around the top of her boot, around her gun. Licking her lips. Not wondering why, not thinking, just anticipating.

Restless.

Eager.

Until they stopped and Susan was gone.

"Something's changed."

She wanted him to shut up. She wasn't blind, she wasn't stupid, she knew all that, he didn't have to keep telling her, for crying out loud.

The carriage slipped into shimmering heat, a mirage fading in a semigreen desert. For a moment there was only the red triangle, hanging in the air.

The horses left the tree for a drink in a creek that meandered through the pasture.

She touched her thighs, and they were hot.

"Gonna fry, gonna fry," Stan muttered. "Gonna fry sure as hell."

"Jesus Christ!" she snapped.

"What? What?"

She had no chance to tell him.

"It's time to go, children," Susan said behind them.

Lupé whirled, tried to get to her feet and fell while Stan giggled at her. A glare shut him up.

"I've changed my mind."

"About what?" Stan asked.

She stood above them, little more than a silhouette against the sky.

Lupé shivered.

"It's time to go."

2

In the automobile cave there was no music, no instructions, no talk at all except one more, "It's time to go."

They kept to the two-lane road, winding through the hills, the landscape a smear of no color, no shapes, the sun dying behind them.

Lupé sat as still as she could, thinking of the mountains she had left behind. Maybe she missed them, maybe she didn't, probably they belonged to the memory of a woman who didn't exist anymore and for whom no one mourned, no one ever said, *whatever happened to . . .*, no one dreamt about when the wind took the road down through the canyons to scour through the city and leave it behind.

She heard Stan say, "How far?"

She heard Susan answer, "To the end."

She looked into the corner at the bundle huddled there and looked away.

Not thinking.

Not wondering.

"I'm hungry," Stan whined softly.

"You'll feed," Susan answered.

Lupé wiped a hand across her stomach, up over her breasts to her throat, where it stayed, pulling idly at the skin there, massaging, drifting away. He used to touch her here, the goddamn gringo; he used to touch her here, with his lips.

The bundle giggled.

Lupé frowned. "What do you know?"—in a soft voice.

"Everything."

Lupé grinned. "Yeah, right."

"More than you."

"Oh yeah?"

"Yeah."

"Prove it."

"I don't have to if I don't want to."

"And you don't want to, right?"

"Yeah."

"Hush," Susan said gently without turning around.

The sun began to fade.

"Hey," said Stan, leaning forward, pointing. "Be damned, it's a cloud. Two of them. No, three. You think we'll get some rain?"

Susan glanced at him, and he started, pushed against the door and stared out the window.

Lupé knew what he had seen.

Vampires and werewolves.

3

Lupé's eyelids began to flutter, her head to nod, lulled by the rhythmic sound the car made on the road.

It was mostly concrete, or cement, she never could tell the difference, and its sections had been repaired over the years by thick ribbons of tar. The wheels hit them quickly, two and two, thump and thump.

*Thump*and*thump*.

It took her a few minutes, but she finally put a memory to the rhythm and the sound.

Hoofbeats.

It was hoofbeats.

4

1

He told them in a voice he didn't recognize as his to leave him alone. And they did. Without protest.

Then he brushed angrily, nearly snarling, at the dust the dead moths had left on his shirt and pants, swiped at the feel of it on his cheeks as he went inside and closed the doors. More out of obligation than conviction he checked the bell tower, not at all surprised to find no one there, oddly hopeful when he saw clouds building over the low mountains he could see out there in Pennsylvania.

If nothing else, there might be rain.

No one in the church.

No one in his office.

The wise thing would be to leave. Clean up. Use the water and its thunder to give him time to think. Get some distance between himself and whatever the hell was going on. Get hold of his fraying temper. Only then would he speak to the others.

The problem was, God help him, he didn't know what he would say.

So he sat by the aisle in the first pew on the left, legs

extended, ankles crossed, left hand in his pocket. He had pulled the cross out of his shirt, fingered it thoughtfully while he stared at the one on the altar.

"Something's happening," he said far more calmly than he felt, and closed his eyes briefly at a quick chill in his lungs. He cleared his throat, did it again. "You want to let me know what it is?"

Fading sunlight did not dull the brass's gleam.

"I have to tell You, Lord, whatever it is, I really think You've picked the wrong guy here." He shifted uncomfortably. Expelled a long, loud breath. "Let's face it, I haven't been thinking much quicker than Moss's old beagle in this miserable heat. That doesn't take any genius to figure out.

"I waited too long to do something about poor Cora, I'm messing things up pretty fierce with Helen and hurting Kay, and I . . ." He shook his head, shifted his gaze to the toes of his boots. "They used to call it hubris. I'm not fool enough not to see it. So full of myself, I figured I got this town under my wing, nothing's going to hurt them they don't do to themselves." He shook his head again, once and slowly. "Walking the streets like some damn gunfighter marshal. Lord, what a fool. I don't know why You just don't send the lightning and be done with it, teach me a lesson, except probably I'm probably too thick to learn it.

"I know I should've talked to Arlo right away, look what happened when I didn't. A man's dead, a killer's on the loose, people around here talking this and that and making things out that . . ."

He covered his eyes with his free hand.

Had he not feared what it would loosen, he would have let himself sob.

"He wasn't dead," he finally whispered, and the chill touched him again. "That second there, when I touched him . . . he wasn't dead, was he."

The trembling began somewhere around his stomach, spread and intensified until he had to hug himself so tightly he thought he would scream. Big man shaking like a child waking from a nightmare; big man wishing his momma were still alive; big man sitting in a little backwater church, terrified his own shadow would rise up and bite him.

He drew his feet back sharply and leaned forward, arms still wrapped around his stomach, pressing hard, rocking now, watching the floor come at him and slip away, watching the toe of his left boot beat some indefinable time, looking up and watching the cross for a sign.

Big man.

Stained glass darkening.

He felt the heat.

A single strand of hair tickling his brow above his eye.

Like the wing of a moth.

The trembling passed; still he rocked.

Slowly. Slower. Until he unfolded his arms and sat back, stretched out his legs again, and said, with a faint lopsided smile that held no humor at all, "I can't read minds, you know. Especially not Yours. If I'm supposed to be fixin' to do something, I really have to have a hint."

This is my church, he had told it.

Whatever it was.

You will not keep me out.

Whatever it was.

Yet the wind had flown the moths and the church bell had rung and the bees had fled and that man more char than flesh . . . that dead man . . .

He felt the anger.

Being played with, being nudged this way and that.

Suddenly he shoved himself to his feet with a decisive grunt and walked up the aisle, lightly slapping the back of each pew as he went, not looking back when he entered the vestibule, not looking anywhere when he closed and locked the doors behind him and walked down the street.

If they were watching, he couldn't feel them; if they were whispering, he couldn't hear them.

All there was, was the sun, directly in his eyes, turning everything black-and-white and setting fire to his eyes.

When he reached the rectory he kicked the gate open, ignoring the scream of the snapped rusted hinges.

On the porch he tore off his clothes, and naked he flung them as far away as he could.

In the shower he let the waterfall do its work, refusing to check what might be gathering at the drain. Twice he soaped himself and twice he rinsed, three times he washed his hair and let the water pound his scalp.

Once, he nearly fell when he thought he heard the bell.

He paid no attention to the time he spent there, nor to the time he took to dry himself without looking at the reflection in the misted mirror.

There was no thought; he didn't need it. There had been too much of that already. What he did need, what he wanted, was to look at things without wondering or analyzing or turning this way and that. If he found answers he could understand in light of what he knew, then so be it; and if there were answers that made no sense but were true, then maybe, just maybe, he would know what to do.

He sat on the bed, black jeans in his hands, staring at them, getting angry again, finally tossing them aside with a grunt, and rummaging in the dresser's bottom drawer until he found a pair of blue ones, faded and loose, a tiny rip in the thigh. In the closet he shoved aside all the black shirts and pulled out one he hadn't worn in months—a red-and-dark-green hunter's plaid. Helen had given it to him last Christmas, telling him he shouldn't always have to wear the uniform, colors were not a true abomination; he could see still the creases where the shirt had been folded into its box. Tan boots so scuffed they were nearly white across the toes.

The cross he left in a silver tray atop the dresser.

A chair he dragged out onto the porch, where he sat and watched the last of Friday's sun spear whitely through the last of the trees.

The only time he smiled was when he saw a picture of himself, sitting on the porch, feet on the rail, chair tipped back, country squire, country fool.

No more, he decided; damnit, no more.

The only time he moved was when Todd stood at the gate, staring at it, frowning, making up his mind whether to come along or not—Casey folded his hands and put them to his lips, to hide the grin. It was a wonder any one of them had been able to last this long.

He supposed that was one of the many reasons why he loved them.

He knew it was one of the reasons why he was so afraid.

2

Eventually Todd chose to walk through the shattered gate, scuffing his feet on the flagstones, taking the steps as he nodded, dropping onto the top one, his back against the post, so obviously uncomfortable that Casey had to smile again. "Nobody bites here, Todd."

His friend didn't return the smile. He sat with one leg up, hand draped over his knees. "Case . . ." He stopped, sniffed, rubbed a finger under his nose. "Case, I'd guess this is more your territory than mine, but we have to talk about what's going on here. I mean, there's people out there, they're ready to set up a shrine or something, you know what I mean?"

"Enid."

Todd nodded.

Casey took a deep breath, let it out in spurts.

"She'll do what she has to do. Petyr will take care of her."

"Pete's gone. Took his car and left as soon as she started."

This time it was Helen he spotted on the road. She didn't bother to come as far as the gate; she cut across the driveway and lawn.

Casey grinned. "You call a meeting or what?"

This time Todd grinned back. "It's either here or be up on the Crest, listening to that idiot."

"She's in the middle of the street, for God's sake," Helen complained. She went inside, fetched another chair from the table, and set it beside Todd. "Standing there yelling Bible stuff at the top of her voice." Her face was taut, her eyes puffed and faintly red. "And there are people listening to her,

Casey. Maybe a dozen, I don't know. It's spooky. It's really spooky."

"Name of the game these days," Todd said.

The backfire of a truck buried whatever she answered. Micah parked on the far side of the road, took his time climbing out of the cab with two others, took his time crossing, glancing around as though he expected something to leap out and yell, "Boo!" His captain's cap was in one hand, an unlit cigarette between his lips. He sat on the bench swing while Mel in his shirtsleeves sat below Todd, his back to them all. Tessa took the swing.

She sneezed.

Casey blessed her.

She wore jeans now and an untucked white shirt, sockless in tennis shoes. "Mabel's got Moss doing something in the hardware. Big secret. He's got the door locked. Beagle's whining on the bench, driving the place nuts."

"Aliens," Mel told her with disgust. "She wants him to rig some spotlights she can put in the meadow so the aliens will know where to land."

"And he's doing it?" Helen said.

"Sometimes," Casey said, "love doesn't make you blind, it makes you stupid."

"But aliens?"

"What do I know? I'm just a poor preacher trying to do his job."

"In those clothes?" Todd said, his expression a sudden realization of what Casey wore.

Tessa giggled and Helen allowed a smile, although she wouldn't stop fiddling with the buttons of her shirt.

"Looks like it's going to get cooler," Casey allowed with an exaggerated drawl, a languid gesture toward the river. "Have you noticed the clouds?"

"About time," Micah said. "You think maybe it's over?"

Mel pointed west at the treeline. Clouds rimmed in silver and gold, bottomed in dark grey. "What do you think?"

"I think," Micah growled, "I don't know what the hell's going on, that's what I think."

Loud voices on the road.

Reed and Cora, arms and hands in waving debate.

"Talk about love making you stupid," Todd muttered.

"Oh, don't be so hard on them," Helen chided. "They don't know it yet. They'll work it out sooner or later."

Rina was behind them, staying well out of the argument, kicking at pebbles, looking so miserable Casey wanted to leap up and hug her. The trio faltered when they saw who was on the porch, but Reed marched forward anyway, greeting everyone with a sharp nod, taking a position on the railing at the end of the porch, to Casey's right.

Casey looked over his shoulder. "Rina, where's Nate?"

"I don't know." Her hair was braided and pulled over one shoulder. She fussed with it, refused to look up. "At work, I guess."

"Work?" Micah almost rose from the swing. "Work? Who the hell can work? For that matter, who can do anything around here anymore? After what happened, we're lucky the place isn't deserted."

Casey finally scraped his chair back until he could see all of them without effort. "What happened?" he asked mildly. "What do you think happened?"

No one answered right away.

The Landing suddenly felt very large and very cold.

It took a moment for him to realize they were waiting for Todd to say something. Somehow they had managed to appoint him their spokesman, and Casey felt for him because he knew what the man had to say.

The creak of the swing's chains, the creak of the boards as Tessa planted her feet to stop the swinging.

"Case." Todd's right hand wouldn't stay still until Mel reached around and stilled it. He thanked him with a look, and cleared his throat. "Casey, we've got explanations for everything, right? Explanations up the wazoo, and I don't mean that real-estate crap with Arlo."

Casey nodded.

"But they don't mean jack, and you know it. What's been going on around here for I don't know how long isn't natural.

It isn't right. Doc here can talk about muscle stuff this and postmortem that, and Cora there, she's been telling poor Dimmy the birds have gone because there's no food here anymore, and you can tell me until you're blue in the face that those bees took off because we made too much noise, but damnit, Case, I don't believe it anymore. Not after today.''

Casey waited.

"It isn't natural,'' Todd repeated softly.

"Cora.'' Casey looked at her again. "You okay? All set up?''

Startled, she nodded, seemingly unaware that Reed had taken her hand. Her feet were hooked around the spindles, squeezing, her thigh muscles taut.

Casey watched her for a moment, watched them all and saw them wondering. He would have sent the kids away, but by Reed's expression, all that would have done was make things worse.

Whatever *things* were.

"What about it, Doc?'' he asked. "You're the man of science around here. What about it? Are we talking miracles or what?''

Mel flopped a hand in his lap. "I'll be honest, Case. After today, I think I'm out of my province here.'' He pushed a palm back across his hair. "I think . . . I think this is more in your line of work now.''

"Maybe, maybe not, Mel,'' he answered gently. "But that's not what I asked you.''

Farber didn't move, but it was clear he wanted to squirm, to leave, that he regretted leaving the sanctum of his clinic. As with Todd, Casey felt for him, but offered no help.

Mel nodded once, decisively. "Okay. Okay. Todd's right. We have more explanations, more rational explanations, than we know what to do with. And there's no reason at all why we should be bothering you about it.'' He clamped a hand on Todd's leg to stop it from bouncing. "So tell me about the bell, Casey. I know you didn't find anyone up there, or any kind of rigged mechanism, so tell me about the damn bell.''

3

In the small workshop behind Tully's hardware store, Beagle sat on a three-legged chair in the corner, tongue poking from the corner of his mouth, evidently glad to be at last inside, out of the heat.

"Nuts," Moss told him. "She's nuts; why the hell am I doing this? She's out of her goddamn mind."

On the workbench were three sections of two-by-sixes. It had taken him the better part of three hours, and a couple of mashed fingers, but he had managed to rig four spotlights to each section.

"Somebody come up to me and told me that's the woman I'm gonna marry, I'd punch him in the mouth."

Beagle cocked his head.

When Moss was finished, he was supposed to have four sections in all. Then he was supposed to take them down to the meadow and lay them out in a big square. Then he was supposed to rig them all to a battery so they would light, and not die, when Mabel threw a switch.

"You really think space guys are going to see this?"

Beagle whimpered.

"Dumbest thing I ever heard of." He spat dryly and wiped a rag over his sweaty scalp. "Somebody finds out about this, boy, they're gonna wrap her in white and haul her ass away. Then they're going to come for me."

Still, he kept working.

Since the bell had rung that afternoon, she had plunged into a frenzy that unnerved him, and he would have agreed to build a spaceship of his own just to get away from all that energy. It was like she had turned into another person. Even her eyes were different. Burning, sort of. Looking at him and not really seeing him.

He nearly whacked his hand while setting a brace, and decided it was time he took a break. He and Beagle went through the store to the bench outside, sat, and watched the shadows born of the setting sun.

"Awfully quiet," he said.

Beagle wagged his tail.

He wondered if Arlo was still hiding in the bar. Not that it mattered. If he went in there now, he probably wouldn't come out until he couldn't walk. Vinia had left like her beehive was on fire, and he hadn't seen her since. He could see Nate Dane in the Moonglow, alone in a booth, a glass of water cupped between his hands.

On the air he could hear Enid still preaching, or whatever the hell it was she was doing. She sounded damn hoarse. She sounded like her husband.

Suddenly she was silent.

"Awfully quiet."

Mabel appeared in the grocery doorway, hands mad on her hips. "You done?" she called.

He shook his head.

"Then hurry!"

"Taking a break," he called back. "Gimme a break. It's an oven in there."

She took a step toward him, raised a hand in disgust, and went back inside, slamming the door.

He waited a second longer, just in case she changed her mind, then rose, said, "Screw it," and headed for the bar.

After his fourth glass of water, and it not looking like anyone was coming back very soon, Nate slid out of the booth and went into the restroom. He looked at his reflection, lifted the toilet lid, and threw up.

Kay sat on her high stool behind the counter, waiting for customers she knew in her gut wouldn't come. No one would come today, not even Enid. The poor woman had driven all her listeners away when spittle began to fly from her mouth. Kay had watched her, wanted to go out and shake some sense

into her, but she hadn't moved, only listened, and felt Nate's
fumbling hands. When the street emptied, she decided that as
soon as the sun was down, she would leave. It wouldn't take
very long—a few clothes, what little jewelry she had, check-
book, the register cash. She would leave and not come back,
and Casey would wonder for a while, but he wouldn't wonder
long. Eventually they would have one of their damn meetings,
and someone new would take over the store.

Maybe Sissy and Ed, they could offer home delivery on one
of their horses.

She giggled while she wept.

Dimitri sat with his sister as far under the backyard trees as
they could, holding hands, watching the still water in the pool,
listening to the silence.

"Is Momma okay?" Sonya asked, chin up, fighting the
tears.

"Sure."

"She was yelling."

"But it wasn't that kind of yelling. She was just telling
people things."

"I don't know what she said."

"She said what we saw at the church, that's all."

She looked up at him, eyes brimming. "What did we see,
Dimmy? What did we see?"

"The wind." He nudged her playfully. "Just the stupid
wind."

They watched the house for signs of movement.

She nudged him back. "What about the bell?"

Dimitri didn't answer right away. He tugged at a strand of
hair and stared at the water, wishing Poppa were home and
not at the store somewhere, getting supper like he said he
would. He wished the birds were back. He wished Cora were
here to dive-bomb the pool and make him laugh. He wished
he really knew what was wrong with his mother.

He stood, and pulled Sonya to her feet.

"Where are we going?"

"To see Reverend Chisholm."

"Why?"

They left the hot shade and crossed the yard.

"I don't know. Just because."

Arlo sat at the bar, an empty beer bottle in front of him. It was the first one he had had since leaving the church and the bell. It had taken him forever to get the courage to drink it, forever more to finish it, and now it took forever for him to wait for Bobby the Beautiful Barmaid so he wouldn't have to get himself another.

"Peace," he said to the bottle. "Love. All that shit."

Bobby wasn't coming back.

He had a feeling.

Then Moss came in and said, "Christ Almighty, Arlo, I'm thirsty."

The world doesn't change.

Arlo pointed listlessly at the liquor ranged on the shelf. "Help yourself, man, help yourself."

4

The fire demon waited in the living room.

Diño Escobar watched it from the kitchen doorway. Smiling. Gloating. Stepped toward it, and embraced it, and didn't feel a thing.

He heard it, though.

He heard it screaming.

And he heard it tell him, *wait.*

5

Listen, Casey said, keeping his voice low as if afraid the clouds would overhear, but unable to keep all the anger from his voice, only hoping they would think it was something else.

Listen, I have to be honest with you. I don't know what's going on. I don't know why the bell rang, or anything else. I do know these are strange times. Todd said weird shit's going on, and he's right. It's not new, though, it's happened before. The Millennium comes along and people go nuts. The religion, it doesn't matter which one, comes apart a little, and that little goes off on a tear, like Chicken Little, except it isn't the sky that's falling. It's everything. Before you know it, you've got an infection. People catch it, it doesn't matter how smart or dumb they are. They see signs and portents, faces in the sky and faces on the wall and faces where no faces ought to be. They give it up, everything they own, and they climb a mountain to wait for the end.

But it doesn't end.

Not then.

So they come down from the mountains and go about their business, feeling, I bet, a little foolish, a lot angry, wondering who they can trust to tell them what's what.

I'm thinking out loud here, so bear with me a bit.

Used to be—maybe still is, for all I know—you went to a house on Sunday afternoon. A man in the parlor, he's playing something on a guitar, folks are listening, maybe keeping time with a hand or a toe. Over there in the dining room you've got another man, he's playing an old piano, louder, maybe not, and folks are keeping time. Out in the kitchen there's a couple of them, maybe a guitar and a banjo this time. Keeping time.

Out on the porch there's a fiddler, and he's the best of the lot. He's playing a waltz, kind of sad, kind of slow, and on the lawn kids are dancing, while on the porch and under the trees grown-ups are watching and smiling and nodding and letting the dinner settle down in their bellies. Soon the guitar in the living room picks up the tune, and the piano in the dining room, and those boys in the kitchen. Autoharp, maybe, and maybe some old guy pulls a Jew's harp from his pocket, you got a harmonica going, the next thing you know, a dozen couples are on the grass, listening to the symphony.

Waltzing to a tune nobody knows, nobody ever wrote down.

When it ends, they say their pieces and head on home.

Come again, hear? Next Sunday, same time, maybe another place.

It doesn't matter.

What matters is the symphony waltz.

I don't know who started it this time, the fiddler or the guitar player. But it seems to me, now that I'm talking, that these last few months, maybe even years, they've all started playing the same tune.

If it was just the people—all the killing and the burning and the lies and the drugs—I'd be sad, but I wouldn't be afraid. People get stupid now and then, and then people get smart. I never did believe we were anything like lemmings.

It's more than the people now, though.

It's like . . . I don't know . . . it's like everything, every living thing has started listening. And dancing.

Look at the moths.

Look at the birds.

I don't know why the bell rings like that, Mel.

I wish I did.

I wish to God every day that I was the man you all think I am, or want me to be.

You think I'm mad?

Damn right I am.

Madder than I can ever remember being in my life.

I wish to God I could make sense of a drought that doesn't end and bells that ring and birds that fall out of the sky and bees that rise from a tree and everything else. If I could, then maybe you wouldn't look at me the way you do. If I could, then maybe I'd get some sleep at night.

Of course, maybe it's only Mabel's aliens on the way. I wouldn't mind that. It might be fun.

But if it's not . . .

If it's true what people are saying, that this is the Millennium that ends it all . . .

Then the fiddler's on horseback.

And he's riding this way.

6

There were several attempts to talk, to make comment, to respond, but finally they saw his face, saw the creases, and began to leave, one by one. Saying nothing, their expressions etched and shadowed with disappointment.

Only Helen stayed behind, moving to the swing where she used her heels to rock her back and forth.

"Do you really believe that, Case?"

He hadn't moved. "Believe what?"

"The end of the world is coming."

"I didn't say that."

"Well, excuse me, but it certainly sounded like it." She nodded toward the road. "And if they're not scared, they think you're out of your mind."

"What I said was, what I wanted to say was that I don't know, Helen." He rubbed his face with the heels of his hands. "I honest to God don't know."

"You're supposed to know."

"Why? Because I'm a preacher? I'm supposed to have a direct line to God? He's supposed to let me in on all His secrets?"

"That's pretty much it, yes."

"You've been watching those TV evangelists too much. They don't know any more than I do."

"What if they do?"

She patted the swing lightly until he sat beside her. Her hand in his was hot, sweaty, and he could see moist diamonds gathering around her neck, darkening the ends of her hair.

"Nice shirt," she said, straightening his collar.

"Thanks."

She tilted her head this way, that way. "It's not you."

"It is now."

Her hand left his; he didn't try to take it back.

"Casey?"

They faced west along the length of the porch. The sun had

dropped below the Pennsylvania mountains, slowly laying strips of black across the clouds.

"The other night I was outside, you know? I had to get out of the house, Tessa and Bobby sometimes drive me crazy. I was coming back to bed and I heard a horse on the street."

He didn't look.

"I couldn't see it, Case. It wasn't that dark, and I couldn't see it."

Another voice said, "Dimmy saw it."

They jumped and turned, saw Reed standing below the railing, grinning.

"Sorry."

"Young man," Casey said, half closing one eye, "you are not supposed to eavesdrop on your elders."

"I wanted to tell you something," he answered, all innocent except for that grin. "I heard you talking, that's all."

"What about the horse?" Helen asked.

Reed told them about the afternoon he thought the heat had gotten to Dimitri, how the boy had panicked, screaming about a horse chasing him down the middle of the street.

Except there wasn't any horse; there was only Mrs. Racine.

"And if you don't believe me, you can ask him yourself."

He snapped a thumb at the gate, and they saw Dimitri and his sister staring at the broken hinges. Casey stood and called them, beckoning with a smile that eventually got them moving. He met them on the steps, hunkering down, leaning a shoulder against the post. Reed didn't take the easy way; he climbed over the railing and sat beside Helen.

"You know," Casey said, "you're not supposed to be walking down the road all by yourselves. You know how the tourists drive, they don't bother to look."

Sonya told him it was okay, she was with her brother, and besides, Cora wasn't around, and was it true that all the birds had gone away because there wasn't any food left to feed them?

"I expect so," he answered carefully, just as solemnly as she had asked the question.

"Then why can't we buy food to give them?"

"We could," he admitted. "I don't think it would be enough, though."

While Sonya considered it, he looked to Dimitri, who looked back without blinking.

"Are you all right, son?"

Dimitri took his time nodding.

"Reed here was telling me about the horse."

Dimitri stiffened.

"Hey." Casey reached out to touch his shoulder, but the boy shied away. "It's all right, son. Reed doesn't keep secrets very well, but I do."

Sonya smiled.

Dimitri didn't.

Casey waited patiently, feeling the others watching.

"It scared me," the boy said at last, so low Casey barely heard it.

"Me, too."

Dimitri cocked his head.

"I've heard it, son. Didn't see it, but I heard it. A couple of times."

"What is it? A ghost?"

The swing creaked.

Dimitri waited.

And Sonya said, "I'm hungry. I haven't had anything to eat all day, and I'm hungry."

"Well." Casey straightened, the moment gone when Dimitri looked away. "As a matter of fact, young lady, you're just in time. Helen here was just telling me she had to get back to work before Todd gave her the boot, and I was kind of looking for a gorgeous lady to have dinner with." He made a show of checking his wallet, counting his money, figuring in his head. "You have a date, Sonya?"

She blushed and shook her head.

"Me neither," Reed said, standing so quickly Helen nearly slipped off the swing. "Are you buying, Reverend Chisholm?"

"Yes, he is," Helen said. "He's buying, I'm cooking."

Dimitri said nothing.

But he stayed close to Casey as they walked up the road, bumping into him now and then, as if making sure he was still there.

The temperature was still high, and a mottled dusk had taken over as the clouds sailed and thickened, softening the shadows and blending them with the dark that began to expand through the woods.

They reached the Moonglow, were about to go in when Reed said, "Hey, guys, look."

At the point where Black Oak took its dive onto the flat, an automobile idled in the middle of the road. Its headlamps were on, too bright, too large.

They could only see the outline of hood and windshield.

"Stupid tourists can't even see the white line," Helen said, and herded the children inside. Reed followed.

Casey stayed.

The car didn't move, and no one got out. If its engine was running, it didn't make a sound.

He took a step toward it without knowing why, and another before he changed his mind. Helen was right. Tourists lost again.

But as soon as he stepped inside, the car began to move.

5

Stan Hogan reached down between his legs to be sure his backpack was still there on the floor. He didn't know why he needed to know; he just knew it was a comfort.

Right now, though, it seemed kind of silly.

There was nothing in this place that should make him feel the way he did. In all his travels, here and there, over hills and mountains, humming, hitching, singing a song, he was pretty damn sure he had seen single estates bigger than this. A lot prettier, too. This reminded him of cornfields after the harvest, all those husks and stalks dried out and waiting for someone to come along and knock them down.

"I don't know," he said, mostly to himself. "I don't know."

Susan had parked in front of a bar that didn't seem to have a name. Without a word, not a look, she had gotten out without shutting off the engine, walked around the hood and walked straight inside. It was the first time he had seen her do anything like that. Leave the car when they were in a town. Go into a building. Leave them alone.

He didn't like it.

He didn't like this place.

He didn't like the fact that there was nobody on the street, just a dog on a bench, and the streetlamps were dim, barely holding back the night.

He didn't like the people over there in that diner place with the neon trim, staring out the window. They couldn't see him, he knew that, but they watched him just the same. He could see their mouths moving, heads bobbing, eyes and brains trying to figure it out, this big old car parked with the engine running in the middle of their town.

Lupé said, very quietly in his ear, "I don't get it, I don't feel it."

He knew exactly what she meant. This wasn't like the other times. This wasn't the way it was done. Susan hadn't told them to stretch their legs, visit, talk, smile, laugh, and wait for the blood. The other places, they had a feel.

This place felt like nothing, like it had nothing inside it, like the sun had taken it away with all the water.

He pulled at his cheek.

No, that was wrong.

Lupé was wrong.

There *was* something here, it wasn't empty, it was just different. Very different. He wished he knew why, maybe he wouldn't be so nervous.

"Try again," he said without turning around.

She shifted, but said nothing.

His gaze drifted from the bar's recessed doorway to the Moonglow's large windows.

Back and forth.

One foot tapping.

Bar. Moonglow.

"What's she doing in there?" Lupé wanted to know, on the verge of whining.

"Maybe she's thirsty."

Lupé snorted a laugh. "Sure."

"Why not?"

"Come on, *amigo*, you ever see her eat? You ever see her drink anything?"

"I sleep a lot."

She snorted again.

Moonglow. Bar.

Feeling the faint soothing vibration of the car, the soft breeze of the air-conditioning, the baby skin softness of the leather beneath his hand.

Moonglow, but this time he was interrupted by the dashboard glow, and he frowned a little, checked the bar door, and scooted over until he could see the instrumentation array. Big old speedometer. Lights for oil and water and this and that and little signs and a needle on the gas gauge that quivered just enough to make him stare.

And smile.

"Hey."

He felt Lupé lean against the seat. "What?"

He pointed. "Nearly full."

The engine whispered.

"Before you," she said, hesitating, waiting for her thoughts to catch up. "Before you, we never stopped. Not once. Not for gas, anyway. I swear to God."

He didn't answer. He moved back to his place before Susan could see him, and smiled at the windshield. All his life on the open empty road he had never once believed he was anything special. Susan came along. He's still nothing special, although he understood he was doing pretty special things. But all those years and miles on the road, almost every time he was picked up, sooner or later he was dropped off at a gas station because the driver had to fill up, take the fuel to take him on and leave Stan behind.

Susan came along.

Never stopped for gas.

He nodded, humming.

Now that was something special.

She wasn't going to leave him behind.

"Hey," Lupé whispered.

He started, rubbed his eyes as if waking from a nap, saw Susan leave the bar.

Oh boy, he thought eagerly; oh boy, here we go.

She stood at the corner for a moment, looking at the car,

looking at the sky Stan knew was packed with clouds. She did not, not once, look across the street. Not even when she came around to the driver's side, opened the door, slid in, and grabbed the wheel.

He didn't ask when she closed the door, he didn't ask when she released the brake, he didn't ask when she let the car drift on its own, steering around the corner and past the bar, cutting across the street and pulling into the driveway of a small house, the first one past the back of a drugstore.

There was no garage.

The headlamps looked at nothing but trees behind the house, and maybe, though he wasn't sure, another house beyond them.

She cut the ignition and opened the door again.

"We're here, children," she said without looking at them. "Grab your stuff and come inside."

Shaking with anticipation, doing his best to hold his tongue, he snatched up his backpack and fairly leapt from the car, scuttling after her to the steps of a porch so narrow there was barely room for the old ladder-back chair that sat beside the door. He heard Lupé and the other one following more slowly, whispering excitedly to each other, probably asking the same questions that filled his own mind like the urgent rustle of a dry wind.

Susan unlocked the door and pushed it in, stepped back and made a soft noise.

Stan, right behind her, shuddered when he smelled the dead air, was perplexed when he smelled the blood.

She stepped up to the threshold, reached around the jamb and flicked a switch. Somewhere in the front room a lamp went on. She turned and looked down at them.

"We'll stay here tonight. The gentleman in the bar was kind enough to rent it to me. There's not a lot of room, but I think you'll be able to work things out and get the rest you need. If there's no food in the kitchen, Lupé, you'll have to go over to that grocery store and get some, there's money in your pocket. Stan, when you're ready, check the other houses on this street, tell me if anyone lives there. Little one, you stay with me, don't go wandering off. We're in the middle of the woods. It could be dangerous out there.''

Stan grinned, grinned more broadly when he heard Lupé's quick laugh.

Susan smiled with them. ''Nevertheless,'' she cautioned. ''Nevertheless.''

She stepped aside, and let them in.

Stan waited for the others—he was still a gentleman after all—and bounded into the room, smiling, looking, stopping with a silent grunt when he saw the man in the kitchen doorway, wearing nothing but a bath towel darkly stained and sagging.

''Who the hell are you?'' Lupé demanded.

Susan held up a hand. ''It's all right, Lupé. I want you all to meet Diño Escobar. Señor Escobar is a special man.'' She smiled. ''He's going to help us practice.''

It took less than fifteen minutes for Stan to check the other houses. They were empty, closed up, reeking of dry heat, reminding him of the husks of dead insects he had seen curled by the roadside. When he returned to their house, he walked around the outside twice, made his way through a weedy jungle to the end of the backyard and went halfway through the stand of twisted maple before he was satisfied the house back there was empty as well.

He didn't think about this Escobar.

The man was there, Susan obviously knew him, there was nothing he could do about it, no sense complaining.

Lupé was on the porch when he returned, smoking furiously, pacing loudly.

''Son of a bitch,'' she said when she saw him. ''You believe that? What the hell is so special about him?''

Stan shrugged.

''Son of a bitch, Stan, this is our party, right? I mean, what the hell do we have to practice for? It looks to me like we're already pretty good.''

He shrugged again, not liking her this way. She was hard, tight, waiting for someone to light the fuse.

Angrily she flicked the cigarette into the street. "Son of a bitch." Angrily she slipped the knife from her boot, stabbed the railing, slipped the knife back. "Son of a bitch."

"There's a reason," he said at last, with a twitch of a smile. "You know there's a reason. You know Susan."

"Oh, yeah, sure I do." But she stopped herself before she lit another cigarette. Inhaled deeply, closed her eyes, and blew her breath at the roof in an explosive gust. "You're right, *mi amigo*. You're right." She took his arm. "So what do you say we go in and see what's so special about this Señor Escobar. Then, if you can believe it, I have to go shopping."

An hour later Stan knew what it was that made this man special.

Escobar lay on his back on the kitchen table, the filthy towel draped modestly over his midsection. He hadn't said a word. He only stared at the ceiling and giggled hoarsely, once in a while laughing with teeth bared like a wolf, all the while never moving a muscle.

Lupé had used her knife; the little one, teeth and nails.

Stan had only watched, dumbfounded, because the giggling man could not die.

"Oh, yes, he can," Susan said, startling him. "And he will, Stan, he will. But only when I let him." She gestured toward the bathroom. "The mop, please, Stan. I don't want you slipping in the blood."

Later, much later, after Lupé had returned with two bags filled with groceries and the most amazing stories about the woman who ran the store, he sat on the porch railing with her, smoking one of her cigarettes, listening to the night wind sneak out of the starless sky.

There was no sense of time, although he suspected it was close to midnight; there was no sense of movement other than

the wind, although he suspected the townspeople had already
checked them out, one way or another.

"Practice," Lupé whispered in disgust. "What was that all
about? Nothing we haven't already done."

He could feel the weight of the clouds, but he couldn't smell
the rain. Other nights, other days, he could smell the coming
rain, like an extra scent in a garden. He shook his head slowly,
massaged his right shoulder. It was up there, the rain, but he
just couldn't smell it.

"I don't get it," she said around a jaw-popping yawn.

The radio played inside. Music, weather, news of the outside world falling apart. A man talking with a woman about
the storm that didn't seem to want to let loose its water, talking
about heat wave records and brushfires and forest fires and
making jokes about people going half-naked in the streets.
More music, more weather, more news about the world falling
apart.

Suddenly Stan straightened and stared at Lupé.

"What?" she asked sleepily.

"This is the end."

"What?"

"This." He waved the cigarette at the street, at the darkened
bar, at the greylit main street. "The road. I come to a place,
it don't matter how or why I got there, I always knew, for that
day anyway, it was the end of the road. Even if I got there
first thing in the morning." He gestured again. "This is it."

"You mean we're not leaving?"

He shrugged. "All I know is what I know."

He heard the front door open, didn't hear Susan but felt her
as she came up behind them.

"I'm right, huh?" he said.

"Yes," Susan said.

"That man you talked about. Not the one inside, the other
one." He felt a bubble in his chest, at once chilled and warm.
"He's here, huh?"

"Yes," Susan said.

"We're going to do what we do, right? Do what we do?"
He paused, checked the sky he couldn't see, watched the cig-

arette he had tossed into the street explode into sparks that didn't make a sound. "We're doing, then we're going."

"Yes," Susan said.

"But . . . but we're not going with you."

A hand on his shoulder, a gentle shake, a finger trailing across the back of his hair.

"Yes," Susan said.

And she was gone.

He couldn't speak, didn't want to speak, didn't want to move, didn't want to sleep, didn't want to respond when Lupé touched his arm.

"You know a lot," she said.

He swallowed. "I been on the road a long time."

"Well, I know something you don't know."

He couldn't look, didn't want to look, didn't want to turn his head to see her profile, see the one eye that watched him, see the way her cheek was sucked in, making her face look like a skull.

"What?" he asked, but only because he already knew, had already heard it in that one simple word.

Yes.

Lupé slid off the railing and waited for him to join her. She opened the door and stepped in, turned suddenly and kissed his cheek.

"She's afraid, *amigo.* She's afraid."

Part 5

SYMPHONY

1

1

The day was made for monsters.

Dawn was nothing more than a shift from black to light.

On the radio, talk about the appearance of the clouds, how fronts and isobars and pressure systems denied them. But they were there nonetheless, streaked with black and grey, bulging downward, pressing downward, arcs and tails and veils dangling from the mass of them, while old-timers nodded and agreed that someone was getting rain today.

Somewhere out there.

Out there, but not here.

A breeze the breath of a dry oven, curling leaves on twigs while leaves quivered on the ground, shifting dust on Black Oak Road in and out of the gutters, avoiding the surface of the Balanovs' pool, coasting across the river without the trace of a ripple, ruffling the feathers of two crows in the meadow while they walked like old men through the trembling weeds, searching for food, eyeing each other.

In the Palmers' stable, horses kicked and snorted in their stalls. A mare with her ears back. A gelding who wouldn't stop staring at the door. In the corral a young stallion gnawed at the rawhide that held the gate shut.

The temperature rose.

The clouds hovered, and baked the air.

No sound at all.

2

Lupé lay on her bed, hands behind her head, staring at the ceiling while Stan, in the bed beside her, snored comfortably. Escobar had been given the front-room couch. She didn't know where the little one was, and she hadn't seen Susan since daybreak.

She yawned, and shivered, a goose walking over her grave, and for the first time in memory, since her mother had died, she crossed herself without thinking, glanced toward the kitchen and mouthed, *I'm sorry.*

Although she hadn't noticed any units in any windows last night, the gentle breeze of an air conditioner kept a sheet over her, made her drowsy the way she used to be, when times were good and getting up in the morning was a pleasant chore, not a sacrifice.

The shades were down.

Not much light out there, she thought as she checked her watch, surprised at the hour coming up on noon. Rolling over gave her a way to pull aside the shade beside the bed, and what she saw, all that grey, reminded her of November.

She lay flat again and scratched her head, massaged her face, sat up and held the sheet against her breasts. "Stan."

He snorted.

"Stan."

He woke up slowly, stretching, making her smile at the way he got used to sleeping on a mattress, decent food, something to do. For him, this must be close to heaven.

When he saw her, he turned away. "Sorry."

She grinned. "What for?"

"You're . . . not dressed."

She shrugged one bare shoulder. "Come on, Stan, you never saw a woman before?"

He didn't answer right away. When he did, it was, "Not you."

For some reason that made her unimaginably sad. She smiled anyway. "I'll tell you, *gringo*, it ain't much to look at, believe me."

He looked back, head still on his pillow. "He hurt you real bad, didn't he."

A nod, nothing more.

His hair like wire, his face sagging with sleep, he scowled and said, "The stupid son of a bitch."

The connecting door to the bathroom was open, and movement in the kitchen distracted her, made her realize how hungry she was. Not bothering with false modesty, she leaned over, scooped up her clothes and said, "I think we're getting food. And I get the first shower."

He watched her cross the room.

She felt the gaze, and couldn't help it. As she closed the door she looked over her shoulder and winked at him. "You and me, *amigo*," she said. "When this is over, you and me are going to party."

When this is over.

The water was hot and smooth.

When this is over.

The towel was fresh and soft.

She looked in the mirror as she brushed her hair.

Lupé, she told herself, this ain't never going to be over.

3

They sat at the kitchen table, Lupé and Stan facing the counter, Escobar facing them, the little one at the head, while Susan fried and mixed and poured and squeezed.

Lupé ate as if she hadn't eaten in a week, joking with Stan, teasing the little one, but not looking at the man who sat opposite her. He gave her the creeps.

He had dressed in a suit, but it was stained with blood and grass, with bits of grass and leaves clinging to the lapels and to his trousers. One sleeve was torn at the shoulder. His shirt was white and dark red. Scorch marks. The clear stench of gasoline and smoke.

She reminded him of one of those zombie things she had seen in a movie one time, lurching across a field, sagging jaw and dead eyes.

Escobar's eyes weren't dead, they were bright.

Susan fed them and answered no questions.

Escobar didn't say a word.

Lupé felt a giggle and suppressed it. Instead: "Stan and I are going to elope when we're done here."

Stan choked a piece of bread into his palm and his face turned red, the little one laughed, Escobar stared at his plate and kept on eating.

"If you wish," Susan said calmly, pouring them each a cup of coffee.

Lupé watched the steam rise. "We *are* getting out of here, aren't we? Like the other times, I mean. They can't stop us, right?"

Escobar ate.

Susan poured a glass of milk, placed it on the table, and moved to the back door, rubbing her upper arms as if to drive away a chill. Faded curtains hid the view, as did the curtains drawn across the window over the sink. When she finally turned around, Lupé didn't feel like eating anymore.

Neither did anyone else.

But it was Stan who said, "Who are you?"

4

Susan wore blue jeans and a denim shirt; her feet were bare, her hair brushed carelessly back over her ears.

After today, she said, it won't matter who I am, you can do what you like.

Stan, the road is yours again, to go wherever you want for as long as you want it.

Lupé, you can go back to your mountains and your desert, there won't be anyone left there to hurt you.

Diño, you will have everything you want.

Little one, only the little one, will come with me when it's over.

I'm telling you this because, no, Lupé, this won't be at all like the other times. This place, this insignificant little hole in the wall, is different. Smaller, but that's not it. Fewer people, but that's not it.

Every End has a Beginning; it all has to start somewhere, and it might as well be, it will be, here.

This is the place where Time stops and waits, where I stop and wait to see if I, and Time, will ever move again.

I am not alone.

But I am, this time, and don't look so miserable, it has nothing to do with you. You should see yourselves, you look like children whose party has just been canceled.

Poor things.

When you're finished here, every scrap gone from your plates, I want you all to go out there, walk around, see the place, know it, find the dens and the lairs and the holes and the traps. When they speak to you, speak back and say nothing. Or say it all, it doesn't matter, because they won't understand then any more than you do now.

But do not speak to the man, not even if he speaks to you first.

You'll know who he is.

Stay away; he's mine.

Talk, look, but do absolutely nothing.

Do you understand?

Nothing.

Don't make me angry.

*   *   *

I will let you know when to bring the fire down.

I will let you know when to start the games.

Don't worry about a signal, that's for people like them, not people like you.

No matter where you are, you'll know it's time.

All you have to do is listen.

2

1

Casey woke up with one hand clenching his throat, as if he could throttle the cry the hand twisted into a whimper.

There may have been light, he didn't know, his eyes were closed; there may still be clouds, he didn't know, he wouldn't open his eyes.

If he did, he would see.

If he did, he would know.

the fiddler's on horseback

Lord, he prayed; I told You before, You've got the wrong man.

Points of light, pricks of pain, the sound of the blood pounding in his ears was the sound of hoofbeats racing down Black Oak Road.

Lord, no.

and he's riding this way

A fan on the dresser blew ice across his bare chest, swiveled away and there was fire on his skin until the ice wind blew again.

Points of light, pricks of pain, and a girl-child behind a

counter shrieking as he towered over her, fury in his eyes, murder in his fist.

And hate.

Hate for the warmth she worked in, in the winter; hate for the money in her purse beneath the counter; hate for the meal she had had at dinner.

Hate for those who had lost faith and refused to search it out again, blaming the God they didn't believe in for the God they didn't have; hate for the bishops bejeweled and berobed who wrote checks for the poor while the chauffeur waited patiently in the limo in the street; hate for the man he saw in a dusty mirror, whose so-called down-home, homespun, easy way with God was only a shield to protect him from making up his mind just how far his fear went. How deep. How strong.

He kept his eyes closed. A child's game. If you can't see them, then they can't see you.

But he could hear them.

The fiddle and the harmonica and the guitar and the banjo, the soft horns and gentle woodwinds, the distant drums, the distant bells.

Symphony for the End.

No, he thought.

No.

2

Mabel Jonsen sat at her makeshift desk behind the counter. Crumpled papers piled in drifts on the floor around her; had been flung across the counter into the aisles; were stacked to overflowing in the Claridge Casino wastebasket beside her. On the desk were photo albums thick with newspaper clippings, so fiercely opened that some of the bindings had buckled and some had torn. The only light was the fake brass gooseneck lamp she had nailed to the wall years before.

On a narrow shelf beneath the lamp was her collection of fat plastic cups, from every casino on the Atlantic City board-walk, every one once filled with quarters, dimes, and nickels, every one commemorating a major winning streak. Now they held sharpened pencils, ballpoint pens, pencils with fancy erasers, receipts, casino chips, scraps of paper she hadn't looked at in ages.

She grabbed another pencil from its cup, tried to write on a fresh sheet of notebook paper, but the point snapped, the lead bouncing off the wall and onto the floor.

The paper tore.

Mabel wept—anger, with a large dose of frustration.

She tried again.

She would keep on trying until she got it right.

It had already taken her most of the night; she had barely had three hours of sleep before she started again, keeping the store closed, ignoring those who banged on the door.

She didn't care.

They laughed at her.

She knew that, and until last night, it hadn't really been a bother. A kind of dumpy, middle-aged woman living in a place not big enough for any map, looking for those who would visit her from the stars. Correspondence she had received from all over the world told her she wasn't alone; laughter was something you got used to, that's all. The kidding, the teasing, the not-quite-condescending pat on the shoulder. It hadn't mattered, not really.

Until last night.

Until the stranger, a woman, had come in and began piling food on the counter. Canned stuff, mostly, some bread, milk, a little bit of junk food, two boxes of cookies. A lean woman, not unattractive, who said very little; dark-skinned, Spanish accent, but definitely not from anywhere near here. A few words exchanged, and Mabel learned she had rented the place behind Vinia's drugstore, her and her friends.

Nothing so odd about that, although the timing was weird, and Mabel had packed the groceries in two bags, rang up the charges, and nearly gasped aloud when the woman dropped a handful of new bills on the counter and said, "Is this enough?"

Like she didn't know how much she had.

Like she didn't fully understand the currency system.

Mabel had counted it, nodded, reached into the register for the woman's change, but the woman had said, "Keep it, I don't need it," and left without another word.

Mabel didn't know whether to laugh, to sing, to cry, or to chase after her.

Instead she had stood there, dumbfounded, blinking so rapidly she had nearly gotten a headache. Then she had gathered the woman's money carefully and stuffed it into an envelope, sealed it, and set it on the shelf below the counter, all the while cursing for not having recognized the signs before—the bell, the wind, the clouds, the sudden stillness, the early dark.

They were here.

Dear Lord, They were here.

Not long afterward, Moss had come in, stood swaying on the threshold as if battling a high wind.

"They're here," Mabel had told him excitedly, her voice high as a girl's.

He had belched, staggered to one side and grabbed the jamb for support. "Who cares? I'm not building those damn lights, Mabe. It's stupid, a waste of time, and it's still too damn hot. You're crazy." He laughed and backed out to the sidewalk. "Stupid!" he yelled, and tacked across the street against the force of his giggles.

She had wanted to run after him, shake him, bring him to his knees and make him understand; what she had done instead was close and lock the door, turn the *Closed* sign around, and run to her desk, where she began the first draft of her welcoming speech.

It was awful. They were all awful. All of them echoing Moss Tully's drunken laughter.

Sleep, then, restless and clammy and tangling the sheets around her ankles. Waking with a cry, hastening to dress, making toast and coffee and finally back to the store.

To try again.

Fail again.

And she couldn't stop the tears no matter how hard she tried.

At last, hunched with defeat, she fumbled her reading glasses off her nose and onto the desk, rubbed her eyes, and kicked to her feet. A glance at the doorway that would take her to the stairs that would take her home and the rest of needed sleep, and she switched off the lamp and went outside.

The clouds didn't excite her.

The dry breeze sapped her and made her stride short.

Walking east toward the Crest. Head down. Tears dripping from her chin to the pavement. Forcing herself not to sob. Letting the weight of the clouds press on her shoulders as if it were the punishment due her. For thinking they would believe. For thinking she was special enough to greet Them on her own.

"Oh . . . yes!" a hoarse voice tried to cry.

She was abreast of Trinity Church, saw Enid Balanov at the foot of the walk, and stopped, using a sleeve to dry her face.

"Mabel."

The woman wore a summer-blue dress, pearls at her throat, white dress shoes. Sunday best. Except, Mabel thought, she looked as if she had been run over by a truck. Her eyes were bright, but ringed with black; her hair was tangled as if combed with claws; her legs had no strength, she had to lean against the picket fence. Her clothes looked as though she had slept in them all night, or hadn't changed them for days.

In her left hand she held a Bible.

"Mabel, it's coming."

Mabel winced. Enid's voice was painful to listen to, half rasp, half beseeching.

"Mabel, please."

Mabel wiped her face again and walked over, shaking her head. "Enid, you want me to get Petyr for you?"

Enid smiled; lipstick stained her teeth. "He's gone, dear. He came back late last night, left early this morning." Her eyes searched the shifting keel of the clouds. "To prepare, he told me. *He* knows." She looked at Mabel. "You know, and you won't believe."

Mabel looked around for someone to help her, but the street was deserted.

A dust devil danced down by the bar.

"Believe what?" she asked calmly.

"The Light," Enid said breathlessly. "The Coming." She giggled. "The End."

Mabel stepped back. "Enid, you need to rest, honey." She gestured toward the Crest. "I bet you haven't eaten for hours."

Enid lowered her voice. "I heard them, you know."

Mabel held her breath.

Enid smiled again as she pointed the Bible at the sky. "They rode out of the storm." Her voice lower still. "They rode all night"—the voice rose to a sudden screech—"and I can't get the damn church open to pray!" Whispering: "Locked, the doors are locked."

Mabel decided it was time to get some help, drag Petyr down here to take his wife home. She sidestepped slowly. "Can't be," she said, hoping to sound reasonable. "Casey always opens the doors first thing in the morning."

"Locked." Enid glared. "Locked."

Mabel said, "Wait here, honey, I'll see what I can do," and hurried off as fast she could without running, a slow-growing anger tightening her chest.

Enid watched her. "Locked!" she called, and looked over her shoulder at the steeple, hitched a sigh, and pressed the Bible hard to her chest. "It's locked, and they're here."

She swayed and grabbed the fence with her free hand. She couldn't see very well, her vision had become foggy, and she wondered where that crazy woman had gone. Probably to find her flying saucer friends. She giggled. She closed her eyes. She tasted bile and felt acid in her stomach and listened to the soundless breeze as it gently scoured her cheeks.

She decided to get Reverend Chisholm herself. He would understand. He read the Bible. He knew. He *knew*.

She headed toward the river. Small steps to keep from falling. Praying softly. Not for her, but for her children, that they would be spared, that they would be, when it was over, in the hands of their Lord.

Moving slowly. Very slowly.

Telling herself she wasn't scared, that she had been waiting for this time all her life, this escape to a better place, the end of the world not being the end of it all but the beginning of something that would keep her family safe.

"Hey, Mrs. Balanov, are you okay?"

She didn't stop. She looked left and saw that filthy man, that gas station man, sitting outside his filthy gas station office. Smoking a filthy cigarette. Wearing filthy clothes.

"Are you ready?" she asked, feeling the tears in her eyes.

Ozzie Gorn frowned. "What?" And cupped a hand around one ear.

It didn't matter. He wasn't. And she prayed for him as she moved on.

Moving slowly. Very slowly.

"Mrs. Balanov?" Ozzie called, concern in his tone.

She ignored him, prayed for him, stopped abruptly when a little man stood in her way, his clothes just a little too large for his frame, his large eyes smiling at her gently.

"Lady, are you all right?"

"I'm fine," she said primly. "I'm praying, that's all. And I have to find Reverend Chisholm." She fluttered a hand back toward the church. "It's locked."

He nodded. "Okay." He looked around, shrugged. "You need some help or something?"

She stared at him, a blur, and grew angry that this stranger should bother her now, angry that Reverend Chisholm hadn't opened the church in the very hour of its need.

She looked back at Ozzie, who opened his mouth to call again, and changed his mind when he saw the little man speak to Enid and turn her attention. One of those new people, he figured; so let him have to listen to the woman's ranting for a while, the hell with it.

He wondered, then, about Mabel, why she had been in such a hurry to get to the Crest. Not that he had expected her to stop and talk to him. She thought him about the lowest on the Maple Landing food chain, like just about everyone else. Pump the gas, fix the cars and trucks, get me to work, get me to the mall, but otherwise don't bother to try to fit in, good heavens, no. It had been that way since he had been eighteen, working the garage with his uncle, taking it over when his uncle had had one too many bottles and tried to swim the Delaware down to the sea.

He was three days without a shave, the stubble comforting when he passed a palm across it, watching Enid walk stiffly on, the stranger persistent at her side. To his left, at the edge of the station property were four automobiles waiting for his touch. Magic fingers, that's what he had. Ford, Mercedes, some Japanese thing, it didn't matter, he could fix it.

Until last night.

He had been in the pit, the lift had creaked, the bell had rung, and suddenly he had known he was going to die if he stayed down there much longer. It didn't matter that he knew the tracks the Jeep sat on were too wide and too long to descend into the pit; it didn't matter that he knew the lift could sink and he'd be trapped but someone would hear him shouting; it didn't matter. When it creaked a third time, and he realized it was going to slam down and trap him, he had stood there, trembling, unable to move.

He knew, he just knew, that if he tried to climb out, that thing would crush him, cut him in half, and he wouldn't die right away, it would take him all night.

He knew it, and he couldn't move, and the lift had shuddered and the Jeep had creaked and he figured he would rather die than have to sit there in the dark, smelling the gas and the grease and the sour sweat that had turned his face slick.

He couldn't move.

The lift shuddered, and lowered just a little, and that's all he needed—he had moaned and grabbed the lip and hauled himself out lengthwise, rolled onto his back and watched as the Jeep lowered itself slowly. Slowly. Creaking and shuddering until the pit was covered.

Coffin lid; that's all he could think of.

Coffin lid.

So he had dragged a chair from the office just as grimy as he was, brought it outside, sat, tilted it until the back rested against the dirt-smeared stucco wall, and chain-smoked, and listened, until his hands had stopped shaking.

He waited for the sun to rise.

He waited for someone to come out into the street.

He looked up and waited for the damn rain to start.

He wondered about the woman he had seen leaving the grocery the night before, figured she was probably with the guy walking now with Enid. Another frown. Enid may be a little tough in the religion department, but she had always been gentle with him. Unlike her prick husband. Maybe he should do something before she got in trouble.

What the hell, he didn't have anything else to do right now. He sure as hell wasn't going back in there, in the bay where the Jeep sat, waiting for his magic fingers.

He tipped the chair forward and stood, put his hands in his jeans pockets, and headed down toward the Moonglow. Just as he reached the clinic, Bobby Karnagan walked out, all snug jeans and T-shirt, hair glowing even in the clouds' greylight.

"Hi." He didn't bother to disguise his admiration, or his lust.

Her face was slightly puffy, her eyes fresh from crying. She glared and stepped around him. "Go away," she muttered.

He almost grabbed her arm, caught himself, and turned around. "The hell with you," he said. "Hell, the hell with them all, they hadn't even asked him to help search for the guy who'd run away from the crash.

"The hell with you!" he shouted.

Bobby didn't turn around, just held up one hand and slowly lifted her middle finger.

"Oh, nice," Ozzie said, sneering. "Real nice."

She ignored him, forgot him as soon as she had crossed the street, walking past the bar to the drugstore entrance. It was too soon to go to Todd, to tell him what Doc Farber had just told her. It wasn't his feelings she was concerned about now; first she had to figure out what she was going to do. Vinia would give her something for her queasy stomach. After that . . .

She swallowed, checked the clouds, and couldn't bring herself to open the door.

Vinia would know.

As soon as Bobby opened her mouth, Vinia would know. The woman was strange like that, like she could read people's minds. You'd walk into the store, she'd look up from the rear counter where she kept the drugs and prescription records, and before you were halfway back there, she already knew what you needed.

Maybe Reverend Chisholm, but she had already tried the church once, and she didn't think she had the nerve to do it again. Not now, now that she knew.

Tears burned; she lashed them away with her fingers.

Helen.

She turned around.

Helen would know what to do. Helen always knew the right thing to do. She lifted her chin, straightened her shoulders. Ever since they were kids, Helen had known what to say to keep them out of serious trouble.

She laughed silently, bitterly.

Okay, so it was too late for that, but it wasn't too late to figure out the next step. The right next step.

But Helen had to swear not to tell Tessa. That jealous bitch would ruin everything if she found out too soon.

Heat spread across her forehead as she passed the Moonglow without glancing in.

Tessa. Slutting around Todd as if she had a claim, when she knew damn well Bobby's claim had been staked first. She didn't blame Todd, he just needed a little work, that's all, a little smoothing of his bachelor edges.

Another laugh, this one aloud.

Well, if this doesn't smooth them, it'll kill him, that's for sure.

She stood in front of the little house. Hers, Helen's, Tessa's. It was empty. She could tell. Something about it told her there was no help in there, no place to hide, no one to talk to.

Her fingers attacked the tears again, but they wouldn't go away.

She sobbed, and didn't move when a voice said behind her, "I don't want to butt in, Bobby, but I think I can help you."

"I doubt it."

"I don't."

She turned then, rubbing her eyes, blinking, trying not to cry and failing so badly it made her chest hurt.

"It's okay, Bobby, it's okay." A hand caressed her arm. "Let's find someplace cool and quiet to talk, all right? Before you know it, we'll have it all worked out, no problem."

Bobby let the hand grip her arm lightly, let it pull her along the street.

"By the way, Bobby, let's not be strangers, okay? You can call me Lupé."

3

1

Casey stood in the useless shade of the porch and watched as Helen scowled for a second at the busted gate before coming through.

"Afternoon," he said, tucking his hands loosely into his pockets, leaning a shoulder against the post.

She stopped halfway up the walk and shook her head at him. "What," she said, nodding to his clothes, "do you call that?"

He wore a blue-striped white shirt, white chinos, sneakers and white socks. Spreading his arms, he said, "You ever hear of Sunday-go-to-meeting clothes?"

She nodded warily.

"Well, these are my Saturday-go-to-hell clothes." He brushed at his shirt. "A little wrinkled, but not too bad, wouldn't you say? Found them in my trunk."

She only said, "I missed you at breakfast. Todd was going to make your favorite."

An apologetic nod toward his door. "I decided to eat in,

keep my hand in on the skillet and such." He laughed. "Todd has nothing to worry about, believe me."

"Come down here."

"What?"

She pointed at the walk in front of her. "Come here, Casey. It's like talking to a statue with you so big up there."

He took the steps at a leap, landed lightly, paid no attention to the puzzled look on her face. "I was thinking," he said, rubbing his hands together, "maybe you'd like to go to the mall with me, huh? It's been forever since I've been, and since I don't have anything special planned for today, I'd like to get some new—"

"Casey." She grabbed his arm and squeezed it. "Casey, what's going on?"

He patted her hand. "Not a thing, darlin'. Not a thing."

But he refused to meet her skeptical look, choosing instead to make a show of checking the clouds and shaking his head at the perversity of all that rain up there and not a drop down here. Although the sky had darkened over the past hour, the light was still bright enough to make him squint as he took her unprotesting hand and led her to the road.

"It's nearly two, I'm starving, let's get some lunch."

"Casey," she said quietly, "you look silly."

"Only because you're not used to it."

"Neither are you."

Maybe, he thought grimly, but he would be if it killed him. They walked on, taking the easy slope slowly.

"Are you going to drop in on the new people?"

"What new people?" It was a moment before he remembered the car. "Oh. Are they vacationers? Surely not fishermen."

She shrugged. "I don't know. Nobody does." She tugged his hand playfully. "That's what we depend on you for. To snoop around a little."

"Well, I don't think so."

Her fingers tightened around his. "Why not? You always do."

"Not this time."

She stopped then and yanked until they faced each other. "Casey, what the hell is going on? Yesterday you're talking about the end of the world, and now this stuff. What's the matter with you?"

He looked up and down the road. "Helen, this isn't the time or the place."

"For what, Casey?" She moved closer, still gripping his hand. "For what?"

"On an empty stomach like mine," he answered with a grin, "anything."

She scowled.

"Listen," he said, moving them both on, "I had a lousy night, all right? Not much sleep, too much heat, and breakfast was a dud. The weather sucks, and I can't think straight, much less try to answer your questions."

When they reached the flat, it was his turn to stop, and he wiped the palm of his free hand on his hip.

The feeling was so strong, it made his jaw tighten—*they've all gone, nobody's left but Helen and me.*

In spite of the breeze, absolutely nothing moved on the deserted road.

Not even Beagle was in his place on Tully's bench.

A ghost town.

He looked at the steeple, and his fingers twitched around invisible keys, reminding him that he hadn't opened the church yet today. For the first time in years, he hadn't unlocked the doors.

Oh, Lord, he thought, and hid the shudder of a chill that worked on his spine.

From a great distance: "Casey."

He felt pressure on his arm, a pulling.

"Casey, you need to sit down."

He didn't resist until he realized she wanted them in the Moonglow. He shook his head and nodded at the hardware store, at the bench. He ducked under the awning's fringe and sat with his legs out, his right hand on his thigh; Helen kept her grip on the left.

"You're still sick, aren't you."

He didn't answer.

The back of her fingers against his cheek, a palm against his brow and drawn back in haste. "My God, Case, you're hot and cold at the same time."

What he wanted to say was: *you want to know what's going on, you want to know if I know what's happening, and I think I do, Helen, I think I do, and I don't want to do it, I can't do it, and I'm not going to do it because it's wrong, it's all wrong, I'm not the one.*

What he did say was, "Just a little setback, nothing to worry about."

"Then let's get you something to eat."

"I'm not hungry."

"You just said you were starving. At least get something to drink before you dehydrate."

What he wanted to say was: *I don't want to go in there and have them looking at me like that, thinking I'm something special because of what they think they saw, because of what they think is going on.*

What he did say was, "I'm all right. Just a little tired, that's all. I told you, I had a bad night."

She released his hand and slapped his leg, hard. "Damn, but you're stubborn."

"Pigheaded," he suggested.

"That, too." She stood and offered him a hand up. "Now get off your butt, Reverend, and let's go. I'm frying out here."

He almost did.

He almost took the hand.

"Casey." She was angry, said his name like his mother used to, low and firm, brooking no argument, demanding his obedience because it was her due. Singsong, rising at the end: "Casey."

He heard a sob and thought it was her, looked up and saw it wasn't, looked to his right and saw Enid Balanov stagger past the bar, one hand pawing the air as if hoping to find purchase to keep her from falling. He was on his feet before Helen could move, called Enid's name, and trotted down to the corner.

Enid turned and faced him blindly.

"Enid."

"Reverend Chisholm?"

"Enid, what's wrong?"

She reached for him with a hand smeared with dirt. Her lower lip quivered violently, but she couldn't say his name again before her knees gave way.

He caught her, cradled her easily in his arms and told Helen to get to a phone and call Petyr. Then he carried the moaning woman to the clinic, kicked the door, and pushed Farber aside when he answered.

"Jesus," Mel said, following Casey down a short hall into an examination room. "What—"

"I don't know. She was like this when I saw her, out there on the street."

Lying on the paper-sheeted table, moaning, pawing the air, holding her Bible so tightly to her chest neither man could pry it loose from her fingers.

"Heat prostration," Farber guessed. "Shock, maybe. You see anything?"

"No."

"She say anything?"

"No." He took her hand gently and forced it to stop, winced at the power of her grip when he just as gently forced her arm down at her side. When he released her, and she him, she didn't move except for the erratic rise and fall of her chest.

Tessa hurried into the room. "Helen told me. Holy Moses, what happened to her?"

Farber muttered something, and Casey backed slowly out into the waiting room as Tessa began the task of disrobing the woman while whispering her name, telling her she was all right, she'd be all right in a minute.

Then Enid screamed, "He locked the goddamn doors!"

2

Cora stood in the swimming pool, knees slightly bent, submerged to her shoulders. Sonya lay along the edge, idly paddling. Dimitri floated in a red inner tube, shading his eyes to see the clouds better.

The morning had been awful, and the afternoon hadn't been much better. Sonya had turned sullen, whining about everything from the lunch to the water; Dimitri hadn't said a word, although he had done what he was told.

Cora felt as though she were living in a bubble, her voice sounding muffled, her brain turned to cotton. She had to force herself to blink hard every once in a while just to clear her vision, and the water that was supposed to cool her off made her feel like she was sweating.

Reed wasn't home, Rina was working, Nate was God-only-knew-where.

"Oh," Sonya said, surprised, and sat up.

Cora turned, and held her breath.

Her father walked around the side of the house, still in his stupid manhunting fatigues, a rifle slung by its strap over his shoulder. Beneath the water, her hand clutched near her stomach.

With him was a little girl not much older than Sonya.

"Found her wandering around," he said, staring at Cora as if it were her fault. "You know who she is?"

Dimitri had managed to kick the tube around; Sonya had slipped quickly into the pool.

"No," Cora said flatly. "What are you doing here? You're not supposed to talk to me."

"I just told you." He gave the girl a shove. "I'm seeing a lawyer today," he said as he left. "You get your ass back to your own house."

Cora dog-paddled to the side and lifted herself up on her forearms.

The little girl had shining black hair with straight bangs that ended above large black eyes, dusky skin, heavy lips. She wore coveralls over a short-sleeved T-shirt, and red sneakers on her feet.

"Hi," she said with a white-tooth smile. "My name is Anita. What's yours?"

Cora was shocked when she heard Dimitri say, "Go away, we don't like you."

Before she could scold him, however, the girl said, "It's too late, Dimmy. Do you want to see me swim? I can sing, too. Just like a bird."

3

Casey leaned heavily against the clinic wall, head down, trying to understand what had happened to Enid, almost grateful when Petyr swept down from the Crest and braked hard at the curb in front of him. He entered the building without a word, without a look, returned what seemed a lifetime later, and said, "You did this."

Casey straightened. "No, sir, I just found her."

The man's eyes narrowed. "No, you did it. You did this thing. You made her this way, all this talk, all those things, all your . . ." He waved a hand in disgust. "You. No one else."

"Now look," Casey began, but Balanov shoved him, one hand to his chest.

"You made her crazy, Chisholm. You made her see things and hear things, and . . ." His face reddened, his jaw trembled. "And you did this, you sanctimonious son of a bitch." This time the shove was a punch to Casey's shoulder. "You!" Another punch, lips curled in loathing. "You!"

Casey grabbed the wrist before the fist reached him a third time, held it just hard enough to keep Balanov from taking it back. "Don't, Petyr," he said without raising his voice. "Enid doesn't need this now."

Balanov strained to free himself, a thick vein bulging across his forehead, cheeks sucked in.

"Petyr."

Spittle foamed at the corner of the man's mouth; he wouldn't give up, although he didn't use his other hand.

"Petyr."

"What's going on?" Helen demanded from the sidewalk.

"Petyr's understandably concerned about his wife," Casey told her without looking away. "He's worried, and it looks like I'm a pretty good target to get it all out."

Petyr's expression softened, but just a little, as he relaxed his arm and Casey released it.

"Petyr," Helen said, false smile, false concern.

"Oh, shut up, you whore," he snapped, and stormed inside, slamming the door behind him.

"Well," she said with mock indignation, "I guess he sure told me."

"He's upset, as he should be." A sigh, a shake of his head, and he touched the shoulder where Balanov had struck him. "Man packs a punch."

"You're kidding. You didn't even flinch."

"Righteous armor," he said wryly. "Now, let's eat, if you don't mind. There's nothing more we can do—"

The shot interrupted him, and made Helen rush up the walk to hold his arm.

It was William Bowes, marching with a pronounced limp down from the Crest, slinging his rifle back over his arm. His fatigues were sweat-stained, his face pale, the cap he wore shoved to the back of his head.

"Chisholm!"

"Helen, maybe you'd better go inside."

"I want my daughter back!"

Casey stepped away from the building, intending to meet the man at the curb, but Bowes made to grab his weapon again, and Casey froze, hands out.

"Mr. Bowes—"

Bowes stopped in the middle of the street, legs apart, thumb hooked in the rifle's sling. "Chisholm, I am not going to argue with you. I don't care what you heard, what that bitch told you, if she isn't back in my house before sunset, I'm calling my lawyer, the police, and then I'm coming to see you."

Casey did his best not to smile. The man wasn't quite drunk yet, and he was clearly eager for any excuse to throw a punch or pull a trigger, but Casey couldn't help being reminded of a man with more liquor than sense trying to call the local gunfighter out.

"You hear me, boy?"

"Casey," Helen warned behind him. "Casey, easy."

He realized then that his right hand had become a fist, and he swallowed hard as he opened his fingers and flexed them until the tension was lost.

"Mr. Bowes," he said carefully, "you do what you have to do, that's your right."

"Goddamn right."

"But if you want Cora back, you're going to have to get that lawyer and the police. I'm not going to help you."

The rifle came off the shoulder.

"Casey," Helen stage-whispered.

Bowes pointed it at the ground, thinking hard, looking first to the clinic, then back at Casey.

"If you want her back," Casey said, "you won't do it."

A second passed before Bowes said, "Don't bet on it," and march-limped away.

Casey didn't move until the man was gone, then let his shoulders sag abruptly, just as the door snapped open and Mel in his clinical whites poked his head out and looked around. "Oh, good, you're still here." He jerked a thumb. "You'd better come inside."

"Not now, Mel," Casey protested. "And Petyr—"

Farber jerked his thumb again, angrily. "Casey, get in here."

Casey exchanged puzzled frowns with Helen, and hurried in, past Tessa, who sat with Petyr on one of the waiting room's two dark leather couches.

"Moonlighting?" she asked with an impudent grin.

"Huh?"

"Good Humor man," she explained. "You're moonlighting, right?"

Again Mel forestalled a response, pushing him urgently into the examination room. Enid still lay on the table, breathing calmly, it appeared, her eyes closed, her hands folded over the Bible resting on her stomach.

"Enid," Mel said softly. "Enid, Reverend Chisholm is here."

Her eyelids fluttered open, but it took a few seconds for her to focus on Casey, standing at the foot.

"Exhaustion mostly," Mel said to his unspoken question. "And the heat. And . . ." He rested a hand on Enid's shoulder. "Enid, you promised me you wouldn't get excited if I let you do this, right?"

She nodded.

"How are you, Enid?" Casey asked, smiling.

"An angel," she answered with a tremulous smile. "You look like an angel."

"Not likely." He ducked his head as if blushing. "Too many black marks, you know what I mean?"

Her eyes closed slowly.

"On a horse," she said. "I saw her on a horse."

A nice man, young but not well-dressed, had volunteered to take me to see Reverend Chisholm after that awful Gorn had made lewd remarks to me. I didn't know him, but I wasn't feeling too well, so I accepted, thinking people would see, people would help if I needed it.

But he didn't take me to Reverend Chisholm.

He took me up the street past where Arlo has his bar.

He took me to a house just behind Vinia's place, where a woman stood on a porch. A young woman, an old woman, I couldn't tell, my eyes were too fuzzy.

The young man, who told me his name was Stan, said to the woman, "Here's one, what do you think, is it time yet?"

I didn't know what was going on, but I couldn't get the man to let go of my arm. He didn't hurt me, but he wouldn't let go, he just stood there and I felt him shaking.

The woman was angry. She came down off the porch and yelled at the man without raising her voice. She called him "fool" and kept coming, kept calling him "fool," kept telling him to do what she told him and don't get into trouble.

He let go of my arm then, and I almost fell. I wanted Petyr

so badly, but he wasn't there, there was no one there, so I tried to move so those two wouldn't notice.

She was so angry, Reverend. She was so very, very angry.

I didn't stop, though, even though I was sure she would do something terrible if she saw me. I didn't stop.

And I saw her.

I saw her on a horse, a huge white horse, and I saw her reach down and slap this man on his face, and I saw blood, Reverend, I saw so much blood and I heard the man cry and I saw him fall and I saw the woman grab his hair and lift him to his feet and she hit him again, she called him ''fool'' and hit him again, and the next thing I knew . . . the next thing I knew . . .

Mel gripped her hand as it fumbled through the air, whispering, calming her.

Hysterical? Casey mouthed to him.

No.

She wasn't hurt?

Farber shook his head as he patted Enid's shoulder until her breathing settled. ''I gave her a sedative,'' he said quietly, leaving the woman to her sleep. ''Tessa, come in here and watch for a while, will you?''

The other room was empty except for Helen; Petyr had gone.

Mel dropped onto a couch, rubbed his face hard with the heels of his hands. ''Man, this has been a class-A crappy day.''

''Is she all right?'' Casey said.

''Yeah.'' His hands dropped to his lap. ''Exhaustion, like I said. I don't think she's had any sleep at all, and she's been working herself up ever since the other day. Since . . . you know.''

Casey nodded.

''You get emotional like that, on top of no rest which is on top of this weather, and . . .'' He gestured toward the doorway.

"Delusions, things get twisted." He sighed loudly. "Where the hell's her husband?"

Helen shook her head. "He said something about taking care of business."

"Swell. Enid needs him, and he's . . . ah, the hell with him."

"So the horse wasn't real?" Casey said.

Mel looked at him sharply. "No, of course not. You heard her. It was there and it was gone. The magic of a brain that wants to shut down for a while." His expression softened. "So what do you make of it, Case?"

Casey didn't get it. "What do you mean? You said she's suffering from exhaustion. What's to make of it?"

"Well, let's put it this way—the last time I saw Bobby, that woman, if it is the same woman Enid saw, was with her, and they were heading for that house, I think."

"Bobby?" Helen leaned forward anxiously. "What was she doing here?"

Farber looked at them both, pulled his lower lip between his teeth, and put a hand over his mouth, stared at the floor for a while.

Casey waited.

"Well, hell, you're going to find out sooner or later, just don't tell her I was the one," said Farber.

"One what?" Helen said.

"The one who told you she was pregnant."

4

"Oh, boy," Sonya cried. "Hey, Cora, it's raining! It's raining!" She scrambled from the pool and began to run around the yard. "Raining, Cora, raining!"

More a mist than rain, Cora thought from her place at the edge of the pool. But it sure felt good.

The first good thing to happen today.

The girl named Anita was next to the sandbox, and she

clapped her hands in delight, although her lips formed no smile.

Dimitri was on the redwood deck, where he had run when Bowes had left, paying no attention to her call to come back. His bathing suit still dripped on the floor. He was hugging himself, and Cora could see him shivering so violently he could barely stand up.

"Rain, rain, rain, it's raining!" Sonya sang as she ran.

Anita applauded.

Dimitri sank to the floor, still hugging himself, looked at Cora, and wept.

"Well, I'll be a son of a bitch," said Micah from his throne on the dock.

He grinned, tipped his cap to the sky, and reached for another beer. From inside the boathouse he heard Reed start to whistle, then laugh, then swear at a canoe that wouldn't fit into its slip.

No customers today, but who gave a damn? The drought looked to be on the way out, and the tourists would be back, his retirement would be saved, and maybe even the damn bees would start making honey again.

He toasted the blasted oak.

He toasted the mist.

He toasted Reed when the boy came onto the dock, but Reed only nodded absently and hurried to the dock's far end, dropped to his hands and knees and looked over.

"Micah, look."

Micah rolled his eyes. "I've seen fish before, boy."

"Micah, come here."

Making a loud noise that would do a martyr proud, he pushed off the piling and walked over. "What?"

"Look." Reed pointed.

So the water was a little oily, a little slick. So what? It wasn't unusual when the river was low. It—

He looked again.

"Holy shit."

It wasn't an oil slick; it was bees floating on the surface, their wings spread to catch the dim light, in numbers so great he couldn't see the bottom.

Nate couldn't stand it anymore.

He had left the house early that morning, hoping Kay would be back from wherever she'd gone. But when he found the shop still locked the way he'd left it the night before, he decided to try to find her. First he went around the corner to her house on Sycamore Road, but all the doors were locked, the shades were down, and no one answered his knock at either the front or back. On a hunch he continued on down the street to the Palmer stables; no luck there, either. In fact, both Sissy and Ed were too busy with nervous horses to do more than shake their heads when he asked about Kay. She still wasn't at the house when he returned, and the garage door was locked and the windows so dirty he couldn't see inside. By that time he began to feel guilty about deserting the shop, so he opened it, and sat behind the counter, pleased with himself because business became oddly brisk until shortly before three.

Then he saw the mist.

Not five minutes later Mabel Jonsen walked in and said, "You're a witness, Nathan Dane. I'm going to kill that bald bastard."

And she pulled a gun from beneath her shirt.

Arlo spun around three times on the end stool, moved to the next one and spun three, four at the next one, two at the next, and couldn't stand long enough to sit on the next, had to flatten his palms on the bar to keep from sliding off. He slid off anyway.

His laugh was a high cackle shot through with hiccups, and lasted until he was able to grab a stool and haul himself up. From there he flopped over the bar, hands dangling in the dry sink on the other side.

"Oh, God," he gasped, and hiccupped. "Oh, God, I think I'm going to sick."

"Then you can clean it up."

He cackled, squeezed his eyes shut, snapped them open and shoved himself onto a stool, grabbing the bar's surface when the seat began to revolve. "No sweat, man, no sweat."

Kay Pollard sat at a table farthest from the door, a shadow in the faint light, features obscured, only a pale smudge where her face was. "Is this some kind of ritual or something? You do this before you open up?"

Arlo took off his glasses and cleaned them with the tail of his Hawaiian shirt, put them back on, and reached behind his head to be sure his ponytail hadn't shaken loose. "No offense, movie lady," he said with a stupid grin, "but when the hell are you going home?"

"Never."

"Bad news, man, bad news."

"You don't know the half of it." The smudge vanished for a moment, and he heard the sound of her purse dropping onto the table. "So are you open yet?"

As much as his monumental hangover would permit him, he shook his head.

"Damn," she said. Then, in an eerie falsetto she asked, "Mackey, do you think I'm sexy?"

Tact kept him from laughing. Instead, he stared hard at the ceiling so he couldn't see her face, back there in the gloom.

"Arlo, I asked you a question."

"Damn," he said, and slipped off the stool, cleaned his glasses again, and looked up. "Well . . . damn."

"Damnit, Arlo!"

"Damnit yourself, movie lady," he snapped. "Some bastard's stolen my protection."

He heard her chair scrape across the floor, felt her at his side. "What do you mean?"

He pointed.

The peace sign on the ceiling was gone.

There was nothing left but a ragged circle where the plaster gleamed like new.

* * *

Todd Odam poked his head through the serving gap, scratched his head, and smiled. "Hey. Am I nuts or is that rain?"

Rina crawled into an empty booth, cupped her hands around her eyes to cut her reflection off the window, and grinned a *yes* over her shoulder.

"More like a mist or fog," declared Vinia Leary from the counter.

"Who cares?" he said. "It's better'n nothing."

Mrs. Racine lifted her cup of coffee and sipped. "It'll make the roads slick. Too dangerous to drive."

Who cares? he thought, and wondered if the new people were ever going to come out of that house. He had half a mind to wander over, just taking a stroll, and see what he could find out. It would certainly be better than waiting around here for someone to come in who had some decent news.

He scowled at his hands.

First he catches Bobby walking across the street with some woman, then sees Enid getting carried off by Casey toward the clinic. Normally he would have sent someone along to find out what was what, but the diner had been so busy, he'd barely had time to get the meals done, much less figure out who had done what to whom.

It was driving him nuts.

It was driving Rina nuts too, he could tell, and when she finished taking care of the customers in the booths, and only Vinia was left at the counter, he beckoned her with a finger, leaned over and said, "Haul ass to the clinic."

She didn't have to ask why; she dropped her towel on the shelf, dropped her order pad in his hand, and was gone before he would ask her to sneak up the block and see if she could find out where Bobby went.

"Drizzle," said Mrs. Racine, sipping.

"Better than a heavy rain," Vinia answered. "A heavy rain won't soak in, it'll just run off and take half the topsoil with it."

Down to the left, two families from the Crest, arguing over

which movie they were going to watch first, interrupted their debate with a clamor for service. Todd smiled stiffly and backed out of the gap, rolled his eyes for patience—and maybe, if it wasn't asking too much, Helen to show up—and pushed into the dining room just as Bobby slammed through the back door. He heard the racket, looked through the gap, and saw her pick up his guitar.

"Hey!" he shouted.

"You bastard!" she yelled, and smashed the guitar on the grill. Twice, before he could get to her, and once against his hip, knocking him to the floor.

"Bastard!" she screamed, flung the battered instrument against the wall, and was gone before he could get to his feet. He leaned heavily against the butcher block, panting, only vaguely aware of an ache in his side until he touched it and stared dumbly at his palm.

At the blood.

5

Casey stood with his back to the wall, chin tucked toward his chest. To his left he could see down the short hall to the examination room where Enid lay asleep. Tessa appeared in the open doorway, fussing then vanishing, reappearing to leave the room for one of the other of the three at the rear of the clinic. No more trouble there, he hoped, and didn't believe it for a minute.

He lifted his gaze to Mel, who sat on a couch opposite him, beneath a print of Paris in the autumn. The man looked much older than his years now, his lab jacket rumpled, black hair curling across his brow. The couch against the entrance wall was just as long, and Helen looked as if she wanted nothing more than to stretch out and close her eyes. Above her head was a long window, fogged with falling mist.

"You know," Mel said, his voice rumbling slightly, "it isn't your fault."

They both looked at him, and he laughed quickly. "Okay,

neither one of you, all right? Consciously or unconsciously, she blew it." He rubbed a finger against the inner corner of one eye, and lowered his voice. "I'm more concerned about Tessa, if you want to know the truth."

"Hell to pay," Helen agreed wearily. A sour smile at Casey. "You think I can sleep in your office tonight? Home is definitely not going to be any fun."

Casey didn't answer; he was still thinking about the horse Enid claimed she saw.

It was stupid, and he knew it. She was delusional, nothing more, but he couldn't get the image out of his mind.

Suddenly the door slammed open, making him jump aside, bringing the others to their feet as Todd stumbled in, a bloody towel folded and pressed to his temple, his apron streaked with fresh blood.

"Jesus," Mel said, and called, "Tessa! Tessa, get Two ready, we've got another one."

Casey had no time for questions, but as the two men turned the hall corner, he heard Tessa yell, "She hit you with *what*?"

"That's it," Casey said to Helen. "I'm gone, outta here."

"I'm with you," she said quickly, following him out the door. "I'd better get to work. Rina's probably having a break-down." She touched his elbow. "Come with me, okay? You still need something to eat."

He exaggerated a frown. "What, are you my momma or something?"

"Something," she said, bumped him with a hip, and whirled when they heard Nate call out.

Mabel Jonsen was on the sidewalk, stomping furiously off the Crest, Nate dancing hysterically behind her.

Casey saw the gun.

"Oh, Lord," Helen said.

"Out of my way!" Mabel yelled even though she was still half a block away. "Out of my way, I'm gonna shoot that bald bastard!"

Casey nudged Helen to one side and stood on the sidewalk, hands loose at his sides.

Mabel waved the gun and her free hand wildly, her hair

matted by the drizzle. She didn't pay any attention when Nate darted around her to cut across the lawn; still bouncing on his toes, desperate to do something and not knowing what to do.

"Mabel," said Casey sternly.

She stopped immediately, squinted, and startled them all by throwing up her hands and shrieking, "You're here! My Lord, you're here!"

The gun flew from her hand and landed at Nate's feet. He gaped at it, made to pick it up, changed his mind, and sat on it instead.

Mabel raced to Casey—"You're here, you're here!"—and embraced him tightly, making him grunt and nearly lose his balance.

"Mabel," he said to the top of her head. "Mabel, it's me."

Squinting she looked up, blinked the water from her eyes, and stared.

He smiled. "Just me, Mabel, just me."

"Oh." But she didn't let go. "Oh."

His grip became a hug, and he rubbed her back gently. "It's okay, Mabel, it's okay." He looked over at Helen and Nate. "I'm getting the message white isn't my color."

A flush spread across the woman's cheeks, and after a moment's muttering and sniffling, she nodded that she was all right. He held her a second longer, one more rub, a tender pat, and lowered his head, lowered his voice as their arms dropped away. "You want to go home? You want someone to go with you?"

She shook her head, too embarrassed to speak.

"How about a cup of coffee?"

She tried to smooth her shirt, fix her hair, and gave him a sheepish smile. "Sure. Sure, okay." But her face changed as she walked around him. "I'm still gonna shoot him, though, that sorry son of a bitch."

At his nod, Helen caught up with her, her head cocked as she listened to whatever had set the woman off. When they reached the corner, Casey walked over to Nate, gave him a hand up, and picked up the gun.

"Is it loaded?"

"I don't know, son, I don't know."

"You could shoot it to see."

"Nate." He lifted an eyebrow. "You've done just fine, and I thank you for the warning, but aren't you supposed to be at the Pavilion or somewhere?"

Nate scuffed one toe on the grass. "I guess. Yeah."

Casey laughed, grabbed the side of the boy's head and gave him a gentle shove. "Then go to it, boy, go to it. I'll make sure they know you're the hero again."

Nate grinned self-consciously and trotted off without looking back.

Casey watched until he reached the slope, then looked up the street and over. The steeple seemed much taller, much brighter in the mist, and he started toward it, hunching his shoulder briefly as he recalled Enid's bitter accusation, heard the despair, felt the guilt. It wasn't until he was halfway up the walk that he remembered the keys were back on the bedroom dresser.

He closed his eyes and shook his head.

Idiot.

He turned and saw the couple in the street, staring at him. No; watching him.

6

Stan couldn't see the man very well. Water kept getting into his eyes. But the guy was big, no question about it, all that white kind of smearing, like he was standing behind a curtain or something.

"Is that him?" he asked, refusing to believe this was the one that was supposed to give them a problem. He was big, sure, but he wasn't that big.

Lupé said, "Yes, I think so."

"Good afternoon," the man said. "Can I help you with something?"

Stan swallowed, finally thought to shake his head.

That voice. My God, he thought, what the hell was that voice?

The man took a step toward them. "Are you sure?"

"*Madre Dios,*" Lupé whispered. "*Madre Dios.*" She grabbed Stan's arm and dragged him away.

He didn't argue.

There was no way he wanted to be anywhere near that giant. Especially not if Lupé was as scared as she sounded.

7

Casey watched the curious pair hurry down the street, suddenly remembered the little man who had pretended to help Enid.

"Hey!" he called.

The couple broke into a run, scattering the mist around them, fading into it before they reached Mackey's.

Casey didn't hurry. He knew where they were going.

Outrage fueled him as he swung onto the sidewalk, trying not to speculate on what that man had or had not done to terrify Enid so. But whatever it had been, he would find an explanation.

The drizzle lightened.

The breeze returned.

He glanced over his shoulder when he thought he heard the sound of an engine, thinking maybe Petyr was on his way back to pick up his wife. But the road was empty, and when he passed the clinic Balanov's car wasn't at the curb.

He felt the weight of the water in his hair.

He felt the crawl of water down his neck.

Nervously, without knowing why, he rubbed the ball of his left thumb over the tips of his fingers.

At Mackey's he swung north into Hickory Street, hadn't reached the end of the bar before a woman stepped into the road, some ten yards away.

A different woman.

He stopped, and she said, "Good afternoon, Reverend Chisholm."

A little startled, he ducked his head. "Good afternoon." A glance toward the only house on the block with lighted windows. "I think I may have upset a couple of your friends." He smiled. "I wanted to apologize."

"No need," she told him easily. "I'm sure they understand."

They do if they're guilty, he thought.

"The man," he said. "A friend of mine, Mrs. Balanov, said that young man sort of frightened her."

The woman shrugged. "Yes?"

He kept his voice flat. "Why?"

She shrugged again. "You'd have to ask him. I know nothing about it."

He stepped off the curb, and something about the way she backed off at the same time made him stop. Like a mother protecting her cubs, he thought. Then: no, like a guard dog. Protecting something else.

He took another step toward the house, she another step back.

"Something wrong, ma'am?" he asked politely.

Another step, another step back.

And he saw the car in the driveway, facing out.

The hood ornament glittered with raindrops, even when the woman stood beside it and stroked the silver mane. Slowly. Caressing it. Her gaze not leaving his face.

"Reverend Chisholm."

At his name the afternoon's greylight shimmered and became night, and all he could see was her, and the car; all he could feel was the weakness that made his legs cold and his stomach leaden and his lungs not able to take in enough air; all he could hear was a voice, his voice, pleading for mercy, begging not to be killed, even though his lips didn't move.

All he could smell was the stench of his own fear.

"Reverend Chisholm."

Fingers curled into helpless fists, nothing inside strong enough for anger.

"You know me," he said, despising the sound of his voice, too thin and too high. "I don't know you."

Night snapped to greylight and he took a step to one side as if he'd been using the dark for support. Confused, uncertain, he lifted a useless hand in a useless, feeble farewell and walked away, not sure where he was going.

She said, "Oh, you know me, Reverend Chisholm. It's a little too late, but you do."

He didn't look back.

Not even when he heard the rhythmic sound of the engine.

4

Stan paced across the kitchen, wrapped in his trench coat, one hand scratching through his beard, the other through his hair he was sure had turned from blond to white no matter how often he had checked the bathroom mirror since he'd gotten back.

"*Basta*, Stan, for God's sake," Lupé said from her place by the sink. "You're driving me crazy."

"*Loco*," he told her. "That's Spanish for crazy."

She looked at him, grinned, then laughed as she lit a cigarette. "Yeah." She nodded. "Crazy, *loco*, what's the difference, man, knock it off, okay?"

He couldn't stop.

The voice, the man, he couldn't stop moving, but no matter how much he moved he couldn't get far enough away.

Escobar sat at the table, hands flat on his thighs, staring at the refrigerator. As far as Stan could tell, he hadn't moved since breakfast.

"She was right, you know." Pacing to the door, peeking around the shade. "This place is different. It feels weird. I don't like it. That woman with the book, she was weird, Lupé. And that . . .'' He shuddered and paced into the living room, made a circuit without looking outside and returned to the kitchen, avoiding Lupé's grab for him by going around the other side of the table.

"Damnit, Stan!"

"I can't help it," he said, big eyes bigger, hardly blinking at all. "You saw. You saw."

He could see it in her eyes, the way the cigarette trembled between her fingers.

"Oh, man." He paced back to the living room and looked through the door window. "Oh, shit."

"What?"

"Come here. Quick."

She came up behind him, leaned over his shoulder.

The driveway was empty.

Stan put a hand on the doorknob. "Do you think . . . ?"

She didn't answer, and he pulled it open, grimacing at the humidity that wrapped him in damp wool, peering through the light rain up and down the block.

"I don't hear nothing," he said.

She moved to his side, pulled up one jeans leg and took the knife from her boot. Grinned at him over the blade.

"Yes, you do, *amigo*. Yes, you do."

Through the water dripping from the roof, from the branches, from the leaves, he could hear it. Not clearly, but it was there.

He heard Escobar stand.

"Time to go," Lupé said quietly, pushed the screen door open, and stepped onto the porch. "Tell you what, Stan, I make you a promise. When we're done, I'll take you to my place in New Mexico. I think you'll like it there."

"I don't have a passport."

She looked at him, she laughed, and she stepped into the rain with a wave over her shoulder.

Laughing all the way down the block.

But not loud enough to drown out the hoofbeats that sounded like rolling thunder.

5

Casey sat on his stool beside the register and spoke to no
one. His third bowl of steaming soup sat in front of him,
and although he put spoon to bowl, spoon to mouth, he barely
tasted a thing. Barely heard the clatter of silverware, barely
heard the chatter and the laughs. An impromptu celebration.
Doors were open, lamps were lit, people came out of their
homes, stretching and pointing as if they had been in hiber-
nation; they stood in the streets and gawked at the rain, decided it was time to eat out for a change.

There was no room in the diner.

People stood patiently by the door for a place to sit down,
swapping weather and news reports, grinning as they *tsk*ed and
tutted over riots and murder.

No one carried an umbrella or wore a raincoat.

Rina and Helen worked the booths and counter, every so
often Helen ducking into the kitchen where Todd, with a pad
of gauze taped to the side of his head, a splendid bruise blos-
soming on his cheek, cursed at the grill and insisted he needed
no help in spite of the cannonade echoing in his skull.

Casey stared at the bowl. Chicken with rice, and he couldn't remember what the other two had been.

The lights were too bright, the noise too loud.

Spoon to bowl, spoon to mouth.

His hands had stopped shaking maybe an hour ago, but he still felt cold, as if his insides had been carved from a rough block of ice.

People spoke to him in passing, and he responded with a smile or a nod or a word or two without conscious meaning; people clapped him on the back, and he stiffened every time.

This is nuts, he thought; I've got to go home, I'm getting sick again.

But he didn't move beyond looking outside at the rain. A rain so fine and soft it was merely a faint ripple in the air. Silver sparkles caught in the diner's glow, in the streetlights, slowly adding neon reflections to the shining tarmac.

Mist rising from the street in swirling pools, lifting into the trees to soften the dying leaves. Scattering and regathering whenever someone walked through it.

A tranquil summer's night, a heat wave broken, a drought finally on the way to being a drought no more.

Then a natural lull, with nothing but the hiss and spatter of the grill, the squeak of Rina's sneakers on the floor, Helen dropping change into the register drawer, slapping the drawer shut, nearly silent groans and sighs of contentment.

People drifting away, conversation low.

Rina gathering tips as she wiped the tabletops, change jingling heavily in her apron pocket.

Helen took a break and sat beside him, rocked toward him until their shoulders touched, rocked away and said, "So what did she say?"

"What?" Too loud, too quick. He couldn't keep her gaze.

"We saw you talking to that woman. What did she say? Who is she?"

Spoon to bowl, spoon to mouth.

The soup was cold.

"I don't know."

yes you do

"Casey."

"How is Bobby?" he asked instead, a smile so false it felt grotesque and he killed it.

She shrugged. She had discovered Bobby tightly curled in her bed, sobbing and refusing to move. "I gave up. Tessa's with her now."

His eyes widened a bit. "Tessa?"

"A common enemy," she said, nodding toward the man bent over the stove. "I guess they've been friends for too long." She inhaled quickly, deeply, and plucked the spoon from his hand, set it on the plate, trying to force him to look at her. "Casey, you've got to talk to me."

He stared at the bowl dumbly. "About what?"

She slapped his arm; it wasn't a playful tap. "What do you think, you jerk? Mabel and her gun, Bobby trying to knock Todd's head off, Enid . . . you name it." Her hand covered his before it could escape to his lap. "This place is going nuts, has been for a week, and if you blame it on the heat, I'm going to strangle you, Casey Chisholm. I swear to God, I'll strangle you."

Pressure in his chest, in his head.

As he swiveled his seat around, hand slipping from beneath hers, he saw Mabel in the far booth, pale and looking older, laughing silently at something Mrs. Racine had said; Nate at the end of the counter flirting with Rina, but not very well; Mel standing in the doorway slapping rain from his shoulders.

No one else.

The rest had gone home.

Silver flashes outside; an early night in the rain.

"The bell," Todd said behind him, making him jump. "Don't forget the goddamn bell." In a voice loud enough to silence the others, turn their faces toward him. Waiting.

It was yesterday on his porch all over again, but this time, this night, there was urgency and demand.

His hands wouldn't stop moving while he struggled for an answer—from his face to his lap to patterns around his chest, from a mime for understanding to a mime for ignorance and confusion, from his lap to patterns to covering his face until he knew he couldn't run anymore.

"It's the goddamn Millennium, isn't it," Todd said.

And Casey answered, "Yes."

Cora didn't know what to do. She had let the girls run around in the rain while she sat cross-legged on the deck with Dimitri, trying everything she could think of to stop him from crying. It had lasted so long he had run out of tears, and she had finally cajoled him to his feet and brought him inside, sitting him at the kitchen table while she tried to find out where his parents had gone. She called everyone she knew, every place she could think of, but Mr. Balanov had either just left or hadn't been seen, while his wife hadn't been seen since just before noon.

She called Reverend Chisholm half a dozen times, both at home and at the church, but the phone kept ringing, an odd hollow sound.

"I don't know," she said to the room. "I don't know what else."

Dimitri didn't move.

She hurried to the back door and held it open while she called the girls. She still didn't know who that Anita kid was, but it made her mad that her father had stuck the kid here without even bothering to tell Cora where she lived.

"Come on, guys," she called. "It's getting dark. Come on in."

Sonya stood by the near side of the pool. "Aw, Cora, do we have to?"

Anita was at the other end.

"Yes, you have to. You don't want to get sick just when the heat's gone, do you? And look at you, silly," she added. "You're shivering so hard your skin's going to fall off."

Sonya giggled. "That's yucky."

Cora leaned over the railing. "Not as yucky as you'll look if the Cora Shark gets you. Now move your butt, kid." She raised her voice. "You, too, Anita. Come on, hurry up."

Sonya scrambled up the steps and into the house, still gig-

gling, saying she was going to put on her clothes before her
face fell off.

Anita didn't move.

Cora waved. "Anita, come on."

Although the rain wasn't hard, it was still hard to see her
clearly, and Cora had to look twice when she thought she saw
a spark jump in the girl's hand. "Anita, what are you doing?
Come in here. Now!"

A faint buzz beneath her feet made Cora start, then the
underwater lights came on in the pool. The surface rippled and
cast rippling shadows across the little girl's figure, and this
time Cora did see a spark in the girl's hand.

"Anita." She headed for the stairs. "Anita, do you have
matches?"

A third spark, and Cora froze on the top step.

A flame added shadow to the child's face, and there was
something in her other hand.

"For God's sake, do you have a firecracker?"

Anita laughed. Not a child's laugh; a woman's.

Flame touched fuse.

"Anita!" But Cora couldn't move. "Anita!"

An orange glow spiraled up from the girl's hand, end over
end, and landed in the pool.

"Anita, damnit!"

The explosion threw Cora onto her rump, the monstrous
geyser that rose from the center of the pool spread in white
fire and foam and landed on the deck, slamming her onto her
back and sliding her into the wall. She screamed and tried to
get to her feet, spitting water, shaking her head, finally standing and wiping her eyes clear.

"What the hell are you doing?"

A futile scream; Anita had another one.

"I'll give you to three," the little girl called, and laughed.
"One."

Cora slipped and skidded across the deck, screaming for
Dimitri and Sonya to get out of the house.

"Two."

Punching the door open, skidding across the cold kitchen

floor, grabbing a stunned Dimitri's arm and dragging him into the hall.

"Two-and-a-half," she heard, and shrieked Sonya's name, saw her charging down the staircase, and shoved Dimitri toward the front door.

"Two-and-three-quarters!" And a laugh.

Sonya froze, and Cora scooped her up under one arm.

"Three!"

Todd came around the counter and sat sideways in the booth directly opposite Casey, fussing with the surgical tape that had come loose around his hair. The others moved closer. Helen remained at his side. This, he could tell, was no philosophical discussion about to get under way. They were afraid, badly afraid, and they were angry because they didn't know why.

"It's funny," he said, keeping his voice steady, not looking at them, looking everywhere but at them, "but we can believe or not in ghosts and monsters and aliens from outer space, life after death or nothing at all, but when it comes right down to it, none of it matters.

"If this is truly the end, none of it will matter."

"What do you mean, if?" Nate demanded weakly, his voice shaking a little.

"I mean, son, I don't know. Not for sure."

Rina stood behind Nate, her hands on his shoulders, her face drawn with fear. "Yesterday you said some fiddler was riding. I don't . . . are you talking, like, those guys I saw once on TV? The ones on the horses?"

No one answered.

They all knew what they had heard.

"They're called the Four Horsemen," Casey said at last. "In the *Book of Revelations* they ride into the world to herald the last days."

"What?" Todd said, his disbelief clear, disbelief uncertain. "Come on, Case, are you saying those Horsemen are actually real?" He leaned away and shook his head, winced, and touched his bandage. "What the hell—you should pardon the expression—are they doing here, then? In Maple Landing? Why not New York, someplace like that?''

"Nonsense," said Mrs. Racine calmly, still in the last booth, still sipping her coffee. "Nonsense."

"Assuming," Farber said casually, leaning against the door, "you take the Bible literally, of course."

Casey looked at him, at the sprinkle of water across his face that made him seem almost transparent. "Like I said, Mel: if they're here, it doesn't matter what you believe, does it?"

"It does to me."

Lights too bright, voice too loud, Nate shaking off Rina's hands and slipping off his stool, saying, "You guys are nuts," saying something else about getting home, his mother will be worried, crossing the space between the counter and the booths, no one stopping him, until Casey cleared his throat.

Nate's eyes shone; he swallowed several times.

"You know me, Nate." Quiet, excluding the others, excluding the world.

Nate nodded shakily, not protesting when Rina came up beside him and took hold of his hand.

"I can only tell you what I think. What I believe. I can speak for no one else. Do you want to know? Do you really want to know?"

Nate sniffed, wanting to leave, wanting to listen.

Terrified.

"One minute," Casey said. "Give me one minute."

Arlo stood behind the bar, juggling four empty beer bottles while Kay watched unimpressed from a stool. He hadn't dropped a one, and he considered adding a fifth when something pounded against the back door.

Kay swiveled around quickly. "What the hell?"

The bottles fell, smashing one by one.

"Delivery?" she asked.

Arlo shook his head. No deliveries due today. It was Saturday, it was late, the back door was locked, his act interrupted just when it was getting good. And now he had to clean up the mess that crunched at his feet. The worst of it was, he wasn't even drunk.

Something hit the door again.

"Hey," he shouted, hands cupped around his mouth, "go around the front, it's open!"

Kay leaned over the bar. "You got a broom, Arlo?"

The back door slammed open, rebounded off the wall, and was kicked open again. A dark figure stood on the threshold, winks of rain on its shoulders.

Kay uttered a small scream and hustled around to stand beside Arlo, but not so close, he noticed, that she couldn't make a break for the front door if she had to.

"We're open, you idiot," Arlo said angrily. "You could've used the front, you know. Man, that's going to cost me a fortune, getting fixed and all. Hope you brought your wallet, I don't take checks."

The figure stepped inside, cloaked by the shadows that clung to the back.

Arlo heard the rain drip from the eaves, splatter on the gravel in the back driveway. He felt Kay easing away to the end of the bar. Like he needed this crap; like he really needed this crap. He rubbed a thumb along the side of his nose. "So what are you? Like, the Shadow or something?"

"No."

Arlo frowned, ignoring Kay's desperate gesturing for him to stop talking and get out of here. This was a guy he knew, but he couldn't put a face to the sound of the voice. Maybe a guy who started out drunk at home and decided to finish it here, at Mackey's. Maybe a guy who thought he was cute, being spooky, being cool, being an asshole who liked to smash in bar doors so he could brag about it to his friends.

"So shut what's left of the door and come in, for God's sake," he said in disgust. "But you better have money, man, or you're not getting a drop."

"Yes, I am," the figure said, and began to make his way around the tables. Into the light.

"Arlo?" Kay whispered.

Arlo barely stopped himself from bolting, grinned instead,

and without looking away reached into the cooler for a fresh bottle of beer. "Well, peace, love, all that good shit, man. Looks like you survived."

Diño Escobar stopped in the middle of the room, and traced a circle on the table beside him. "Yes. No thanks to you."

Arlo snapped off the lid with a church key and set the bottle on the bar, hard enough to make Kay jump. "Old business? New business? Your buddy's toast, you know. And I don't think my karma can stand another round, okay?" With his free hand he pulled the shotgun from its clip, tipped it back against his shoulder.

All very smooth, he thought, all very calm, all very not how he felt when he saw the charring on the man's suit, the debris from the forest floor, the raw red flesh and scratches and cuts across his dark-skinned face. The man was ugly before; he was damn sinful now.

"I think I'm going to leave," Kay said nervously.

Escobar shook his head.

He didn't say a word; he just shook his head.

"They've always ridden, Nate," Casey said, knowing he had to hurry, seeing the boy leaning, about ready to bolt. "Over every battlefield, every drought-dry farm, every village where people are sick and dying and have no way to cure themselves, have no one on the outside who can cure them if they knew.

"It's not just in the last days.

"They're always out there. Always have been."

He sighed.

"Always."

Nate couldn't speak. His lips moved, his eyes pleaded, but he still couldn't speak.

Rina spoke instead: "But this isn't like that. This is my home. This isn't like that. There's nothing here that they want."

"Nonsense," said Mrs. Racine. "Can I get another cup of coffee, dear? This one's gone cold."

"You're nuts," Nate said to Casey. He shook his head

sharply, pulling Rina after him toward the door. "You're nuts, you know that? You're not making any sense. It's the end of the world, but maybe it isn't . . . Jesus, Cora rang the damn bell, don't you know that? She must have, and all that other stuff you're talking about . . . you're nuts. You're talking nuts."

"Nate!" he snapped.

The boy stopped, although Rina kept pushing at him, urging him to go on.

"Nate."

Tessa sat on the edge of the bed, head bowed, hands clasped between her knees. She was pretty much all cried out, pretty exhausted by the rage she had felt, first at Bobby for bashing Todd with his own guitar, then at Todd when she found out why. But Farber had been clever enough to chase her out of the room once the wound had been cleaned. Not that it was very much, just a small gash across the scalp, no more than three or four stitches she would have killed to do herself. And once all the paperwork had been done and Todd sent back to the diner, Farber had said nothing, just let her go.

"To enjoy the rain," he had told her. "Think of it as a bonus."

Her laugh was dutiful, her direction straight for the house, with a stop along the way at Mackey's for a quick shot, paying no attention to whoever it was who sat in silence at the back, and not giving a damn. Sociable was the last thing she felt like right now.

Helen, however, had beaten her to it, and when she stomped into the bedroom, Helen had said, "Think about it, girl, before you say anything."

Then Bobby had rolled over, saw her, and burst into new tears that Tessa couldn't resist. Cursing Todd and men over and over, mumbling something about some woman who told her what men were really like, showing her what she could do, sobbing, subsiding, falling into a fitful sleep.

"Oh, brother," she whispered, stood and stretched and

walked to the window to look over the hedge at the Moon-glow. Listen to the light rain. Wishing there were thunder and lightning and a powerful wind to suit her mood.

A footfall in the hallway.

"Helen?"

Bobby stirred but didn't waken.

"Goddamnit, if that's you, Todd . . ."

A woman stepped into the room. "Sorry," she said, lifting her dark eyebrows in a careless shrug. "It's only me."

"And who the hell are you?"

"It don't matter," Lupé said, and showed Tessa the knife.

"Nate."

Casey kept his voice steady, already thinking the boy was probably right, that he was indeed crazy, that his sickness and the heat and the charges he had taken upon himself without thinking had tipped him over without warning.

"So? What?"

Knowing, however, finally knowing that being insane was simply wishful thinking.

"There aren't four out there, son."

Nate sneered.

"There's only one, Nate. There's only one."

Nate opened his mouth, then elbowed Mel away from the door and yanked it open, just as an explosion filled the night with fire and light.

Casey was off the stool before he even knew he was moving, shoving Nate, Rina, and Mel ahead of him through the door onto the sidewalk.

It wasn't hard to find.

A fireball was in the process of implosion up on the Crest, but unlike the other night, this one didn't die. It lashed sparks and tongues against the bottom of the clouds, and in contrast set the flatland into deeper darkness.

Casey ran while others shouted instructions for phone calls

and volunteers, Mel yelling for someone to fetch Tessa, he would need her.

The fire took a voice, a low rumbling roar, and debris began to plummet out of the sky.

Part of a burning plank bounced off the sidewalk in front of the clinic, raising a cloud of sparks; smaller pieces of wood and melted plastic pattered like hail along the street, smoking, glowing black and red; a length of burning cloth held by the breeze–turned–slow wind danced above the slope as Casey approached the church, eyeing the steeple nervously for signs of sparks and flame; what was left of a wood chair bounced off a roof and fell in flames into the yard.

The voice of the fire.

Another voice behind him, and he looked over his shoulder, saw Kay racing toward him through a pocket of mist, waving her arms and screaming, shoving someone away who tried to stop her. He slowed, backpedaled, then paused in hesitation, then hurried toward her.

"Arlo!" she cried, and fell into his arms, pushed away, and said, "Arlo. That man. The man in the car. That man. Casey, that man!"

Indecision froze him until she yanked frantically on his arms, pulling him, forcing him to trot, to run, while the others raced in the opposite direction. As they passed the hardware store, Moss Tully stumbled out, hauling up his trousers, agape at the chaos, not arguing when Casey said, "The bar! Arlo!" and following behind.

The front window blew out, neon tubing and sparks spraying over the street. A second later, Arlo tripped and fell outside, shotgun in one hand, scrambled on hands and knees over the curb onto the blacktop where he rolled onto his back and aimed the weapon at the door. Kay stopped, but Casey kept running, one hand out to keep Arlo from firing, the other reaching for the closing door and snapping back when Diño Escobar stepped out.

"Holy shit!" Moss yelled, slipped on the sidewalk and fell against the wall.

"*Padre,*" Escobar said, teeth white in a shark's smile.

The voice of the fire.

A horn blowing, shouts and cries, muffled explosions ranging over the Crest.

"I hit him!" Arlo shouted. "Jesus, I hit him, get away, Reverend, Jesus, get away, I can't see him, get away!"

Pockets of smoke steamed from Escobar's chest, a narrow strip of flesh dangled beneath his chin.

Casey didn't bother to think or to question; he swung a fist and knocked the man into the recess, swung again and doubled Escobar over.

"Get away, damnit, Reverend, get away, let me shoot him again!"

Escobar straightened, slapped Casey's next punch away, and lashed him across the cheek with the back of his hand. Casey's head snapped to one side, seeing sparks that had nothing to do with the fire. Another slap, and Casey backed away, swinging and missing, tasting blood, vision threatening to blur, wondering how it was that this man, shot and practically dead, could be so damn strong.

Escobar landed an overhand left on the side of his head, and he went down to one knee.

"Reverend!" Moss yelled, just as Arlo fired over Casey's bowed head.

Escobar took most of the blast in his chest, suit jacket fluttering and smoking, a tiny, short-lived fire near his heart, a slow insolent turn as Moss came in low, aiming to tackle him and bring him down. Deliberately, swiftly, Escobar brought a fist up and turned it into a club, catching Moss squarely on the back of his neck.

Even through the voice of the fire, Casey heard the bone snap.

Arlo, still on his back and squirming away and trying to stand at the same time, fired again, hitting nothing but air and the edge of the roof. Splinters kicked into the air and were scattered by the slow wind that mixed them with more black and fire hail from the Crest.

Escobar laughed and stepped out to the curb.

Casey, his breath in short supply, tried to stand, but the man whirled deftly and caught him in the ribs with an instep, flipping him over, landing him next to Tully, whose face was turned toward him, bleeding through the nose, his lips parted in an astonished grin. His eyes wide open, weeping rain.

Arlo fired again.

Escobar laughed again. "Aim next time, you old bastard," he said. "I'll wait. I'm in no hurry."

Casey used the building to brace himself as he stood, one hand briefly brushing across Tully's back in a silent promise and farewell. Kay was gone. Escobar was on the corner, a hand in a pocket, his battered face twisted in derision as he watched Arlo make it to his knees, and fall back again when another explosion highlighted the clouds.

This time Mackey didn't hesitate, didn't slip—he scrambled to his feet and ran, toward the new fire, the roaring, toward the people whose silhouettes flickered on and off at the top of the slope.

"Any time, my friend," Escobar called after him. "Any time, I'll be here," and with a smile of disdain for Casey, he walked back into the bar.

Casey wanted to follow, to finish what had been started, but he also knew this was one fight he couldn't handle alone, so he let the fire draw him while he held his side, pressing against the pain, waiting for the buzzing and the screams in his head to make way, to go away.

He got as far as the church before he saw Cora.

She sat on the flagstone, face raised to the clouds, rocking Dimitri in her arms, Sonya sitting beside her, sucking her thumb and staring and not seeing a thing.

"Cora?"

Cora rocked.

"Cora."

He stood over her.

She looked up, lips pulled away from her teeth.

Dear God, he thought; all those tears.

"She blew it up," Cora said, blinking slowly. "She blew the house up." Her face began to change its shape. "She was a little kid, Reverend Chisholm, and she blew the house up."

He knelt in front of her, tried to take Dimitri from her, but she snarled and pulled away.

"No! You can't have him! You can't save him, you son of a bitch."

He saw it then, the blood in the boy's hair, gleaming and still running, the blood on his bare back, gleaming and still running.

"The birds," Cora sobbed, resting her cheek on Dimitri's head. "Oh, God, he couldn't hear the birds."

"Reverend Chisholm?" Sonya said, still staring, still sucking her thumb. "Reverend Chisholm, is Momma still alive? Did the bad girl hurt her?"

A vehicle braked hard.

"Cora!" Reed called. "Cora, what—?"

Unsteadily Casey rocked to his feet while Cora rocked Dimitri. As Reed rushed past him, he turned stiffly, walked to Lambert's pickup and almost said, "Take them inside, Micah, they should be safe there."

He didn't.

He couldn't.

The church was still locked.

"Come on, boy," Micah said, ignoring Casey completely. "There's folks up there need us, we gotta go. We'll send the doc down for them."

Casey saw someone running across the top of the slope; he couldn't tell if they were afire or not.

He looked up at the steeple, and the belfry windows were black, edged with shimmering orange.

"Aw, hell, Dimmy," he heard Reed say through a crack in his too-young voice.

Casey walked away.

*   *   *

He walked west, and slowly.

He could smell smoke on his clothes, could smell smoke on the air, could feel pinpoints of fire where embers had landed on his shirt and neck.

He smelled blood.

He walked past Mackey's and heard laughter inside, and the crash of breaking bottles.

He walked past the Moonglow, and there was no one inside, just the too-bright lights, and a crack across the window.

Two men ran past him toward the Crest, as if he weren't there.

He heard someone call his name, but he didn't turn until he heard it again.

She stood in the road, arms folded loosely across her chest, the fire above and behind her, reaching through the smoke, dragging the clouds down.

The horse waited behind her.

"Good-bye," she said grimly. "Good-bye, Mr. Chisholm."

He turned away and kept on walking.

6

1

Todd was exhausted, angry, frustrated.

Scared to death.

The Balanov house was nothing more than two walls and the foundation now, the roof collapsed, pools of fire eating at the front yard. Even the chimney had collapsed. The explosion had blown out most of the windows of the nearest houses, as well as the school and shops on the other side of the road. Although volunteers were still busily pouring water on the houses adjacent to the ruined building, he didn't have much hope. Put a fire pocket out here and another one pops up there.

Propane tank, someone had guessed, but it didn't matter; the destruction was nearly complete.

It didn't matter, either, to those he had helped down to the clinic—burns, a broken arm, an unconscious woman whose leg had been fractured. Mel was doing the best he could, but Todd didn't think his best, this time, would be good enough.

It would have been easier to call outside for help, but the explosion had knocked the telephone lines down, and no one's cellular phones seemed to work.

"Jesus Christ, find Tessa, will you?" was the last thing Farber had said before shoving him out the clinic door.

A second explosion, not as bad as the first, froze him on the sidewalk. He didn't even look. Another tank, a car, what did it matter, the whole place was going up and there was nothing he could do to stop it.

He tried to run down to Hickory Street, but his head hurt too much, and he had to slow to a walk. Everything moved, everything shifted, and before he reached the corner, he dropped to his knees and threw up.

The voice of the fire above and behind him; the rain on his head and neck, soaking through his shirt, making the pavement slick when he stood, scrubbed his face hard, and started off again.

He didn't think anymore about Casey. He had seen the reverend walking away not all that long ago, heading back for his house. Not running; walking. Not looking back. A blur of white soon swallowed by the dark.

Rage had urged him to chase after the man and drag his sorry ass back, but there had been, at the time, more important things to take care of, like the injured and the fire, and now he had to find Tessa.

He saw a light on the second floor. The bedroom.

He frowned, hurried to the steps, and started calling her name even before he was inside.

No one answered.

Using the banister as a pulley, he hauled himself up to the second floor, rounded the hall corner, and stumbled into the room.

"Tessa?"

A small lamp, milk white with pale flowers, burned on the nightstand. Tessa wasn't here, but he saw Bobby on the bed, curled up, face to the wall.

"Bobby, for God's sake, get up," he said, putting one knee on the mattress, one hand on her shoulder to roll her over. "Bobby, come on, don't you know what's going on?"

She didn't move, and he tugged, grunted angrily, and tugged again until he had her on her back.

At first he didn't know what he was looking at, didn't recognize what had been smeared on the wall, what had turned her T-shirt into a wrinkled dark sponge.

When he did, he shoved away from the bed, arms batting the air to drive the image away. He wasn't sure, but he thought he screamed, a harsh strangled noise that followed him as he staggered into the hall and down the stairs, a noise that turned into Tessa's name when he pushed into the kitchen, into the dining room, into the living room, and out into the street. Trying to breath, trying to rid his nostrils of the stench of all that blood.

"Todd!"

He turned, swaying drunkenly, and saw her, was about to ask what had happened, who had done it, when he also saw a woman standing behind her and to one side. One hand gripped Tessa's shoulder, the other held a knife up for him to see.

"Hello, *gringo*," the woman said.

Todd took a step toward them.

"Todd, please," Tessa begged. Her legs trembled, her hands were clasped hard across her stomach. "Todd?"

He took another step.

The woman said, "It isn't going to do you any good, you know. You can't be the hero." And she laughed without a sound.

He took another step, could almost reach Tessa. His head ached, burns on the backs of his hands and on his face flared. The night filled with fire and distant shouts and a horn, but he only heard Tessa whisper his name over and over while her eyes rolled like a frightened horse's.

He stopped, ignoring the sweat and the rain that dripped into his eyes. "Mel needs you," he said to Tessa as calmly as he could. "There's people hurt at the clinic."

Tessa tilted her head as if she hadn't understood.

"Dimitri's dead," he said flatly, "Petyr's gone, and some folks have been hurt." He gestured sharply. "Go."

She hesitated, glanced at the hand on her shoulder, then

wrenched free and ran, snatching at and missing his arm as she passed.

He wouldn't move. He watched the woman and the blade and the faint flicker of firelight at the corners of his vision.

He waited while she checked him over, seeing the grime, the bandage, probably figuring he would be easy, too easy, making up her mind if she was going to bother or not.

"Who the hell *are* you?" he demanded, shoulders slumping, trying to stay on his feet.

"Lupé," she said.

He gestured with a palm. "That's not what I meant."

"No kidding. And who cares?"

She stepped forward without warning, and her arm swept around, the blade intended to slash across his throat, but she was surprised when he grabbed her wrist with his right hand, stepped in and wrenched the arm up while, at the same time, he kicked her leg from under her.

Her head smacked against the blacktop, her fingers opened, and he snatched the knife away. Stared at her blinking away the confusion. Leaned in and thrust the blade into her stomach. As she gasped and nearly sat up, he jerked the blade upward, released it, and stepped aside.

"Oh . . . Jesus!" she said, doubling over, rolling onto her back, her side. "Jesus!" Rolling onto her knees, her forehead against the street.

Todd wiped his face with a sleeve.

Lupé coughed, choked, and rose unsteadily to rest on her heels. "Oh . . . God!"

The knife was in her hand.

"Don't run," she said, rocking forward now, and back, trying to get to her feet. "Don't run."

Then she smiled.

2

Stan wandered down a side street, ignoring the chaos, following a little old lady dressed in summer white. He thought she looked like some kind of ghost. But she didn't float like ghosts were supposed to; she took quick little steps, like she was in a hurry, but her shoes hurt too much.

Don't know about this, he worried as he lengthened his stride; don't know about this; she's so old, where's the fun, where's the game?

She turned then, and squinted through the rain at him. "Reed Turner, is that you?"

"No, ma'am," he said politely. "Just me. Just Stan."

"And who is Stan?"

She sounded like a librarian, the kind who sneered at him every time he walked into one of their dusty old buildings, the kind who liked to talk like schoolteachers and scare him half to death.

He didn't like them very much.

"I asked you a question, young man. I'm getting soaked out here."

She made him angry.

She humphed and walked away, quick little steps, dismissing him like he was nobody. With quick little steps.

Very angry.

He caught her in three strides, grabbed her arm, and spun her around so hard she fell against him, gasping in terror, clutching her silly-looking purse to her silly flat chest.

"Go away!"

"Not yet," he said, and raised a fist, widened his large eyes, and grinned when she cringed, too weak to break his grip.

"Hey!"

He looked over the old lady's head, and couldn't believe it. Hurrying down the street toward them was a guy in some kind of army outfit, the kind they wore when they were in the jungle and stuff, but he couldn't remember the name.

"Let her go, punk, before I kick your ass."

"Mr. Bowes," the old lady called, her voice shaky and high, "he's hurting me."

William Bowes unslung the rifle he had over his shoulder. "Oh really?"

He was about ten yards away when Stan switched his grip

from the old lady's arm to her hair and tossed her to one side, not bothering to look when he heard her hit the street.

"Oh, that does it," the army guy said. "You're mine, now, you punk. You're all mine."

Stan didn't mind.

This would be more fun.

And when the army man used the butt of his rifle against Stan's head, and Stan managed to stay on his feet, with a grin, he knew he was right—this really was going to be more fun than the little old lady.

3

Nate found the little girl standing in front of the grade school, across the street from the fire. Glitters of broken glass lay around her, and chunks of steaming wood and blackened stone. Her hair was matted to her head by the rain, and she had a thumb stuck in her mouth.

He had been on the fire hose with Micah Lambert, Reed's father, and some other men, but when the pressure decreased as the need did, he had been ordered to check around the school and the nearby houses and shops, to see if anyone needed help, or wanted to help. Until he spotted the kid, he hadn't seen anyone who didn't already have something to do. Most of it, by now, was working on the house three doors up from the Balanovs'. A van had exploded in the driveway, so violently that it had bounced halfway across the lawn, the concussion shattering more windows, and splashing burning gasoline onto the attached garage. Despite the rain, the fire had spread swiftly, but it didn't look to him as if the house would be lost.

He almost passed the kid by. What he wanted to do was find Rina. The last he had seen of her, she had been supporting a woman while they made their way down the street, at the same time swiping at embers that landed in her hair.

"Hey," he said softly. "Hey, kid, you all right?"

She turned large dark eyes on him, and around her thumb said, "I'm Anita Smith. Who are you?"

"Nate." He knelt in front of her, searching for obvious signs of injury. Aside from a tear in her coveralls, though, and some smudges across her face, he couldn't see anything wrong. "Where's your mom?"

The little girl pointed downhill, and closed her eyes against a sudden shudder.

He didn't blame her. After all that heat, this rain felt like ice, and the air was filled with the stench of burning wood and rubber, burning gasoline and things he didn't want to know.

He stroked her arm, and coughed, tasting ash and spitting apologetically to one side. "Your mom got hurt, huh?"

She nodded.

"She's at the clinic with Doc?"

She nodded.

"Where's your daddy? Is he home?"

She shook her head, not taking her gaze from his face.

"All right, no sweat." He rose, and reached out a hand. "Why don't we go down to Doc's and see your mom? I'll bet he's got some candy and stuff. You want to see?"

She shook her head.

"Aw, hey, come on." He gave her his best smile. "It's not far, you know that."

He waggled his hand, an order for her to take it, but she backed away, popping the thumb from her mouth, ducking her hands behind her back.

"Hey, look, kid—"

"Anita."

It was hard not to raise his voice: "Yeah. Anita. Well, look, Anita, we've got a lot of people hurt here, right?, so I can't waste time. We gotta go. Now." Then he groaned when he saw her ready to cry. "Okay, okay, I'm sorry, I didn't mean to yell, all right? But—"

She pointed across the street and pouted. "The fire's almost gone."

He looked, saw flames writhing up the front door, poking

at the ground-floor windows, curling through the glassless windows of the van, and wondered what she was talking about. A few people had connected garden hoses to fight the new blaze, and he could hear Harve Turner's voice shouting orders no one listened to.

He saw Rina.

"Hey!" he called, and waved one arm in a semaphore that nearly wrenched his shoulder. "Hey, Rina!"

She spotted him, waved back, and started to run.

A giggle made him turn around.

The kid's left hand was out, palm up, and in the palm he saw a single red flame.

His mouth opened in disbelief, he took a step toward her to put the fire out, and froze when her other hand came out from behind her back.

At first he thought it was a firecracker.

Anita touched fuse to flame, closed her hand, tossed the stick over her shoulder into the school.

"Fire," she said, smiling sweetly.

Like the second just before a canoe tips over in the deepest part of the river, like the second just before a face twitches and temper explodes.

Like the second between the lightning and the thunder.

"Rina!" Nate yelled, desperately spinning around. "Rina, run!"

4

"I'm *wait*ing," Escobar sang from the entrance to Mackey's. "Come on, you old fart, I'm *wait*ing!"

5

Reed didn't know if he was simply numb or had somehow been turned into some kind of a zombie. All he knew was that he could barely feel a thing anymore, inside or out; all he knew was that somewhere between the first explosion and the first dying, he had decided it wasn't crazy to believe in black magic.

It wasn't crazy to believe in someone called The Horseman.

System shutdown, that's what it was. What he saw, what he heard . . . he couldn't take it any longer unless he pretended it was happening to someone else. Like watching a movie or a TV show.

It began when he lifted Dimmy from Cora's arms and stared at the church and couldn't think of a damn thing to say.

It began when he carried Dimmy across the street and down the block, Cora and Sonya following meekly, holding hands. Doc Farber was in the clinic doorway. When he saw who was in Reed's arms, he slumped heavily against the jamb, said, "Oh my God, no, oh no, not this."

"I don't know what to do," Reed had said helplessly. "I don't know where—"

Doc crooked a finger. "It's all right. Follow me." And led him along a narrow brick path around the side of the building. At the back was a large shed with a roof of corrugated sheet iron. Inside there was nothing but stored cots and cartons, a low pile of blankets on a shelf. He opened one of the cots, and Reed laid Dimmy down.

"I'm sorry," the doc told him, flapping open a thin blanket. "I . . . it's the best I can do for now. His mother's inside. I can't let her . . ."

Reed waited until Dimmy's face had been covered, then walked away. Some distant part of him noted that the rain had begun to fall a little heavier, that mist still swirled and rose from the gutters and drains, that the fires on the Crest had subsided and the clouds seemed to pull away from the dancing light, higher, blacker.

But when he went back to the church, he didn't know exactly why, he saw only the image of Reverend Chisholm's back, moving down the street after Reed had first arrived with Lambert, ignoring them all, slipping into the dark one step at a time.

He had no idea how long ago that had been.

He had no idea now where Cora had taken Sonya, where Nate and Rina had gone to. He supposed he ought to go up there and help the others. Old Micah was probably teasing a heart attack—Reverend Chisholm had run away—and his old man was probably still too drunk to hold a hose—Reverend Chisholm had run away—and he had just watched Todd stagger around into Hickory Street and that son of a bitch Chisholm had turned his back on them all, just when they needed him. If not his words, then his arms and his hands and that voice of his.

He shivered, absently wiping water from his face.

He glanced west and almost found the courage to go down there, go all the way down there, and demand explanations.

Almost.

He couldn't.

He didn't want to know what Reverend Chisholm would say.

What he did was leave the church walk and head up the slope. He didn't hurry. There was no need to hurry now. What was left was probably just cleaning up, making sure there were no fires in the woods, making sure there were no embers burning in someone's yard or on someone's roof.

Halfway there he thought he heard a gunshot up a side street, and shrugged it off as simply wood splitting in the fire's heat. He came over the top and paused, seeing no one running, even a few standing in the street, smoking, talking, taking a break, while those who had spelled them worked to keep the fires where they belonged.

He squinted, coughed as the light wind blew smoke into his eyes and lungs, and thought he saw Nate up there, by the school, Rina trotting toward him. It was too dark to tell, the fire's light too uncertain.

Then he saw the sun rise from the school's roof, and flaming hands reach out from the already shattered windows.

Then Nate was gone, Rina gone, and half the men in the street were on their backs, yelling, one screaming, and someone, a ghost, smacked him in the chest with a plank and he, too, was on his back, blinking into the rain.

Only then did he hear the explosion, and night turned back into day again, the rain laced with bubbling sections of tar paper, with whole bricks and brick shards and things that were nothing but balls of stinging fire.

As he lay on his back, waiting for his lungs to start working again, he was afraid for a moment that he had gone stone deaf. When the moment passed, however, he could hear things, all kinds of things, but he couldn't tell what they were because they were too muffled.

Nate.

"Nate," he groaned, and got to his feet in painful stages, swayed and fell to his knees.

Rina.

He gasped and swallowed.

Most of the school's front wall had been blown outward, fire lurking there like the fire in a furnace waiting to be fed. A voice pleaded for help, another for a new hose, another for someone to get in a goddamn car and get to the nearest town, they were dying like flies here.

A shadow in front of him: "Boy, are you all right?"

A hand gripped his arm and helped him to his feet.

"You all right?"

There were too many speckles of red and grey in the air; it took him several seconds and several more questions before he said, "Fine, I'm fine."

Mabel Jonsen nodded sharply and hurried away.

Reed was all right; she couldn't waste her time.

"Nate," he said, but there was no one there to hear him.

He headed for the school, half turning when a cloud of thick smoke rolled in his direction; when it passed, he had turned all the way and was on his way down toward the flat. His left leg bothered him, but he was able to run a little; his ears were still stuffed and there were whistles in his head, but he was able to understand just where he was going.

When he was opposite Mackey's he saw a man lying against the base of the wall, another man standing in the doorway, watching him, saying nothing.

When the road sloped downward again he realized he had a shadow, faint and uncertain.

When the slope flattened again, he realized he was crying. Soundlessly. Hard. Chips of rusty steel tearing his lungs and throat.

His legs were slow to obey, and he veered helplessly to the left, nearly tumbling into the trees he could no longer see. Once he regained control, he had to walk or he would fall; once he walked, he stopped crying, but the steel chips were still there, at least one of them, he thought, lodged in his heart.

He stopped when he finally reached the last house on the road.

There were no lights.

Not even the fire reached down this far.

Maybe down by the river? he wondered, and wondered if he could make it there and back. Or maybe he should just break a window or break the door down and go inside and wait. Or maybe he should just go back, because this wasn't getting him anywhere while other people were up there, getting themselves killed.

Maybe, he thought, it didn't matter anymore.

And a voice whispered behind him, " ' "Vengeance is *mine*," sayeth the Lord.' "

7

As Casey walked up the center of Black Oak Road, Reed straggling behind, he saw Hell sketched across the bottom of the clouds, reached out with his right hand and caught Reed's shirt and dragged him alongside.

"Where is she?" he said, looking nowhere but straight ahead.

The boy stumbled; Casey held him until his hand was slapped away.

"I don't know who you're talking about," Reed snapped. "And I don't care. You've got those powers and things, and you ran away, goddamnit. I don't have to—"

Casey grabbed him again, both hands, and stopped, holding him close, forcing him up on his toes. "I don't know who or what you think I am, son," he said kindly, sternly, "but I'm only who I am, no one else, and don't you forget it." He pulled him higher. "If you don't know who I mean, then get out there and find her. You'll know her when you see her."

He released him, and Reed staggered backward a few paces, turning to keep his balance, turning again to make a stand.

"Reed."

He knew what the boy saw before the boy bolted, and it gave him no pleasure.

He walked on, neither slow nor fast, and there were no fantasies with him this time around. The gunslinger was gone, the marshal cleaning up the town, the priest who had all the answers because God spoke to him on the hour every hour, the miracle worker, maybe even the coward.

He hadn't lied: he was only who he was, nothing more, nothing less.

He wore black from shirt to boots, but he didn't wear his collar because he still hated the stupid thing, it still felt like a starched noose. Around his neck was the gold chain, the cross tucked between the second and third buttons of his shirt, shifting lightly against his chest. His heels came down hard, very hard, on the blacktop, not for any sense of the dramatic, but because he knew she would hear him.

When he reached the flat, he paused, and shook his head sadly at what he saw: the debris on the ground, still smoldering in the rain, Moss still lying over there at Mackey's, the cracked window at the Moonglow, the smoke crawling off the Crest and mingling with the mist and raindrops. And firelight like a fading sunrise.

He was the only one on the street.

Alone, for the moment, with the voice of the fire.

He could still leave.

He could still turn around and take off the black, maybe go down to the river and take one of Micah's boats and let the current carry him as far south as it could.

He could.

He smiled a little ruefully.

Sure.

He flexed his fingers, tried to blow out the fear that walked with him as he walked forward, tried to remember that it was no crime, no shame in being afraid. And it had been anger, it had been shame, that had driven him away tonight, back to the house where he had stood in the yard and stared at the sky and waited for a sign that would tell him what to do, how to make amends for his failure in protecting those who had counted on him for protection.

There was none.

Not a comet, not a star, not even a burning bush.

When he realized how idiotic he must look, drenched to the skin, whining for special favors, beating his breast and checking out hair shirts, he had thrown up his hands and laughed, laughed all the way inside where he stripped and toweled dry, and pulled out the clothes he should have worn all along.

They were neither a shield nor a uniform, they were simply what he was.

Closer to the Moonglow now, the pink neon hazed by the rain, the crack a dark silver.

He didn't know precisely what he would do when she finally came. He had no spells or special weapons or a blessed amulet or his Bible. And he reckoned words weren't going to be all he would need.

At the intersection at Hickory, he looked left toward the rented house, snapped his head around when he heard a moan.

And saw Todd. Crawling on his stomach, using his elbows and hands to drag him along, hunched in the middle as if he couldn't bear to let his stomach touch the ground. With a moan of his own he ran over, went down on one knee, and put his hand on Odam's head to tell him he was there.

Todd looked up, resting on one elbow. "Aw, Jeez, Case," he said, "where the hell've you been?" Pulled himself higher as Casey lowered the other knee and rested his friend's head in his lap. "She killed Bobby."

Casey frowned. "She? Who?"

Todd managed to point down the darkened street. "A demon, Case. Damn, but . . . she was a . . . demon."

Casey smelled the blood, tipped Odam over a little and saw it seeping through the jagged edges of the rip in his open shirt. "Todd."

"Demons, Case. They can't die. I tried. Those new people are demons."

No, he thought. It would be easier if they were. If they were in fact the clichéd monsters from Hell, swarming across the globe to do Satan's work, it would be so much easier.

"Case." Todd sagged, and Casey hurried to grab his shoulders and hold him close, leaning over to shield him, at least from the rain. "Case, it ain't the UFOs."

"I know."

He heard voices, distant and high and angry.

"Case."

"Come on, Todd, let's get you to Mel's."

Todd shook his head, more like a shudder, and pushed weakly until Casey let him lie on the ground. Rain spattering on his face and side, rain spattering on the street.

"Aw, Case," he said, and said no more; he closed his eyes.

Casey lay a hand on his head, whispered a prayer and a promise nothing like a prayer at all, and looked down the street. A woman stood there, only her face visible, but none of her features.

. You're not her, he thought as the face disappeared. He brushed rain from Todd's cheek, kissed his fingertips and placed them on Todd's forehead, and rocked to his feet against a gust that tried to shove him.

He wouldn't let it.

He walked on.

Looking side to side, searching shadows and houses and trees and gutters.

But she wasn't there; she wasn't anywhere.

Be patient, he cautioned; be patient, she knows.

Midway up the next block he looked over at the clinic as the door opened with a shrill creak, and Mel stepped out. He lifted his face to the rain for a second, groaned loudly, and was about to return inside when he saw him.

"Casey, God, is that you?"

"Yep."

Farber started for him, but stopped when he reached the curb, his hands quivering at his side. Tessa came to the doorway, calling Mel, she needed his help, and cut herself off. She didn't say a word.

"Casey," Mel said, bewildered and exhausted, "we're cut

off. What were you doing? The whole place is blowing up, we needed you, damnit, people have—''

''I couldn't have stopped it,'' he said calmly. ''Not then. I would have died myself.''

''Maybe you should have,'' Tessa said from the doorway without a trace of emotion.

He tilted his head—*maybe*—and walked on, ignoring Mel's calls, hearing Tessa order him to stop wasting his time, watching the firelight grow stronger, pulsing like a heartbeat within the clouds now, watching a group of people stagger over the rise like black ghosts, supporting each other, their voices low, urging, cursing, in pain.

Looking side to side.

And still he couldn't find her, and he wondered if he was wrong, if he was too late for whatever it was he had to do.

At the next intersection he looked right and saw nothing, looked left and saw the little man in the trench coat standing near the block's solitary streetlamp, the light to one side, turning half of him black. The little man swayed side to side, and Casey was sure he heard him humming.

''Reverend Chisholm!''

Ahead, one of the black ghosts had already reached the flat and had broken into a run.

Reed, nearly tripping in his haste, slipping on the oil slicks on the road, lunging for him, grabbing his arms. Casey didn't know the word for what he saw in the boy's face.

''Nate,'' Reed said, in anguish, in despair. ''Oh, God, Reverend Chisholm, Nate. And Rina.''

Casey hugged him tightly, one hand pressing the boy's cheek to his chest. The children. They were killing the children, and here he was, still playing games, still walking the streets as if he owned them.

He stroked the boy's back and let his sobs wrench from grief to rage and back again; he shook his head when Mel came up beside him and asked if Reed was hurt; he didn't move at first when Tessa came to his other side and glared at him, daring him to say something, daring him to explain.

Then he turned his head slowly, and when she saw his expression she covered her mouth with a hand and moved to leave.

"Helen," he said. Steady. Deep. The voice of the pulpit in the voice of the fire and rain. "Where is she?"

Tessa shook her head. "I don't know. I . . . she was at the house when that woman . . ." Her eyes widened. "Oh my God, Todd!" And she turned to run.

"Helen," he repeated.

Tessa stopped abruptly, leaning away, unable to leave. "She left me with Bobby, Casey. Then that woman . . ." Frantic hands through her hair. "She dragged me into the street, and then Todd showed up and he got her to let me go and . . ."

Casey nodded, and eased Reed away, still holding his upper arms. "Wait here," he said. He looked first at Tessa, then at Mel. "Both of you wait here."

"I have a gun," Mel offered. "In the clinic. I have a gun. We can get her, Case. We'll find Helen, and we'll get that woman."

"No," he said, and let his hands drop. "No, you won't. You can't." He didn't smile. "Not yet."

"Then what the hell are we doing here?" Farber demanded.

"Waiting," he answered.

Then he did smile.

"For her."

And it was for her that a path opened through them, averting his face from the brunt of a gust, flexing his fingers, wishing he could do something about the cold that had begun to spread through his gut, his lungs, his limbs, deadening all sound but the sound of his heels as he made his way across the street and up the flagstone walk to the steps, to the double doors.

A small explosion on the Crest startled him, made others cry out wearily.

He looked down at the knobs and closed his eyes briefly, found a number of different ways to call himself an idiot, because the keys, the damn keys, were still back at his house.

Feet on the blacktop, shuffling, kicking aside or stumbling

over chunks of plaster and wood, brick and stone; whispers without words; the rain pattering on the grass; the wind humming through the steeple.

He didn't want to do this.

He was in a cave without light, forced to move, too far from the walls, knowing that in the center was a pit filled with blood, knowing that the entrance was on the other side, and no one had told him why he was here or what he had to do to avoid drowning.

In the blood.

He didn't want to do this.

The cold intensified.

He grabbed the doorknobs and remembered how foolish, how vain he had been.

"You can't keep me out," he whispered. "This is *my* church."

He braced himself, and he pulled, and the doors rattled in protest, the hinges groaned, and the wind keened through the steeple.

"Mine."

He pulled, and the doors opened with a scream when the hinges snapped and the wood cracked.

And there was silence.

Move now or run, he told himself.

No lights inside, but he could see as clearly as if fragments of the sun rested in each of the segments of stained glass.

He stepped in, hesitated, wiped the rain from his face, and walked into the sanctuary, and saw her in the aisle.

"Well," she said. Hands on her hips. Shirt bulging around her waist. Short brown hair perfectly dry. Jeans neither snug nor baggy. Shoes on her feet that reminded him of slippers. "Well."

Had she been a demon, as Todd had said, he would have felt the defilement, the blasphemy; had she been a demon, he would have presented her with the cross and banished her to her Master; had she been a demon . . . but she wasn't.

Her presence in this place felt as natural as his.

In a sense, he knew, in a very real sense, they had the same boss.

"I don't know what to do with you," he said, standing behind the last pew, running a hand along its curved polished back.

"That's too bad," she said. "I've come a long way to meet you."

He shook his head. "Why? Why me?"

Her smile was brief. "Too big a question, Reverend. Everybody asks that one."

"Not everybody brought life back to a dead man."

It was almost a question, and she spoke as if it were: "Did you, Reverend? Did you really?"

The cold; he felt the cold, and it made him dizzy.

"Where . . ." He stopped, refused to look at her. "Where are . . ."

Say it, Casey, and it's true; say it, and the world is over.

That smile again, taunting. "The others?" She gestured at the windows. "Not those, don't worry about that. Those are only friends I've picked up along the way. You mean the Others, I'm sure." She dusted a pew's back with one finger. "You could call them, I suppose, my comrades-in-arms."

It took all he had left not to speak, just to nod.

Belief was one thing; seeing its proof was something else.

Her face took on angles as the taunting smile faded; her eyes narrowed. "What do you care, priest? I'm the one who's here." The next pew up, the finger still moving. "I'm the one who's going to kill you."

The windows brightened for a second, but he couldn't hear the explosion.

Another pew, only three away, and her face changed again; subtly, but it changed.

"You were right, you know, Reverend. That little story you told? Maybe it was a parable, I don't know, I don't have to worry about those things. I just do what I'm told, go where I have to." Her head was down; she looked up without raising it. "They're all dancing now. The same song. It took a little

while, but now they're all in step. And the funny thing is, they
don't even know it.

"And if they do, they don't really believe it."

Another pew.

He tensed, but he didn't move. Her voice was smooth, her
voice was hard, her voice was as old as any voice he had ever
heard; it was the voice of a snake, the voice of ancient fire,
and when her eyes tried to hold him, he didn't move, he only
shook his head and said, "If I'm going to die, you won't be
the one."

Feeling the cold, burning through him.

She lifted her head. "Arrogance doesn't become you, Reverend Chisholm."

He didn't argue, but suddenly he knew it was as true as the
reality of this harbinger who stood before him. He knew a lot
of things now, some of them confusing, some of them so clear
he was nearly blinded.

He tried twice to speak, and twice he failed, because he
couldn't keep the terror in hand as she took another pace, and
they were separated only by the width of a double pew.

He could feel her breath; he could smell her skin; he could
hear her shoes brush across the old red carpet in the aisle.

A woman screamed, long and high.

Quickly he looked through the vestibule to the open doors,
but all he saw was the slant of rain, and fire shadows in the
street.

He felt the cold.

Nate and Todd; Dimitri and Rina.

He felt the burning.

"Leave this place," he said, pulpit deep.

"Too late, Casey. This place is dead."

He felt the heat.

She moved too quickly, but he didn't flinch when she
touched his cheek, ran her palm down his chest, making sure
he knew she could feel the cross beneath the cloth. And he
didn't move when she frowned and did it again, harder this
time, and faster.

And didn't move when she slapped him.
But when she stepped back, he finally smiled.

No one moved.

He heard a shot.

No one moved.

Until she lunged for his throat, and he grabbed her wrists and easily tossed her aside, spilling her into the gap between the last two pews. Surprised when she was on her feet before he could follow, and tried to bury a fist in his stomach.

He doubled over, his breath gone, and she made a club with her two fists and brought it down on his skull, driving him to one knee, one hand braced against the pew's armrest, using his foot to drive him upward, catching her under the chin with his head, knocking her back again.

This time she didn't fall.

This time she grabbed a hymnal and used it as a bat, swinging the spine across his mouth, laughing softly as he toppled onto his rump and tasted blood.

The slippers became heavy boots, and she waited until he stood before she lashed one against his left shin and brought him down again.

"One way or another," she said, barely breathing hard, giving him a smile. "One way or another."

He pulled himself up, ducked another swing, and slammed a fist against her chest, stepped in and used the other above her eye, splitting the skin, drawing blood, forcing her back, the boots sliding on the carpet, making her grab for the pew's back to keep from falling.

He struck her again, *feeling the heat*, and she bounced off the pew, the back splintering onto the carpet.

And still she smiled.

The only sound the rasp of their feet on the floor, the dull connection of her fist on his jaw, his fist on her hip, the grunt as she grabbed his wrist, came with him as he pulled, suddenly spun and whipped him into the vestibule where he landed against the edge of the announcement table with his side.

Feeling the heat.

Watching her smile lose its humor.

Circling, searching, blood smeared across her eye and cheek, blood smeared across his teeth and chin.

They came together in a silent shout like grapplers, and she was down and under him, and he was in the air and on his back before he could think. Rolling over to avoid the boots. Seeing a spark burst from beneath her sole as she tried to stomp on his knee and missed. Seeing the look on her face, however brief, that told him it wasn't supposed to be like this.

She was one of four, and no one was supposed to stand in her way.

Seeing the smile.

Seeing the lie.

Watching her from the floor as she stood beside the table, grabbed its edge, and shoved it as if it were cardboard across the floor toward his head.

When she missed, he stood under it, bringing it up and over and pinning her against the wall. Pushing. Seeing nothing but her hands on either side slip away, and suddenly the table pushed him instead, and he gave ground until it fell away and he saw her race to the belfry stairwell.

No, he thought, and followed, slapping his hands against the walls to give him momentum, using the sparks of her ascent to give him light through the door and into the belfry.

Feeling the heat.

Feeling the wind.

Looking behind him and seeing a dozen fires on the Crest, except the Crest was below him, and he caught his breath and backed away, made the mistake of looking south where he saw the lights of Farber's clinic, and a group of people in the street far below in the rain.

Breathing through his mouth, reaching up and behind him, half turning when he touched a bell and felt it shift until he snatched his hand away.

"You can't kill me, you know."

She stood in the west archway, her hands braced against the frame on either side. Her shirt rippled as the wind tried to take it, and her hair was pulled sharply away from her brow.

"I don't have to," he told her, and was on her before she could move, one arm around waist, crushing her to him, squeezing while he stared at her face because he didn't dare look anywhere else, his other hand in a fist and raised above his head.

He nearly screamed when she smiled and stopped her struggling.

And then her lips moved: "Please don't hurt me, please don't hurt me, please don't, please don't."

In a voice that wasn't hers.

He knew it wasn't hers, and he froze just the same.

please don't kill me

Smiling; always smiling.

please don't please don't o Jesus please don't hurt me

The wind gusted and nudged him forward and he couldn't help but look down.

please don't

Smiling; always smiling.

Waiting for the crash of glass, waiting for the cop, waiting for the gun that would send him someplace warm.

please

"Don't," she said, the smile gone, one eye red with blood.

"Yes," he said, and brought his fist down.

Stan crept to the corner and watched the people in the street watching something in the air. He couldn't see much with all the rain, and he wondered if he dared show himself, just for a second. They were so busy, they wouldn't notice anyway, and they certainly wouldn't see the stupid hole that stupid army man had put in his favorite coat, right there above the heart. It had scared him to death even though he knew it wouldn't hurt him. Just as it hadn't scared him when he had grabbed the rifle from him and used it as a whip to send him to his knees and then to the ground where Stan used it to make sure no one would ever recognize him again. Then he had thrown it away because he didn't need it, and heard the commotion and saw the people.

"Hey."

He froze, relaxed, and turned around. Hummed and rubbed his palms together when he saw the old lady and saw the rifle in her hands. Damn, but she could barely hold it; and damn, but she looked bad, that white coat all torn, her hair all messed and looking like a witch.

She pulled the trigger and missed him.

"Lady," he said.

She fired again.

He felt the impact; nothing more.

And he brought it down again.

Helen knelt in the diner's kitchen, holding her upper arm just above where the woman's knife had sliced through it. She had tied a dish towel around it, praying it would do for a tourniquet until she could get to Mel for help, then snuck out the back door and forced her way through the hedge, biting her lips against the twigs that gouged at her face and breasts, that clawed at the bloody arm, that tried to flay her hands.

When the screen door opened, she thought to run, and changed her mind. Instead, she tensed against the pain and rose slowly, leaning against the stove.

"You know," Lupé said, "I don't have all night."

Helen grabbed the cleaver from the butcher block and waited.

"You don't get it," Lupé said, almost sadly. "You don't get it, do you?" She wiped her knife on her jeans and shook her head again. "It doesn't matter, you know? Since the mountains, it doesn't matter."

She lashed out and stepped too close.

The cleaver slipped into her chest.

And he brought it down again.

Harve Turner surprised himself by being just about the last one to pack it in. There were too many fires despite all the rain. Every time one was taken care of, another explosion changed the rules. It had been too much. Surrender had finally become the order of the day, and when he decided it was time to get down to Mackey's and get himself a drink, it didn't bother him a bit.

What did bother him was the kid he spotted wandering down the street. What the hell was she doing here?

"Hey, kid," he called.

She turned.

"Get the hell home, okay? Jesus, are you stupid or what?"

Then he saw what she held in her right hand.

"My God, where'd you get that dynamite?"

The flame in the palm of her left hand.

Harve didn't know which way to run when the flame touched the fuse; he didn't know what to make of the way the damn kid giggled; he didn't make it to the curb before the explosion lifted him off his feet and carried him to the sidewalk where he landed on his shoulder and heard the bones split, had no breath to scream, was just alert enough to see the little pillar of fire in the middle of the street and think, *Stupid damn kid*, just before he passed out.

And he brought it down again.

*   *   *

And again.

Until the smile was gone, replaced by a silent scream of a silent question, a fierce look, a spit of blood, both eyes blinded now by shimmering red.

He hesitated, his arm shaking, not sure.

"Reverend Chisholm," she said, and wrapped her arms around him.

And threw herself backward.

Falling in the rain, listening to the wind, was the sweetest thing he had ever done.

And he didn't mind a bit.

Because he was what he was.

No matter how hard he hit the ground.

Part 6

Coda

1

There was nothing left but the rain, and a few smoldering shards of wood, and a shattered brick at the door of Mabel onsen's store. The mist had long since been beaten away. The treets had long since been emptied.

"I can't stay here," Cora said. Her hair was burned, her heeks and brow and chin and arms dark with wet ash, her hirt ripped, her jeans stained with too many drops of blood.

"I know." Reed sat beside her on the top step of the church. 3ehind them the doors hung, broken on their broken hinges. 'Me neither."

Nate, he thought, and couldn't cry anymore.

Rina, he thought, and threw a pebble angrily out toward the urb.

Too weary to move, too weary to sleep, they sat in the rain ind waited, neither one looking at the place where Reverend Casey had come down.

The woman was gone.

As far as he could tell, no one else had seen her but Cora, ind maybe Helen. Maybe Doc Farber, too, but they were still at the hospital, sitting in a room that was warm and light, waiting for the surgeon to tell them if Reverend Casey would live to see the dawn.

The woman was gone.

They sat in the rain, not smiling, not talking, until Beagle trotted over and squeezed between them, and whimpered.

"Hungry," Reed guessed.

"Probably," Cora answered, hugging the dog to her side. "Probably."

He almost said something, but had nothing else to say. To want to tally the dead, to feel for them, to miss them, was, for now, too big a chore.

Mourning would have to come some other time.

The rain was cold; they didn't feel it.

"I should have helped him."

Cora cupped a hand around the back of his head, stroked it once, and the hand fell away. "Where will we go?" she asked instead.

He lifted one shoulder. "Anywhere."

"Good enough." She hugged the dog again. "Want a pet?"

"I think Miss Jonsen will want to look out for him, don't you?"

Cora nearly made it to a smile. "Help her look for UFOs or something."

Reed too. "They'd probably scare the poor mutt to death."

The sound of a car over the sound of the rain.

Beagle whimpered.

Reed remembered, but he didn't hear the hoofbeats.

They had vanished with the woman.

Headlights split the rain into sparkling motes and slashes. The car passed them at a crawl, stopped and backed up.

They didn't move.

Helen slid out, one arm bandaged from elbow to shoulder, a bandage over her right eye. She wore no coat and didn't bother with an umbrella.

Reed didn't have the strength to stand. "Well?"

"Too soon to really tell," she said, standing at the first step. She smiled, though. "But it looks good." She chuckled. "

eard one of the nurses call it a miracle when she found out
ow it happened.''

Reed nodded. "Cool. Because it was."

Cora said, "Yeah. Maybe." Not really a contradiction.

Helen leaned over and tapped their shoulders. "Let's get
nside, okay? He wouldn't want you guys to catch pneumonia.
Ie's got enough problems now as it is."

He looked over his shoulder and saw the dark beyond the
hreshold. "Can we go to the Moonglow instead?"

Helen balked for a second, then nodded. "Sure. Why not?
'll turn on the coffee."

Halfway there, Cora stopped them with a touch.

There were no fires left; just the rain.

"What happened?" she asked.

Helen said, "I don't know. Maybe he does, but he can't
alk. Not for a while, anyway."

But Reed walked on, Beagle trotting at his side.

I know, he thought, and wouldn't say it aloud; I know what
t was. It was the end of the world, and Reverend Chisholm
topped it. At least for a while.

He did smile then.

No one saw it but the dog.

2

Please don't
    Casey knew he was alive, knew he was hurt badly, knew
there was an even chance he would never see the Landing
again. Or anything else, for that matter.

He knew in the cloud that carried him through the comforting dark that he had wrestled with Death, and neither one
of them had won.

What he didn't know was what it meant.

What he didn't know was why, from the edge of the cloud, he
could see through the dark to a Tennessee autumn hillside, and
the funeral down there, a big man in black reading softly from a
Bible over the grave of a woman who finally knew her son.

What he didn't know was why the pain wouldn't stop.

please don't hurt

What he did know was that he was tired. Almighty tired.
Tired enough to let the cloud take him wherever it wanted to
go. Tired enough to want to stay here, drifting through the
dark, Tennessee autumn below, flickering visions of a steeple
once in a while passing by.

Tired enough to decide that if this was how you died, it wasn't so bad. Not so bad after all.

He only hoped that whatever it was he was supposed to do, that he had done it, and that it hadn't been too late, and that someone out there, maybe Helen, maybe the kids, knew that Casey Chisholm wasn't a coward after all.

casey

Not so bad. A little too quiet. It would do to have someone sing now and then; maybe play the organ the way Helen did on Sundays, or when she practiced and he sat in the office without her knowing he was listening; maybe get out a guitar and play it in the kitchen while someone else played the piano over there in the parlor, and

Casey

Someone else danced a waltz out there on the lawn.

Aw, damn, he thought; aw, damn I'm going to miss it.

"Casey."

Maybe his eyes opened, maybe he could see now without them. Whatever it was, Mel Farber was so close, Casey could smell the fear and anxiety on his breath, on his skin.

The young man looked old, and there were pocks of burned flesh across his face.

"You look like hell, Doc," he managed, and gasped at the pain, closed his eyes, and gasped again.

A muttering, a woman responding, a few seconds later, the pain receding but too slowly.

"Casey."

"I hear you. Stop shouting."

"Don't talk, Case, it probably hurts."

No kidding, he thought, but for a change he obeyed.

"You're going to be all right. Eventually. I think. Better shape than the Landing, that's for sure."

Casey moistened his lips. "Feels. Every bone. Broken."

"Damn near." Closer. "You never heard this, Case, but I think it's a goddamn miracle."

Casey hoped he smiled; he couldn't feel a thing. "Nothing. Goddamn. About it. Then." Moistened his lips again. "The kids? Helen?"

Silence for too long.

He was afraid.

He couldn't move.

"Reed and Cora, pretty good. They're home. Helen was banged up by that madwoman. The other one, I mean. Helen chopped her with a cleaver. She's with the kids now, just called from the Moonglow." Chuckling, macabre chuckling. "Would you believe Mrs. Racine put a hole through that little man's head? She claims it was one shot."

Casey floated for a while, no longer quite so comfortable with the cloud and the dark, wishing someone would turn on a light so he could see better, so he could see more. The Tennessee autumn hillside would just have to wait.

"Arlo. The others."

"Word's still coming in, Case. Don't know where Arlo is, but we found Escobar in the bar. Burned to death. Sliced to ribbons." Closer, again. "Not a single drop of blood, and no burn marks on the floor."

Floating.

Listening to his heart working overtime; listening to the silence.

"Case?"

"What?"

"Is . . . is it what you said? Was that woman . . . you know."

What he wanted to say was, *It wasn't a woman, Mel, and you know it now. Not a woman. She was one of them. Maybe it was a test, I'm not sure. Maybe it was a warning, I'm not sure. No matter what I say, old friend, you'll believe what you want to and the hell with what I say. That's the way of it. The way it always was, the way it always will be.*

Believe what you want. It'll get you through the night.

What he did say was, with what he hoped was a smile: "We'll never know, will we? I don't think we'll ever really know."

Silence, moving around the room, whispers, the smell of ointments and bandages and healing flesh and broken bones and flowers that had no right to smell so lovely.

A straw between his lips.

Blessed water.

"Casey?"

"Now what?"

"There's something else."

A moment of panic: "I'm crippled."

"No, no, good Lord, no. Just about everything's busted but that dumb back of yours. Don't worry. You get through this, you'll walk. Limping, for sure, but walking."

"Then what?"

"It's your hair."

He couldn't move his arms; they both hung in traction.

"What about it? You had to shave it off?"

"No. It's . . . I don't know, maybe I should let Helen—"

"Mel." The voice, without the look.

"It's white, Case. Your hair has turned pure white."

There may have been an explanation, but he couldn't hear it and didn't try. He was tired. Almighty tired. He let the cloud take him away for a while. To rest. Maybe dream. Maybe listen to the music, watch the people dance.

He had done his best.

With any kind of luck now, not all of them were in step.

3

And the church bell rang.

In the Mood

the second movement of
the Millennium Quartet
by Charles Grant

a preview

1

Midway down the block, on the wide top step of a four-step stoop, two men sat on folding lawn chairs on either side of the wood-and-glass door entrance. A dim light in the foyer gave them outline, without substance.

They had been there for two hours, as they were most every night, watching the occasional pedestrian, sneering at the cars cutting through from Eighth Avenue to Ninth, speculating on the few silhouettes they could see on the shades across the way. Long stretches of conversation broken by long stretches of silence. Staccato condemnations of the Yankees and the Jets, dirges and sighs for the Giants and Mets. Neither cared about hockey, so the Rangers were ignored; both thought basketball an overpaid game, so the Knicks were never mentioned at all.

Best friends for half a century, in this neighborhood and others, with too many birthdays and funerals between them to bother counting.

"I think," said Tony Garza, "I'm going down to the Korean's for something to eat."

"Eat? What are you, nuts? It's nearly midnight, for God's sake."

"I'm hungry."

"You'll get heartburn."

"I never get heartburn."

Ari Lowe shook his head, rolled his eyes. A short man in loose dark trousers, white shirt, open vest, open cardigan. A slight triangular head that deepened his cheeks and pointed his chin, with wavy white hair he touched once in a while as if to make sure it was still there.

"Heartburn," Garza told him, "is for little men like you, who don't trust their stomachs."

Lowe was short, with a genteel paunch; he was seventy-four, and looked it.

Garza was not tall, but everything about him made it seem so. He was large without a suggestion of fat, his long heavy face barely marked by wrinkles. Far less hair than his friend, still dark and combed straight back from a high forehead. A deep voice somewhat rough; a smile that always exposed his still-white teeth. Even when silent, he talked with his hands.

He looked to his left and saw a little woman on the sidewalk, wearing a scarf over her hair and a long black coat. She puffed behind a small dog more hair than meat that insisted on checking out every tree on the block, and every section of the wrought iron fencing that fronted most of the buildings. She had a newspaper tucked under her arm, and as she passed he cleared his throat.

"Good evening, Mrs. Lefcowitz."

She didn't stop, but she looked over. "Mr. Lowe. Mr. Garza."

The dog yipped and tried to climb the stairs.

Lowe nodded toward the paper. "They catch him yet?"

"No," she snapped, and hurried away.

Another killer loose in the city. Nothing new, Garza thought; comes with the territory, even in the suburbs. Even in the country. This one cut throats, Slasher they call him. This one showed up all over the damn place, from Chelsea to the Village. No one had seen him yet. The cops didn't have a clue.

"You remember that thing last year?" Ari said, scratching between the buttons of his shirt.

"Which thing? I'm a mind reader now?"

"In Jersey. When it was hot. Some gang took out practically a whole town?"

He remembered.

"Jersey, Nebraska, who cares?" He flicked the cigarette into the street. "The place is going to hell in a handbasket, we got troubles of our own." He patted his breast pocket, decided it was too soon for another smoke. "End of the world is coming, my friend. And I'm still hungry."

A lone figure down at the corner, the way he was shifting, he wasn't sure whether to use this block to go crosstown or go up another one.

A long moment passed before Ari nodded. He stood, groaning, and folded his chair. "You coming?"

"I'm hungry. The Korean will feed me."

"Heartburn."

"Screw the heartburn."

"Mazel tov, you bastard."

"Same to you."

They shook hands, and Ari went inside, the old glass in the door distorting him before he was gone through the heavy inner entrance.

Garza rubbed his stomach and stood, stretched his arms out sideways, and yawned. He rubbed his stomach again and checked the figure coming toward him, not very fast. For a second he wondered if he should bother, shrugged, and decided he would let Fate do all the thinking. If it worked, it worked; if it didn't, it didn't.

What the hell.

By the time he had folded his chair and propped it up against the door, then stepped down to the sidewalk, it looked as if the timing would be right.

Then again, maybe not.

What the goddamn hell.

There were blocks, he knew, scores of them all over the world, that had blind spots, like that place in the rear view mirror where a car in another lane comes up on you and you can't see him. On many blocks on most neighborhoods, all the conditions being right, it was the same principle—walk along, reach the spot, and no one can see you from any window on any floor in any building.

He walked down toward Ninth, right hand in his pocket, left swinging loosely. Maybe he would get roast beef for a change. It was expensive these days. Cows dying all over because the grain wasn't growing right, and they had to ship the meat in; he read someplace it came from Argentina or Australia, he couldn't remember which. Some kind of riot down in Philly because a guy was accused of hoarding, even though it wasn't illegal. At least not yet.

It didn't really matter when you could barely afford it anymore.

Even bread cost too much, for crying out loud.

The figure passed under a streetlamp. A young man in a sweatshirt and fatigue pants, his boots slamming on the pavement like he owned the place.

Garza couldn't figure out why kids just didn't wear ordinary clothes anymore. What was so wonderful about looking like you were in the army? He grunted softly.

He checked over his shoulder; his stoop was quiet, Ari hadn't come back out.

For most buildings, like his, the iron fencing was less decorative than to keep people from falling down the flight of concrete steps that led belowground, to the basement apartment. Trash cans were stored there, under the main steps. Litter was tossed there. He smiled as he remembered a time a couple of years ago when he and that blonde he'd met at St. John's had a little fun down there, just to see if they could do it without getting caught.

The dance of danger, he had called it.

He did the dance again now, because the timing was perfect, and because he had never done it on his own street before.

His right hand left his pocket and pressed lightly against his leg, thumb caressing the mother-of-pearl handle tucked in his palm.

The young man heard him approach, looked up, didn't even
nod a hello.

Garza, however, smiled.

As soon as they were abreast, the dance began.

Four easy steps.

Silently, smoothly, he turned as his left hand grabbed the
young man's hair and yanked the head back; his right hand
brought up the straight razor and slashed it deeply across the
exposed throat; he shifted the razor-hand to the back of the
kid's neck, grabbed the seat of his pants, and hoisted him
effortlessly over the fencing; and dropped him into the well.

Into the dark.

Not a sound but a startled grunt, and the dull thud of the
body landing.

Not a single wasted motion.

Not a single pause.

He stood for a moment, staring down, absently folding the
razor into his pocket.

Then he blinked, once, and walked away.

When he reached the streetlamp, he didn't look down,
didn't check for blood.

He didn't have to.

It was never there.

Horseradish, he thought then as he headed for the corner;
if he was going to have roast beef, he couldn't forget the
horseradish.

And maybe he'd bring a little something back for Ari.

2

John stood in the bathroom, watching his reflection listen to the ghost. Stanley Arlington Hovinskal. A thirty-four-year-old man whose death-row cell had been vacated sixteen months ago. Nothing quite so dramatic as lights dimming or smoke drifting from beneath a specially-made cap banded in iron or fingers convulsing or lips screaming.

He had died.

Period.

Only the voice remained.

You look a little confused, Mr. Bannock.

I can't help it, Stan, I'm sorry. You had a decent life, a decent job, you were getting ready to start a family, your fiancé had the wedding all planned . . . I'm sorry, but I just don't get it.

Well . . . things change.

Forgive me, Stan, really, but . . . let's face it, you pushed someone in front of a subway train in Washington, you cut

e throats of three women and two men in the Midwest, you
rew a teenager off a bridge in San Francisco, and you ran a
affic cop over four times with your car in Pennsylvania.

Yes. But it took me three years to do it all.

Is that important? The timing?

Ask the shrinks, Mr. Bannock; I wouldn't know. You know,
he of them actually said I had spells? Like I was some kind
old Southern lady with the vapors or something? Some kind
state, I don't know what the word is.

Fugue.

Yeah, maybe. Another one, she wanted to tie it all up with
he anniversaries of my parents' deaths. Didn't work. She had
harts and everything, but she couldn't make it work.

Stan, I—

Look, Mr. Bannock, there's nothing all that complicated
bout this. I keep telling you. When I felt like it, I did it; when
didn't, I didn't.

No voices.

Nope.

No messages from another dimension.

God, no.

No seeing your parents' faces superimposed over those of
our victims.

Are you kidding?

No demons.

. . .

Stan?

. . .

Stan?

ohn held his breath. The reflection cocked its head, waiting.

he exhaled loudly and lowered his head, hands braced on
ither side of the porcelain basin. A minute passed, and an-
ther, before he straightened and rolled his shoulders, feeling
he joints pop softly. An unexpected yawn made him grin. His

watch was in the other room, but he had a feeling it was close to midnight. He sniffed, rubbed his nose, and wondered if he was up for another ghost tonight.

This time he laughed aloud. Shortly. Sharply.

Hell, no.

Then maybe it was time to hit the downstairs bar before it closed. Something to help him sleep.

"Yeah," he whispered. "Right."

He stretched then, and strained to reach the ceiling with his fingers.

He almost made it.

He had always been tall, but never quite tall enough. Even in high school, the basketball players had tended toward giants, and he had never had enough weight to make it in football, or coordination for baseball. His hair was just long enough to cover his ears and his neck, dark hair flecked with early silver that seemed to sparkle in the right light, add years where they didn't belong; stray waves in front refused to stay off his forehead. In college he had tried dramatics, his soft rasping voice an oddity there, but the first time they slapped a beard on, his thick eyebrows and deep eyes, the high cheeks and prominent nose, made him look like Abraham Lincoln.

It gave him "Prez" as a nickname that lasted all four years.

"Four score," said the reflection.

"Up yours," said John, gave the face a grin and a lazy two-finger salute, and walked into the other room, picked up his wallet and key from the low dresser, reached for the suit jacket thrown on the bedspread . . . and stopped.

He stared at the tape recorder on the table.

That drink would be nice.

The company, even if it was only the bartender, would be nice.

But it wouldn't be just one drink. The first, taken quickly, would choke him and water his eyes, hardly any taste at all; the second, sipped, but not too slowly, would eventually numb his throat; and he wouldn't be able to keep track of those that followed. Certainly not the way he was feeling now. Certainly not if history were any kind of teacher at all.

With a grunt part relief, part regret, part sneering gratitude
this display of false strength, he dropped wallet and room
y onto the bed and went to the window, pulled aside the
apes and looked out at the city, his hands still gripping the
ges of the stiff cloth.

A few droplets shimmered on the wide pane, catching frag-
ents of neon as they slipped down toward the sill.

He could see up a fair portion of Canal Street six stories
low, watched a handful of pedestrians turn into the Quarter,
atched two more leave, holding on to each other as they
ossed the empty street. They were too small, however; they
eren't real, just clumsy clockwork figures that would vanish
hen he looked away. The Quarter itself was little more than
hazy glow that turned the buildings around it black.

e stands at a crossroads in lower Custer County, right in the
nter of the intersection. He has never seen land so flat in his
fe. Two lanes in four directions all the way to the horizon a
illion miles away and nothing on them but dust drifting out
f the fields, out of the roadside ditches, lazily swirling across
e blacktop. The wind isn't strong enough to lift it into
louds, and not cool enough to dry the running sweat that
ains his shirt. He knows he should be looking at horizon-
eep corn waiting for the harvest; he knows he should be
stening to the sound of giant machines that roll through the
ws and take the stalks and swallow them; he knows there
ught to be something out here but nothing.

There isn't.

The corn, what's left of it, what little has grown despite
rigation and prayers, is the color of the dust.

So is the sky.

So is the sun.

And the machines are still back in their sheds, in their barns,
nused for the most part because there's little for them to do.

But right now, in this place, he doesn't care.

He's waiting for his son.

His hands cup his mouth and he calls, "Joey!"

A crow answers.

"Joey!"

A wobbling dust dervish patters and dies against his leg.

"Joey!"

In the heat and the dry air his voice doesn't carry.

He looks down all the roads, stares across the dead and dying fields, even checks the sky.

He sees them.

Eastward, walking down the center line away from him— two figures, one not much taller than the other, holding hands, the shorter one every few steps playfully bumping into the other and dodging a playful slap.

He runs.

"Joey, damnit!"

A crow flies beside him, off his left shoulder. It's joined by another on the right, and he feels like some World War I bomber on a suicide mission, escorts on the wings, and that makes him run faster because these escorts, these crows don't have the dead black eyes such birds usually had.

They're blue.

Startlingly vivid, almost blinding blue.

"Joey!"

Silent wings.

Silent feet.

"Joey!" he cries.

And finally yells, "Patty, wait up, it's me!"

While the crows with the live blue eyes edge closer, and begin to laugh.